Monroe Township Public Library
3 4201 10140797 $

MAN IN THE MIDDLE

Also by Brian Haig

Secret Sanction
Mortal Allies
The Kingmaker
Private Sector
The President's Assassin

MAN IN THE MIDDLE

BRIAN
HAIG

WARNER BOOKS

NEW YORK BOSTON

The events and characters in this book are fictitious. Certain real locations and public figures are mentioned, but all other characters and events described in the book are totally imaginary.

Warner Books
Hachette Book Group USA
1271 Avenue of the Americas
New York, NY 10020

Visit our Web site at www.HachetteBookGroupUSA.com.

Printed in the United States of America

First Printing: January 2007
10 9 8 7 6 5 4 3 2 1

Library of Congress Cataloging-in-Publication Data

Haig, Brian.
Man in the middle / Brian Haig.—1st. ed.
p. cm.
ISBN-13: 978-0-446-53056-9
ISBN-10: 0-446-53056-5
1. Iraq War, 2003—Fiction. I. Title.
PS3608.A54M36 2007
813'.6—dc22 2006024656

For Lisa,
Brian, Pat, Donnie, and Annie

AUTHOR'S NOTE

Like the other Sean Drummond novels, this is not a war book; it is a murder mystery—and a legal mystery—that happens to have a military backdrop, and that backdrop happens to include Iraq.

I thought long and hard before writing a novel that deals with an ongoing conflict. No novelist—no commercially ambitious author, at least—writes a political polemic. The political climate in America is passionately divided, sometimes hysterically, which in my view is mostly for the good. In a healthy, functioning democracy, citizens are supposed to care, to participate, to raise their voices—and war should definitely hold our interest.

I entered the Army just as we shifted from a large draft force to a lean, all-volunteer one. Other issues aside, what most worried me, and many others, was that America's army no longer would be reflective of a very diverse nation, and that the country no longer would regard us as citizen-soldiers, just as soldiers. Fortunately, this second fear never materialized. Americans never have lost their love and unique concern for our people in uniform, and those in power in Washington never have been tempted to regard our soldiers as fodder, as an expeditionary force, a term that sounds too ominously like an expendable one.

Most authors want their books to be enjoyed, read, and bought—not necessarily in that order. This is doubly true for a writer with four wonderful children who demand food, clothing, housing, and, in the not too distant future, somebody to foot their college bills. It was not my intention to write a politically biased novel, and I hope it is not perceived as such.

So why risk a novel about Iraq? Quite simply, we are today at a crossroads over a country—and a region—about which most Americans know surprisingly little. I have met thousands of Americans who have visited Paris or Hong Kong or even Kenya; I have yet to meet one who can tell me about the lovely beaches of Yemen (actually, Yemen's beaches aren't that lovely).

In 1983, as a captain, I found myself laboring for the Joint Chiefs of Staff as an action officer working on Lebanon. We had put a Marine Expeditionary Unit into that country as an experiment in peacekeeping after a disastrous Israeli invasion. Lebanon, formerly the jewel of the region, by then was a scarred relative of its former self, a horrifying spectacle of what happens after a decade of vicious civil war. Long before we came, it was riven and rocked by religious conflicts, tribal competitions, family feuds, and by intruding neighbors who exploited the violence and stoked the hatred, often by terrorism. It was very, very different from modern Iraq; and it was not at all different.

Because of our all-consuming fixation with the cold war, every military officer of that era was an expert on the Soviet threat—or at least sounded like one. Yet, had anybody asked me to name a single difference between Sunnis and Shiites, a major source of intra-Arab friction and conflict yesterday, today, and likely for the foreseeable future, the long silence would have been deafening. Then one morning a suicide bomber drove a truck filled with explosives into a building filled with Marines, and I realized that Captain Haig was not alone in his ignorance—much of our civilian and military leadership had barely the foggiest idea about what we had gotten into. It was scary and confusing at first; ultimately, it was tragic. To this day, I am convinced that 284 fine Marines gave their lives because of our ignorance.

So here we are again, in a country we knew surprisingly little about, and once again *their* disgruntlements, *their* feuds, and *their* conflicts have become ours. As then Secretary of State Colin Powell paraphrased to the President prior to the invasion, "Once you break the pottery, you own it." Yet we, meaning most Americans—meaning most voters—know very little about these broken shards our troops are attempting to glue together with blood, sacrifice, and courage into a functioning democracy.

Thus, *Man in the Middle*. I hope you find the novel fun, entertaining, and stimulating. As I mentioned, it is a mystery, but one that dances around some of the thornier issues regarding Iraq and, I hope, one that broadens your knowledge and interest.

I should also emphasize that the characters are all wholly fictional creatures, though many of you will recognize certain historical parallels and mysteries around which the plot is based.

That said, there are a number of people I must thank. First, for the loan of his fine and honorable name, Lieutenant Colonel Kemp Chester, a great friend, a crackerjack military intelligence officer, and twice over a veteran of Iraq. Another close friend whose name I borrowed, Christopher Yuknis, served brilliantly for nearly thirty years and was one of the smartest officers I ever met. And Jim Tirey, a dear friend who performed countless dangerous missions for this country, and has always been a personal hero of mine. I also borrowed the name of a West Point classmate, Robert Enzenauer, who actually *is* a brilliant doctor, an officer in the Army Reserve, and who at great personal cost served for eighteen months in Afghanistan and Iraq.

Also, Claudia Foster. The real Claudia was in the World Trade Center on September 11, 2001. She was a lovely young lady, smart, loving, and funny. Like so many, she perished and left behind a grieving family, who asked me to find a good place to fit her name into the novel. I hope I found it.

And last, Donnie Workman. The real Donnie Workman was West Point class of 1966, captain of the Army lacrosse team, a goalie with uncommon reflexes and nerves of steel. Goalies in all sports are a special breed; lacrosse goalies, though, are a class of their own. Donnie was a constant presence around our house when my father was on the West Point faculty. He was a model for young high school lacrosse players like me, and in countless other ways an inspiration to any young man. Less than a year after graduation, Donnie stepped on a land mine in Vietnam. A man who we all thought was larger than life, who would one day become a senior general, and a great one, was gone in the blink of an eye—but never forgotten.

For those at Warner Books who have labored so hard to repair my bad writing and to package and sell my novels, I cannot be more thankful or admiring. Colin Fox, my editor, known to all his writers as charming and fun and enormously talented. Mari Okuda, who does the thankless task of copyediting and somehow makes it seem fun, despite all evidence to the contrary. Roland Ottewell, who performs literary alchemy in transforming my fractured manuscripts into readable texts. And Jamie Raab and Larry Kirschbaum, the publisher and now departed CEO, and Rick Horgan, my former editor, who encouraged my writing, have made Warner a label any writer would be proud to have on his jacket cover.

Special thanks to Gerald and Trish Posner, who have done extraordinary research that was very helpful to the book.

And mostly, Luke Janklow, my agent and my friend, who, in both categories, is surpassed by none.

MAN
IN THE
MIDDLE

CHAPTER ONE

Lateness can be a virtue or a sin.

Arrive late to a party, for instance, and that's fashionable. Arrive late for your own funeral and people envy your good fortune. But come late to a possible murder investigation and you have a career problem.

But nearly every problem has a solution, and I turned to the attractive lady in the brown and tan suit who was standing beside me and asked, "Come here often?"

"Hey, that's very funny." She was not laughing, or even smiling.

"It's my best line."

"Is it?"

"You'd be surprised how often it works."

"You're right," she observed. "I'd be surprised." She placed a hand over her mouth and laughed quietly, or maybe yawned.

I stuck out my hand and introduced myself. "Sean Drummond," then added less truthfully, "Special Agent Drummond. FBI."

"Bian Tran." She ignored my hand, and was trying to ignore me.

"Pretty name."

"Is it?"

"I like your outfit."

"I'm busy. Can't you make yourself busy?"

We were off on the wrong foot already. In all fairness, sharing a small space with a lovely lady and a fresh corpse does push charm and wit to a higher level. I directed a finger at the body on the bed. "It's interesting, don't you think?"

"I might choose a different adjective."

"Then let's see if we can agree on nouns—was it suicide or murder?"

Her eyes had been on the corpse since I entered the room, and for the first time she turned and examined me. "What do *you* think?"

"It sure *looks* like suicide."

"Sure does. But was it made to look that way by him . . . or somebody else?"

Funny. I thought that's what I had asked her.

I turned and again eyed the corpse. Unfortunately, a tall, plump forensic examiner was hunched over the body, mining for evidence, and all I could see was the victim's head and two medium-size feet; the territory between was largely obscured.

But here was what I could observe: The victim was male, late-fiftyish, neither ugly nor attractive, tall nor short, skinny nor fat, and so forth. An everyday Joe. A man with bland features and a gray brush cut, physically ordinary and entirely unmemorable.

It occurred to me that if you walked past him on the street or sat beside him on the subway, you would look right past or perhaps through him.

And there, I thought, was one putative motive for going either postal or suicidal—fatal anonymity. "How long have you been here?" I asked Ms. Tran.

"Thirty minutes, more or less." She was jotting notes in a small notebook. She shifted her shoulder and—accidentally, I'm sure—blocked my view of her notebook. She asked, "What about you?"

"Just arrived. How about a little help getting oriented?" What I failed to mention was why I was here in the first place, which had something to do with the victim's phone being tapped by people from the FBI, who were working with people from the CIA, who had overheard a phone call from a distressed lady to the local cops, reporting a corpse.

The victim was what is termed in the intelligence business a target of interest; *was* being the operative tense. Now he was an object of mystery, and in every mystery there are five basic questions. Who died was obvious, as was where, leaving the three questions I was sent here to figure out—when, how, and with any luck, why.

Nobody informed *me* why and in this business, don't ask. If you need to know, they'll tell you. Irritating, certainly, but there are valid and important reasons for this rule. The fate of our nation might depend on it, so you have to swallow your curiosity, avoid speculation, and get on with it.

Anyway, suspicion of espionage—that was my guess. I mean, the FBI and CIA don't even like or trust each other. They are the Mr. Inside and Mr. Outside, except in cases of espionage, when the crap lands on both their doorsteps. Then you have two prima donnas sharing the same small stage, and we all know what that gets you.

Also worth noting, with the country at war—in Afghanistan and Iraq—espionage had become a more noteworthy matter than during the cold war, where spies mostly just gave up other spies, like homicidal incest. By all the spook thrillers and Hollywood flicks you'd think that was what the whole cold war thing was about. In truth, it was little more than the waterboys at a pro football game snapping towels at each other's butts. Entertaining, for sure: Ultimately, however, the successes were never as great, and the failures never as dire, as they sounded. The more serious stuff would be handled by the millions of armed troops glaring across the inter-German border; the genuinely serious issues by a pair of gentlemen with briefcases who could turn out everybody's lights.

Post-9/11, however, was a new world. Times change—espionage today meant falling towers, crushed nations, and soldiers' lives.

About that latter point, you can bet my interest was more than passing.

Which brings us to me—a newly promoted Army lieutenant colonel by rank, attorney by trade, Judge Advocate General Corps by branch, temporarily assigned to the CIA, though neither Ms. Tran nor the local cops were supposed to know any of that. The CIA is really into disguises, covers, and concealment. Inside the United States, usually this means we're impersonating other federal agencies, and you have to get your act straight. CIA people tend to be intelligent, clever, snide, and arrogant, and you have to suppress that. Feds tend to be intense Goody Two-shoes, wholesome, nosy, pushy, and obnoxious, so I was good to go on three out of five. I think it's fairly obvious which three.

Anyway, Ms. Tran had returned to ignoring me, so I asked her, "Are you going to help me out or not?"

"Why should I?"

"I'll make it worth your while."

"Will you? How?"

I smiled. "Afterward, you can take me to lunch, dinner, Bermuda, whatever."

She replied, without visible enthusiasm, "Let me think about it." Apparently she became distracted by something on the other side of the room, and she wandered away.

I should also mention that, at the moment, I was assigned to a small and fairly unique cell inside the CIA titled the Office of Special Projects, or OSP. About the only thing *special* about this cell that I can see is it gets the stuff nobody else wants—this job, for instance. In my view, it should be called the Office Where All the Bad Shit Gets Dumped, but the spooks are really into smoke and mirrors, so nothing is what it seems, which is how they like it.

Anyway, this office works directly for the Director of Central Intelligence, which has advantages, because we don't have a lot of bureaucratic hoops to jump through, and a big disadvantage, since there's nobody else to pin the screwups on, so it's a bit of a high-wire act.

Also, there are large and significant cultural differences between the clandestine service and the Army, and I was experiencing a few adjustment difficulties. I've been warned, in fact, that if I remove my shoe and speak into the heel again, I can look forward to a long overseas trip someplace that really sucks. These people need to lighten up.

Nor is it unusual for Army officers to be loaned, or, in military parlance, seconded to other government agencies. The idea, as it was explained to me, is we each bring something different to the table—different specialties, different mind-sets, different wardrobes—and the whole becomes greater than the sum of its parts. In an organization, the term for this is synergy, and in an individual it's called multiple personality disorder. I'm not really sure about the difference, but there it is.

But for reasons I have yet to understand, the Agency requested me, and for reasons I fully understood, my former Army boss was happy to shove me out the door, so you might say it seemed to work out for everybody; except perhaps me.

But Phyllis Carney, my boss, likes to say she looks for "misfits, mavericks, and oddballs," for their "willingness to apply unorthodox solutions to ordinary problems." It's an interesting management theory, and I think she's started looking into a new one since my arrival.

Ms. Tran now was poking her head inside the victim's closet. I approached her from behind and asked, "Anything interesting?"

She turned around and faced me. "There are three cops, a forensics expert, and four detectives here. Why me?"

"Update me, and I'll get out of your life."

For the first time she looked interested in what I had to say. "Is this because I'm an attractive woman?"

"Absolutely not." *Definitely.* I said, "You look smart and you take notes. Like the girl I sat beside in second grade."

"When was that? Last year?" She smiled at her own joke.

Which brings me to the here and now: 10:30 a.m., Monday, October 25, Apartment 1209 in a mammoth complex of rental units, mostly cramped efficiencies and one- and two-bedrooms, on South Glebe Road. There was no sign in front of the building that advertised, "Cribs for Swinging Singles," though I was aware it had that reputation.

The apartment was small, essentially one bedroom, an efficiency-style kitchen, closet-size living room, and an adjoining dining room. A Realtor's brochure would characterize it as cozy and intimate, which is code for cramped and uninhabitable. The furniture was sparse and looked new, and also cheap, the sort of crap you rent by the month or pick up at a discount furniture warehouse. I observed few personal, and no permanent touches; no books, no artwork, few of the usual trinkets or junk people sprinkle around to individualize their living environment.

You can usually tell a lot about a person from their home. Especially women who tend to think that how they dress, and how they decorate, are reflections of their inner selves. More often it reveals who they'd like to be, though that contrast can also be telling. Men aren't that complicated or interesting—they're usually anal or pigs; usually shallow pigs. Anyway, I judged the inhabitant here to be fairly neat, not showy, highly organized, and thrifty. Or, alternatively, broke, with the personality and interior complexity of an empty milk carton.

I knew the victim's name was Clifford Daniels, a career civil servant, and I knew that he was assigned to the Pentagon's Office of the Under Secretary of Defense for Policy, or USDP, part of the Secretary of Defense's civilian staff.

I also knew this to be a singularly important office in the vast labyrinth of the Pentagon, the equivalent of the military's own State

Department, where strategies for world domination are hatched and war plans are submitted for civilian approval, among other dark and nefarious activities.

Also I knew Clifford was a GS-12, a civilian rank roughly equivalent to an Army colonel, and that he had a Top Secret security clearance. Regarding those facts, I considered it noteworthy that a late-middle-aged man in a serious profession such as he, working in a sensitive and prestigious office such as his, would choose to live in a complex nicknamed the "Fuck Palace."

I should mention one interesting personal touch I observed as I passed through his living room: a silver frame inside which was a studio-posed photograph of a mildly attractive, middle-aged lady, a smiling young boy, and a frowning teenage girl.

This seemed incongruous with Clifford's living arrangements, and could suggest that we had just stumbled into his secret nooky nest, or he was divorced, or something in between.

Finally, we were just inside the border of the county of Arlington, which explained all the Arlington cops, homicide dicks, and forensics people trying to get a fix on this thing.

Were this suicide, they were wrapping up and about to knock off for an early lunch. If murder, on the other hand, their day was just starting.

As I mentioned, the smell was really rank, and I was the only one without a patch of white neutralizing disinfectant under my nose—or the only one still breathing.

At least I looked manly and cool while everybody else looked like character actors in a stunningly pathetic milk commercial. But in my short time with the Agency, I had learned that image is all-important: The image creates the illusion, and the illusion creates the reality. Or maybe it was the other way around. The Agency has a school for this stuff, but I was working on the fly.

Anyway, Bian Tran was staring at her watch, and she sort of sighed and said, "Okay, let's get through this. Quickly." She looked at me and continued, "I spoke with the lead detective when I arrived. It happened last night. Around midnight." She said, "I think your nose is already telling you that. Am I right?"

After five or six hours at room temperature, a body begins purging gases, and in a small and enclosed space such as this, the effect was worse than the men's room in a Mexican restaurant. Whatever Cliff had for dinner the night before was revolting.

She noted, "Statistically, that's the witching hour for suicides. Not the exact hour, per se. Just late at night."

"I had no idea."

"About 70 percent of the time."

"Okay." I was looking at the window. Unfortunately, we were on the twelfth floor of a modern high-rise and the windows were perma-sealed. I would either have to breathe slower or get her to talk faster.

She said, "Think about it. Exhaustion, mental defenses are worn down, darkness means gloominess, and if the victim lives alone, a mood of depression and isolation sets in." I must have looked interested in this tutorial because she continued, "Spring. That's the usual season. Holidays, though, like Christmas, Thanksgiving, and New Year's are also fatally popular."

"Weird."

"Isn't it? When normal people's moods go on the upswing, theirs sink into the danger zone."

"Sounds like you know this stuff."

"I'm certainly no expert. I've helped investigate seven or eight suicides. How about you?"

"Strictly homicides. A little mob stuff, a few fatal kidnappings, that kind of thing." I asked her, "Did you ever investigate a suicide that looked like this?"

"I've never even heard of one like this."

"Was there a note?"

She shook her head. "But that's not conclusive. I've heard of cases where the note was left at the office, or even mailed."

She walked over to the dresser and began a visual inspection of the items on top: a comb and brush, small wooden jewelry box, small mirror, a few male trinkets. I followed her and asked, "How was the body discovered?"

"The victim uses . . . *used* a maid service. The maid had a key, at nine she let herself in and walked into this mess."

"Implying the apartment door was locked when she arrived. Right?"

"It has a self-locking mechanism." She added, "And no . . . there are no signs of burglary or break-in."

"The cops already checked for that?" I knew the same question would later be asked of me, so I asked.

"They did. The front door and a glass slider to the outdoor porch are the only entrances. The slider door was also locked, if you're interested. Anyway, we're on the twelfth floor."

"Who called the police?"

"The maid. She dialed 911, and they switched her to the police department."

I already knew that, but when you fail to raise the predictable questions, people get suspicious and start asking *you* questions. My FBI creds looked genuine enough to get me past the crime recorder at the door; now all I had to do was avoid any serious discussions that would expose what an utter phony I was. I'm good at that.

Checking the next box, I asked, "Where's the maid?"

"In the kitchen. Name's Juanita Perez. Young, about twenty. Hispanic, and very Catholic, probably illegal, and at the moment, extremely distraught."

"I'll bet." I mean, I arrived at this apartment anticipating a corpse, and yet, between the malignant stench and the sight, I was still appalled. Juanita expected perhaps a messy apartment, but not a dead client, definitely not one in his vulgar condition, and for sure not a green card inspection.

I tried to imagine the moment she entered the bedroom, lured, perhaps, by the odor, lugging her cleaning bucket and possibly a duster or some other tool of her trade. She opened the bedroom door, stepped inside, and bingo—a man, totally naked, lying on his back, utterly exposed with the sheets rumpled around his feet. On the bedside table was a full glass of water, and discarded on the floor by the bed was a pile of unfolded garments: black socks, white boxers, dog-eared brown oxfords, a cheap gray two-piece business suit, white polyester shirt, and a really ugly necktie—it had little birds flying on green and brown stripes. His sartorial tastes aside, it looked like the same outfit Cliff wore to the office the day before. For the watchful observer this is a clue of sorts.

Also, nearly beneath the bed with only a corner sticking out, was a worn and scuffed tan leather valise, which for reasons I'll explain later, you can bet I kept a close eye on.

In fact, I edged my way over, gingerly placed a foot on that valise, and pressed down. The contents felt hard and flat—a thick notebook, or maybe a laptop computer. I then nudged the valise farther under the bed and, to distract Ms. Tran, pointed at the pile of clothes and observed, "He undressed in a hurry."

"Well . . . I'll bet messing up his clothes was the least of his worries."

I nodded. Behaviorally, I knew this to be partially consistent with suicide, and partially not. Those about to launch themselves off the cliff of oblivion focus on the here and now, with perhaps a thought to eternity, totally indifferent about tomorrow, because there is no tomorrow.

But neither are suicidal people usually in a careless rush. They are, for once, masters of their own destiny, their own fate. Some wrestle with temptation, others indulge the moment. Whatever stew of miseries brought them to this point is about to be erased, banished—forever. A calm sets in, a moment of contemplation, perhaps. Some compose an informative or angry or apologetic note; many become surprisingly detached, methodical, ritualistic.

A psychiatrist friend once explained all this to me, further mentioning that the precise method of suicide often exposes a great deal about the victim's mood and mind-state.

Dead men tell no tales, as our pirate friends liked to say. But they often do leave road maps.

A common and I suppose reasonable impulse is to arrange a painless ending, or at least a swift one. But *how* they do it, that's what matters.

Scarring, scalding, or defacing their own bodies is often verboten; thus the popularity of overdosing, poisoning, carbon monoxide, or a plastic bag over the head—methods that leave the departed vessel intact, which matters for some reason. Some turn their final act into a public spectacle, flinging themselves off high buildings into busy thoroughfares, or rounding up an audience by calling the cops. Others take the opposite approach, finding an isolated spot to erase all evidence of their existence, anonymously leaping off tall bridges into deep waters, or presetting a fire to incinerate their corpse.

Unfortunately, we were in a bar, the shrink was a she, I was three sheets to the wind, and I was more interested in her 38D than her PhD. I am often ashamed by own pigginess, but anyway, I understood this: Suicide is like performance art. For the investigator, if you know how to read the signs, it's like a message from the dead. The victim is communicating *something*.

Again, I tried peeking around the hefty forensic examiner's shoulder and asked myself, what message was this guy sending, deliberately or otherwise?

His head rested on a pillow that was soaked with dried blood and brain matter, and about two inches from his left ear rested his left hand, in which a Glock 9mm pistol was gripped. His forefinger was still inside the trigger guard, and a silencer was screwed to the end of the barrel, which was interesting. There were no obvious signs of a scuffle or struggle, further presumptive evidence that this was a solo act.

Of course, you need to be careful about hasty conclusions when homicide is a possibility. There's what you see, there's what the killer wants you to see, and there's what you *should* see.

Tran asked, "Do you have a clear view?"

"I . . . Am I missing something?"

This question for some reason elicited a smirk. "Yes, I think you probably are."

I took this as a suggestion and walked across the room to a position on the far side of the body where the forensics dick no longer obscured my view. I began at mid-body and worked up, then back down.

The first thing I noted was a purpling around his butt and upper arms, as you would expect a few hours after his heart went out of business and gravity cornered the market on blood flow. His stomach had already bloated with gas, and I saw no bruising or abrasions on the corpse. His eyes were frozen open, and his facial expression indicated surprise, or shock, or both. I spent a moment thinking about that.

About two inches above his left ear was a small dark hole, roughly the size of a 9mm bullet, which was indicative that the Glock in his left hand was the weapon that did the dirty deed. I took a moment and examined the pistol more closely. As I said, a silencer was screwed to the barrel, and as I also said, it was a Glock, but a specialty model known as the Glock 17 Pro, which I knew to be expensive and usually imported.

The bullet had been fired straight and level, and part of his right ear, half his brain, and chunks of his skull had produced a sort of Jackson Pollock splatter arrangement on the far, formerly white wall.

No wedding ring—thus Cliff Daniels either was not married or, based on the photographic evidence in his living room, was keeping it a secret.

More interesting, for a man who in so many ways seemed so inconspicuous, in one very notable way Clifford Daniels, at least in his present state, was anything but—I mean, I'm fairly comfortable about my own manhood, but I wouldn't want to have a locker beside Cliff's.

And most interesting of all, his right hand was gripped around his other gun, and at the moment of passing he appeared to have been in a state of sexual arousal. Goodness.

I walked back over to Ms. Tran. She looked at me and asked, "You saw it?"

"It?"

Silence.

Somebody had to say something, and eventually she defined *It*. "He's so . . . large."

"Oh . . . that? I don't call that big."

She smiled.

"Of course, it's not about the size," I told her.

"Wrong."

"Right."

We suddenly found ourselves on thin ice. I mean, here we were, a man and a woman, barely acquainted professionals, sharing a small room with a monster Mr. Johnson flying at full mast.

She suggested, "I suppose we have to address his, well . . . his state of . . ."

"His what?"

"You know . . . his . . ."

"Spell it out."

She said, sounding annoyed, "That's enough, Drummond. We're both adults."

"Really? You should ask my boss about that."

"Look . . . the corpse has . . . had an erection—okay? Let's just keep it clinical. Act like professionals. We can deal with this."

"Good idea. After all, you can't ignore the elephant in the room."

She put a hand over her mouth and smiled, or maybe frowned. Then she mustered a stern look and said, "I hope that's out of your system."

"Not a chance."

"Well . . . now, here's the good news. I think we can rule out erectile dysfunction or penile insecurities as motives for suicide."

We laughed.

I mean, we both were affected by this man's death, sympathetic about the miseries that led to such a tragic act, and professionally dedicated to getting to the bottom of this.

Eros and Thanatos—sex and death. When the ancient Greeks wrote about sex, it was comedy, and of death, tragedy. So the scene before us was a combination of sad, nauseating, and ridiculous. As every cop knows, satire is a coping mechanism, a path to detachment, without which you haven't a prayer of catching the bad guys.

Anyway, that was her excuse. My dog ate mine.

I cleared my throat, and tried to clear my mind, and asked, "So, was it murder or was it suicide?"

"Well . . . the lead detective mentioned a few other things you should be aware of."

"Go on."

"When the maid entered the bedroom, the TV was on . . . as was the DVD player, albeit in passive mode."

"So he watched a little tube before he pulled the plug. Maybe he didn't like the show. Rather than get up and turn the channel, maybe he pushed his own stop button." I recalled a lady friend who once made me watch a full episode of *General Hospital*; I thought seriously about killing myself.

She said, "A porn video was in the DVD player."

We exchanged eye contact.

She added, "I've never seen or heard of this with a suicide. Have you?"

"I've read of cases where certain sexual fetishes resulted in death. For example, asphyxiation, or near asphyxiation, apparently heightens the sexual sensation."

"I've heard of it. In those cases, though, death is accidental, an unwanted by-product. That doesn't apply here."

"Maybe he was holding his breath when he blew out his brains."

I thought she was going to make me stand in the corner. She said, "Sexual asphyxia . . . that's the clinical expression for the fetish you've raised. It involves strangulation, a sudden disruption of blood, and therefore of oxygen, to the brain. But that's not what happened here, was it? He watched a dirty movie, he put a pistol to his head, and he blew out his brain."

I had a really funny response to that, having to do with the possibility that he accidentally blew out the wrong brain. But I sometimes obey my better angels, and instead I suggested, "You could theorize that he used the tape as a distraction from a task that was surely unpleasant. A mental diversion . . . a form of mental anesthesia." Recalling the conversation with my lady shrink friend, I informed her,

"Here's another thing to consider. With suicide victims, the manner of their death often expresses what they were thinking, their final thoughts."

"All right . . . I can see where that makes sense." She gazed thoughtfully at Clifford Daniels's body and asked, "What do you think was the last thing that passed through his mind?"

"A 9mm bullet."

I think I had worn out her stamina for my bad jokes. In fact she said, "Try again."

"Well, it's not necessarily a conscious or even deliberate arrangement on the victim's part. Maybe he was experiencing a final narcissistic impulse. You know, like subliminal exhibitionism run amok."

"You think?"

"I think it's fair to say that Clifford had one exemplary feature. Wouldn't you agree? Maybe he wanted to be remembered for that."

I couldn't tell what she was thinking about this, but she remarked, "Men are really strange."

"Check the nearest magazine rack. Males have no monopoly on sexual exhibitionism . . . or oversize organs, or weirdness."

"And you consider who buys those magazines, and why." She then concluded, "You raise an intriguing point, though. I'll be sure to consult with a psychiatrist about this."

Which offered the opening I'd been waiting for. "Why are you here? Have you got a piece of this case?"

"Why are *you* here?"

"Ladies before gentlemen."

"Oh . . . now you're a gentleman?" It wasn't that funny, but she laughed.

I should mention why I asked. Bian Tran's tan- and loam-colored outfit was not your ordinary feminine attire, but a desert-style camouflage battle dress uniform with Uncle Sam's Army embroidered above her right breast.

The Army uniform can be both illustrative and informative. For instance, the insignia on her right collar—crossed dueling pistols—designated her a member of the Military Police Corps, which might have something to do with her presence here. And from the gold leaf on her other collar, she was a major, with the combat patch on her right shoulder indicating she had a full combat tour under her belt, and had done her part to secure Western civilization, such as it is.

Regarding the person inside the uniform: thick, straight hair, parted down the middle, black in color, and shoulder length, as per regulations, which not all women follow. Eyes large, black, Asiatic in cast, with arched eyebrows that were slyly expressive. I estimated her age at about thirty—young for her rank—so she probably was very good at her job, and there was a warm intelligence in her eyes.

"I asked why you're here," she said.

Vietnamese by name and by race, though her English carried no hint of an accent, in fact was flawless—idiomatically correct, native in tone and inflection, and so forth. Light on the makeup and, if you're interested, as I sometimes am, no wedding band, just a practical black plastic runner's watch, tiny gold West Point ring, and a plastic-wrapped dog-tag chain around her neck.

All in all, I thought Bian Tran was an impressive specimen of soldierly attributes—fit, wholesome, and freshly scrubbed; ready to launch a volleyball on the beach, or a fire mission on an enemy village, whichever the occasion calls for.

She now looked a little miffed and said, "Remember as kids when we played I'll show you mine, if you show me yours?"

I raised my eyebrows.

"Would you just tell me why you're here?"

Also she was quite attractive, though of course in the new Army we don't notice those things. A soldier is a soldier, and lust is a weakness monopolized by the hedonists outside the gates.

Oh, yes, and another thing I didn't notice was the lovely body beneath that camouflage. Svelte, muscular, sexy.

Anyway, I had clearly worn out her patience, and I had a good alibi and informed her, "Well . . . an FBI liaison works at the Arlington police headquarters. As the victim is—or *was*—an employee of the Defense Department, our liaison thought we should take a look."

"What does that mean?"

"If it turns out to be murder, we might exercise jurisdiction. If suicide, on the other hand, it's beneath Bureau dignity and interest—we'll let the locals keep it."

"How generous." She stared at me a moment. "Why would the FBI be interested even if it *was* murder?"

"We wouldn't, necessarily. My job is to report back. The big guys make the call."

She nodded.

"And you? Why does the Army have an interest in the death of a Defense Department civilian?"

"I'm not working for the Army right now. I'm assigned to a Special Investigations unit that reports to the Defense Secretary. The office Cliff Daniels worked in was notified by the Arlington police that he was dead. They called my office, and here I am."

"Investigating, or fact-finding?"

"Like you, I'm expected to compile a brief report on the circumstances of Daniels's death. Nothing more."

"Did you know the victim?"

"No."

"Who gets the report?"

"The header will be the Secretary of Defense's Office. However, it will be read by one of his staff assistants, and probably ignored." After a moment, she added, "Unless Mr. Daniels was murdered."

"And then?"

"This is my first case like this. My office doesn't usually handle violent crimes. Fraud, theft, and sexual improprieties are our bread and butter. But my guess would be the Secretary's Office will send a letter to the Arlington Police Department and ask to be kept in the loop."

I smiled. "Hard to believe, isn't it? Death . . . the amount of paperwork it generates."

"Sure is." She smiled back. "Look, I have to go talk to the lead detective again. Do me a favor?"

"I'm all yours."

"I neither need nor want *all* of you, Drummond." She smiled. "Just keep an eye on that briefcase."

"Briefcase? I don't see—"

"That one." She pointed it out. "The one you accidentally nudged under the bed."

"Oh . . . I hadn't—"

She put her finger on my chest. "I intend to have it dusted for prints. Don't let me find yours on it."

CHAPTER [illegible]

The moment Bian Tran stepped out of the bedroom, I shifted position, closer to the bed and directly behind the forensics specialist, who remained bent over the body, manipulating tweezers and picking debris off the sheets. I cleared my throat and asked, "What are we seeing here?"

"It'll all be in my report," he replied.

"Okay, but—"

"Aren't you *listening*? I said it'll be in my report."

I allowed a moment to pass. Then I withdrew a pen and a small green notepad from my pocket. "What's your name?"

"What?"

"Your name—spell it."

He straightened up. "What are you talking about?"

"For *my* report."

"What the—"

"Back at the Bureau they throw monumental fits over silly things like misplaced modifiers and split infinitives. Misspellings really make them pissy." I added, "I think it's because we hire too many lawyers and accountants. You know? Totally anal."

"I still don't know what—"

"It's fairly simple. I can spell 'impeding a federal investigation.' I just need to be sure I get your name right, Mr. . . . ?"

"Reynolds . . . Timothy Reynolds." He turned around and faced me, and in a nasal, whiny voice, said, "I'm just trying to do my job."

"Aren't we all, Tim?" I flashed my phony FBI creds in his face. "Now what are we seeing here?"

Timothy looked around for a moment, obviously torn between doing his job and mollifying the impatient prick with the federal badge. He insisted, "Well, nothing conclusive. On the surface, it appears the victim committed suicide."

I let a moment pass and asked, "What about below the surface?"

"You must understand that I can't answer questions with any accuracy until everything's run through lab analysis."

"Of course."

"Also I haven't yet taken prints from the gun."

"Check."

"Obviously, this is very important, and—"

"Noted."

"A complete toxicology and serology will need to be worked up. If the victim was on drugs or under the influence of alcohol, that can—"

Holy shit. "Shut up, Tim." I took a deep breath and tried to recall my question. "Is there any physical matter we should be concerned about at this stage of the investigation?"

You can lead a horse to water, but you can't make him drink. Tim glanced over his shoulder at the body and replied, "Well, it's interesting. What I think is—"

"Tim . . . did I ask what you *think*? Facts."

"Oh . . . all right. For starters, the sheets on this bed are changed and washed weekly. The maid informed us. This is relevant and important information. It establishes time frame. The particles and residue on this sheet were deposited within the last seven days."

I flipped open my notebook, scribbled, and said, "Time frame . . . yes, yes, always important . . ." Actually, I began sketching Tim, standing perfectly erect, tottering on a chair, noose around his neck, arms straight, extended and . . .

"There are a lot of the victim's hairs on the pillow," Tim continued, "and sweat residue. But you expect that. Everybody sheds and sudates when they sleep. But there are other hair particles and strands as well."

I erased the chair, Tim's legs were kicking furiously, and—I looked up—"Not *his* hair?"

"Well . . . you can see that his hair was gray, coarse, and cropped very short. There are some red hairs, and also some very fine blonde hairs. Both are quite long, which suggests they could be from females . . ." He turned tentative again, and added, "That's a hypothesis on my part. A chromosonal analysis is needed before a firm conclusion can be reached."

"More than one woman?"

"Well . . . I would say at this point—"

"Yes or no."

"Uh . . . yes."

Goodness. Despite Tim's pathological aversion to declarative phrases, this suddenly took an interesting turn. I asked him, "Have you finished the bathroom yet?"

"I did that first. Bathrooms are always gold mines."

"And what did we find there?"

"More hair. Both black and red, as well as some of the victim's hair in the sink, probably from shaving. And the usual pubic traces on the toilet seat."

"Further confirming the presence of more than one female?"

"It appears . . . yes, perhaps as many as three." He knew what my next line of questioning would be and added, "I ran an infrared light over the sheets. There are interesting traces . . . probably semen. I don't know whether these traces are new or old."

Like that, Cliff Daniels went from the ubiquitous man in a gray flannel suit to something far more complicated and mysterious. This raised a number of evocative questions, not to mention a few dark and dubious possibilities.

Anybody who beds two different women inside one week likes to live on the edge. This guy didn't have to whack himself—just arrange for the two or more women to show up together and they'd take care of things for him.

Indeed, *that*, or some variation thereof, might be what happened here. I looked at the corpse on the bed and asked myself the obvious question: What was Clifford doing in the hour before the trigger was pulled? Did he die alone? Or with company?

To Tim I asked, "Is there *any* indication he was having sex at the time of, or shortly prior to, his death?"

"It does seem an obvious conclusion, doesn't it? I intend to take epidural traces from his penis for the lab. However, from what I've seen . . . or didn't see—specifically, no visible traces of sperm, or crust of vaginal fluid on his penis—it's possible the victim was stimulating himself."

Tim looked at me expectantly as I weighed whether to ask him another question or just kill myself. When I remained silent, he said, "Can I return to my work?"

"What's stopping you?"

"Well . . . you are."

"Nonsense."

"Oh . . . that's a joke." He emitted a sort of high-pitched laugh.

I looked at him and said, "If anything interesting pops up, call me immediately. I'll be in the living room." I turned and started to walk away when I was struck by an afterthought, and turned back around. "Uh . . . ?"

He stared at me.

"How many suicides have you investigated?"

"I don't know. A good many. This is a high-stress area code. Within the county, we experience more suicides than homicides."

"How many of those suicides involved guns?"

"A few. Perhaps three this past year. Overdoses and slashed wrists are the norm. A majority of our suicide victims are teenagers who can't afford—"

"I understand . . . thank you." I asked Tim, "Did you observe any blood splatter on the gun?"

"Yes, some. It was fired from very close range, and there was a volume of blowback. Also, even visually, I can detect powder residue on the victim's left temple. That means—"

"I know what it means." I asked, "Have we confirmed if the pistol belonged to the victim?"

"Not yet. The serial number is unobservable until we turn it over. We don't rearrange the evidence until after I've finished my site inspection."

I pointed at the silencer on the end of the pistol. "Have you ever seen a suicide where the victim used one of those?"

"Uh . . ."

I remembered to specify, "Yes or no?"

"No."

"Does the silencer strike you as odd?"

"I leave the conclusions to the detectives."

"As you should. Except I'm asking your opinion."

"Yes. It is unusual." In fact, I was sure Tim regarded it as more than unusual—even suspicious—though, sucked inexorably back into his orbit of qualifiers and modifiers, he suggested, "You could postulate, I suppose, that the victim didn't want to disturb his neighbors. A final act of courtesy, so to speak. Or he didn't want to be discovered. I've seen suicides where the victim went to great lengths to avoid attention."

"I see." Sometimes it's the little things. Essentially, in almost every way this *looked* like a suicide; that is, every way but two. To begin with, that petrified expression on Daniels's face—eyes wide open, mouth contorted, a mixture of frozen shock and amazement. It's my impression that most people, in the millisecond before they blow a bullet through their own flesh, reflexively shut their eyes, purse their lips, and contract their facial muscles—this is going to hurt, a lot, and the mind and the body respond instinctively, even reflexively, toward the anticipation of pain.

Ergo, shock and surprise seemed wrong. After all, the act of suicide was *his* idea. Relief, anger, sadness, pain—these, or some combination of these, are the expressions one would expect on his death mask.

Plus, the silencer *was* weird. If I assumed the pistol was Clifford's weapon, silencers are hard to come by, expensive, and, even for radical gun lovers, an unusual accessory. I mean, gun nuts live for the big booms. No, silencers are an instrument of assassins.

Neither of these incongruities was entirely dissuasive of suicide, and neither alone implied murder. Taken together, however, they raised doubts, and doubts are like termites; ignore them at your own peril.

I was about to ask Tim another question when I heard footsteps. I turned around in time to see Major Bian Tran, accompanied by a tall, lanky black gentleman in a tweed blazer, walk through the doorway into the bedroom. The gentleman looked amazingly like that actor who played Alex Cross in *Along Came a Spider*, down to the pockmarked face, high cheekbones, salt-and-pepper hair, and thoughtful brown eyes. Weird.

The gentleman was staring at me with a pissed-off expression. Major Tran, also with an eye on me, had an amused squint.

CHAPTER THREE

The gentleman marched straight up to me and asked two direct questions I did not want to hear: "Who the hell are you? And what in the fuck are you doing at my crime scene?"

I withdrew my creds and flashed them in his face. "Special Agent Drummond."

He snapped the creds out of my hand and studied them for a moment. I had the impression he knew I was full of shit.

"Who are *you*?" I asked.

"Detective Sergeant Barry Enders. This is my investigation."

I shifted my attention to Major Tran. She was apparently preoccupied, because she avoided my eyes.

Enders pocketed my creds and said, "Look, Drummond—if that's your real name—you logged into a crime scene using a phony federal ID, you entered the premises, and lied to my investigators. Let's see, that's"—he began drawing down fingers—"impersonating a federal officer . . . trespassing . . . interfering with a police investigation, and . . . give me a minute—I'll think of three or four additional charges."

He reached down to his belt and whipped out a pair of metal cuffs, apparently not needing another minute.

I looked at Tran, and this time she returned my stare; actually, she smiled.

"What's going on here?"

Tran informed me, "No veteran agent comes to an indoor homicide without disinfectant. Rookies make that mistake—once. Cause for suspicion, right? So when I stepped out, I asked Barry what he knew about you."

Enders said, "And guess what, smart-ass? There is no FBI liaison at the Arlington Police Department."

To Tran I said, "You're sharper than you look."

"Actually, you just weren't that clever." She added, "We called FBI headquarters and asked them to confirm the employment of Special Agent Sean Drummond. Would you like to guess what they said?"

I did not need to guess, and anyway, Enders weighed in again. "So let's start with your rights. You have the—"

"I have the right not to hear my rights."

"Ah, hell . . . a funny guy. Who are you? A reporter?"

I ignored that insult. "Write down this number."

"Why?"

"Do as you're told, Detective. Now."

He stared back. Clearly he and I were in a macho pissing contest; we would either stare at each other forever or somebody had to take a swing. Women are better at this; they smile, say something nice and conciliatory, and get revenge later.

But Tran withdrew a pencil and notebook from her pocket and said, "Give me the number."

She copied as I said, "Local, 555-4290. Call and ask what you should do with me."

Enders, taking a threatening step in my direction, insisted, "The next call anybody's making around here will be you—from lockup. Hands up for the cuffs."

"Don't be stupid, make the call."

Tran, who had already shown she was clever and alert, put a hand on Enders's arm and advised, "I don't see how it can hurt."

Reluctantly, he took a step back, then flipped open his cell and dialed as Bian read him the number.

I waited patiently as he listened to the phone ring, then somebody answered, and he identified himself, then explained his problem—moi—and, after a long moment, he said, "And how do I know you're who you claim . . . Uh-huh . . . okay . . . Yes ma'am . . . Uh-huh." He looked at me and listened for a long moment. "No, no need, ma'am . . . Yeah, that would be acceptable . . . Yes, in fact, he's standing right here."

He handed me the phone and rubbed his ear. To Tran he said, somewhere between impressed and annoyed, "This guy's CIA. That was the assistant to the Director." Then, to me, "She wants a word with you."

Shit. I took the phone from Enders and stared at it, while I toyed with the idea of just punching off.

The lady on the other end, Ms. Phyllis Carney, was my presumptive boss, an elderly lady with the looks and bearing of a fairy-tale grandmother and the avuncular temperament of the Big Bad Wolf. About eighty, and thus long past mandatory retirement, which showed she was either irreplaceable at her job, or she knows the apartment number where the chairman of the House Intelligence Oversight Subcommittee keeps his mistress. Probably both—Phyllis doesn't like loose ends.

Her official title is Special Assistant to the Director of Central Intelligence, an amorphous designation, which seems to suit her fine. I had been working for her for six months and had yet to figure out exactly what she does, or who she is. You feel you know her, and on the surface you do. At the same time, something about her is chronically elusive, a maddening mystique, as our writer friends might say. But partly her job is to cover her boss's butt, a Sisyphean task in a democratic land such as ours, where the head spook is always distrusted by the President, despised by the press, pilloried by the left, demonized by the right, and at any given moment is the object of no less than thirty ongoing congressional investigations and inquiries.

It said something about Phyllis that her boss chose her for this punishing and thankless task. It said something more that she accepted it when her high school classmates were either six feet under or dodging skin cancer and hurricanes in America's elephant dying grounds.

She must've been a good choice, however, because her boss was already the second-longest-serving Director in a job where few occupants are around long enough to have overdue books at the library.

Enders reminded me, "Drummond . . . the phone. Your boss."

I actually like Phyllis. She's courtly and well-mannered in that nice, old-fashioned way, and also businesslike and intelligent. At times, too, I think she actually likes me. However, spooks and soldiers have a relationship that, to be charitable, is best characterized as complicated. Partly this is because Army folks, when not covering their own butts, live by the soldier's code, a credo that frowns upon such mannerisms as betrayal, deceit, sneakiness, and moral hedging. These of course are the very qualities that make the CIA the world-class organization it is. But mostly, I think, we just don't trust each other.

Actually, I had no real cause to doubt this lady. And neither could I think of a single reason not to.

"Drummond," Enders barked, "you're wasting my county minutes."

I cleared my throat and put the phone to my ear. "Sorry for the wait. I was killing an international terrorist." Pause. "I strangled him with my bare hands. He really suffered. I knew you'd like that."

She made no reply, though I could hear her breathing heavily. I hate when women do that.

After a long moment I suggested, "Why don't I just hold this conversation with myself? At least I'll like the responses."

She answered, very tartly, "This is no laughing matter, Drummond. Do you know the cardinal sin in our business?"

I could tell she wanted to answer that, so I made no reply.

"You've just blown your cover." She said, "I shouldn't need to remind you that the CIA has no legal authority to investigate domestic homicides. If that detective decides to make a stink—"

"Thank you. I'm a lawyer. I understand."

"Are you? Well . . . *Cucullus non facit monachum.*"

Translated, the cowl does not make the monk. That really hurt. "Look, Phyllis—"

"No—you listen, I speak. Apologize to that detective. Kiss his . . . his fanny as much as it takes, then be gone. I promised him you'd depart immediately."

I glanced again at the briefcase by the foot of the bed. Bian Tran's eyes followed mine, and she smiled. I needed to even the score, and I knew how to do it.

I informed Phyllis, and by extension Enders and Tran, who were being rude and eavesdropping, "Of course. I'll just tell Enders you changed your mind."

"I . . . What?"

"Problem—? No . . . Detective Enders looks like a bright guy with good sense—"

"You'll explain nothing. I told you—"

"Complications? Just one. Call the Office of the Secretary of Defense."

"Drummond, are you listening to—"

"Exactly—what *is* a military police officer doing in a civilian apartment building outside military jurisdiction and poking her nose into this?"

Enders recognized something was amiss, and he was now staring with some annoyance at Tran. For some reason she had lost her smile. Actually, she looked pissed.

Phyllis, also annoyed, was saying, "Drummond, you're out of your mind. The last thing we want—"

"Tell Jim . . . I mean, the Director . . . tell him we'll discuss this when I return." I punched off and handed the phone to Enders, who regarded me with newfound appreciation.

Major Tran also was looking at me, probably wondering how she was going to spend the rest of her day. She suggested to me, with a tiny note of apprehension, "We need to have a word. Alone."

Enders demanded, "What's going on here?"

I turned to Enders. "Understand that the victim was a Pentagon employee. He worked in a very sensitive office and possibly there are highly classified materials in his briefcase. I suspect that's why the major is here." I gave Tran a pointed look and added, "I know that's why I'm here."

"Why didn't you say so in the first place?"

"I'm CIA. We lie."

He thought this was funny and chuckled.

I told him, "Don't touch that briefcase while Tran and I straighten this out."

She and I left and walked together through the living room, through the glass sliders, and outside onto the porch. It was narrow, not long, perhaps four feet, so we ended up about a foot apart, maybe less. Below us, Glebe Road was in its usual state of congested agony, and I pictured Cliff Daniels when he was still alive, standing where now we stood, cocktail in hand, perhaps observing the swarm below, and also perhaps meditating upon the unhappy causes that would make him snuff out his own life. Rarely is suicide a spontaneous act, and I wondered what concoction of miseries and maladies convinced Cliff to remove himself from the gene pool.

Or perhaps Cliff never had that conversation with himself; maybe somebody had that conversation for him.

For a few moments neither Tran nor I said a word. Her arms were crossed and she was staring off into the distance at a mushy formation of cumulus clouds that didn't look all that interesting. Despite this conversation being her idea, she was forcing me to make the first move.

So, to get this off on the right foot, I commented, "You ratted me out back there."

"Well . . . what can I say?"

" 'I'm sorry'?"

"Screw off."

"Close enough." I smiled.

She shook her head. "All right . . . I'm sorry. Look, Sean—"

"*Colonel* Drummond to you, sister."

"You're—?" She looked at me with surprise, then disbelief. "Hold on—you've lied about your identity once. And I'm supposed to believe you now?"

I opened my wallet and withdrew my military ID, which, as per regulations, I had only the week before updated to reflect my new rank and, more happily, my new paycheck. I allowed her a long moment to study it, and watched her expression shift from skeptical to irritated.

I slid the ID back into my wallet. She said, "I overheard you tell the lady on the phone that you're a lawyer. I . . . an Army lawyer at the Agency?"

"I didn't ask for this gig."

"Weird."

"Right." Of course higher rank is a license to bully, so wasting no time, I said, "Major, you have three seconds—what's going on here?"

"I told you."

"Tell me again. You have my permission to alter your story."

"Why would I change it?"

"Fine. I'm sure you'll have no objection when I leave with Mr. Daniels's briefcase."

"Actually, I'll mind a lot."

"Aha."

She looked annoyed. "Let me remind you, Colonel, Clifford Daniels was a Pentagon employee. The contents inside his briefcase are possibly military property. It's my responsibility and my duty to secure it."

"No, the contents are U.S. government property. The Supreme Court decided this issue long ago."

"What are you talking about?"

"*Big Dog vs. Small Dog.* Famous precedent. I'm surprised you're unfamiliar with it." She looked clueless, so I offered her a brief technical summary of the decision. "When the big dog pisses on a tree, the little dog gets lost."

She did not find this amusing. In fact, her eyes sort of narrowed and she said, "I'm a law enforcement officer; you're not. That briefcase *will* leave with me."

"Not outside a military gate you're not, Major. Out here, you're just a lady who doesn't get the dress code."

She cleared her throat. "You're putting me on the spot."

"You put yourself on the spot."

"Don't get carried away by that civilian suit, Colonel," she said with a hard stare. "You're still a military officer. It would be a bad idea to get your loyalties twisted."

"What does that mean?"

"Think about it."

I leaned my butt against the railing and thought about it. Though her face communicated other emotions, I sensed she was under considerable duress to bring home that briefcase. Like me, she might not have been told why, and also like me, she might only be guessing it was something important; I suspected otherwise, though. I said, "I'll pretend you didn't say that."

"Pretend what you like."

I asked, "Do you have reason to suspect there's sensitive or compromising material in Cliff Daniels's possession?"

"How would I know?"

"That's not the right answer, Major."

She hesitated, probably tempted to say fuck you, but instead she suggested, "Colonel, let's keep this friendly. Okay?"

"*You* made it unfriendly."

"I realize that. And that was a big mistake on my part." She smiled warmly. "Hey, I'm woman enough to admit it." She stuck out her hand. "I apologize. Come on—let's start over."

"I'm enjoying where we're at right now." I ignored her hand.

"Well . . . I'm not. I'm sure we can come to an accommodation. Just lose the attitude. I don't respond well to overbearing men."

"What do you respond to?"

"The same things *you* should respond to. Duty, honor, country . . . the higher needs of the society we're both sworn to protect."

"No . . . seriously."

She laughed. And I, too, laughed.

Indeed, this was an intriguing lady. Of course, it never pays to underestimate the competition. Clearly Bian Tran was a fascinating and surprisingly complex woman—self-confident, forceful, spirited, and, I thought on a more contradictory note, sly, brazen, bawdy, and slightly cynical. Beneath that cool intelligence and soldierly veneer, I sensed, was a woman of considerable passion, of suppressed spontaneity, of independent motives—qualities any smart female in the military keeps in check, if not repressed, if she wants a successful career.

It's a little strange. Here was this physically exotic Asian woman, and you expect her to exhibit the manners of the old country, to be inscrutable, demure, subservient to males, and all the rest of that misogynistic crap the occidental male typically associates with oriental ladies. This is why in the great and immutable melting pot of America, stereotypes are such dangerous stuff; they narrow *your* frame of mind, and shape *your* reference and behavior. The object of that stereotype can stuff it up your butt.

At any rate, this seemed like the right moment to put everything on the table. I informed her, "Cliff Daniels was under watch by the FBI and CIA."

She stared at me blankly.

I wasn't buying that and said, "I think you already know this."

"How would I know that?"

"You tell me."

She looked annoyed. "Maybe this conversation would move faster if you enlighten me."

"Maybe it would, but I wasn't informed."

"You weren't . . . You must have an idea?"

"I have better than an idea. Think of the one thing that brings these two brotherly agencies together."

"Oh . . ." She did appear genuinely startled by this news, then said, "Seriously, I had no idea."

"Now you do. And as a cop, you're aware that espionage takes it out of the hands of the Defense Department and into the pockets of the FBI and CIA. That briefcase is leaving with me."

She took a short moment and mentally explored her options. She had no options, but took a stab anyway and said, "On one condition."

"Did I give you the idea I'm asking for permission?"

"Just hear me out. Okay? Let's work out an arrangement."

"I neither need, nor do I want . . . an arrangement."

"Oh . . . yes, you do. We leave together with the briefcase, and we'll search it together." She put a hand on my arm. "This is a good deal for you. I'm both a military police officer and I'm assigned to the Office of Special Investigations. Suppose we do find something inside that case. I can get to the bottom of it faster than you can."

After a long moment, during which I made no response, she added, "My office reports directly to the Secretary of Defense, and we play for keeps. When we ask, people answer."

"Sounds like the Gestapo."

She looked me in the eye. "We're not that nice." After a moment she handed me her cell phone. "Call your boss. Tell him to cancel that call to the Pentagon."

"Her." I took her cell phone. "Give me a moment. She's going to throw a fit."

"Sounds like a tough woman." She gave me a sympathetic look and added, "I'll say it again . . . I'm sorry. I didn't mean to get you in hot water."

She opened the glass door and stepped back inside, then moved to the far corner of the living room, where she crossed her arms, pretended to study the carpet, and I could observe her observing me.

I flipped open her cell phone and dialed Phyllis. Miss Teri Jung, her lovely and very affable secretary, answered and said to hold on.

Phyllis made me wait a full minute before she came to the phone. I sensed she was in an unhappy mood when she opened by saying, "Drummond, I am exceedingly unhappy with you."

"I understand."

"You had better be calling from your car."

"I understand."

"I'm expecting a good explanation for your silliness during that phone call."

"I understand."

"If you say that again, I'll—"

"Are *you* ready to listen?"

I heard her draw a sharp breath. I tend not to draw out the best qualities in my bosses. She said something I already knew. "This better be good."

So I succinctly recounted what I had observed and what I surmised, including that Cliff might have had a helping hand when he killed himself, that Major Tran was suspiciously territorial toward that briefcase, and that perhaps it contained something incriminating, or worse. Phyllis is a good listener—at least a patient one—and she did not interject or comment until I finished. Then she said, "This is curious."

"I know why it's curious to me. Why is it curious to *you*?"

"Well . . ."

We were already off to a bad start. "Start over."

Silence.

"Phyllis, I'm involved. Tell me what's going on here, now, or I'll let Tran walk out with that briefcase."

"You're too nosy for your own good."

She meant for her own good, but with her that might be the same thing. I said, "Three questions. Who is Cliff Daniels? Why are you and the Feds interested in him? And why am I here?"

"This is . . . inconvenient. I can hardly elaborate over an insecure cellular phone connection." After a moment, she added, "Had you been following the news you would have noted in last week's *Post* that Clifford Daniels has been ordered to testify before the House Intelligence Oversight Subcommittee."

"Why?"

"I suppose because Cliff Daniels was Mahmoud Charabi's handler."

A lot of Arabs are in the news these days, but I was familiar with that name. Twenty years before, Mahmoud Charabi had fled Iraq, two steps ahead of a posse of Saddam Hussein's goons, who stayed on his tail and had a clear agenda. There followed a few attempted whacks, including a nasty affair with a hatchet in a London hotel and a shotgun ambush outside a Parisian nightclub. Then Saddam called off the dogs; either other Iraqi exiles bumped Charabi down on the hit list or he was no longer worth the effort. Thus he entered his rootless and peripatetic figure stage, seeking haven first in Switzerland, then London, then Paris, and eventually setting up shop in Washington. As with many exiles driven by restless ambitions and old grudges, he founded an organization for the liberation of his homeland, the Iraqi National Symposium.

Many of these so-called liberation and opposition groups are little more than social clubs for nostalgic expats, associations for preposterously lost causes, or scams for gullible fools to throw money at. The world is indeed a wicked place, filled with nasty tyrants, hateful prejudices, ancient crimes unrepented, starvation, diseases, genocide, and fratricide; all of which, of course, is Pandora's fault—though I suspect human nature also may have something to do with it. And for every wrong, there is somebody who wants to make it right.

In Washington, there are literally thousands of these expat revolutionaries in the wings, organized into hundreds of groups and organizations, all vying to get their dreams and their causes on Uncle Sam's to-do list. The lucky few even find rich and/or powerful patrons to bankroll and lobby their causes. But there is, I suppose, something romantic and adventurous about these foreign people peddling grand ideas for miserable places, because they are highly sought figures on the Hollywood Stars Seeking Grand Causes tours, the D.C. cocktail circuit, and in Georgetown's more storied salons. And why not? Listening to Xian discuss why anguished Tibet must be liberated and free certainly makes for more ennobling table talk than the hubbies bitching about greens fees at the Congressional Country Club. Personally, I prefer uncomplicated company when I eat—definitely when I drink.

But it's clear what draws these galvanized exiles to our shores: our unimaginable power, and their deplorable lack of it; our "light on the shining hill" mentality, and their fingers pointed at dark places; our uniquely American sense of can-do compassion, and their desire, no matter how selfless, to exploit it.

Indeed, America has a grand record of knocking over other nations, even if our history of installing lasting new regimes is a bit checkered. Plus, I suppose it's hard these days to find a great power willing to kick a little butt for a righteous cause. The Europeans have been there, done that; they have lost their appetite, if not their flair, for foreign empires, intrigues, and escapades that often turn out badly. As for the Russians and Chinese, they lack charitable impulses. They liberate like the mob lends money; the vig sucks. But Americans are a generous if slightly naive people, with a distinct messianic bent and the animating conviction that what works for us must work equally well for others. We are the New World, they are the Old; new is always better. Right?

But as I said, Washington attracts a lot of these zealots yearning to borrow Uncle Sam's checkbook and a few legions to rearrange the decor at home. Some are the real deal and their tales of oppression and woe, and their sad optimism, are deeply affecting, even heartbreaking; others are charlatans, schemers, phonies, and scoundrels. Unfortunately they are hard to tell apart, and when you guess wrong, you have a long supply of corpses with a short list of excuses. A happy few, like Shah Pahlavi or Aristide, get their wish; but possibly these are not the best examples.

It's interesting. Having Irish heritage, I find all this a little ironic. Rather than enlist others to fight their battles, my ancestors had the literally unsettling habit of migrating in vast, freckled flocks to fight other people's causes.

There is, in fact, an almost embarrassingly long tradition of this in the Drummond strain. In 1862, Great-great-grandpa Alfonso fled Ireland, he claimed to escape the potato famine; and a pregnant lady and an aggravated father with a shotgun might have added a little impetus. While still scratching his ass on the dock in New York harbor, he promptly accepted one hundred greenbacks from a prosperous New Yorker to take his place in the Civil War draft. He spent three years as an infantryman in a war he understood nothing about, killing people he felt no animus toward, at the behest of somebody who *deserved* to be there, and decided America truly was the Promised Land.

Great-grandpa Seamon served nearly a year in the trenches as an infantryman in the War to End All Wars—subsequently renamed the First World War, after that turned confusing. He insisted to his grave that he shipped out without the slightest idea the Germans, whom he had no particular feelings toward, were killing the English, whom he truly detested, and the French, whom he regarded as uppity bastards who would benefit from a Hun boot on their throat. At least Seamon read the newspaper, cover to cover, every morning the rest of his life.

Grandpa Erasmus waded ashore at Normandy, got lost in the Huertgen Forest, and spent the final months of his war cooling his heels in Stalag Eighteen. Afterward, he swore those were the most relaxing and luxurious years of his life. But maybe you had to know Grandma Mary.

My own father became a lifer, and made a full-blown career of fighting wars in hilly and jungled places with obscure and unpronounceable names. He battled the commies in Korea and completed nearly two full tours in Vietnam—the former referred to as the Forgotten War, and the latter as the War Everybody Wishes They Could Forget.

But as I look back on this extended family chronicle, it strikes me that the Drummonds make good infantrymen—at least we survive—though, as they warn about mutual funds, past successes never guarantee future returns.

Also the wars that five generations of Drummonds have fought have become increasingly less popular, less fashionable, and more morally confused. I myself was an infantryman before I became a lawyer and saw action in Panama, the first Gulf War, Bosnia, and Mogadishu—messy war, good war, utterly confused war, total fuckup.

As I grow older, I find myself less tolerant of people with well-expressed causes they want Sean Drummond to fight for.

Anyway, Phyllis must have been reading my thoughts, because she suggested, "So you're familiar with Mr. Charabi?"

I allowed that question to linger in the air, then said, "What was . . . or what *is*, the Agency's relationship with Charabi?"

"None. He approached us many years ago. We did some backgrounding and didn't like what we saw."

"I know the official line. Try the truth."

"I'm telling you the truth. We took a pass." She emphasized, "Charabi was, and *is*, the Pentagon's creature. Start to finish."

"And how did the dead guy on the bed end up as Charabi's . . . as his *what*?"

"Technically, his controller. But it's more complicated than that . . . Before he moved to the Pentagon, Cliff Daniels was a career officer at the Defense Intelligence Agency. About a decade ago he befriended Mahmoud Charabi, or possibly vice versa." She concluded, "That's it. As far as I can go on an unsecure line."

I thought about this a moment. From the news reports, I had read that Charabi spent about twenty years peddling his plans and scams for a free Iraq. I'll bet he thought his train had come in when this President decided that Saddam needed the boot, if only somebody could help him justify why.

I wasn't sure why or how Charabi became that go-to guy; but he did, and apparently the dead guy on the bed played a big hand in it. Also, as I recalled from the news reports, Charabi was supposed to be the Pentagon's man to run Iraq after the invasion, though obviously that hadn't worked out exactly as planned, since nobody seemed to be in charge in Iraq now, at least no Iraqis, and possibly not even the U.S. military.

Then, somehow, Daniels himself ended up as a target of intelligence interest, with an invitation to explain his activities in front of a congressional panel. Interesting.

Anyway, Phyllis repeated herself, saying, "I really can't go any deeper on the phone." She added, "I've told you more than you should know, as it is. Unless you're part of the investigation."

"I didn't know there was an investigation."

"With Daniels dead, it's now imperative to learn *why*. An investigation is how we usually handle these things."

"Maybe it was suicide. Sure looks like suicide."

"Maybe it was. But knowing what you now know, the alternative gains a little added weight . . . don't you think?" She gave me a moment to think about it, then said, "Now you persuade the Arlington police that it *was* suicide. And bring back that briefcase."

"Are you ordering me to lie to the police? I want to be clear on this."

"Did I say that?"

"In so many words . . . yes."

I couldn't see her smile, but I could picture it. She said, "You're a lawyer, Drummond. Handle it."

"Am I part of this investigation?"

"Do you want to be?"

"No."

"Then now you are. Is that settled?"

"Not yet. Who am I working for?"

"You report to me."

"And who do you report to?"

She ignored my question and said, "The Agency inspector general and the FBI already have an ongoing investigation, of which Daniels was a subject. But we'll handle them as parallel efforts. Ours will be kept separate, quiet, distinct."

Interesting. "And will one hand know what the other hand is doing?"

"I receive ongoing updates on what they're doing."

"That's not what I asked."

"Figure it out."

I figured it out. Phyllis would hold *all* the cards. I asked, "What am I investigating?"

"Whether Daniels was murdered or not. We'll see where it leads from there."

"And Major Tran?"

"Yes . . . I'm glad you brought her up. Do you feel you can trust her?"

"As much as I trust you."

Now I was sure she was smiling. She asked, "More relevantly, does Major Tran trust you?"

"Absolutely. As we speak, she's on the other side of a glass slider, trying to read my lips."

Phyllis laughed. She asked, "Can you *work* with her?"

"I can work with *you*, so I'm sure I can work with her."

I thought I heard a sharp breath. I think I had just worn out her patience for my insolence. Part of the fun of this job was seeing how far I could push it. The Army, peculiar institution that it is, tends to be fairly stiff regarding such issues as insubordination and disrespect to superiors. Candor is permitted, even encouraged, so long as it is rendered respectfully. Of course, one senior officer's interpretation of respect can differ substantially from another's, so you have to watch your P's and Q's. The CIA, also a fairly hierarchical organization, is sort of a halfway house between a martial culture and a civilian one, and you have a little more leeway to be a pain in the ass.

Back to Phyllis. She said, "I think it would be invaluable to have the Defense Secretary's own investigative staff in on this. The Pentagon is, after all, a fortress of sorts. You should . . . partner with her."

"You mean, use her as a Trojan horse?"

"You know how much I dislike analogies. You shouldn't oversimplify complex situations." She added, after a long pause, "But yes, that one fits."

Lest you think I'm a complete fool, it was Phyllis, after all, who dispatched me to this death scene in the first place, and nothing she does, or thinks, is serendipitous. She is well aware of my nosy, mulish ways, my propensity to rush around corners, my . . . well, enough virtues. The larger point is, I was the sole military person in her office, Mr. Daniels was an employee of the Pentagon, and it was suddenly clear why she picked me for this job.

And now she was exploiting one Trojan horse to recruit another—a frightening display of how her mind works.

The truth is, our relationship is no more or less complicated than that between a cat and a mouse. I'm nimble and quick. And so is she, with a facile mind and razorlike paws. It's sort of fun, also scary, and often dangerous. But the larger truth is, I wanted a piece of this case.

Phyllis mentioned, "Incidentally, *Bis dat qui cito dat.*"

In plain English, he gives twice who gives promptly—and I understood what she meant, and why. As soon as Clifford Daniels's identity was nailed down, via witnesses, personal identity cards, dental records, and/or fingerprints, the Arlington Police Department public affairs people would issue a standard public notice. With luck, the local press might not recognize the significance of Daniels's name before they filed their late edition; without luck, some enterprising reporter would run Clifford's name through Lexis, Google, or Yahoo! and get an interesting hit. Either way, by morning, the nuts and junkies would be on this like flies on poop.

Washington has always thrived on juicy rumors and corpulent conspiracy theories, fueled by amateur Oliver Stones—people with dark outlooks, overheated imaginations, whose mental bolts could stand a good tightening. But the proliferation of cable news channels, talk radio, and Internet blogs has changed a beltway pastime into a national frenzy. Every paranoid idiot now has an outlet and an audience. A few even have network anchor jobs.

I informed Phyllis, "That isn't my problem."

"It is now. Speed, Drummond. Get this done quickly." Right.

She agreed to call Major Tran's office and work out some kind of bureaucratic entente, and I told her what I needed when I returned to the office . . . starting with a new job.

I snapped shut the cell, stepped back inside, and rejoined Major Tran, who was still pretending to study a piece of faux artwork on the wall.

I nodded at her. She nodded back.

"When did you first figure me out?" I asked her.

"I don't know. Maybe . . . the instant you claimed you're FBI."

"Really? I was obnoxious, overbearing, and a prick. What gave me away?"

"You were all of the above. You just don't fit the mold."

"I'm . . . devastated."

"You'll get over it."

"I'm even wearing fresh undershorts."

"Thank you for sharing that." She smiled. "You forgot your look of wholesome goodliness."

We walked together, she and I, back to the bedroom and Detective Sergeant Enders.

CHAPTER FOUR

If possible the smell had worsened to the point that Bian Tran refreshened her disinfectant the moment we reentered the bedroom. Our newly erected partnership apparently had limits; she never offered me a dab.

Tim Reynolds was still painstakingly lifting lint and particles off the bed and dropping them into labeled plastic Baggies.

Enders, still with an eye on the briefcase, was conferring with another gent, who also wore a cheap sports coat and bad necktie—it had green and yellow polka dots. As he spoke, he kept glancing at his notebook, presumptive evidence that he also was a detective.

Clifford Daniels remained naked—and dead.

In fact, as we entered the detective was informing Enders, ". . . suicide. Yeah, I'm comfortable with that. I guess I'd feel better if I knew something about his life, whether he fits into a suicidal profile. But . . . look . . . gun in his own hand, no break-in, the overall physical arrangement . . . it's fairly clear-cut."

"Yeah . . . but . . ."

Before he could finish that "but," I chose to intervene. "Major Tran and I are equally satisfied it was suicide."

Enders glanced in my direction. "Did I ask your opinion?"

"That was more than an opinion."

It got a little frosty in the room. "What are you talking about?"

"As there's no apparent reason to suspect foul play, Major Tran and I are seizing Daniels's briefcase as government property. It's immaterial to your investigation and we're asserting the right of higher domain."

"The . . . ? What in the hell are you talking about?"

For his edification, Bian explained, "It's a complicated legal theory. Something to do with big dogs, small dogs, and, if I recall correctly . . . urinating on trees."

Enders looked at me like I was nuts.

"That briefcase is mine," I said, and stepped toward the bed and the briefcase.

He put a hand on my arm. "Welcome to Arlington County, pal. Higher domain, my ass—*my* beat, *my* briefcase. I decide what's relevant and what's not."

"Not this time."

"This time, every time." I took another step toward the bed, and he said, "Touch that case and I'll slap cuffs on you."

Bian and I traded looks and shared the same disquieting thought. Somebody needed to play good cop. I can do that, though it's not really my forte, and in any event, the slip was already showing beneath my sheep's clothing. Besides, differences in uniforms aside, a cop is a cop, and Bian was a cop, and she could talk the talk. She said to Enders, "Barry, do you have doubts about this being suicide?"

"Well . . . I . . . uh . . ." It seemed Enders either had none, or at least none sufficiently evolved to be expressed.

"Because I agree with Drummond," Bian continued. "So does your detective. He called it clear-cut and he's right. The man killed himself."

"Nothing's firm until I get results from forensics, and until I know something about the victim . . . what might've led to this. You're a cop. You know that."

"I know how it works procedurally, Barry. I'm also aware that you have certain leeway for extraordinary circumstances."

He looked at her. "I have an ongoing investigation here. That briefcase could contain evidence relevant to my investigation, and until I know otherwise, it stays in my custody."

"Should we find any, I'll call immediately. Promise."

"Come on. I shouldn't need to remind you about chain of custody issues."

"I . . ." Bian paused and looked at me: Cop-to-cop, she was getting the crap kicked out of her.

This sounded like a good time for a little expert legal advice—meaning vague, selective, and possibly misleading advice. I turned to Bian and asked, "Your office—is it an investigative agency or a law enforcement office?"

"Both—I have the power to make arrests, as well as the legal authority to refer for prosecution."

"Well, there you have it." I turned to Enders. "Just sign an evidence transfer statement, from you to her. Right?"

"And if it don't stand up in court, I'm left holding the bag. The county prosecutors here are real . . . Look, I'm two years short of retirement. I don't need trouble."

"I'm a government lawyer. Trust me."

Maybe that was a poor choice of words. He replied, "I don't even know who the hell you are. You claimed to be FBI, then CIA, now you're a lawyer. You better figure out who you are before you start offering advice."

Bian assured him, "He *is* a lawyer, Barry. Also an Army lieutenant colonel . . . a JAG officer."

My identities and jobs were switching so fast, poor Enders looked like he needed a flowchart to keep me straight. I explained, "Look, Detective, it's no different than forwarding samples to a state forensics facility or an FBI lab. Major Bian has an investigative specialty—to wit, a security clearance—that affords her the ability to examine and interpret evidence neither you nor your department possess."

I was making this up, of course. It did sound good, though, and Enders seemed to be impressed by my grasp of legal technicalities, or my inventive bullshit, which are actually the same thing. Still, he insisted, "I'm going to see what's inside that briefcase."

Bian started to object, before I said, "Fine. He's doing his job. Let's just make sure there's no cover sheet that says Top Secret."

I walked to the bed, bent down, and picked up the briefcase. As I mentioned, it was a valise-style case—so no lock, just a brass clasp that I undid then peeked inside.

There were no loose papers, certainly no Top Secret cover sheets, nor did I see a helpful and illuminating suicide note, just a slim gray Gateway laptop computer and a thick store-bought address book. I carried the valise over to Enders and allowed him to peek inside and observe the contents.

Bian, peering over his left shoulder, predictably concluded, "Looks innocent enough."

Enders asked, "Is that an office or a personal computer?"

"I'd have to turn it on to tell," Bian replied. "But not in your presence. It's irrelevant, anyway."

Bian reached into her pocket and withdrew her business card, which she thrust into Enders's hand. "If this causes you problems, Barry, refer them to me."

I said to Enders, "When you get the results from forensics, call. Also, we'd like to know if the gun belonged to Daniels or somebody else."

He looked at me and replied, "I can't tell you how fucking pleased I am to be of service."

"Incidentally, we were never here."

"You know what?" he replied. "I wish that were true."

In the parking lot, Tran and I decided that as she had arrived in her own car and I in a government sedan, we would depart together in mine. The subtext here: Neither of us trusted the other alone with the briefcase. Also my car, a big blue Crown Victoria, used taxpayers' gas. This is called interagency cooperation.

As soon as we were seated and buckled in, she said, "Don't take this the wrong way . . . but your place or mine?"

"I'm driving. Mine."

"I knew you had an ulterior motive."

"What did you expect? I'm CIA."

I put the car in gear, backed out of the parking space, and headed east in the general direction of Crystal City, specifically toward the large brick warehouse where my office is located.

I should mention that the Office of Special Projects is located not, as you might expect, at the sprawling headquarters at Langley but in the aforementioned warehouse. The warehouse is a front, or in the lingo of the trade, an offsite, with a sign out front that reads "Ferguson Home Security Electronics." A double entendre is supposed to be located in there somewhere. Don't ask.

I was still new to all this, but as I understand it, OSP handles important projects for the Director that are highly sensitive and confidential in nature. And CIA people are, by training and instinct, nosy, cunning, and intrusive—at least the better ones are. So the purported intent of this geographic separation is to reduce the chances of leaks, thefts, or competitive sabotage. I guess it's no secret that the CIA distrusts other governments or even its own government. But it is somewhat surprising how little it trusts even itself.

After a moment of companionable silence, Bian said, "I have a confession."

"If this concerns your steamy sex life, keep it to yourself, Major."

She looked at me. "Is this going to be a long day?"

"You'll earn your paycheck."

"Well . . . okay, here goes. About Cliff Daniels . . . I may have—actually I *wasn't* entirely forthcoming."

When I failed to reply to this bold revelation, she said, "I was sent because Daniels was the controller for a man named Charabi. Are you familiar with that name?"

"Sure. Simon Charabi. Delivers my laundry."

She was obviously getting to know me and said, "I'll assume that means yes." She paused, then said, "Because of Daniels's relationship with Charabi, a House investigating subcommittee ordered him to testify. He was scheduled to appear next week."

"I don't think he's going to make it."

"Probably not. Anyway, his death is going to require an explanation to the panel members."

"Why are you telling me this now?"

"As long as we're working together, I . . ." She paused for a moment and reconsidered her words. "Cooperation is a sharing experience." She touched my arm and said, "I expect you to reciprocate. We're partners, right?"

She stuck out a hand. We shook.

She was a good liar, but not that good. What she really meant to say was that she thought Phyllis might have already let me in on this secret, or soon would. But rather than harm our plastic mood of amity, I asked, "Where'd you get that combat patch?"

"Iraq. During the invasion, and a year afterward."

"You should fire your travel agent."

She smiled and said, "We have the same travel agent." She added, "I was the operations officer of an MP battalion during the invasion. Afterward, during the first year of the occupation phase, I was with the corps intelligence staff. My alternate specialty is military intelligence and I'm a fluent Arabic speaker. A lot of my time was spent interrogating prisoners, or performing liaison with local Iraqi police in our sector."

"I'll bet the Iraqis got a kick out of that."

"Out of what?"

"An attractive Asian-American woman speaking their lingo. Was it a problem?"

She shrugged. "It was awkward. Not the language part, the female part. They have fairly medieval views toward women. It's not a fundamentalist society, but in Arab countries the notion of male supremacy is more cultural than religious."

"No kidding? Hey, I might even like it there."

She wisely ignored my chauvinism and added, "You have to learn the tricks."

"Like what?"

"Show them your gun and speak with blunt authority. If they're still leering, knee them in the nuts." She added, "They grew accustomed to that under Saddam. It helps them get over it."

"Does it? I don't recall that technique from the textbook."

"I'm speaking metaphorically. But Iraq *is* different. The textbook doesn't work there. You have to make certain . . . adjustments."

"Every war is different."

"I'm talking about something else. One minute the people are smiling and waving at you, and then . . . the moment you're out of sight, those same people are planting artillery shells and bombs in the road to blow you to pieces."

"Maybe you misinterpreted their waves. Maybe they meant 'au revoir, asshole.' "

"That's not funny."

"That wasn't meant to be funny."

She took a deep breath, and then we made eye contact and she said, "One day, I watched a car pull up to a checkpoint. A woman in a black veil was driving and yelling out the window for help. A little kid was in the passenger seat, for Godsakes. Two of my MPs let down their guard, they approached her and— It was really awful. Body parts flew all over the place." She held my eyes for a moment, then added, "They don't play by *any* rules—that leaves you no choice. What kind of people blow up their own children? You have to throw away the rule books over there."

"Do you?"

"Oh . . . I forgot. You're a lawyer."

"Meaning what?"

"You know what it means."

"I really don't. Explain it."

"Nothing. Drop it." I glanced at her and she said, "I wasn't trying . . . I wasn't implying—"

"Did it ever strike you that maybe the people there are pissed off because we invaded their country, and now they view us as unwelcome occupiers? Unreasonable, I know, but maybe it's why they're trying to kill us."

Apparently I struck a raw nerve because she said, "Spare me the armchair moralizing. Here you see these news reports of people having their heads lopped off, or being blown to bits by roadside bombs, and you think, oh goodness, how awful. Over there, you lay awake at night wondering if you're next."

She started to say something else, but apparently changed her mind.

"When you throw away the rule book, Bian, you get Abu Ghraibs. Play by those rules, they lose *and* you lose."

She decided to change the topic, because she asked, "How did you wind up at the Agency?"

"One day I came into work and everybody was gone. All the furniture was gone, too, except a desk with my nametag on it."

She laughed.

"Countries, governments, office buildings . . . that's how they do things." After a moment, I added, "They're not completely bad people, though. I got to keep my parking space."

"Seriously."

"Seriously . . . I don't have a clue."

She changed subjects again, and asked, "So what do you think? About Daniels? Did he kill himself or was he murdered?"

"What do *you* think?"

"To be frank, a few elements appeared out of sync for a suicide. You must have noticed the silencer. Also, his nudeness—that makes me uncomfortable."

"Nothing to feel bad about. He was pretty big."

She elbowed my arm. "You know what I'm saying. There's a contradiction here."

"Explain it."

"All right. He uses a silencer, presumably not to disturb the neighbors. The inference here is that even as he's contemplating suicide, he's concerned about how those neighbors will remember him. Yet he's willing to expose himself as a vulgar idiot as a corpse. Does that make sense to you?"

I hadn't even considered that angle. I mean, anyone contemplating suicide, by definition, needs to get his or her head screwed on straight. She said, "Incompatibilities are clues in themselves."

"Right. And did you notice his dying expression?"

"I know what you mean. Scared, frightened . . . actually, surprised. Also out of character for the situation."

"Was he married?"

"Was. I was told he was divorced."

"What else were you told?"

"I was in a rush. There wasn't time to run a full background check."

"Okay. Well, we'll soon learn more about this guy and what made him tick."

After a long moment, she replied, "Perhaps we'll learn more than we want to know."

In retrospect, that turned out to be the ugly truth.

We turned in to the parking lot of Ferguson Home Security Electronics.

CHAPTER FIVE

Ferguson Home Security Electronics: There actually is a store directly inside the front entrance that would appeal to the most paranoid citizens, including shelves bristling with high-tech bric-a-brac to keep burglars out of your home or unwanted husbands out of your life, whichever ails you.

If that doesn't fool you, there is also a helpful female receptionist, Mrs. Lila Moore, who does actually possess expert knowledge of home security devices; in her spare time she also happens to be an officer in the Agency's security service, with a gun inside her desk and a license to kill, which is one of the reasons I'm nice to her. The other is she's really pretty.

Lila looked up as we entered, awarded us a vacuous smile, and asked me, "What can I do to assist you, sir? We're having a big sale on a spectacular line of window alarms. Would that interest you?"

Bian looked around, obviously wondering if we had wandered into the wrong place.

"I'm interested in you," I informed Lila.

She stared back, wide-eyed.

"Hands where I can see them. Your money or your life."

Lila raised her hands in pretended alarm. "Please, sir . . . I'm a mere employee. Don't hurt me." She frowned and added, "There is no money. Basically, business really sucks here."

"Well . . . I already knew that. What do you have?"

"Let's see . . ." She smiled. "How about a pissed-off senior citizen waiting for some guy named Drummond?"

"Oh . . ."

Lila laughed and shoved the sign-in sheet across her desk. "You know the drill." I scrawled Bian's name on the page, while Lila handed her a white guest pass. This is a controlled facility, with obviously questionable standards, because they let me in. She informed us, "Some Pentagon bigwig arrived a few minutes ago. Phyllis logged him in."

I saw a name on the log and pointed it out to Bian.

"Mark Waterbury," she informed me. "My boss. An SES 1. A man you don't want to tangle with." She gave me a pointed look. "You might want to exercise a little . . . rhetorical restraint."

"How do you spell that?" I knew, of course, that SES 1 stands for Senior Executive Service, Level One—a politically appointed rank roughly equivalent to a brigadier general. I told Bian, "Right this way," and led her to the door at the rear of the store, which I opened, and through which we entered into a large cavernous space, essentially a converted warehouse.

The government does not believe in spoiling its employees, and the home of OSP sets a shining exemplar; clearly the lowest bidder furnished it, and it is poorly lit enough to provoke suicidal fits. There actually are a few genuine offices for the more senior people, none of which read Drummond on the nameplate; mostly, however, it's a congested, sprawling cube farm. The lack of walls and privacy are designed to engender teamwork and a sense of community, and the communal sparseness to encourage a feeling of proletarian solidarity. Anyway, that's the theory; reality is a roomful of people who whisper a lot and act sneaky.

A few people said hi as Bian and I made our way to the rear where Phyllis had her office. I knocked twice, and she called for us to enter.

Phyllis was behind her desk, and to her front was seated a gentleman of late middle age, bald head, intense brown eyes, who at that moment appeared to be experiencing unhappy thoughts. Phyllis stood and said, "Mr. Waterbury, obviously this is Sean Drummond." Phyllis walked from around her desk and extended her hand to Bian, saying, "And you're obviously Major Tran."

Mr. Waterbury did not rise to shake my hand, which was interesting, and revealing. But now that we knew who we all obviously were, Bian and I took the chairs against the far wall. I placed Clifford Daniels's briefcase prominently on my lap, and like the good subordinate I sometimes pretend to be, allowed my boss to make the opening move.

Phyllis had returned to the seat behind her desk, which I knew to be her standard practice whenever she needs a physical barrier from an asshole. She looked at me. "Mr. Waterbury is the director of the Office of Special Investigations."

I nodded at Mr. Waterbury, who was studying me.

Phyllis continued, "He's not completely convinced that a joint investigation is the best way to proceed."

"Why not?" I asked.

"He believes this matter falls squarely under his jurisdiction. As he pointed out to me—rightly—the CIA has no business investigating a domestic death, be it suicide or homicide."

"A very persuasive point," I noted diplomatically as I stifled a yawn.

I took a moment and studied Mr. Mark Waterbury even as he continued to study me. From his upright, wooden posture, trim figure, neat attire, and severe expression, I was sure he was former military.

But of a certain type. Some are drawn to military service as a patriotic calling, others by a yearning for glory, others in an effort to reform a life going wrong, and others to put a dent in their college tuition. I do it because I happen to look really good in a uniform. A select few, however, are enthralled by the lifestyle—the rarefied military sense of order, discipline, and a rigidly hierarchical universe where everything has its place, and everybody has their place. Hollywood caricatures are often based upon these stereotypes, and while by no means are they a majority of people in uniform, they are out there, and they do stand out. They tend not to be clever or resourceful, but they do keep you on your toes.

This, of course, was a lot to read from a brief glance. It was in his eyes, though—a pair of compressed little anal slits with tiny ball bearings for irises.

In fact, Waterbury's first words to me were, "You had no business being at Daniels's apartment."

"Nonsense."

"Is it? This agency is barred by law from involvement in domestic matters."

"A man was reported dead and I went to look. Simple prurient curiosity. Where in the federal statutes does it say CIA employees can't look?" I smiled at Mr. Waterbury.

We exchanged looks that were fairly uncomplicated, essentially telling each other to fuck off. This was not one of my better Dale Carnegie moments, but why waste time acting civil and friendly when you already know where it's going to end up?

He pointed at the briefcase on my lap and, with a nasty smile, said, "Yes . . . well, you walked out of a possible homicide investigation with material evidence, Drummond. That, in fact, is a serious violation of the federal statutes."

I love it when idiots try to play lawyer with me. I live for moments like this. I held up Daniels's briefcase. "*Evidence?* Did you say this case contains evidence?"

"I . . . what?"

"Evidence, Mr. Waterbury. You claimed this case contains evidence."

"I did not say—"

"I'm sure you did." I looked at Phyllis, who appeared amused, and asked her, "Isn't that what he said?"

"It's definitely what he implied."

I turned back to Waterbury, whose face was reddening. "By inference, you have relevant, prior knowledge about what's inside this case." He stared back without comment, and I continued, "By implication, something inside this case is pertinent to Cliff Daniels's death. That's news to me. Wow! I need to turn this case over to the proper authority."

"Don't play games with me, Drummond. You'll hand that case over to me."

"Not likely."

Mark Waterbury apparently was not accustomed to having his orders questioned and was experiencing some trouble maintaining his equanimity. In fact, his face reddened, he clenched his fingers, and a snort erupted through his nostrils.

I continued, "You're a political appointee, not a law enforcement official. And since you raised the issue of jurisdiction, surely you must be aware that your office lacks authority to investigate matters outside of military property." I smiled. "If I give you this briefcase, *that* would be a felony."

Waterbury was giving me a stone face, as if he didn't have a clue what I was talking about. I knew how to fix that.

I looked again at Phyllis. "This briefcase has to go to the FBI. And I will of course inform our federal friends that Mr. Waterbury has foreknowledge about whatever they'll find." I looked at Waterbury and noted, "They love it when the evidence comes with somebody to explain what it means. Saves time."

I stood but did not walk out.

As though it needed to be said, Phyllis mentioned to Waterbury, "Did I fail to mention that Drummond is an attorney?"

Waterbury mumbled under his breath, something fairly short, about two syllables, I'm sure about what a good lawyer I am.

To Phyllis I said, "So . . . if you'll excuse me . . ."

Waterbury had gone from red in the face to worried. He said to me, "Sit down."

"I don't take orders from you, pal."

Phyllis said, "You do from me. Please sit until we get this matter resolved."

I sat.

Phyllis took my cue and turned to Waterbury. She asked him, "What's on that laptop?"

"I have no idea."

"You might not know the particulars, or you might, but you have some idea or you wouldn't be here."

"It's none of your business." He looked at Phyllis. "Tell Drummond to hand over that briefcase."

Phyllis ignored this request and Waterbury looked increasingly ill at ease. As I said, the man was not clever, and clearly he lost his sea legs in an environment where the lines of authority were ambiguous and the solution to a dispute cannot be found in the manual.

He needed another little nudge, though. I leaned forward and advised Phyllis, "You don't want to hear what's inside the briefcase. Once you *know* what he knows, it could implicate you in a criminal conspiracy." I looked at Waterbury. "It's his problem. Don't let him make it yours."

Nobody spoke. I had just uttered the golden phrase—criminal conspiracy—with all it's nasty echoes of Teapot Dome, Watergate, Iran-Contra. Nothing strikes greater fear into the heart of a government bureaucrat—and from Waterbury's change of expression, I had clearly hit a nerve. Phyllis had a hand over her mouth, but I couldn't tell if she was choking back laughter or biting her lip. As for Waterbury, his lack of cleverness notwithstanding, clearly he had enough feral cunning to understand what he had just heard—the last lifeboat was being lowered over the side.

"Uh . . . okay . . ." He reluctantly said, "It's possible Daniels was carrying on correspondence with some of his Iraqi friends. Freelancing. Outside of work. It's also possible that some of that correspondence is classified."

Phyllis asked, "Do you suspect this, or do you know this?"

"We merely suspect it."

I said, "It's possible, or probable, or definitely he was?"

"Don't push me, Drummond."

"Waterbury, friends of mine are across the waters right now. I attended two funerals last month, good men who died much too young. If somebody back here is playing games with their lives, I'll push you into an ocean of shit so deep your feet will never touch bottom. Are we clear?"

"It might surprise you to know, that would piss me off, too."

"That would surprise me." Clearly we were both getting on each other's nerves; the difference was I was enjoying it.

Phyllis interrupted our little pissing contest, and said to Waterbury, somewhat dryly, "Explain what you mean by correspondence."

"We really don't know. Daniels was a senior employee. He had leeway to operate independently."

Phyllis skillfully allowed Waterbury a moment to reconsider his position, then suggested in a sly tone, "Mark, I think it would be in our mutual interests to pool our efforts and get to the bottom of this. Don't you?"

Still staring at me, Waterbury replied, "Are you giving me a choice?"

"Drummond just explained your choice."

Of course, he had to get in his last licks, and insisted, "Here's the terms. Whatever we find goes to the Secretary of Defense for disposition. There is a war on, and if Daniels did something harmful to . . . that effort . . . it must be weighed against the larger needs of national security. Take it or leave it."

He made a threatening glower at Phyllis, then at me. I'm not overly Pollyannaish about the public's right to know, but I meant every word I said to Waterbury. My brothers and sisters in arms were getting blown to pieces over there. Depending on what I found, I would make up my own mind about how to deal with it.

I turned to Waterbury and assured him, "Sounds good to me." Of course my fingers were crossed.

Phyllis, displaying more honesty than I, insisted, "Whatever we find will also go to the Director. I will abide with his decision."

Waterbury studied her face, and although it went against his obvious grain, he nodded. Phyllis said, "Good. Please allow me a moment to speak with Drummond."

Waterbury and Bian stood. They left the room, and the door closed with a loud crack.

Phyllis smiled at me and said, "You handled that well."

"He's a dimwit."

"And don't you underestimate him," she replied sharply. "He won't be so easily dealt with if you don't have him by the balls." She added, "I'll do my best to watch your back, but you had better watch your own ass."

Either my coarse soldier talk was starting to rub off on Phyllis or she was taking it down a notch to make sure the message got through. I have that effect on people. Anyway, I already had figured out that my future dealings with Mr. Waterbury were likely to be stormy, perhaps hazardous.

There was something I did not understand, however. "What's going on here? What has Waterbury all worked up?"

"You don't know?"

Obviously not.

She said, "I've already told you that Daniels was career DIA. Here's what I didn't mention. In the run-up to the war, as you might've read in the newspapers, the Office of the Under Secretary of Defense for Policy decided it did not like, or perhaps trust, the intelligence the Agency was providing the White House. They therefore formed their own small intelligence cell to . . . in their words, to vet and decipher the intelligence on Iraq. This cell had a straight pipeline to the Secretary of Defense, and via him, to the White House."

"And Daniels was part of this cell?"

"Yes. A founding member." Phyllis continued, "Now the question Congress wants answered is who cooked up the evidence that led our nation to war on phony premises. Specifically, the Iraqi nuclear progress that turned out not to exist. The stockpiles of chemical weapons that have never been found. The terrorist connections that haven't materialized. The White House and the Pentagon have been madly leaking to the press and pointing their fingers at us. Clifford Daniels knew where the truth is buried. Follow his path and you shall learn that truth."

"And the truth shall set you free."

"Not this time." She stared off into the distance a moment, contemplating how much to tell, or not to tell me. She eventually said, "Bear this in mind also. Lord knows what Daniels has been involved in since the war started. With luck, it's possible you might uncover that as well."

"Would that be good luck or bad luck?"

"You'll know when you find it."

"Phyllis, this isn't doing it for me."

"Well, then ask anything you like."

"Are we talking espionage? Was Cliff Daniels betraying our country?"

When she made no reply, I said, "I need you to clarify this."

"I can't make it any clearer."

"Can't or won't?"

She smiled. When you ask a senior officer in the Army an impertinent question, you get a direct rebuke, like, "That's enough, Drummond," or the less ambiguous, "Have you ever seen the prison at Leavenworth? It sucks." Senior CIA officers are shrewder, more austere, polished. They tend to couch their responses nonverbally, like they know there's a hidden recorder in the room. So you get a frozen stare, or a slight knit of the eyebrows, or an icy smile. You need to listen with your eyes, because somewhere between the polite nod and the slight twitch of the left nostril, you've just had your balls cut off.

I moved on and asked, "If I find something, how am I supposed to handle it?"

"You'll know when you find it."

"That's not good enough. Are we talking damage to my career, or damage to my life?"

We looked at each other and I realized I was getting in way over my head. She informed me, "This man Daniels was involved with the Iraqis for nearly twenty years. He knew where a lot of bodies were buried, and I think you'll find his fingerprints on a lot of things that were hazardous for his health." She added ominously, "Don't let those things become hazardous for your health."

Suddenly, I could see why a lot of people would want Clifford Daniels dead, quietly buried, and long forgotten.

When I walked out of Phyllis's office, Waterbury was gone, and Bian Tran was standing alone, beside the water cooler, smiling.

CHAPTER SIX

We carried Daniels's briefcase to a small windowless side office whose occupant had been told to get lost so a pair of prodigies from the Agency's Office of Technical Support could perform a little on-the-spot forensics on Clifford's computer. Bian and I entered the office and made our introductions. They were named Will and John. They looked like Delbert and Elbert.

Will had thicker glasses than John, with wider black rims, and he had more pens and pencils in his pocket protector. Based on the geekiness factor, I handed the computer to Will, who immediately popped it open, flipped it on, and they both erupted in giggles.

Apparently thinking I cared, Will and John tried explaining their intentions—decoding Daniels's password, breaking through any firewalls that were erected, then digging through the hard drive, where the really good stuff would be found.

From my experience, too much time on a computer alters your physical appearance, and your outlook. Will, for instance, was almost transparently pale, with a large, flat butt, a scary, myopic stare, and he seemed totally clueless about how to interact with people who aren't connected to a joystick. John was the type who seems to believe all of life's problems can be fixed or repaired with a thorough virus scan. I mean, they were probably good guys, and competent, too. A lot of nontechnical people become uncomfortable in the presence of computer geniuses, and I'm one of them. I felt ashamed of my small-mindedness.

Anyway, it was all very interesting. In fact, John was just winding up a comprehensive and, dare I say, spellbinding explanation about the protocols involved with firewalls when I pulled out my gun and plugged them both. Just kidding.

Actually, I wasn't armed, so I did the next best thing—I fled.

Even Bian, who had showed enough familiarity with the subject to ask them a few probing and intelligent-sounding questions, looked relieved to get out of there.

We stopped off at the coffee machine, filled a cup for me, a cup for her, and proceeded to my cramped office carrel, where we sat.

I mentioned, "Why did you ask *questions*? It only encourages them."

She smiled. "The expression on your face when I asked about code-mapping made it all worth it."

Obviously needing to change the subject, I mentioned, "Incidentally, I was very impressed with your boss. Does he ever pull his head out of his butt?"

"I could see you two hit it off. Is this the start of something beautiful and lasting?"

"Personally, I like the guy. I really do. I'm going to do my best to develop a warm and amicable relationship."

"Bullshit."

"Right. Who is he?"

"Former military. A retired MP colonel, in fact. Look, I know he's a little intense, somewhat rigid . . . but he's good at his job. Very deliberate, by-the-book."

"Like Adolf Eichmann."

"Good analogy. But, well . . ." She searched her mind for something nice to say and came up with, "At least there's never a mystery about where he's coming from."

"Okay. Where is he coming from on Clifford Daniels?"

"Who the hell knows?" She laughed.

"He knows." After a moment, I asked, "So, how should we approach this thing?"

Bian understood exactly what I was asking, and why. At the start of a murder investigation you usually have a corpse, if you're lucky, also a murder weapon, and you have to dig for the rest—things like motives, suspects, and, for good measure, sufficient evidence, eyewitnesses, and elements of proof to get the bad guy an appointment on the hot seat. Sometimes—very often, in fact—the killer is an idiot and leaves a mother lode of clues and leads that draw a straight line from victim to killer—such as fingerprints, sperm cells, DNA markers, witnesses, and, increasingly in this cinematic age, the deed might even be captured on videotape. Killers, at least most killers, really aren't that clever or deceitful.

This wasn't one of those cases. Here, I suspected, we had that rare criminal who operated on a higher plane—thus, where we began, and how we began, would determine how fast we went and how many dead ends we hit.

She sipped her coffee. She suggested, "Okay, let's *assume* it was murder. I think we're both leaning that way. Procedurally, approach it like a standard homicide case."

"Good idea."

"Why don't we start with suspects?"

"Okay. I think there are lots of people who wanted Daniels's mouth sealed. People here, perhaps, Americans who are worried about the political fallout and/or the damage to their careers if he spilled the beans to a congressional committee. So that includes the people he worked with, and the people he worked for, up to and including the Secretary of Defense and the President of the United States."

She nodded.

I continued, "Possibly, there were some Iraqis who wanted him dead. And—"

"Can't you be more specific?"

"Well . . . there are some Iraqis who might carry a grudge because our friend played a heavy role in persuading the President to invade their country. Small-minded, of course—but people can be petty. Or maybe Charabi, or some of his associates, wanted to keep him from exposing some nasty secrets."

"This is pretty open-ended, isn't it?"

"Not yet. We're only at about thirty million suspects. Don't rule out enemies with more intimate motives—teed-off girlfriends, angry husbands whose wives Cliff may have been popping, a jealous ex-wife, a greedy brother who stands to inherit the full family fortune, or—"

"Okay—thank you. I think that covers the range."

"No it doesn't. The range is everything you expect, and everything you don't." In fact, I once prosecuted a murder that turned out to be over a pair of running shoes. Premeditated murder, too. The victim's parents were in the courtroom, and I'll never forget the shattered looks on their faces when they learned their son took three bullets in the gut over a pair of hundred-dollar athletic shoes that in six months would be vogued-out, worn-out garbage. The reasons people kill other people are almost endless, sometimes picayune, and often ridiculous. I looked at Bian and said, "Killers have limitless imaginations. Don't narrow yours."

"I've got it," she said. "Forget the suspect angle. Let's try reconstruction."

"Good decision."

"I'll raise the facts we know. You suggest the hypotheses."

"Bad decision. Why don't I ask? You're the cop."

"It *was* my idea." She punched my arm. "Besides, lawyers are more creative bullshitters."

Right.

After a moment, she said, "There was no sign of burglary. What does this suggest?"

"That Daniels let the murderer into his apartment, suggesting further that this was someone he knew. Or the murderer had a key, suggesting someone he knew even better. Or the murderer was an expert lock picker. Or Daniels's lock malfunctioned."

"The lock works. After I left you in the bedroom, I checked."

"Between ratting me out, you found time to inspect the lock?"

"Oh, get over it."

"I did. You made up for it."

"How's that?"

"You could have informed Waterbury that I entered Daniels's apartment with a false ID. But you didn't. Or you could have contradicted me and confirmed that I already suspected that Daniels's briefcase contained evidence. Again, you didn't."

She nodded but made no reply.

I looked her in the eye. "Why didn't you?"

"What would be the point?"

"That's what I'm asking." After a moment, I again asked, "Why?"

Instead of replying, she asked me, "Why do *you* think?"

"I think you don't like or trust your boss."

"He is a . . . difficult and . . . an aggravating man to work under."

"He's an asshole."

"That too." She laughed.

I did not laugh. "Also, I think you're worried that your own department wants this thing buried. Not covered up, necessarily—but we both know an internal investigation would move at a snail's pace, in very oblique directions, and only a small circle of friends would be exposed to the sequel."

She did not confirm this, but instead asked, "And why would I care about that?"

"You want me to assume it's because you're motivated by higher sensibilities. A West Pointer, that duty, honor, country thing." I looked her in the eye and said truthfully, "In fact, I believe you are motivated by these factors."

"But you think there are other motives, too. Right?"

Right. I looked at her. "If we're going to be working together, I'd like to know about them."

"You don't trust me?"

I did not, but there was no point in saying that. Instead, I said, "We could find things that will be very embarrassing and possibly very damaging for your bosses. I'd like to know where you stand, how you're going to react."

"You've read too much into this." She looked at me and said, "I think you're very clever, very observant, and you seem to have a firm grasp of investigations. I want to solve this, and you'll make a good partner. That's the professional reason." After another moment, she added, "And maybe I like you. Perhaps this is clichéd . . . you remind me of somebody."

"You're right. It's clichéd."

"And true. My fiancé. He's in Iraq, a major with the First Armored Division." She examined me a moment with those warm eyes. "You don't look alike, but you share so many quirks and mannerisms. It's almost uncanny."

It did not escape my notice that she had changed the subject, but this sounded more interesting and certainly more pleasant than the topic of murder. "Such as?"

"Mark . . . that's his name . . . Mark has a certain swagger, a way of moving. Sexy. Self-assured. And you both have this unnerving habit of shoving people around when you think you're right and they're in your way."

"And you're engaged to this guy?"

"He has some rough edges." She laughed. "I'll fix him *after* we're married."

That's what I love about women.

She looked at me. "Also like you, he doesn't know when to keep his mouth shut, he has no sense of self-preservation, and—"

"Excuse me—weren't we talking about a crime reconstruction?"

She smiled, sort of.

Back to the matter of how Daniels died, I said, "Fact two. The man was dead on his own bed with the gun in his hand."

"Yes. Why?"

"He either put it there himself, or it was placed there. If you're building a mental flowchart, this one's fifty-fifty."

"All right. Fact three. He was naked with a hard-on. What do you deduce from *that*?"

I stared at her.

She asked, "Should I rephrase that?"

"Too late." I suggested to her, "The most innocent explanation is that he was enjoying a moment of sexual solitude before he killed himself. We already discussed this."

She did not ask me to review that discussion, but instead wisely suggested, "But there are also less innocent explanations, right?"

"Apparently. He had company, and the company did not behave the way he anticipated."

"Female company."

"Well . . . don't discount the possibility that Mr. Daniels's taste ran the other way, or that he was a switch-hitter. But we'll work with that assumption until we know otherwise." I said, "And here's where it gets interesting. Why would he have a dirty video in the machine?"

"You tell me."

"This is beyond my experience or imagination."

"And you think I know something about this?"

I smiled.

She smiled back, a little coolly. She decided to be a good sport, though, and said, "All right, I'll take a stab. Some people use pornographic images to create a romantic or sensual mood, a prelude or warm-up before they get into the real article. In fact, it's not unhealthy . . . not even aberrant. A lot of sexual therapists actually recommend it." She looked at me and noted, "Also, the video wasn't necessarily his idea—maybe it was hers."

"Okay, his or hers. That's still a little hard to explain to a first date. Some women or men might find it a little bizarre and respond negatively."

"Yes, I think that would be a little awkward."

"So this suggests somebody he knew fairly well. This wasn't the first time they were together, was it?" She nodded, and I continued, "So that's where we start: a woman, someone he had already . . . somebody he already had intimate relations with."

"That was nicely put."

"I'm working on cleaning up my act."

"Keep working on it."

"Good point. Bear in mind, though, it's still possible a person he did *not* know entered the apartment, Cliff was asleep, they blew out his brains and planted the gun in his hand. Don't get hung up on opening assumptions."

"I'm not. But it helps to have something to work with." Bian crossed her legs and went back to sipping her coffee. I put Daniels's address book in my lap and began leafing through the pages.

The book was thick and organized alphabetically, and I noted that Cliff's handwriting was surprisingly neat, with a light touch and precisely formed and uniformly sized letters. I'm no expert in handwriting analysis, but with males such orthographic neatness is often a sign of a Catholic-based education, or a school experience dominated by bossy women who care about such things. My own handwriting has never been mistaken for having a light touch.

Bian, watching me, observed, "You know what? I've never actually seen a crime solved through an address book."

I made no response to that observation.

"It's odd," she continued. "Something like 90 precent of murders are committed by people the victim knew."

"I'm aware of the statistics."

"Good. So you would think an address book would be like a road map from the victim to the killer. In fact, often, the killer *was* in the victim's address book . . . unfortunately you don't *know* that until you've already ID'd the killer through other means." She concluded, "A very low percentage of crimes have been solved through address books."

"Am I wasting my time?"

"Well . . . I thought you should know."

"Now I know. Thank you."

"Statistics can be useful criminological tools."

I looked at her.

"Are you sensitive to criticism?" she asked.

"Me? . . . No. Would you like a punch in the nose?" I explained,

"I'm not looking for the killer, Bian. I'm trying to see who this guy associated with, get an idea of his life."

"I see." She pointed at a name and asked me, "And what does that name tell you?"

I looked at the name Albert Tigerman. "It's a statistical fact that only .0001 percent of killers are named Albert, and less than .0001 percent of those have the surname Tigerman. Ergo, Albert moves to the bottom of our suspect pool." I smiled at her. "I love statistics."

She smiled back tightly. "Try again."

"Should I know Albert?"

"Were you a Pentagon insider . . . yes, you would instantly recognize the name."

"That's why I have you."

"Tigerman was Daniels's boss, a very powerful and influential man. He's the deputy to the Under Secretary of Defense for Policy, Thomas Hirschfield—roughly the third-highest-ranking official in the Pentagon."

"Is there a point to this?"

"You catch on quick. Why don't I leaf through the address book and you look over my shoulder? I might recognize some of these people."

I tossed her the book. She started with the A's and ran her finger down the pages quickly, moving on to the B's, and down the line. Occasionally she used a pen and stabbed a checkmark or slashed an X beside a name. I had not a clue what significance was attached to those names or to these symbols.

As you might expect, the majority of names in Cliff's book were males, some with military ranks, most not. From what I could discern, Cliff's world was the usual amalgam of work colleagues, professional contacts, and people who were important or relevant to him personally; a few doctors, his dry cleaner, and presumably some friends and social acquaintances. Less than a third were women. Also, only about a third had listed addresses, the majority limited to phone numbers, predominately from area codes 202—Washington—and 703—northern Virginia.

A few names were recognizable to me, however—several well-known members of the National Security Council staff, some senior CIA officials, assorted Pentagon muckety-mucks, and General Nicholas Westfall, commander of the Defense Intelligence Agency. For a midlevel bureaucrat, Clifford was surprisingly well connected and inside the beltway loop.

Bian was now on the T's, and she flipped back to the D's and pointed to several people with the surname Daniels she had put X's next to—a Theresa with a northern Virginia area code and a South Arlington address; a Matthew with a Manhattan address; and a Marilyn in Plano, Texas.

Bian placed her right forefinger on Theresa from South Arlington. "What do you want to bet that's his ex? This address is only a few blocks from his apartment. The other two could be his parents, siblings, or maybe cousins."

At that moment Will popped his head around the corner. In a shrill and exhilarated voice, he reported, "We broke his code word. We're diddling his hard drive."

This sounded either vulgar or ridiculous, but Bian diplomatically asked Will, "And what are you finding?"

"Well . . . it's quite intriguing. Mr. Daniels stored a lot of personal materials on his computer. Financial information. Checkbook. He did his taxes on the computer. Lots of personal correspondence, too." He added, with fraternal approval, "He was very computer-savvy . . ." then added, "but it's really weird."

Will was really weird. I kept that thought to myself, however, and asked, very sweetly, "What's weird?"

"The three encrypted folders."

"Folders?"

"Yeah . . . folders . . ." He stared at me through his thick spectacles before concluding, accurately, that his interrogator was a technological dimwit. "Like a dresser drawer in the hard drive, where you store common items . . . say, socks or underwear. Judging by the large amount of storage space, they must contain multiple files. But as I said, they're encoded. Indecipherable."

I asked, "Are we talking socks or underwear?" Actually, I'm not that much of a dimwit—I knew what folders were—but this was my way of getting him to tone down the cyber gibberish. He stared back, I'm sure wishing he, or I, were someplace else, but I'm sure he got the point.

Bian decided to be helpful and asked Will, "Can you describe the code?"

"Well . . . it looks like a commercial version. The FBI and CIA tried to get Congress to ban these commercial codes, but that hasn't worked. So now there are a number of these applications out there." He looked thoughtful and added, "Mostly, though, they're employed by businesses, not individuals."

Bian and I traded glances. The obvious question was: Why would a Defense Department official suspected of espionage have a private code installed on his personal computer? Then again, the obvious is sometimes the enemy of the truth.

Will, sort of verbally rubbing his hands together, informed us, "Wow . . . I'd love to take a whack at those codes myself."

Being an idiot, I asked, "So why don't you?"

"Frankly, that could take months, particularly if it's a VPN version. That ISP protocol is . . . well, with all those symmetric ciphers . . ." He shook his head. "Now, if it's SSL, that would be better luck."

Bian was nodding. I had not a clue what Will was whining about, nor was I about to ask another stupid question and risk another stream of what passes for technical jargon with these people and actually is alphabet diarrhea. Bian, ever the diplomat, suggested to Will, "Thank you. But wouldn't it make better sense to bring these encrypted files to the National Security Agency? They have a lot of expertise in codes and codebreaking."

This was not what Will hoped to hear, and he made a mopey little nod.

"How long will that take?" I asked Will.

"Maybe they already have experience with this code. If they have to break it from scratch, depending on the sophistication . . . a day . . . two days . . . three months. How badly do you want it?"

"Yesterday sounds about right. Tell Phyllis. She'll know whose ass to kiss or kick."

"Sure." He started to walk away, then slapped his forehead and spun around. "Oh . . . there're some letters John thinks you should see."

Carrying our coffee, Bian and I got up and followed Will back to the office, where John had his nose pressed against the computer screen.

I said to John, "Will mentioned letters."

"Uh . . . yeah. I thought you should see these," John replied. "Hold on." Without looking up, he manipulated the little cursor as though it was connected to his fingertip and quickly brought a Microsoft Word file up on the screen. He said, "There are a number of these. This one's a little nastier . . . yet generally representative of what we're seeing."

Bian and I leaned over his left shoulder. I read out loud:

You Bitch,

Your bloodsucking fuck of a lawyer called me again today. At work!

Wow. I stopped reading out loud, and we both read to ourselves:

I'm tired of your bullshit threats about taking me back to court, and I'm REALLY tired of your efforts to destroy my career. I will not put up with it. You tell your hired asshole not to call me at the office anymore or he'll regret it. I'll take care of him myself.

Get it through your thick, bitchy brain: I have no more money to give. You have sucked me dry, you contemptible leech. So Lizzie has college bills—Whoopty Doo. Tell her to get off her ass and get a job. I've got to eat, live, get on with my life.

Sell the goddamn house that's too big for you anyway. I don't live there anymore. By the way I drove by the house the other day. The lawn looks like shit. The car looks like shit. And what happened to the money I gave you to repair the roof? You obviously spent it on something else, you bitch. On what? It's my right to know. It was MY money.

I would ask you to pass my love to the kids . . . of course, you won't. Anyway, you've already poisoned their minds and hearts against me. I rue the day I ever met you. What in the hell was I thinking when I married you? Just don't forget, if your lawyer calls me at work again, I'll make him regret it. You too. Don't underestimate me. Cliff.

I looked up from the screen. Bian and I exchanged glances. My goodness. Clearly theirs had not been a divorce on amicable terms.

Fortunately, JAG officers don't go near divorces—just wars, which generally suck, though they have one saving grace: When they're over, usually they're over.

Bian turned to John and asked, "There are more letters like this?"

"Yeah. I'm still browsing . . . but the titles don't tell if it's hate mail to his ex-wife."

I asked, "Anything else?"

"One thing. It's interesting, I guess. Mr. Daniels belonged to several online dating clubs and chat rooms."

"Tell us about that."

"Oh . . . well, he tried to erase the entries and e-mails. Everything on a hard drive is recoverable, of course. But you know how you can meet people online?"

I suppose I looked confused, because he explained, "It's more efficient. Easier."

"What is?"

"Meeting women on the computer. No need to hang around bars trying to think up clever things to say to real women."

I could see where that might be a problem for John.

Bian looked at me and remarked to him, "I've heard Drummond's best line." She suggested, "Why don't you do him a big favor and explain how this works?"

I smiled back. *Bitch.*

John said, "With online services you pay a fee and fill out a questionnaire. It's very convenient—you answer a few questions about your likes, dislikes, hobbies, the type of person you'd prefer to date. The service culls through similar profiles filled out by women, looks for commonalities, and hooks you up electronically. Chat rooms are a free-for-all. Log in to the conversation, and maybe another member likes your style and becomes interested in you."

"You're telling me my computer's a pimp?"

"No . . . I—"

"What happens if you both lie?"

"Well . . . that can happen but—"

"And you get together and it turns out you're both stupider and ickier-looking than you said?"

Bian was stifling a laugh.

John was now staring at me like I was weird. Truly, it's a whole new world. I'm part of the older world; I don't really like being reminded of it. However, I said to John, "You've done great work. Thank you." I asked Bian, "Who notifies his ex he's dead?"

"The Arlington police."

"You know this for a fact?"

"I do. I checked before I left the office. I hate notification detail." She added, "The obligation for a military notification pertains only to uniformed military."

"Not this time. Call your pal Detective Enders. Tell him he's off the hook."

"You think that's a good idea?"

"Is it ever a bad idea to observe a suspect's expression at the instant she learns the body was discovered?"

She paused for a moment, then said, "I should've thought of that."

"Yes, you should have."

Bian made the call, and I stood looking over John's shoulder and read more letters from Cliff to his ex, and about his ex. All were post-divorce, uniformly bitter, angry, insulting, and frequently they were threatening. On a hunch, I mentioned to Bian, who was still talking with Enders, "Tell him to check for past reports of domestic violence. Restraining orders, protection orders, whatever."

That Cliff was corresponding by mail with his ex suggested, at the very least, a geographic restraining order, perhaps extending to a telephonic order. Or alternatively, this physical excommunication may have been self-imposed. When it comes to divorce, nothing ever makes sense, and you never know. It was too early to jump to conclusions, but based on the tenor of that note, I wouldn't be at all surprised if she wanted to put a bullet through his brain.

And for sure it would be easy for us, and convenient for many, were it to turn out Cliff was popped by a pissed-off ex. Frankly, I would be a little disappointed; also, a lot relieved.

Well, we would see.

CHAPTER SEVEN

The house was on South 28th Street, a winding lane of small, double-storied, red-brick colonial homes that looked like two long lines of red-coated soldiers. The lots were tiny quarter-acre jobs, with mature oaks and elms; everything looked tidy and well-kept. The street held an old-fashioned charm; the homes were uniformly older, constructed in the late forties or the early fifties, a middle-class enclave for men who had just survived and returned from a world war, relieved to be in one piece, ready to enjoy peacetime employment, build families, and get on with their lives. It still looked wholesome, yet dated enough that any second I expected to see Wally Cleaver come dashing around a corner chasing the Beav.

I parked the Crown Vic directly in front of Theresa's house and Bian and I got out. Cliff was right; Theresa's yard was unkempt and overgrown with weeds, a swath of tiles was missing from the roof, and the Chrysler minivan in the driveway was long overdue for a paint job, probably an oil change, a tire rotation, or better yet, a complete replacement.

Bian and I proceeded to the front stoop. I pushed the bell and we waited. After a few seconds, a woman opened the door, dressed casually in dark sweatpants and a ratty T-shirt festooned with a snarling Georgetown University bulldog and the words "Up Yours." Bian handled the introductions, remaining deliberately vague about our purpose, and very politely asked if we could step inside.

It took a stretch, yet from the photograph in Clifford's apartment, I recognized the lady. She had aged considerably, or, more charitably, her face had acquired a new character since the photograph. It was Winston Churchill who said that by the time a person reaches fifty, the story of their life is written on their face. Apparently not always, because the smiling Theresa Daniels I had observed in the photo was about fifty then; somehow, in a few intervening years, a whole new story had been etched on her face.

I guessed she had once been moderately attractive—not necessarily pretty, not even sexy, but striking in a certain sharp-featured way. Cliff, as I mentioned, was fairly plain in appearance, so at least physically he had married above himself.

She was of medium size, possessing a narrow face with good bone structure, high but overly sharp cheekbones, attractive blue eyes, and a trim figure, with thin hips and wide shoulders. But, as with her house and her car, Theresa Daniels had let things slide. Her leathery skin and husky voice suggested she was a heavy smoker, possibly a heavy drinker, and we had caught her sans makeup, which, for all concerned, was seriously unfortunate. In the photo, I recalled, her hair had been brunette and coiffed in a stylish pageboy cut; it now hung below her shoulders, gray, untended, shaggy—less a bad hair day, more a bad hair decade.

Also, I detected something in her posture and movement, a disjointed looseness, as if the spirit inside the body had run out of breath.

Anyway, she had a wary expression as she studied us, Bian in her Army field uniform and me looking natty and businesslike in my blue Brooks Brothers suit. She asked Bian, "Would you tell me what this is about?"

"I . . . it would be better if we discussed this inside."

Mrs. Daniels hooked a languid hand and we followed her inside, turning right into a living room that was small and cramped. To our left, a pair of French doors led to a matchbox dining room, and to our rear a narrow staircase led to the second floor; this was a home designed to induce claustrophobic fits.

That aside, the interior was nicely decorated—overdecorated, actually—and, to the extent I can judge these things, the furniture, which looked colonial in motif, was fairly expensive, tasteful stuff. Also there was a lived-in feel, which is a polite way of saying the house smelled moldy and musty. This was a home, and possibly a life, in need of a good airing out.

Theresa fell into a high-backed, green-and-red-striped chair beside the fireplace, and she motioned for us to be seated on a plush brown couch against the wall. She crossed her legs and her head lolled backward, with her chin pointed upward. She did not offer us refreshments, indicating she either recognized our visit was official or her hospitality, like her home, needed a makeover.

Without further ado Theresa Daniels said, "Tell me what this is about."

I have been on death notification details several times in my career; it always sucks. You never know how the bereaved is going to take the news, and you have to stay on your toes. Often the response is sadness, sometimes shock, usually anger, and often all of the above.

Divorced spouses, particularly, tend to be unpredictable. I have one pal who swears a divorcée dragged him to her bedroom for three hours of wild and sweaty solace; another got a knee in the nuts.

With both memories in mind, I crossed my hands over my crotch and informed Mrs. Daniels, "We have bad news. Your ex-husband, Clifford, died last night. The circumstances are still unclear."

She looked down at the carpet with an expression that reflected nothing. After a brief contemplation, she asked, "Unclear? What's that supposed to mean?"

"It means, Mrs. Daniels, that your ex-husband was discovered in bed, with a pistol in his hand and a hole in his head." I studied her face to see if this was new news or old news. "Circumstantially, it appears to have been suicide . . . but we're withholding final judgment."

Feeling the need to justify her presence, Bian chirped in, "We extend our deepest sympathies. Despite your divorce, I'm sure your feelings are very complicated right now."

Actually, her feelings appeared not at all complex. Theresa stood and turned her back to us. On the fireplace mantel, Bian and I now noticed, was a wedding picture in a nice silver frame showing a younger, beaming Clifford in an Army sergeant's uniform with his arm around a pretty bride with a large toothy smile.

Over half of all marriages in America end in divorce, and another quarter are bitterly unhappy, the couple remaining together for a variety of reasons—children, financial motives, habit, or the simple conjugal satisfaction of pissing each other off. And for every one, happy, broken, or otherwise, there is a photo like this, showing a young, sappy, optimistic couple, totally clueless to the hell or happiness they are about to inflict on each other.

Theresa stared at the photo for a few moments, then lifted it up and placed it facedown on the mantel. She turned back around and faced us. She said to Bian, "I don't understand why I'm being informed of this by a military police officer."

"You recognize my insignia?"

"I hope I do. My father was career military. A brat. I was raised on Army posts."

Bian looked at me. I informed Mrs. Daniels, "Major Tran and I are helping to investigate the causes of Clifford's death. We were hoping to ask you some questions." After a moment, I remembered to add, "But if our timing is inappropriate . . ."

I fully expected to be tossed out on our butts; instead she asked, "Would either of you care for a refreshment? Coffee, tea . . . ?"

On the heels of what she had just been informed, this offer was, to say the least, bizarre. As I said, you never know. I squeezed Bian's leg and said, "I'll pass, thank you," and Bian seconded with a shake of her head.

Theresa Daniels studied us for a moment. She said, "You look disappointed, Mr. Drummond. Were you expecting me to collapse in grief? Pull my hair out, wail, shed a tear?"

"We weren't *expecting* any particular reaction, Mrs. Daniels." But yes, some small gesture of regret or loss would be reassuring.

She studied me a moment. "You're wondering what I feel, aren't you?" When I did not respond, she said, "Frankly, nothing. The Clifford Daniels I knew . . . the man I married, he died years ago."

"Perhaps in your heart. But in a purely clinical sense, his heart stopped beating last night, around midnight. It's now our job to determine if it was suicide . . . or something else."

"Why don't you just say murder? That's what you're alluding to, isn't it?"

"Yes . . . murder." I looked her in the eye. "You don't seem surprised by this suspicion."

She shrugged.

"Did Clifford own a gun?"

"He did. A pistol of some sort."

"What—"

"Don't ask me the type. I hate guns. I begged him to get it out of this house."

"But it was a pistol?"

"I do know the difference between a pistol and a rifle, Mr. Drummond."

"He had this pistol while you were married?"

"Yes. He acquired it a year or two before our separation. He assured me it was properly registered."

"And did he have a silencer?" I explained: "A small tube you screw on the end of the barrel."

"I'm not sure. He had a full gun kit, though. He used to sit here"—she pointed to the dining room table—"at night, after work, cleaning and oiling it. He took better care of the gun than me. I don't think he ever fired it, so what was the point?"

"And he took the gun when you separated?"

"Damn right he did."

"Why would a civil servant need a gun?"

"It was . . . it was a token of his flowering self-importance. No particular reason . . . no threat or anything, if that's what you're looking for."

"I'm not sure what you're getting at."

"It's not complicated, Mr. Drummond. He believed he had become noteworthy enough that somebody might want to hurt or kill him. He was very proud of that thought. That . . . weapon . . . that was his affirmation." She added, "You know how men are with guns—like penises."

Despite this assault on my gender—with its embarrassing ring of truth—this had turned into a very interesting line of discussion, but Bian asked, "How long were you married, Mrs. Daniels?"

"Thirty-three years."

"Long time. When were you divorced?"

"We legally separated four years ago. The divorce finalized a year later."

"And do you have children?"

"Two. Elizabeth, our daughter . . . and Jack, our son."

"Where are they now?" Initially I was annoyed by this diversion from more promising territory into what struck me as mundane familial stuff—then I realized *why* Bian was inquiring. The children also were suspects. She added nicely, "If I'm not being too nosy."

"Elizabeth is a senior at Georgetown," Theresa informed us. "She lives here, at home. She commutes. Saves money."

"And Jack?"

"Jack dropped out of school two years ago. He's in Florida, and has . . . let's say Jack's working through a few problems."

Bian glanced in my direction. "Would it be too rude of me to ask what kind of problems?"

"Well, the . . . the divorce . . . You have to understand, Jack was three years younger than his sister. Also he's a boy, he looked up to his father, and . . . the circumstances were . . ." She recognized she was saying more than we needed or possibly wanted to hear, and quickly concluded, "There were a few school problems . . . drugs, a few legal scrapes. He's now in a special center outside of Tampa."

I said, "It's a mere formality, but I have to ask you something." There are no formalities in criminal investigations, incidentally.

She stared at me without comment.

"Can you think of anyone who would want or who would benefit from Cliff being dead?"

"You bet I can." She looked me in the eye. "Me—I wanted that bastard deader than a doornail." She inquired, after a moment, "Would you happen to know if he kept up his insurance payments? The kids are beneficiaries. We could sure as hell use the money."

Bian coughed.

A moment passed during which Theresa and I never broke eye contact. I said, "You mentioned coffee."

This seemed to amuse her and she chuckled. "I was just making a pot. Join me in the kitchen. It wouldn't be good for your careers if your key suspect escaped out the window."

"You're not a suspect, Mrs. Daniels." *Yet.*

There was a long silence, then she said, "Don't be so sure of yourself."

CHAPTER EIGHT

On that auspicious note, we rose and followed her through the dining room and into the kitchen, essentially a narrow strip, about six feet in length and three feet in width, with old, scarred white cabinetry on both sides. The floor was a checkerboard of scuffed black-and-white vinyl squares, and the counters were some kind of awful lime green plasterboard. Aside from a few appliances and the occupants, since about 1950 the kitchen looked frozen in time.

We all three somehow shuffled and squeezed into the narrow space. Theresa stood by the sink where an asthmatic drip coffeemaker coughed and spit its last drops into a dungy glass beaker. I counted three plants—all withered into gnarled brown papyrus, which seemed to me to be appropriate decorations for the house, and its owner.

Theresa asked us, "Do either of you take cream or sugar?"

"Both, please," I replied. Bian and I traded uneasy glances. I mean, this woman had just been notified that the man she had shared her life with for thirty-three years—slept with, bred and raised two children with—now was in the morgue. No, I hadn't expected her to wail or yank her hair or anything. But neither had I expected such chilling indifference, and I wondered if it was exaggerated, a defense mechanism or something else.

Whatever had soured this marriage must've been catastrophic—but was it enough to pump a bullet through her ex's head? She seemed to want us to believe that she did, but was that the truth or a perverse case of wishful thinking?

Theresa reached into the fridge and pulled out a carton of half-and-half, then opened a cabinet and withdrew a bowl of sugar so old it had metastasized into white granite. She poured two cups and handed them to Bian and me.

While I added half-and-half and made a big mess trying to chip off a spoonful of sugar, Theresa looked away from us and mentioned, "I need a little sherry to settle my stomach."

She stepped out for a moment. When she returned, in her hand was a tall cocktail glass filled to the lip with ice cubes and some blend of sherry that was peculiarly colorless. She said, "I'm sure it won't bother you if I smoke."

A cigarette was already dangling from her lips, spewing pollution into the tiny room.

"Do you mind discussing Cliff?" I asked her, stirring my coffee. "It helps when the investigators know something about the victim."

"Shouldn't you begin by asking where I was around midnight last night?" I took that for a yes.

So I asked her.

"Where I am every night." She laughed. "David Letterman is my alibi. Why don't you quiz me on his top ten?"

I smiled. This was getting weird.

Bian allowed a moment to pass, then said, "I'm not sure how to ask this."

"Just ask." She shrugged and added, "If I don't like your question, you won't get an answer."

"Fair enough. What made your marriage fail? In the wedding picture over the mantel . . . your expressions . . . you seemed to be in love once."

"The official grounds, the cause my lawyer filed, was infidelity." She added, "There was enough of that. Near the end. But that's only the superficial reason."

I don't really like to start a story at the end, so I asked, "How did you two meet?"

"At Fort Meade, in the late sixties. My father was a colonel working in the post headquarters. Cliff was a buck sergeant, an Arabic and Farsi linguist. I was young, eighteen, and I used to hang out at the NCO club. Officers' kids aren't supposed to mingle with enlisted soldiers, but I was too young for the officers and it was . . . I suppose . . . a way of thumbing my nose at my father. It was the sixties, after all. Everybody back then was dropping acid and screwing perfect strangers. I flirted with enlisted soldiers." She emitted a smoker's hack and took a long gulp of "sherry." "We dated. A few months later he asked me to marry him."

"It sounds like you were swept off your feet," Bian commented.

"Yes. I suppose I was. I loved Cliff. He was . . . back then . . . intelligent, kind, ambitious . . . not much to look at, but as you're going to learn, he could be very charming . . ." Also he could pole vault over tall buildings with his third leg, but she didn't mention it. Neither did I.

And so on, for the next twenty minutes, Theresa described what sounded like an ideal beginning, an ideal marriage, an ideal life.

Cliff completed his tour in the Army and happily took his discharge. His next step, due to his Army intelligence experience and language competencies, was to apply for a position in the Defense Intelligence Agency, or DIA, where he was immediately accepted. Theresa worked administrative jobs for about ten years to add extra bucks to the kitty, Cliff and Theresa bought this house, the biological clock began wheezing—bang, bang—two wonderful kids, she quit working, became a Kool-Aid mom, and so on. By the numbers, the American dream in the making.

On the professional side, Cliff was bright, hardworking, diligent, and highly regarded by his bosses; in the early years, promotions and step raises came through like clockwork. Ultimately, however, the role of DIA is support for our warfighters, and during the cold war the action was with Sovietologists and Kremlinologists; the Middle East was a strategic backwater and Arabists ended up with their noses pressed against a glass ceiling. According to Theresa, by the time Cliff awoke to the unhappy reality that he had a big career problem, he was in his early forties, too late to change his specialty or his professional fate.

As she spoke, we occasionally interrupted to ask for a point of clarification, or to steer her back on track. She had become chatty, and it was clear she needed to talk about this, not cathartically, I thought, but more as somebody indulging a tale they now knew ended on a satisfying note.

At times her narrative was chronological and organized, at times free-flowing and disconnected. Theresa frequently paused to light a fresh cigarette, and she twice left the kitchen to refresh her "sherry." It was late afternoon; at the rate she was "refreshing," she would be in the cups before dinnertime.

As a general rule, incidentally, I never put ex-wives on the stand. They make awful witnesses. They cannot recite the past objectively—they know their Sir Galahad on the shimmering white steed turned out to be a self-indulgent cad riding a fetid pig.

Yet, if I listened carefully, I was starting to form a picture of this man who died so weirdly in his bed the night before.

Cliff was raised in a small upstate New York town, father a garage mechanic, one brother, one sister. A local parish priest saw a young boy with spunk and intelligence and awarded him a free ticket through the local parish school. Cliff became the only one from his family to matriculate from high school, then college—to wit, Colgate—doing it the hard way—on brains, sleep deprivation, part-time jobs, and desperation. As with so many young men of his era, no sooner had the sheepskin greased his palm than Uncle Sam intervened to borrow a few years of his life. He was sent first to the Defense Language Institute at Monterey, where he mastered Arabic, then Farsi, followed by an assignment to a military intelligence center, at Fort Meade, Maryland, which, for sure, beat the alternative enjoyed by so many of his hapless peers—humping a ninety-pound ruck in the boonies of Southeast Asia.

And what jumped out from this narrative arc, in my view, was the moxie of the man. Having escaped a deeply impoverished background, he put himself through college, then was selected by the Army for advanced schooling, then for high-level intelligence work, and the pièce de résistance, he bagged a colonel's daughter. Given the Army's fraternization codes, this is akin to a commoner laying wood on a princess and, for Cliff, a big bump up in the social registry. With his entry into the Defense Intelligence Agency, he became a white-collar professional, an educated man in an honorable line of work, which—with luck, skill, and the right breaks—could lead to bigger things.

In the end, as Freudians say, it's all about ego, and in my experience, self-made types are particularly susceptible to an omnivorous sense of self-worth.

So now we were past the early years, the marriage, the house, the two children, and Theresa, now past her fourth gin, was starting to slur and giggle at inappropriate moments. She said, "Throughout the seventies he was on the Iranian desk. In 1982 he was shifted to the Iraqi section, a real backwater. He thought it was the end of the world. Nobody cared about Iraq. Back then, Iran was the career-maker, and as I said, Cliff knew Farsi. He complained bitterly to his bosses and they claimed that's where they needed him."

Incidentally, Bian's questions seemed more oriented toward their marriage and family life, which, I think, is one of those X versus Y chromosome deals. I, being a male, am confident that life's mysteries and puzzles are all rooted in money, power, and lust. Men and women investigators bring different things to the party, but it seems to work out.

Predictably, Bian asked, "How did this affect your marriage?"

"If anything, Cliff became a more attentive husband, a better father. He always worked long hours . . . he began to scale back. He coached Little League, learned to play golf, spent more time with the kids."

She lit another cigarette and drew a long breath. "The eighties were good for us. Happy years. He was professionally bitter, but our marriage was healthy. No fights, no stresses." After a moment, she added, "Until 1991."

"When Iraq invaded Kuwait," I guessed.

"You've got it."

"What happened then?" Bian asked.

"The beginning of the end . . . or maybe the end of the beginning. Those thoughts are so interchangeable, don't you think?"

No, I didn't think, and I found it instructive that she would.

"What were those problems?" Bian prodded.

"A lot of things came together. Midlife crisis . . . job dissatisfaction . . . I don't know. Something inside Cliff snapped."

Bian, who had obviously been paying attention, suggested, "Or was reawakened."

Theresa took another long sip. "He was one of the few men in Washington who knew anything about Saddam. About Iraq. Ironic, if you think about it. The very thing that got him stuck in quicksand suddenly vaulted him into great demand everywhere. He briefed Schwarzkopf, Powell, and Cheney. He visited the White House a number of times."

She stubbed out her cigarette and immediately fired up another. "Overnight, he was briefing the Joint Chiefs of Staff, eating lunches in the White House mess, being flown on government jets to Tampa and Kuwait, getting calls in the middle of the night from reporters begging for tips and insights."

I remembered a pithy quote and told her, "Our virtues are most frequently but vices in disguise."

This was a little too philosophical for a lady on her fourth gin, and she glanced at me with frustration and maybe annoyance. "I'm just saying he wasn't equipped to handle it. For nine months, he was at the center of the storm . . . that was the play on words he liked to use. Then it suddenly ended."

"Because the war ended?" I suggested.

"Why else?"

"Was he disappointed?"

"Disappointed?" She contemplated this question a moment, then asked, "Are you an ambitious man, Mr. Drummond?"

"That's a complicated question."

"Is it?" She blew a long plume of smoke in my direction.

Bian commented to her, "He's a man and a lawyer. What did you expect? Introspective questions confuse him."

They both laughed. This was funny?

Theresa stopped laughing, and opined to Bian, "I'll bet that's why he's not married. That's not a criticism, incidentally. Before he marries, a man should understand his ambition." She looked at me. "Do you understand what I'm talking about, Mr. Drummond?"

"Well, I . . ." No, and I didn't care.

She turned back to Bian. "We had children, for Godsakes. A home, a good marriage. Wasn't that enough? . . ." and so on for another minute or so.

Suddenly, I found myself trapped in an extended episode of *General Hospital.* I offered Mrs. Daniels a sympathetic smile and eyed the exit.

Fortunately, Bian changed the channel and got us back to the good stuff. She suggested to Theresa, "You're telling us he had a taste and he wasn't going to relinquish it."

"In his own words, he wasn't going to slink back into the muck of anonymity. He had big ideas, big ambitions . . . big-shot new friends."

Bian seemed to know where this was going and said, "Albert Tigerman and Thomas Hirschfield—that's who you're referring to, right?"

Theresa nodded.

Bian explained for my benefit, "Hirschfield and Tigerman both held senior Pentagon jobs during the first Gulf War. When that administration ended, Hirschfield went to a Washington think tank, and Tigerman returned to his law firm. As you know, now they're back in the Pentagon."

I remarked, "But they were out of power during most of the nineties."

Bian said, "You mean they were no longer connected to a President. They still had Republicans on the Hill, the Republican Party itself, the web of Republican think tanks . . . Heritage Foundation, et cetera." She observed, "Out of power these days is an illusion."

I guess I knew what she meant. Like musical chairs, the winners take over the government buildings and the losers move a few blocks away into the office space recently vacated by the winners, where they proceed to cash in on their fame, connections, and influence. They collect great gobs of money and connive and hatch plots to get back into power so they can go back to residing in crappier government offices, making less money and working longer hours. How can anybody vote for people who think like this?

Bian turned to Theresa and asked a very good question. "Exactly how did Cliff remain connected to these men?"

"Well . . . as you might remember, Iraq stayed in the news over those years. There was the attempt on President Bush's life in Kuwait, the UN sanctions, our Air Force planes constantly being shot at . . . Would you like me to recount the entire history? It dominated our lives for over a decade."

I assured her we would check it ourselves, thank you.

She continued, "Everything became ridiculously hush-hush when he was home. Which wasn't often. But Albert Tigerman called the house a lot."

"Do you know what they talked about?" Bian asked.

"As I said, Cliff never shared it." She waved her glass around the cramped kitchen and house. "But how could I not overhear what Cliff was saying?"

She paused to fire up another cigarette, and Bian and I stared at her expectantly.

Eventually she said, "They were like some silly cabal. They believed Saddam needed to be overthrown. Cliff, as a career civil servant, was still on the inside, still able to influence perceptions and to work actions inside the administration. Tigerman and Hirschfield were the thinkers. Cliff became their tool. They exploited him."

I asked, "They were using him, or was he using them?"

She gave me a look, like I had asked a dumb question. "He was way out of his league with those two."

"How?"

"Well . . . I wouldn't know the particulars, would I? I'll tell you this, though. Very often, after they spoke, he went on long overseas trips."

"Where?"

"Sometimes Europe, sometimes the Middle East."

"What did he do on these trips?"

"I think they were putting him in contact with various Arabs. I suppose Iraqis . . . people willing to help overthrow Saddam."

"Was Cliff freelancing or were these trips authorized?"

"I can only tell you we weren't paying for it. I suppose DIA for some reason authorized and financed his travel."

This was curious, but I thought I understood the underlying reasons. I recalled that in the mid- to late nineties, the previous administration had ordered the intelligence community to engineer an effort to dethrone Saddam. Unfortunately, my knowledge of the details was somewhat sketchy. And, knowing my CIA friends, everybody now had an onset of amnesia. It must be something in the water at Langley. I mean, these people can't even remember what color socks they're wearing.

From news reports around that period, however, I recalled that there had been an effort, sometime in the mid-nineties, to bribe a bunch of high-level Iraqi generals to overthrow Saddam. Saddam somehow got wind of it and the generals were subsequently invited over to his house for a barbecue and swim party—half the generals got put on spits and were barbecued, the other half got to paddle around the pool with Saddam's pet alligators.

I vaguely recalled reading about other attempts as well, mostly half-assed affairs, employing Kurds or Iraqi expats, all of which came to naught and were swiftly and quietly aborted. Usually Agency people are pretty good at this kind of thing—practice makes perfect as they say—so it was a tribute to Saddam's paranoia that, this time, good wasn't good enough. I mentioned some of this to Theresa, then asked, "Was Cliff involved in any of these efforts?"

"I'm sure he was."

"And Hirschfield and Tigerman? Were they also involved?"

"They helped . . . in the wings, advising him . . . I think helping him plot and putting him in touch with various Iraqis who might be useful."

"Why? By that I mean why would they become implicated in these affairs? It wasn't their watch."

"Ask them."

"What was Cliff's motive?" I remembered to add, "I can't ask him."

"Isn't that obvious?"

It was, but I needed to hear her say it. "Tell me."

After a moment she said to me, "We're back to ambition, Mr. Drummond."

Bian asked, "Meaning there was a quid pro quo from Hirschfield and Tigerman, right?"

Theresa nodded. "Put it this way. The moment the new administration took over, Cliff was pulled out of DIA, given a promotion, and was hired to work for them at the Pentagon."

"What kind of work?"

"We were separated by then. Talking through lawyers. I wouldn't know."

We were now edging into hearsay, which was informative and even juicy, though not necessarily accurate. I checked my watch—4:30 p.m. If we hurried, it might be possible to arrange an interview with Hirschfield, or possibly Tigerman, or possibly both. But there remained one nagging question, and I asked Theresa, "Can you think of any reason Cliff would kill himself?"

She mulled this over for a long period. Eventually she said, "You remember I told you that Cliff was already dead?"

I nodded.

"About five, maybe six years ago, he began . . . self-destructing. It wasn't an overnight thing. Just gradually, he changed."

"How?"

"I think . . . you have to understand, he was essentially a desk jockey at DIA. The most adventurous thing he did was to drive home on the beltway. I know this sounds . . . maybe crazy, maybe nutty . . . but Cliff began to think he was a character in a movie. Like James Bond."

She was right, it did sound crazy, and nutty, and I suppose that showed on my face.

She immediately said, "No . . . not literally, Mr. Drummond."

"Then how about unliterally?"

"The undercover work, the trips, the involvement in espionage, the clandestine meetings in the Kasbah . . . you know what I'm talking about?"

She was staring at me as though I, a male, would have a proprietary chromosonal insight into this cryptic accusation. Actually, I did know and replied, "He was seduced by the adventure and excitement."

"Seduced? . . . No—consumed. He changed, became moody, sneaky . . . but also short-fused, testy, self-absorbed, full of himself. You asked about that pistol earlier." She stared into her drink. "When he brought it home and showed it to me . . . I knew then he had lost it."

"Lost what?"

"Interest in the house. In the kids. In me. He was so proud of that damned gun." She looked at Bian and confided, "He came back from trips, and I could tell . . . I could just tell . . ."

"He was having an affair?" Bian suggested.

"*An* affair? . . ." She laughed bitterly.

I gave her a moment to get it out of her system, then asked, "Would you happen to know the names of the women he slept with?"

"You'll need a thicker notebook." She laughed. "If it couldn't outrun him, he fucked it."

Neither Bian nor I commented on this sordid revelation. Sexual betrayal is, of course, the most ubiquitous cause for divorce, and Theresa had already confided to us that infidelity provided the legal foundation filed by her attorney. There are many reasons husbands cheat on wives, and wives cheat on husbands, nearly all of which boil down to boredom, weak libidos, revenge, or narcissistic lust. Well, unless you're French; then the whole reason for marriage is to have illicit affairs. But in English-speaking lands, we tend to have a lot more hang-ups about sex.

This, however, sounded like something more, something deeper, more twisted. Also, Tim, the forensics examiner, had mentioned hair traces from two or possibly three different females. Added to the overall feng shui at the crime scene, it all hinted at some kind of sexual shenanigans.

I tuned back in, and Theresa was confiding to Bian, "I knew it was happening. I followed him one night to a local motel. I got pictures of him with some woman. You know what really hurt? She wasn't even pretty. In fact, she had a big fat butt."

"I'm sorry," I told her, and I didn't mean about the fat butt.

Not to be uncharitable, but as I looked around—at this suffocating house, at Theresa groping her fifth gin, at the unchanging neighborhood—and added to that mixture a stale and frustrated professional life, I thought Cliff Daniels was an accident waiting to happen. I could see a man trapped in this professional and marital quagmire committing suicide. But I could not see a man who had escaped into a new life—who had put this behind him—taking that drastic step.

To a greater or lesser extent, we all lead lives of quiet desperation; metaphysically and, often in reality, we're all lined up at the convenience store counter, praying for that lucky lottery ticket that will change our lives. Men, of course, will settle for a lovely nymphomaniac who's a football fanatic and owns her own beer company. We're pigs.

I asked Mrs. Daniels, "Incidentally, was Cliff left- or right-handed?"

"Right-handed. Why?"

"Just one of those weird statistics we're required to keep about human proclivities." I smiled. "You know the federal government—building a great society one statistic at a time." I added, "Maybe you can help with another statistic. It's . . . well . . . a little uncomfortable. Did Cliff ever exhibit any tendency toward homosexuality?"

"Haven't you been listening, Mr. Drummond? The man was a raging heterosexual."

"Of course."

I glanced at Bian. She quietly nodded, and clearly she understood why I asked. Were this murder, the suspect pool had just been cut in half.

After a moment, I again asked Theresa, "Why would Cliff kill himself?"

"You're asking the wrong question." She put her back against the sink and exhaled. "Why wouldn't he kill himself?"

CHAPTER NINE

I went out and started the car while Bian stood by the curb and used her cell phone to call and ask her boss, Oberst Waterbury, to persuade either Hirschfield or Tigerman—or better still, both—to clear a little time on their schedules.

She climbed into the passenger seat and said, "He'll take care of it." She looked at me. "What do you think?"

"I need fresh air."

"Her life needs fresh air." She suggested, "So let's start with her."

"You mean, is she a suspect?"

"She's not. We both know that, don't we? But she'll have happy dreams tonight, imagining she did it. My sense is she wrote him out of her life." She reconsidered her words and said, "That's not exactly true. He was her boogeyman, the fount of all her miseries and unhappiness. Now she'll miss him. You know?"

"I know."

"But is she credible? Bitter people make poor witnesses."

"She's very credible about what counts, and her bitterness is justified."

"You believe she deserves sympathy?"

"I sure do. She built a life and a family around this guy. He turned into an asshole."

"There's a stylish elegy. Can I borrow it for my write-up?"

"You should hear my court summations. Come early. Long lines, and the ticket scalpers make a killing."

"I'll bet you're very . . . entertaining." She thought for a moment, then observed, "We only heard her side of the tale. Every divorce has two sides."

"Good point. If you think of a way we can hear his side, be sure to let me know."

She shook her head. I can be annoying.

I said, "It's an old story with many titles: the starter wife, the first-wife syndrome, middle-age idiotitis. Cliff wasn't very complicated or hard to understand. He wanted to be something he wasn't—dashing, dangerous, mysterious, sexually alluring. Theresa and the kids were part of the old, lesser, disappointing him."

"You make him sound very shallow."

"A lot of men harbor secret dreams of being James Bond, but they wake up and see George Smiley staring back from the mirror." I added, after a moment, "Men have two brains in constant warfare over the body's blood supply. When one wins, the other shuts down."

"It's that simple?"

"It's that simple."

"I see."

"He thought his ship came in, and she got thrown overboard." I looked at her. "I wouldn't be surprised if Cliff secretly dreamed of dumping her for years."

"Well, whatever the reason, she needs to pull herself together. Put it behind her."

"Amnesia is not something you call up at will."

"An old Vietnamese proverb says, 'When the petals leave the rose, you grow a new rose.' "

"They grow roses over there?"

"Well . . . no." She laughed. "I made that up." Then she said, "My point is, she's wallowing in the past. Destroying the marriage may have been his fault—destroying herself is hers."

"You're engaged, right?"

"I told you I am."

"How do you know—what's this guy's name?"

"Mark. Mark Kemble."

"Thank you. How can you be sure Mark Kemble won't turn into an idiot?"

"He won't."

"How do you *know*, Bian? Husbands are unpredictable creatures. Some come with hidden flaws, buried defects. Sometimes a guy wakes up one morning, sees the bald spot, the turkey wattles under the chin, and he turns shallow and stupid. Sometimes a fancy new car cures it, sometimes a fancy new blonde. Do I really need to explain this?"

She made no reply.

"In simple soldier talk—shit happens."

"It won't. Not between us." She looked at me and said, with complete conviction, "There is no past tense to the word love."

"It's a verb. Slap a 'd' on the end."

"Look, I've known Mark since we were cadets. This might sound trite, but I was in love the moment I first saw him. I . . ." She looked away for a moment, then concluded, "He won't change—ever. I'm sure."

"You've dated this same guy for ten years? What does that tell you?"

"Well . . . that's not how it happened. I mooned over him when we were cadets, but he was two years ahead of me. Regulations at West Point forbade dating upperclassmen. He also had a girlfriend he was serious about."

"What happened to her?"

"Oh . . . well, she died. A suspicious fire . . . arson, actually. Most unfortunate and very mysterious. The arsonist was never found."

I looked at her, and she smiled. "That was a joke."

I smiled back.

Bian said, "She was from a wealthy family in a ritzy community in Connecticut. New Caanan, maybe Westport. After Mark graduated she got a look at Army life, instead of cadet life. The idea of scraping by on a lieutenant's pay in Louisiana or Georgia was a little much for her. So Mark got a Dear John letter and she got a new boyfriend, at Harvard Business School. They ended up married."

"And you were waiting in the wings?"

"Not really. We didn't get together until later, about three years ago."

"Three years. If you're so confident, why aren't you married to him now?"

"We . . . we decided to wait until conditions improved." My question unsettled her and she had to pause and swallow. "Army life—you're single, you understand how it is."

I did understand. In the old Army they used to say that if they wanted you to have a wife, they'd issue you one. It now is considered both passé and politically incorrect, and nobody says that anymore. Indeed, today's soldiers are mostly married. The underlying philosophy hasn't changed a whit, though. In fact, the Global War on Terror, or whatever buzzword they were calling it these days, was not doing much for military romance, unless your *amore* happens to be a terrorist.

After a moment she added, "During these three years, between Bosnia, Kosovo, 9/11, now Afghanistan, and now Iraq—"

"Whose idea was it to wait?"

"Why did it have to be either of our ideas?"

"These things are never mutual." She tried looking away, but I caught her eye and asked, more insistently, "Yours or his?"

"All right . . . his. He was in Kosovo, then Afghanistan. I was in Afghanistan, after his tour ended, then Iraq, also at a different time. After he finished a year at the Command and General Staff College at Leavenworth, he was reassigned to the First Armored Division and redeployed to Iraq for another tour. He didn't want me to become a widow or spend my life caring for a cripple. I couldn't argue him out of it. Besides, what did it matter? We were going to be apart anyway."

No doubt, a number of sober and practical reasons passed through Mark Kemble's head and heart, all of which seemed logical, persuasive, even compelling. But in my view, with a woman like Bian Tran, you observe a different logic. I wouldn't let this woman ten feet out of my sight without the Rock of Gibraltar on her finger, an unpickable chastity belt around her groin, and a note around her neck—"Touch her and I'll feed you your own nuts."

Well, as I mentioned, she was very attractive, and I found her company quite pleasant: I couldn't imagine a man who wouldn't.

"Do you have a picture of this guy?"

Of course she did, and she reached into the side leg pocket of her Army trousers, withdrew her wallet, and fumbled out a small photograph, which she handed to me as I drove. I gave it a brief look, then handed it back.

The photo was color, taken perhaps at a military ball, and Mark Kemble, attired in his formal dinner mess dress, had a major's rank on his sleeve, yellow cloth on his lapels—a tanker—with enough badges and medals on his chest to shame a Christmas tree. He was looking directly into the camera with a large friendly grin, was slender and broad-shouldered, dark-haired and dark-eyed, with a strong jaw and cleft chin. I could see where some women might get a little sweaty over him. Handsome. Dashing.

I predicted, "You two will produce beautiful little babies together."

No reply.

I glanced over and Bian was staring out the window in a sort of sulky trance. I suppose this was all a little overwhelming for her—the love of her life in a war zone, a politically hazardous murder case on her hands, and me. I can be annoying.

"Are you okay?"

She continued to stare out the window.

I don't like talking to myself, and we drove without speaking for a few minutes. It was almost six o'clock, and the sky had already turned dark, the wind was whipping the trees, and a gusty, gloomy squall was moving in—a typical late October day in the moody, blustery city of Washington, D.C.

Out of the blue, she informed me, "I really want to break this case."

"Think like a cop, Bian. It's not personal." After a moment, I advised her, "What you should be hoping is to make it through this with your career intact."

"What does that mean?"

"Think Oliver North and Bud McFarlane."

"Who?"

"How old are you?"

"Thirty-one. What's your point?"

"The Iran-Contra scandal?"

"Nope—never heard of it."

"Ronald Reagan?"

"Was he the guy before Lincoln, or just after?" She nudged me in the ribs. "Okay, tell me about . . . who were these two again?"

"Ollie and Bud. Bud was a former lieutenant colonel who became President Reagan's National Security Advisor. Ollie was a serving lieutenant colonel on his staff."

She noted, "You should always keep a close eye on lieutenant colonels."

"I just pinned on a few days ago."

"Oh. Then . . . congratulations. How's it feel?"

"Not bad. They say it takes a full year before it sinks in that they're paying you more to act stupider. I'm still getting used to it."

"Well . . . you seem to be off to a good start." She laughed. "Back to your story."

"Not a story. It's a D.C. passion tale. Ollie and Bud—good guys, well-intentioned, patriotic, salt-of-the-earth types. There was a law at the time banning our government from sending money or weapons to the Contra rebels who were battling the communist government in Nicaragua. On the other side of the world, the Iranians and their Hezbollah pals in Lebanon were kidnapping American officials and torturing them to death."

"That last thing, that sounds ugly."

I nodded and continued, "Among others, one hostage was CIA, another a Marine officer. Our official diplomatic response was summed up as—problem too hard, tough shit."

"And how were these two events connected?"

"They weren't. Not until Ollie talked Bud into a plan to kill two birds with one stone. Under the table, we would sell weapons and ammunition from our military stocks to Iran for their war against Iraq. These munitions would be sold at bargain basement prices, the Great Satan's image in Iran would gain a little luster . . . with a subrosa understanding that the Iranians would release the hostages. To come full circle, the cash from these arms sales would go straight to the Contras, who would use it to buy arms and supplies to kill more commies. Symmetry, right?"

I looked at her to be sure she understood. Apparently so, because she remarked, "That sounds like a really stupid idea."

"Why?"

"Where do I start? Because you can't trust Iranians, for one thing. And if you think about it, you're offering them an incentive to take more hostages so they can blackmail you for more arms. Because it sounds like you're talking many tons of equipment and hundreds of millions of dollars. Because this means complicated logistics, middlemen, and money-laundering."

"All of the above. Anything else?"

"Those are difficult, maybe impossible, things to disguise or hide. Lots of loose ends, lots of people involved, lots of moving parts that could spring a leak."

"But if it worked, nobody would be the wiser. Our hostages would be saved, and the Contras would kill more commies. What's not to like?"

"It was breaking the law."

"A slight technicality."

"I believe it's called theft of government property and criminal conspiracy. That's a ten-to-twenty technicality."

"Very good." I explained, "And yes, it did leak, and yes, the scandal nearly brought down Reagan's house."

"I'm sorry, does this have something to do with Daniels, Hirschfield, or Tigerman?"

"Bear with me."

"I'm trying." She added, "But you're very trying."

Indeed, I am. I explained, "Ollie and Bud were both very ambitious types, but in their hearts, and in their minds I think, the ends were noble and the means were justified. When they were caught, they were forced to resign. They're still testifying at congressional investigating committees."

"Am I now seeing the connection to Daniels?"

"If you're paying attention . . ."

"Well . . . spell it out for me."

"Bud and Ollie were two fairly average guys, over their heads in very important jobs, in a very complicated and treacherous world."

"I see."

"A lot of other senior officials were implicated, including the Secretaries of Defense and State. Several senior officials were forced to resign. A few were led off in handcuffs."

She shifted around in her seat. "You're implying that perhaps that scandal is a parable or a parallel for this case?"

I said nothing.

"You think this case goes that high? Spreads that wide?"

"I have no idea—yet."

"Then what are you saying?"

"Consider what we just heard from Theresa Daniels about what Cliff has been doing over the past decade, and whom he has been doing it with." I continued, "He may have been operating with permission, or even with orders, from his bosses—and from their bosses—including people in the White House. These things always begin small—like that Watergate security guard performing his nightly rounds and finding a piece of burglar's tape stuck on a door lock. At that moment in time, he had no idea he had the President of the United States by the balls." I looked her in the eye. "We know that Clifford was a subject in an espionage investigation, and we now know that, for many years, he was connected at the hip to two senior Defense officials. My instincts are telling me this is much bigger than just Clifford, and probably much wider."

She replied, "We don't know that he broke any law."

"He did."

"How do you know that?"

I looked at her. "I want to be sure you know what we're getting into."

"I do know."

"Do you? Because, should there be other people with their hands in the same cookie jar, once we walk into Hirschfield's or Tigerman's office, the shit could hit the fan. After that, there's no turning back."

"Well . . . how far are you from retirement?"

"Your problem's bigger than mine. I at least have a boss who might run a little interference for me." Or might not.

"I'm an Asian-American woman with a military academy degree, and fluency in three languages. Corporate quota hunters have sticky dreams about people like me. You, on the other hand, are an average white male with a law degree." She smiled. "Worry about yourself."

"I love America."

We lapsed back into thoughtful silence. I pulled into North Parking at the Pentagon. It was 6:15, well into happy hour, and I had no trouble finding a parking space close to the building. I turned off the ignition, and we got out and began our trek up the long walkway.

"As a matter of interest," Bian asked as we walked, "Ollie and Bud? What happened to them?"

"Ollie was slick and managed to spin it to become a hero to conservatives. He was canonized, the good Marine doing his best for the nation he adores. It helped that it was heartfelt, I think. So he got the usual raw deal accorded to disgraced officials: a radio show and a fortune from books and the speech circuit."

"And Bud?"

"Yes, Bud. He went home one night and ate a bottle of pills." I allowed her a moment to think about that, then said, "Happy ending. He was discovered before it was too late. The point is, in Washington even well-intended people can do bad things."

"But there's a larger moral here, isn't there?"

I nodded.

"You're using this story as a parable. Cliff is one of those two guys."

Right again.

She said, "You're telling me he was swept up in something, something bigger than him, something more complicated than he could fathom."

"Eight points. Go for the full ten."

We walked in silence for a few minutes. Eventually Bian understood the real significance, and she asked, "But how did Cliff respond—like Ollie, or like Bud? That's the question, isn't it?"

"Good. There's a big prize for the extra credit."

"From what we now know about Cliff, he was not like Bud. His life suggests Cliff was durable, resilient, a survivor. More Ollie than Bud. Right?"

I nodded.

"So you believe he was murdered."

I asked, "Do you have a firearm?"

"What does that—"

"Do you have a firearm?"

"Yes . . . in the safe. At work."

"Start carrying it."

CHAPTER TEN

Bian flashed her Department of Defense building pass and got us quickly past the security checkpoint and into the fluorescent bowels of the beast. Every time I enter this building I feel a flutter in my stomach; it's called panic. In civilian life, only two things are certain, death and taxes, whereas the career military officer faces a third, worse certainty: an assignment inside this building. I had so far managed to avoid this fate. So far. Yet, like bullets on the battlefield, I knew that somewhere inside the Pentagon was a desk with my name on it.

"My office is upstairs. Fifth floor," Bian informed me. "Mr. Waterbury asked me to check in before the interview."

"Let's not, and just say we did."

"He'll notice. He's sharper than you think."

"Fooled me."

She chuckled, and we kept walking.

In the eyes of the great American public, the Pentagon is a huge and confusing labyrinth that somehow burns through some four hundred billion dollars of taxpayer cash per year.

The building, however, in nearly every human and architectural sense, is amazing. There actually are tours, and the guides will inform you this is the earth's largest office structure, comprising some 6,636,360 square feet, occupying 29 acres, able to house about 23,000 workers, in varying levels of comfort and discomfort.

In short, it is a gigantic memorial to function over form, and incredibly, the entire thing was constructed in a sixteen-month span of hyper-frantic activity during the heyday of the Second World War, at the amazing price of less than fifty million bucks.

I once cited this remarkable statistic to a defense contractor pal. He laughed and commented, "Morons. We're gettin' ten times that just to refurbish the basement. And we stretch it out for years."

Other interesting esoterica—the building boasts some 284 restrooms, the world's largest collection of white porcelain bowls under one roof, over 2,000 freestanding commodes, and half as many wall-mounted urinals. Regarding this inviting statistic, I'll restrict myself to one useful observation: You would be an idiot to buy a home downstream.

In fact, three of the four military services have their headquarters within these walls; the Marine Corps has its own sandbox within walking distance uphill. The underlying spirit behind this shotgun marriage is that proximity will force the services to work together in neighborly harmony. The official term is unification, and it would seem to make sense, because after all, the four military services perform the same basic mission, the same rudimentary purpose—laying waste to nations that piss us off. And why it makes sense is exactly why it doesn't work: We're all vying for the same taxpayer bucks, pool of human talent, and opportunities to strut our stuff.

Bian and I walked past a wall on which were hung, in a neat, orderly line, the official seals of the United States Army, Air Force, Navy, and Marine Corps. The message here—all for one, one for all, *e pluribus unum.*

Maybe the tourists believe this.

My own service, the Army, is the oldest, the largest, the smartest, with obviously the most primo JAG Corps. The Marine Corps are also fairly good guys, primarily because they act and think like the Army, except they're a lot more hormonal, with a truly monumental gift for blowing smoke up your butt.

The Air Force, newest of the services, is like an orphan teenager with a fat trust fund—prematurely arrogant and totally obsessed with all the cool shit it can buy. Nobody likes them, but we all envy them.

Last, our seafaring comrades, an overdressed yachting club whose main contribution to national security seems to be propping up bars and bordellos in strange and exotic ports.

The other services might have a different take on all this—of course, it's a well-known fact that their outlooks are distorted by their small-minded prejudices.

But in fact, how each service does its job does tend to color its culture, traditions, worldview, and strategic perspective.

The Navy, for instance, sees the globe as three-quarters water, with several largely irrelevant landmasses called continents populated by quarrelsome people who somehow become scared shitless the instant an aircraft carrier rolls up off their shore.

For the Air Force the world is this really neat target range, conveniently dotted with cities and towns to drop stuff on—so long as it doesn't interfere with happy hour.

But for the Army, combat is neither a balmy voyage nor a fleeting glimpse from a cockpit window—it's a destination, a commitment, a long, messy affair from which there are only two roads home: victory or retreat, with your shield or on it.

The Marine Corps, as I said because it does essentially the same thing as the Army, *thinks* like the Army. But because its purse is controlled by the squids, it quacks like a duck. Get a Marine away from his naval overseers, however, put a few free drinks into him or her, and you'll get an earful about the Navy. Message to my aquatic friends: They don't really like you.

The point is, the Pentagon is a large melting pot of pent-up passions, jealousies, and conflicting strategic visions, so to help things along, a joint staff, manned by officers drawn from the four services, are supposed to shelve their loyalties, and their career aspirations, to direct the services to work together cooperatively, rationally, and efficiently. This is like hiring the marriage counselor who's fucking your wife to fix your marriage.

As if there aren't enough staffs, there is one more, the Office of the Secretary of Defense, or OSD, comprised largely of civilian bureaucrats—a mixture of career civil servants and political appointees—with a smattering of uniformed people to fetch the coffee and man the copiers. The purpose of this curious institution is to perform the constitutional function of civilian oversight. Bottom line here: Americans don't want to wake up one morning in a banana republic run by guys in funny suits.

All this aside, however, where it counts, on the battlefield, soldiers, sailors, airmen, and Marines could care less who's humping who in the Pentagon corridors—they willingly give their lives for one another, and they often do.

Anyway, we had walked up a long stairwell and now we were in a long hallway on the fifth floor, the Pentagon's equivalent of an attic. I mean, you can bet the Secretary of Defense's nephew doesn't work on this floor.

Bian stopped in front a steel-encased door and began punching numbers into an electronic keyboard. A placard beside the door read "Office of Special Investigations"; obviously, this was a skiff, like a large walk-in safe.

There was a click and she shoved open the door. We entered a well-lit, windowless office space, a warren of office cubes where about twenty people were performing various activities, from punching computer keys and chatting on phones to the happier few who were gathering their coats and calling it a day.

A number of people looked up and waved or said hello to Bian; she seemed popular with her workmates, always a good sign. We walked directly to the rear of the skiff, where there was an office door; she knocked, and we entered.

Mr. Waterbury was seated behind his desk, hunched over and scribbling on a form. We stood and waited, and he ignored us, pulling more forms out of an in-box and not looking up.

I have a low threshold for self-important pricks, and after thirty seconds of this nonsense, I said to Bian, "I have better things to do. We're outta here."

His head snapped up and he affected a surprised look. "What do—? Oh . . . Drummond, Tran . . . you're here."

"Were you expecting somebody else?"

"I'm a busy man. This is an important office."

"You asked us to drop by. We're here. What do you want?"

He was used to doing the browbeating, so my directness threw him off and he looked confused for a moment.

Anyway, Waterbury's office was physically small, and the room and the top of his desk—like his mind, and like his personality—were neat and barren, devoid of any of the normal signs of human habitation. The lone ornamentation was a photograph of the Secretary of Defense hanging prominently in the middle of the wall. Upon closer examination, I noted that it was neatly autographed with a short inscription that, for all I knew, read, "To the biggest tightass in the building—don't let up." This, of course, is the kind of bureaucratic pornography people normally display to impress guests and underlings. In Waterbury's case, I suspect he did it in the event the

Secretary dropped by for a cup of coffee, unlikely as that might be. People who owe their jobs to patronage are always a little insecure; they turn ass-kissing into a high art.

In addition to the desk, I observed three stand-up wall safes with Top Secret magnetic strips on the drawers, and to his rear, a large mahogany bookshelf filled with about a hundred precisely aligned regulations and manuals. George Orwell dreamed of rooms, and of men, like this.

His eyes studied Bian, then me. He said, motioning at the absence of chairs, "I won't offer you seats. I don't believe in them."

"Then how do you get your ass to levitate like that?"

"I meant I don't encourage subordinates to relax in my office."

I knew what he meant. "I can't imagine anybody relaxing in your presence, Mr. Waterbury." I smiled.

He obviously understood the underlying message and did not appreciate it, because he did not smile back. Lest you think I was screwing with Waterbury just for the fun of it, he was speaking to me in this really condescending tone. To borrow a metaphor, he was the lion back in his own hunting ground, informing the interloper who was the king of this jungle. To stretch that metaphor a bit further, I'm like a hyena—I scavenge where I like, am quicker on my feet, and my sound is very annoying. Also, it *was* fun.

He came to the point and asked us, "Did you learn anything from Mrs. Daniels?"

Bian started to reply, and I cut her off. "Like what?"

"Answer the question, Drummond."

"Oh . . . well . . . she smokes Camels. About three packs a day. She has a thing for cheap gin. Her car and face need paint jobs, her house—"

"I don't care about all that. Anything relevant to Daniels's death?"

I stared down at him. "It will be in my report. When I get around to writing one, you can read all about it."

His eyes narrowed. He said to Bian, "Major, *you* do work for me, right?"

"Yes sir, and—"

"Then answer the question."

After a moment, Bian said, "We learned nothing relevant to Daniels's death. She didn't know why her husband died, or how."

He studied her face, then mine. He informed us, "I think it was suicide."

"It wasn't," I replied.

"That's your view." He added, "I called the Arlington police and had a long conversation with Detective Sergeant Enders. The ballistics results came in. The gun belonged to Daniels."

"We assumed that—"

"*And* a preliminary match was made between the splatter on the pistol and Daniels's blood type."

"We also assumed that," I informed him. "If you'd be so good, keep your nose out of this investigation."

"This investigation is half mine. I'll involve myself as I see fit."

I looked at him and said, "Major Tran informed me that you're a former military policeman."

"That's right. Twenty-five years' service. Damned good one, if I say so. My commands always led in closure rates."

"Twenty-five years. I'll assume then that you know the basic rule of criminal procedure—let the investigators do their job."

As you might expect, I work with the MPs and CID types a lot. As cops go, they tend to be excellent; for some reason the military concepts of discipline and obedience and the societal concepts of law and order are a marriage made in hell. Also, unlike cops in civilian communities, the military cop does not exist in a world apart, feels no disorienting distance from his community, nor is there a blue wall of silence that pops up whenever the poop hits the fan. Rank is rank in the Army, and the military policeman is well advised to remember it. You can give a speeding ticket to the Secretary of the Army, and I know an MP private who did. But there had better be an up-to-date calibration record at the MP station for the speed gun, which explains why the private was a sergeant when he first became my client before his court-martial.

Occasionally, however, one finds an individual who transcends these boundaries and traditions. I suspected that Waterbury was such a man, and I would bet he wasn't fondly remembered by the military communities he oversaw.

In fact, Waterbury told me, "I weighed into investigations whenever I felt it was necessary. My MPs appreciated it, too."

"Well, I don't."

We stared at each other a moment.

Satisfied that he made his petty point, he informed me, "As I said, Enders and his detectives are leaning toward a ruling of suicide."

"Good. That's exactly what we want them to conclude at this stage."

He looked thoughtful for a moment, then leaned toward me and said, "The position of the Defense Department is that we will subscribe to whatever determination the police—the proper civil authorities—whatever they decide."

"Why do I think you have something to add?"

"You're right, Drummond. You and Tran will confine your investigation to the possibility of a security leak. How Daniels died is neither the purpose of this investigation nor is it your business, nor will you interfere with or duplicate the work the civilian authorities are doing." He finally came to the real point of this dialogue and said, "When you speak with Mr. Tigerman, you'll contain your questions to that realm of inquiry."

"The question of Daniels's death and a security leak are possibly related. You know that."

"That's speculation. In the mind of the investigating detective, we're dealing with a suicide, not homocide. Daniels was certainly a ripe candidate . . . a broken marriage, a foundering career . . . Who knows what else was going wrong in his life or his head?"

It appeared that Mr. Waterbury had done a little research and investigation since we last spoke. Or maybe he knew all about Clifford Daniels all along, but he and the boys upstairs—actually, downstairs—had put their heads together and figured out how to handle this thing—and Sean Drummond.

I said, "Why don't I tell you what else? He had an order to testify before a congressional investigating committee."

"Irrelevant. I'll reiterate—this investigation is not about his death."

"Bullshit."

He narrowed his eyes at me. "It also strikes me, Drummond, that I had better remind you that Albert Tigerman is *not* a suspect. Nor will he be treated like one. He is an important man, a busy man. He has agreed to meet with you out of courtesy." He added, "You will have five minutes."

Bian protested, "Sir, five minutes is—"

"Is more than enough. Choose your questions wisely. In fact,

I'm coming with you. Step over the line, and I'll gladly terminate the interview."

I said, "What are you afraid of, Waterbury?"

"Deal with it, Drummond." He stood. "Follow me."

CHAPTER ELEVEN

Albert Tigerman's office was located on the second floor of the E-ring—the outermost ring—which, within this building, is the equivalent of a beachside condo on the Côte d'Azur.

Grand titles are the coin of the realm in Washington, and particularly among political appointees—many of whom paid a fortune for these jobs—the title at least has to *sound* impressive. It can get fairly confusing, and even annoying, as there is this bewildering array of deputy this and assistant that, with the ever-popular stringing together of two or more of these prefixes, and a flowering of suffixes on the caboose to tell you what the guy actually does. So you get things like the Deputy Assistant Under Secretary of Defense for Facilities Management and Building Restoration. Translation: janitor.

I would limit everybody to one prefix, one suffix, and fire the rest. If it takes more than four syllables to describe your job, there is no job. Period.

But the danger is, when you meet one of these clowns with a multisyllabic title, you don't know whether you're dealing with a superfluous taxmuncher or somebody who can really mess up your paycheck. Generally, the more prefixes, the less they can hurt you. Not always, though.

Anyway, the office of Albert Tigerman, Deputy Under Secretary of Defense for Policy, was located on the most prestigious wing, and on the most prestigious floor, a mere six doors from his lordship, the Secretary of Defense. If proximity is influence, this guy had his tongue deep in the boss's ear.

Waterbury gently eased open that door and we entered an anteroom where a pert, efficient-looking young assistant was hidden behind a large wooden desk covered by a forest of computers and phones.

She looked up, and Waterbury said to her, "Please inform Al that we're here for his six-thirty. He's expecting us."

"I know." She lifted the phone, punched a few numbers, and said, "The OSI people are here." She listened and hung up. "He'll be a few minutes. Please have a seat."

I mentioned to Waterbury, "Wow . . . chairs. This guy's a managerial pussy."

He tried to ignore me.

Bian, I noted, had retreated into a sort of meek silence. From my dealings with her this seemed out of character, though I thought I knew what was behind it. She was using me as a foil for the idiot she worked for, which was politically shrewd, and possibly even entertaining for her, and probably dangerous for me.

Well, whatever her reason, she wasn't in a talkative mood, and I wasn't being paid enough to chitchat with Waterbury. What would we talk about, anyway—how many people you can fit inside a boxcar?

So the three of us were seated, somewhat awkwardly, on a stiff leather couch with a coffee table to our front. Neatly organized on that table was a thick stack of magazines I quickly browsed through for something to kill the time. Unfortunately, they all had such interesting titles as *Foreign Affairs*, the *New Republic*, *Orbis*, the *Economist*, and such. I wondered, did the man inside the office actually read this stuff? Probably yes—and probably Albert spent his weekends watching C-SPAN and gardening, and his children rode horses and played squash, and his wife was on a first-name basis with all the helpful salesladies at Bloomingdale's. My lower-middle-class snobbery aside, I didn't think Mr. Tigerman and Mr. Drummond drank the same brand of beer.

So, with nothing better to do, I spent my time reviewing what I knew about this man we were about to meet. Before we departed my building to drop in on Theresa Daniels, Bian had made a trip to the powder room, and I had made a trip on the Internet to see what

I could discover about our presumptive host. I located his official CV on the Defense Department Web site and, a few entries later, a more enlightening article from *Washington Insider* that fleshed out the juicier personal parts.

Chronologically, he was born in the year 1946, in the city of Boston, on the better side of town, to a wealthy family. What followed was a prototypical northeastern rich boy's passage to adulthood: St. Paul's prep, Yale, Yale Law, then a fast-track partnership at a top New York firm. Not exactly a Horatio Alger, rags-to-riches tale; his was the more archetypal American riches-to-riches struggle. I love this country.

Anyway, over the proceeding thirty years, Albert had bounded between Washington jobs when Republicans were in power, and back to the New York money mill when not. Along the way, he acquired a venerated reputation as a defense intellectual.

Regarding this term—"defense intellectual"—for the life of me, I wouldn't recognize one if he pontificated on my lap or blew a brilliant opinion in my ear. For one thing, war is hardly an intellectual exercise; it's visceral, not cerebral, a contest of wills settled by pounding the crap out of each other until one guy screams uncle.

But, from the best I can tell, you get to be a defense intellectual by attending a lot of windbag conferences and writing scholarly articles that employ big theoretical and largely abstract expressions to describe small ideas. The battlefield lab work is left to somebody else.

But, well . . . shame on me for being so small-minded toward my host. I'm sure Albert's heart was in the right place. I might feel better about him, however, if I thought he could distinguish an M1A1 tank from an M1A2 as their treads crushed his shiny Beemer in the Pentagon parking lot.

Also, according to a number of articles I had read, Albert Tigerman and his boss, Thomas Hirschfield, were now in a bit of a jam because they were publicly credited with being the intellectual and bureaucratic forefathers of a war that had run a little longer than they predicted, gotten a lot messier than they had foretold, with casualty lists that were large—with no end in sight.

As Bian mentioned, this was Albert's second time in the Pentagon, in both incarnations working with and under his longtime mentor, Thomas Hirschfield.

Tigerman's door opened, and I looked up. A pair of Air Force generals walked out, thick briefing binders under their arms, and they ignored us, as military folk tend to do toward civilians, which I wasn't, though I was dressed like one. The assistant waited two beats, then said, "You may now enter."

We followed Herr Waterbury into the office, and three feet inside the doorway Albert Tigerman was standing waiting, like a perched bird. His hand shot out to Waterbury.

I took a moment to study our host and was a little surprised to observe that he was not even remotely impressive-looking—short, slightly pudgy, silver-haired, with thick horn-rimmed glasses, sort of a fleshy, characterless face, and a small, pinched mouth. I'm embarrassed to admit, he looked like a lawyer.

He finished shaking Waterbury's hand, saying, "Mark . . . damned good to see you again. I hear you're doing damn fine work up there."

I watched their faces and I knew. What a load of crap. This was not the first time these two were together that day.

There was a long, telling hesitation before Waterbury, unaccustomed as he was to slyness, replied, "Well . . . it's always a pleasure to see you, too, Al. I'm . . . sorry the occasion is such grim business."

"Can't be helped, can it?" Turning to Bian and me, Tigerman announced, "And you must be Drummond and Tran."

Who else would we be?

Bian said to him, "Sir, let me start by thanking you for taking this time out of your busy schedule to see us."

Not wanting him to get the misimpression that *I* regarded this as a big favor, I immediately said, "If you don't mind, sir, we'd like to start." I added, "I'm sure you are very busy. In fact, Waterbury told us our time is limited to five minutes."

I was sort of hoping he would say, "That ass Waterbury said *what*? . . . Why, a good man, a man who worked for me, a lifelong public servant, is dead under mysterious circumstances—of course you can take all the time you want or need." But he did not say that. He pointed at a short conference table near the window. "Is over there okay?"

Over there was fine, and we moved to the table. Tigerman sat at the head, Waterbury took the seat to his right, and Bian and I sat across from him.

Tigerman squirmed around in his seat for a moment, then

leaned across the table and said, "Mark tells me one of our people died. How damned unfortunate."

Bian replied, "The employee's name was Clifford Daniels. He was a GS-12, and for the past three years he worked here, in your organization. We assumed you knew him."

"Yes . . . yes, maybe I recall the name. I'm sure I would recognize his face if I saw him." He removed his glasses from his nose and a handkerchief from his breast pocket and began wiping the lens. "It's damned unfortunate, really . . ."

After a moment, Bian asked, "What's unfortunate, sir?"

"This organization—the Office of the Under Secretary . . ."

"What about it?"

"We have a total of some nine hundred people. As much as you would like to know all of these fine people . . ." He raised his glasses in a pedantic gesture of helplessness. "Well . . . how did he . . . this, uh, Mr. Daniels . . . how did he . . . you know?"

"That's still under investigation," I informed him.

Waterbury said, "Suicide. Blew his brains out."

"I see." Tigerman tapped his fingers on the table. "Again, Mr. Drummond, how can I . . . What?"

"We just have a few questions. Background stuff." I smiled. "Major Tran won't be reading you your rights or anything."

He smiled back. "So it's perfectly harmless?"

"Why wouldn't it be?"

We stared at each other.

I said, "Two weeks ago, Daniels received a notice to appear next week before the House Intelligence Oversight Subcommittee. Were you . . . aware of this?"

"Well . . . let me think . . ." He then spent a brief moment pretending to think. "Yes . . . I believe I was. Several of our people have gotten these summons. It's damned unfortunate . . ."

"Unfortunate?"

"You know . . ." He looked at me, trying to calibrate how much bullshit to throw in my direction. "Washington is a rough-and-tumble town, always has been . . . but with this war, with the political polarization on the Hill, with the election heat, and of course the loud carping from the liberal media . . ."

I was beginning to suspect Albert Tigerman had some weird mental affliction that prevented him from completing a sentence.

I asked, "Can you tell us why the Intelligence Oversight Subcommittee wanted to speak with Daniels?"

"I wish I could."

"You have no idea?"

"They don't share these things with me. No."

"But, well . . . you must at least know the type of work Daniels was doing here?" How's that for smooth?

He turned to Waterbury. "Refresh my memory, Mark. What office was he assigned to?"

"Near East and South Asia. A division chief."

"Ah . . . yes. Then . . . well, I suppose he was working on something to do with our war in Iraq."

"But you can't tell me what, specifically, Daniels was working on?"

"Let me . . . uh, a lot of actions flow through my in-box . . ." He looked thoughtful, then pained, and concluded, "I can't really say, exactly."

I lost it a little bit and said, "How about inexactly?"

He shrugged. I was really striking out here.

I looked at Bian, who was staring tightly at Tigerman's face. She said, "Daniels previously worked in DIA. Did you know him during those years?"

"What years would those be, Major?"

"Late eighties, throughout the nineties."

"Well . . . I wouldn't say . . . after all, I've met a lot of DIA types. That was a long time ago."

"Of course, sir. But it's atypical for career DIA people—intelligence specialists—to end up working in policy jobs, is it not?"

"It's not unheard of. Perhaps he had regional expertise."

"In fact, he was for many years the DIA desk officer for Iraq."

"Was he? Well, there you have it. The past few years, Iraq has become . . . if I might borrow a business euphemism . . . a growth industry in this building." He smiled. "I may even have approved his transfer myself."

"But you don't remember approving it?"

He shrugged. "Maybe one of our assistant secretaries or division chiefs knew him and requested him." Again he pointed at his in-box, which overflowed with memoranda and folders. "I don't . . . well, to be blunt, I can't remember everything I sign, can I?"

My turn. "We met with his ex-wife this afternoon."

"Ah. The poor woman. She must be devastated."

"She high-fived me."

"Oh . . ."

"In fact, I'm a little surprised by *your* reaction to this tragic news."

"Really? Why is that?"

"Mrs. Daniels informed us that you and Cliff spent a great deal of time together during the first Gulf War. She claimed that, afterward, you and he stayed in almost continuous contact. In her words, you were close friends."

He looked surprised. "Friends?"

I forgot. This was Washington. So to help him with this foreign concept, I explained, "People you hang out with and remember afterward. People whose death causes you to grieve."

This annoyed him, as it was intended to do, but he kept his composure. "Does she recall me ever visiting their house? Maybe she came to my house, met my wife . . . ?"

I did not reply.

He said, "In this town, it's not uncommon for lower-level officials to, you know, embellish their careers with their spouses. Or for wives to exaggerate their husband's importance." He winked at me. "My own wife thinks I'm the Secretary of Defense. Promise you won't disabuse her."

He smiled, and I smiled back. Boy, were we having fun.

After a moment, he blurted, "You've made me curious, Mr. Drummond. What exactly is it you think this man was working on, and how might that be connected to his death? Or to me?"

Bingo. Clichéd as it might sound, the guilty ones always fish. He needed to know what we knew; specifically, whether or how we could implicate him. De facto, the man was worried about something, and I spent a moment thinking about what that something might be. Well, for one thing, we could access the phone records for the Daniels household and see how often they spoke, and how far back their relationship extended. Also we could do a little background digging into how exactly Clifford Daniels got transferred from DIA to this office.

But so what? We could possibly prove that Tigerman misled us and, possibly, plumb the depths of his evasions. But evading the truth in Washington is hardly a crime; it's the ticket to higher office.

I looked at Mr. Tigerman and informed him, "I'm afraid our five minutes are up." I stood. "Thank you for your time, sir. We'll be sure to get back to you when it becomes necessary."

This did not sound like a threat, but it was fair warning, and Tigerman heard what I was saying. He stood, as did Waterbury and Bian. Tigerman studied my face a moment, then said, "I believe you need a little free advice, Mr. Drummond."

It was irresistible, and I said, "Okay, why don't you tell me who murdered Clifford Daniels?"

Tigerman suddenly looked very unhappy.

And Waterbury finally had the opportunity to flex his prosecution complex, and barked, "That's enough out of you, Drummond." He looked at Tigerman, to be sure this display of bootlicking was noted, and added, "The police are convinced Daniels killed himself. But Drummond has some wild and incredible fantasy that he might have been murdered. I ordered him not to raise this issue inside this office."

Tigerman produced a forced smile. "It's all right, Mark." He said to me, "You believe he was murdered? Why?"

"Just say I believe in the old saying."

He raised an eyebrow. "What saying would that be?"

"There is no refuge from confession but suicide; and suicide is confession."

Again he tapped his fingers on the table. "That's a very amusing insight. But, Mr. Drummond, it refers to suicide, not murder."

"So it does. But if we find what Daniels had to confess, I think we'll also find his murderer."

This did not appear to amuse him. He said, "You might find that Daniels was involved in very sensitive work in support of our war effort. I have no idea why he . . . why he killed himself. But I hope you do find out, and I hope you treat whatever you discover with the discretion it might deserve."

I looked at him, then at Waterbury. "Since we're giving free advice . . . by tomorrow morning Clifford Daniels's death will be in the public domain. He is a figure of considerable media interest, the press will become nosy about his death, and they can—and I'm sure they will—dig. There is no shortage of people inside this government with issues and agendas who will leak their own theories and suspicions. Are you prepared for that?"

I allowed Tigerman a moment to mull that reality.

I said, "Now, is there any other 'advice' you'd like to offer us?"

He turned his back and walked back to his desk. We walked out, and as the door closed behind us, I heard him say, "Be careful."

CHAPTER TWELVE

Waterbury went back to his office, and Bian and I walked through the long corridors, back toward the exit and North Parking.

After a few moments of silence, she remarked, "I don't think that went well."

"Were you expecting a confession?"

"No. A crack in his veneer would've been helpful, though."

"He's a career lawyer and a government bureaucrat. If he tells the truth, his lips fall off." I asked, "But as a man, what did you think of him?"

"I guess he was slicker than I anticipated. Basically, a very arrogant person, overconfident, high IQ . . . not the type who scares easily. He exposed nothing . . . until the very end." She saw that I was surprised she had picked up on that, and asked, "Why do the guilty ones always fish?"

"Be careful. He could just be curious, concerned for a dead member of his staff, or wondering how this is going to play with the press."

"You really believe that?"

I smiled.

She asked, "Did we accomplish anything?"

"Personally, I found his glibness reassuring."

"You'll have to explain why that's a good thing."

"For the hunter, the complacent prey is always best."

She nodded and thought about that. "That's a good one. Chinese proverb?"

"My Irish grandmother." She smiled, and I noted, "Here's what's important. Mr. Tigerman confirmed that he has something to hide. We should assume that people higher in the chain of command also share that secret." I looked at her. "For instance, he and your boss are in this together."

"Do you think?" She scratched her head and scrunched up her face. "Boy . . . I never picked up on that."

"I'm just saying, be careful how much you disclose to Waterbury. His loyalty is to the people who gave him his job."

"I know that. What's next?"

"I don't know what's next for you. I'm hungry."

"I was hoping you'd say that. I'm famished." She asked, "What do you usually eat? Raw meat?" She thought this was funny and laughed.

I smiled back.

She said, "Let me guess. A meat, potatoes, and beer guy?"

"Right food groups, wrong order."

"Great. I know the perfect place. Give me a lift to my car, then follow. It's less than two miles from Daniels's apartment building."

As we drove, I used my cell to call Phyllis and exchange updates. She informed me that a team of NSA technicians was working furiously on decoding the suspicious file drawers. I advised her to call them every thirty minutes, be a complete pain in the ass. She warmly thanked me for telling her how to do her job, and asked how our meeting went with Tigerman. So I told her, she laughed, reminded me to watch my backside, and signed off. Phyllis is not a micromanager—which I like—but it occurred to me that she knew this case might piss off a lot of powerful people. And further, it occurred to me that "watch your backside" might mean, if you step on the wrong toe, you're on your own. You have to pay attention with these people.

Anyway, we found Bian's car, she started it up, and I followed her for about two miles and into the narrow parking lot of a small, worse-for-wear strip mall on Columbia Pike. She parked, and I parked next to her. As I got out of my car, she approached me, saying, "I hope you like Vietnamese cuisine."

I started to climb back into my car. But she reached over and grabbed the door before I could close it. She laughed and said, "Come on. You'll like it, I promise." She grabbed my arm and yanked me out of the car. Wow. She was strong.

"I hate fish."

"So do I. Fish are disgusting. Trust me."

I was *really* hungry, and out of the corner of my eye, about two blocks from where we stood, was the golden arch of salvation. I started to make a dash before Bian grabbed my arm. "Come on. I know the lady who owns this place. She needs the business." She added, "I'll get you a fortune cookie."

"I thought that was Chinese food."

"All right. I'll read your palm."

The illogical red-lettered sign over the entrance read, "Happy Vietnamese Cuisine." Regarding that, I asked her, "How can the food be happy?"

"What?"

"Happy . . . it says *happy* cuisine."

"Oh, shut up."

Anyway, we crossed the parking lot and entered through a glass door with Asian letters on it, into a small, cramped restaurant; all in all, it resembled a low-scale pizzeria: plastic tables, plastic chairs, checkered tablecloths, but for those seeking a genuine Asian ambiance, on the walls were a few cheesy paintings of sampans and short people plucking rice in misty bogs. The smell was overpowering. I said to Bian, "Call the cops. There's a corpse in here."

She laughed. "It's fish sauce. A delicacy, actually, like a Vietnamese gravy. You squeeze the oils from the fish, store it in a closed vat, and let it simmer for a few weeks. The taste is very tart."

"The smell is very awful."

"Is this really the same tough guy who was too manly to use disinfectant at an indoor murder scene?"

"That was only a rotting corpse."

She stared at me. "Be nice or there'll be another corpse." Anyway, the lady who ran the place spotted Bian and trotted with bouncy, mincing steps across the floor toward us. They embraced, exchanged cheek pecks, and Bian and she began conversing together in Vietnamese. Mentally, it took a moment for me to adjust to Bian's bantering in this strange tongue, with all its gymnastic consonants and antic musical quality—like listening to a record suddenly skip from 33 to 78 rpm. I wonder how we sound to them.

After a moment, the woman led us to a table at the back, directly beneath a large painting of a thatch-roofed village on stilts populated by little people with thatched saucers on their heads. I mean, if you let your imagination roam, you could almost feel the sweat form on the back of your neck.

The woman apparently spoke little English. "You sit . . . you sit . . . you sit . . ." she said, looking at me.

I sat, I sat, I sat.

Bian mentioned to me, "She's the owner," then said something to her and the woman laughed. The owner was basically mid- to late sixties, wore a scarlet silk ao dai—the traditional female garb—and had at one time been what Grandpa Erasmus would call a real looker. She was still slender and very attractive, but she had hard years on her, evidenced by her tired eyes, her deeply creased face, and a pronounced stoop in her shoulders. Bian informed me, "I told her you don't like fish."

"Whatever. I *hate* fish."

"She called you a typical American. No taste buds."

I smiled at the older woman and informed her, "My ancestors are Irish." This, of course, excuses a wide range of human flaws and abnormalities.

Bian translated this, the woman nodded knowingly and mentioned something in reply. Bian laughed and said something back.

Bian informed me, "She said she knows about the Irish. Bloodthirsty savages, sloppy drunks, and weepy poets."

"What did you tell her?"

"You're no poet."

They exchanged more words, and Bian chuckled. The lady poured water in our glasses while Bian informed me, "She says you are very handsome in a very Caucasian way." She added, "She wonders if you have a wife."

"Oh . . ."

"I told her you had asked many women to marry. They all said no."

The two of them erupted in laughter. Women have a weird sense of humor.

Bian then explained something to the woman, who looked at me, and said, "Can do . . . can do." She then said something to Bian, who nodded. The woman rushed off and disappeared into what I presumed was the kitchen where all the poor dead fish went to be squashed into putrid oils.

I looked at Bian. "Where did you learn Vietnamese?"

"Where it's best learned."

"Berlitz?"

She smiled, sort of. "Saigon. I was born there." She shook out her napkin and placed it on her lap. "Have you been to Vietnam?"

I shook my head. "My father vacationed there. Twice. He came back with wild and not wonderful stories about people shooting at one another, mines, bombs." I added, "He returned the second time with a story about somebody who shot *him*."

"I see."

"How did you get here?"

"That's a long and very boring story."

"Nothing about you is boring."

She looked at me. "Is that a compliment?"

"Consider it an observation."

"Well . . . my father was an officer in the South Vietnamese Army. A major, in the Rangers. It was different for him than for American officers who rotated in and out on twelve-month tours. He fought the entire war. Twelve straight years."

"It was *his* country."

She gave me a knowing nod. "I'll bet that had something to do with it."

"You don't look old enough to remember that."

"I wasn't, and I don't. He and my mother were married in 1967. They waited and waited . . . they didn't want to bring a child into such a miserable existence. I was born in 1973."

"The year before the war ended."

"You mean for America it ended. Not for us. And I think he knew the final ending wasn't going to be satisfying. But I suppose he decided he'd waited long enough for a child . . . that . . . if he kept putting it off . . ." She played with her chopsticks. "It's a strange thought. I've always harbored the sense I was conceived as an act of fatalism."

I said nothing.

"My family is Catholic. Worse, my mother's family were rich, decadent landowners. By physical necessity and political conviction, they were staunchly anticommunist, and they knew what defeat would mean. My father fought until the very end, until 1975."

"Then he left?"

"That . . . No, that proved impossible."

"Why not? A lot of Vietnamese came here. Go to San Diego. They're thinking of renaming it Nha Diego."

"Those were the lucky ones."

"What happened to the unlucky ones?"

"The northerners had a lot of time to prepare for their conquest. During the war years, with the help of their southern spies, they compiled long lists of South Vietnamese officers and politicians who were, in their view, corrupted. My father was on a list of people who would benefit from . . . the phrase was 'reform and reeducation.' Two days after the surrender, he was taken to a camp to be taught how to *think* in the new Vietnam."

"I'm sorry."

A little too offhandedly, she replied, "Don't worry about it. This all happened a long time ago."

"Do you know the definition of a long time ago?" She appeared not to know, so I told her, "In somebody else's lifetime."

She did not acknowledge this, but coolly sipped from her water. Eventually she said, "Well . . . my mother remained in Saigon for the next three years. Waiting. As the wife of a traitor, she wasn't employable with the new state, nor did anybody want to get on the wrong side of the new government by hiring her. Don't ask about the things she had to do to get by."

We looked at each other a moment.

She said, "Understand that nobody knew initially what these camps were, how they operated . . . We were told these weren't penal colonies, they were humane facilities to help the Vietnamese build one society, a brave new nation. It sounded so stupidly communist, for a while, everybody believed it."

"Did you hear from your father?"

"External contact was forbidden—we were told it would taint his reeducation effort."

"And you were how old? Three . . . four?"

"Three, the year my father went into the camp. Six when an army comrade of my father's came to Saigon and found us. He had just been released from the same camp. He told us my father had been dead for two years. To inspire other recalcitrant prisoners, he volunteered to be publicly beaten to death."

"I see."

"So we left. We arrived with the last big wave of boat people," she said as though this were the end of the story rather than the beginning.

I didn't know how to respond to this. Like nearly all Americans, I had no frame of reference for what Bian had experienced, for how she had suffered. The closest I came were my own pop's years away at war, the first of which occurred in the early sixties, when I was too young to be frightened for him, or what his loss might mean for little Sean.

His second tour was in 1971—I was ten, friends had lost their fathers, other fathers had returned home missing body parts, and others came back mentally and emotionally different. So I knew. I will never forget the day we dropped Pop at Dulles International Airport for his flight to San Francisco, where he would catch the Southeast Asia express, the strained look on Mom's face, or how hard Pop squeezed me before he uttered his deeply felt parting advice—"Be good, do everything Mom says, or I'll come back and kill you."

What followed was the year of long days and forever nights. Every night I offered the same shopworn deal as so many other kids in my shoes: Dear God, bring Pop home healthy, and I will never commit another sin.

Well, as I mentioned, Pop came back alive, albeit on a stretcher. Boy, was I ever relieved I had stipulated *healthy*—had I stupidly gone for the more exclusive "alive" or "in one piece," I would've lost the best part of my teenage years.

The point is, as Americans, we send our fathers off to war, they are away for a finite period, and while they are gone, we, their families, live in constant dread but also relative tranquillity. Except that they may never come back, they might as well be on an extended business trip.

"What about your mother?" I asked her.

"Still alive. Our boat was picked up about a hundred miles from the Philippines. The voyage was not . . . well, it wasn't pleasant." She looked away a moment. "We spent a few weeks in a hospital, then a settlement camp outside Manila before the American embassy arranged visas and flights to America. A lot of Vietnamese had come before us, mainly to Southern California, Louisiana, and here, around D.C. The State Department made our choice for us. This was where we ended up."

The old woman emerged from the kitchen trailed by a skinny Vietnamese teenage boy with purple hair, nose ring, punk clothes, and wobbly arms hauling a large tray. His parents probably had a tale somewhat like Bian's, joining in the diaspora, fleeing a nightmare and coming here to provide this boy a better life, a good education, promising opportunities. Seeing him now, I'll bet they were having second thoughts.

He set the tray down on a folding stand, and he and the lady began laying out plates on our table. It was mostly boiled vegetables and starchy rice, with two plates filled with stuff that looked scaly and smelled awful. I gave Bian an accusing look. "You said you hated fish."

"I lied." She laughed. "I'm Vietnamese. Of course I love fish."

At least the rice looked somewhat edible and smelled okay.

The owner mentioned something to Bian, who said something back. Bian said to me, "She says there is no beer on the menu because she doesn't have a liquor license. But she keeps a hidden stock for favored customers in her fridge in the back. She'll bring it out in a moment."

Things were looking up.

I smiled at the woman, then at Bian. "Please thank her from the bottom of my heart for her hospitality. Tell her she is most gracious."

Bian translated this, and the woman bowed. I added, "Also, please tell her she has a lovely and very deceitful daughter."

Bian looked away for a moment. Then she looked back at me. "You're very observant."

"And you have your mother's beauty."

"Well . . . thank you."

Her mother said something to her, and Bian patted her arm and said something in reply. Her mother looked at me a moment, then returned to the kitchen.

"What was that about?"

"Because she thinks you are a good man, she says she has a special surprise for you." She added, smiling, "I told her she's a terrible judge of men. She should poison your food."

Bian's mother returned a moment later, carrying a dish upon which sat two Big Macs, still hot and steaming in their boxes. She set the plate in front of me, and two cans of holy water blessed by Pope Budweiser.

I stood and hugged her. She giggled, saying something to her daughter that probably translated as, "Tell this round-eyed idiot to let go of me before I knee him in the nuts."

I sat, and Bian's mother left us. Bian sliced off a piece of fish and, holding it up on her fork, said, "Try a little of this. It's very good."

"No . . . thank you."

"You're sure? It's a freshwater fish. It tastes different."

"Did it swim in scotch?"

She laughed.

We ate in silence for a few moments. She asked, "How much do you remember about Vietnam? Not the country, the war."

"For me, it was a TV war. You know what I mean, right?"

"No. Tell me about that."

"It was the first war piped into America's living rooms. Somebody described that as like seeing a hologram of a war. But for one year of my life—the year of my father's second tour—I was glued to it. I wanted to see him on TV, but I really didn't. You know?"

"I don't know. All I had to do was step out in the backyard and watch the artillery flashes."

"I had a friend who was watching CBS news one night. He actually saw his own father get shot."

"Dead?"

"Wounded. They were in the middle of dinner, though. His mother actually vomited. But for most Americans it was—just as this war is—that moment on the evening news between the trial of the month and the weather forecast."

"Did TV and the media make it unpopular?"

"Wars are never popular."

"You know what I'm talking about. I read in a history book that Walter Cronkite did more damage in one night than the entire Tet offensive."

"I think the media and TV exposed a truth—an unwelcome truth, an unhappy one, but an important one. They were biased and irresponsible in many ways . . . but I also think they did more good than harm, told more truth than lies. On the big truth, they nailed it."

"What big truth?"

"We had become involved in a war we didn't intend to win. Like sex with neither partner able to orgasm—eventually, somebody has to call it quits."

"That's a very . . . unique explanation."

"I'm thinking of writing a political science textbook."

"They come wrapped in brown paper?" She took a bite of her

fish, then reached across the table, grabbed my beer, and took a long swig.

"I can get you your own beer," I told her. "The owner has a big crush on me."

She laughed. And then we found ourselves staring into each other's eyes.

I broke eye contact first—somebody had to before this turned complicated.

Obviously, she and I, somehow, were becoming intimate. There was a natural sensuality to this woman, an unconscious sexuality that I was very conscious of.

The Army, unique institution that it is, has managed, through bureaucratic dictates and brute legal force, to quell or repress nearly all of the flawed human compulsions and quirks, from social inequalities, to racial and religious intolerance, to the inbred American inclinations toward indiscipline, laziness, and disobedience. Send us your bigots, your snobs, your slovenly punks; we will unkink their screwed-up heads and return to you a model citizen, an individual of tolerance, good citizenship, and self-discipline—or a fairly convincing fake.

Yet the attraction between the sexes has eluded even the Army's most Orwellian programs and mind games. Here we are, some thirty years after the congressional order imposing the integration of the sexes, and there still is rutting within the ranks, affairs between married officers and their spouses, sexual favoritism, sexual blackmail, voyeurism, rape, and every other imaginative act two or more horny people can conceive of. The modern battle dress uniform, baggy and shapeless as it is, is as aphrodisiacal as a knee in the groin; yet the fevered male imagination fills in the blanks and primitive impulses take over.

Not to put too fine a point on it, I knew I was attracted to her; for some reason, I think she found me attractive as well. Of course, I don't like to make a move on somebody else's lady. Relationships are hard enough without complications. That's not an ironclad thing, though.

I draw the line, however, when her beau is serving our country, in uniform, overseas, battling our enemies in a theater of war. I do this as a patriotic gesture. After all, the least the home front can do is keep our hands out of their ladies' undies. Also, the fiancé has a gun, and knows how to use it.

Apparently Bian also recognized we were on thin ice, because she immediately shifted the conversation back to safer ground. She broke eye contact for a moment, then said, "Why did America lose the will to keep fighting in Vietnam? Fifty-eight thousand Americans dead. Hundreds of thousands horribly wounded."

"Because somebody finally asked, why make it fifty-nine thousand dead?"

"Still . . . that's a large down payment. How could you walk away from it?"

"That's a question we're still trying to answer. I think you know that."

"The answer is important."

"For you, maybe. For most of us, the war ended thirty years ago. The dead are mourned and buried, and the survivors have their monument." I added, "For most Americans, it's a brief and confusing chapter in a long history book."

"That's a shallow answer."

"Good. I'm a shallow person."

She put down her fork and stared at me. "You are not. I've known you only one day, but . . . you're deeper and more perceptive than you act."

"Eat your fish."

She smiled. "Hey, I didn't call you sensitive."

"That's why you're still alive."

She finished off my beer. I popped the second can.

She said, "I was on the other end of that decision. It cost my father his life. It nearly killed my mother. Look around you—see what it meant for her future."

"Is she happy?"

Bian repeated my question, and then seemed to contemplate this for a long moment. "She opened a Vietnamese restaurant, and after nearly thirty years she barely speaks English. What does that tell you?"

"She doesn't want to die here."

"She misses her own people. Her sister runs an orphanage outside Ho Chi Minh City. My mother and I send every penny we can spare. The boy . . . the one who's helping her, that's where he's from."

"And are you bitter?"

"I . . . no. I'm the good immigrant story. I've adapted to America, and America adopted me." Apparently enough said about this, because she changed the subject again and asked, "About Iraq, though. Could history repeat itself?"

"Why should it?"

"Well, there are obvious similarities . . . historical analogies."

I reached over and took my beer out of her hand. "Every war is different. The only similarities are that they all suck, and good people get killed."

"That's too simplistic."

"Not if one of those dead people is you, or someone you love."

"You know what I'm talking about. A lot of people believe we went to Iraq on false pretenses, that the government lied, that this war has lasted too long, too many casualties . . . clearly things haven't gone as predicted or anticipated. It was sold as short and simple. It's complicated and bloody. That sounds a lot like Vietnam, doesn't it?"

"That was then, this is now. That was a different time, a different world, a different America. The country was at war with itself—black versus white, young versus old, the establishment against the new order. A messy foreign war was one more than we could handle."

I had the sense this was more than casual banter, and she confirmed that, asking, "What if we find that Clifford Daniels did something really bad? Something really stupid?"

"Like what?"

"I have no idea. But look what he was involved with. As you mentioned earlier, consider where he worked, and who he worked with." She took back my beer and drained it. She handed me the empty can. "This case makes me nervous."

"This case is making a lot of people nervous. We'll find what we find, and let the chips fall where they may. It's not our job to calculate or curb the political fallout."

"Are you sure you're right?"

Before I could answer, my cell phone went off. I pulled it from my pocket and answered. It was Phyllis, who, without any preamble, informed me, "Get over here right away."

"Where's here?"

"My office. The decoded transcripts have arrived." She drew a heavy breath. "It's . . . it's worse than we imagined."

CHAPTER THIRTEEN

Bian trailed behind me in her car, a cute little green Mazda Miata—Maseratis for poor chicks. I turned on the radio and listened to the 8:00 p.m. news update.

The newscaster spooled off the results of the latest poll for the upcoming presidential election, just over a week off and picking up steam fast. This poll, like the ten polls that preceded it, showed a nation more or less evenly divided, and an election too close to predict.

A smug blabberperson for the President came on the air and described the poll numbers as a stunning victory for his camp, because after nearly four years his boss had only managed to piss off half the electorate.

The contender's equally self-assured spokesperson used his equal time to proclaim a signal triumph for his man, as, even after two years of energetic campaigning, half the electorate still did not realize what a complete stinker he was.

Though it's possible I paraphrased their words incorrectly.

What I thought it showed was a margin so thin that the smallest political fart could blow the election either way. I wondered if the big guy in the Oval Office had yet been notified about the death of Clifford Daniels—probably yes and probably, somewhere in the White House basement, unsmiling people were burning the midnight oil.

The next news item was casual and succinct: A car bomb went off in Karbala, a Shiite city south of Baghdad, with sixty dead and more than thirty wounded. Somewhere else, north of Baghdad, three U.S. Marines were killed by a roadside bomb. Then we rushed into the weather—chilly and wet for the foreseeable future—which accorded with what I could see through the windshield, and with my mood.

Regarding the discussion a few minutes before, it struck me that I, too, had become inured, even blasé, toward these recurrent reports of death and destruction in Iraq. It's a little like Chinese water torture—either you ignore the incessant drumbeat or it drives you nuts.

But for Bian, who had served there, who had lost soldiers there, whose fiancé was serving there, her emotional investment was bigger—for her, detachment wasn't an option. Nor was it for several hundred thousand other families and loved ones who would spend the next few days cowering each time the doorbell chimed, fearing the sight of a Jarhead officer on their doorstep, delivering the tragic news that one of the dead Marines shared their surname.

Anyway, when we arrived, Will and John were lounging in Phyllis's office. As was a third gent, whose mother must've been acquainted with Will's dad—their resemblance was scary.

Phyllis introduced us to this new gentleman, whose name was Samuel Elkins, from the NSA Office of External Support, whatever that means.

Samuel—not Sam, he stipulated—spent a few moments explaining to Bian and me what he did for a living. Who cared? He eventually suggested, "Why don't we all sit, and I'll go over what we found."

We all sat.

In the middle of the conference table were two imposing stacks of paper, about three inches thick each. A third stack was in front of Phyllis, which, from the bent and misaligned edges, had already been read and digested. But before Bian or I were allowed to indulge our curiosity, we had to go through the usual obligatory self-congratulatory claptrap.

Samuel summed it up, telling us, "The point is, you were lucky. The code on Daniels's computer is one we're familiar with. The patent belongs to a company named NEMOD, a small boutique outfit outside San Francisco."

Apparently, he and Tim had already talked about me, because he glanced in my direction and mentioned, "I'll spare you the technical details, except to make a few points."

I informed him, "My hands are registered weapons. A *very* few points."

Everybody chuckled. I'm a lot of fun at these things.

Samuel continued, "NEMOD creates and handles secure accounts for customer groups. You pay them a fairly stiff monthly fee, certify the individual members of your transmission group or cell, and they send you encoding and decoding software, which you upload on your computer. The messages are routed through NEMOD's proprietary servers directly between correspondents. It's fairly foolproof."

Bian commented, "It's a closed system, right?"

He nodded. "That's why it's fortunate you got that laptop. There's really no other way to detect and read these e-mails." He looked at me and hypothesized, "Whoever owned that computer, maybe he had a background in counterintelligence."

No maybes about it, buster. But Phyllis quickly cut off that line of inquiry and informed me, "NEMOD does mostly private-sector work—as a matter of interest, it has legally binding confidentiality agreements with its clients. But after the CEO and I had a brief and amicable discussion, he became reasonable."

Samuel must've overheard their conversation, because he laughed. He noted, "After Phyllis busted his . . . well, after she talked with him, we e-mailed NEMOD the files, and they promptly decoded and e-mailed back the transcripts."

In a sign of impatience that I shared, Bian reached across the conference table and asked, "May we see these?"

He nodded, and we both ended up with a large stack of messages, all written in English, some short, others long and fairly wordy.

As I thumbed through the tops of the pages, it seemed like all of them were back-and-forth stuff between two parties, labeled Crusader One and Crusader Two.

Bian, also perusing her stack, mentioned, "The headers, the two subjects, they appear to think of themselves—or maybe they relate to each other—as conspirators involving Iraq."

Samuel replied, "That would seem to be correct."

I read through the first few missives. They opened with warm salutations, a little friendly banter and gossip, then segued into the more substantive material. The style of writing was informal and the tone suggested correspondents who were well acquainted, even chummy. A lot of Arab names and Iraqi organizations were cited, which looked to me like alphabet soup.

I turned to Bian. "Do you recognize any of these people?"

"Yes, a lot are familiar. Mostly senior Iraqi political or religious figures."

At this point, Phyllis turned to Tim, John, and Samuel. "I'm sure you three can find something better to do."

Tim, John, and Samuel did not seem to mind, and they gathered their stuff and departed, without the door hitting them in the ass. Actually, she'd done them a favor, a big one, and I think they knew it. If they were subpoenaed later, they could honestly say they left before we got into the real muck. Sean Drummond would've followed them if I had a brain in my head. But I was curious. And we all know where that gets you.

I continued to read. The messages sent by Crusader One to Crusader Two, judging by the language and vernacular, were authored by a native-speaking American—presumably Cliff Daniels.

Crusader Two's English was decent and showed a good command of vocabulary, though he occasionally confused his verb tenses—the land mine of all languages—or he switched his verbs with his nouns, and he polluted a few fairly common idiomatic expressions.

Ergo, Crusader Two wasn't a native speaker; he was someone for whom English was a second language.

I saw no dates on the messages, and no subject headings. Based on the themes and contents, however, the first thirty or so messages seemed to reference the same general time frame.

The initial messages from Crusader One kept Crusader Two abreast on events and moods inside the Office of the Secretary of Defense, the State Department, and occasionally within the White House. Certain figures were mentioned and discussed by name, a few of whom were famous and I recognized. The two names cited most frequently I definitely recognized: Hirschfield and Tigerman.

These particular references were usually in the form of relayed requests or orders from Tigerman and/or Hirschfield—for information, for insights, or imparting special instructions to Crusader Two. For example, one relayed an instruction from Hirschfield ordering Crusader Two to meet with two officials of the Coalition Provisional Authority in Baghdad, and to put them into contact with various Shia authorities in the city of Karbala. Another relayed an order from Tigerman to transfer ten million dollars from Crusader Two's operating account to an account number provided later in the message. And so on.

The initial messages from Crusader Two essentially involved his take on current events inside Iraq, including his personal struggle to form his own militia—recruiting, provisioning, weapons, training, and so forth—and his progress at creating a political power base.

Bian glanced over at Phyllis. "You do recognize the true identity of Crusader Two?"

Phyllis said, with a tiny note of impatience, "Yes, Mahmoud Charabi. Keep reading."

I took the remainder of my stack, roughly a hundred and fifty pages, and divided it into two neat piles: those sent by Crusader One and those by Crusader Two.

To be honest, all these messages were becoming a blur. I have enough trouble with American names—all the Arab names and the inside baseball stuff about Washington and Baghdad were sailing over my head. Also, most of these messages contained replies to other messages, and they made better sense when I compared them side by side. Not full sense. Better sense.

A third of the way through, the tone, mood, and demeanor began to shift—faintly at first, then the anger and sense of betrayal took root and picked up steam. The time frame appeared to be mid- through late in the initial year of the occupation. Daniels, in increasingly purple prose, began accusing Charabi of providing prewar tips, promises, and intelligence that weren't panning out. There were a number of references to various Iraqi weapons depots and factories that Charabi and his pals had pinpointed before the war, now being searched by American forces with an embarrassing absence of bugs, noxious gases, or glow-in-the-dark stuff.

Charabi's initial responses were bluff and confident rejoinders to keep looking, the evidence was there—America and the world would soon witness the wicked elixirs and technological nasties he and his friends had prophesied. At one point, he offered the interesting aphorism, "Persistence is the mother of invention." After a while he changed tack, blaming Ali-this or Mustafa-so-and-so, insisting that he had only passed on, in perfectly good faith, what others had sworn to be fact.

By midway through the stack, the trust and bonhomie between the two men had visibly deteriorated; the opening salutations became shorter, pointed, frostier, with the ensuing language more formal and factual than conversational. No longer were they big pals sharing a most amazing adventure. The prevalent themes became strained negotiations, threats, and counterthreats—Charabi reminding Daniels of his own personal criticality to the American occupation, Daniels reminding him back that if American protection, money, and support dried up, Charabi was toast, his ass was grass, and so on.

Another thought struck me—the time frame of these messages seemed roughly to correspond to the letters in the computer from Daniels to Theresa, his ex. Clearly, this was a man coming apart at the seams, a man with melting wings frantically flapping to stay aloft; betrayed, angry, overwhelmed by events, bitter, and lashing out.

I checked my watch. Ten p.m. I stood and stretched.

Phyllis, despite being twice my age, looked amazingly alert, without a wrinkle in her suit or a hair out of place, like she'd just had an Ovaltine fix.

Bian, also looking perfectly fresh, somehow remained intensely concentrated on her stack, plowing through the pages like a real trencherman. Maybe it was the fish. Maybe Phyllis also was a fish eater.

Phyllis saw me standing and asked, "What do you think?"

"Daniels writes like a man who just discovered his wife's screwing his brother."

She ignored my coarse analogy and asked, "Do you understand *what* you're reading?"

"Do I want to understand?" I replied, half in jest, half not.

She stared at me for a long beat. "Explanations will come later. Break's over. Sit and finish."

Phyllis, incidentally, tends to have the patience and forbearance of Job. My own parents, the older they get the less self-restraint they exhibit. I don't mean they wear diapers or drool or anything. But they tend to blurt the first thing that comes to mind. It can be fairly annoying; my mother, for instance, every time she calls, opens with the same tired question, "Do I have grandchildren yet?" To which I always reply, "Not with your last name." Pop thinks this is a riot. Mom's checking into whether it's too late to arrange an adoption.

Anyway, Phyllis seemed uncharacteristically wound up, and maybe a little agitated, and for sure, her patience was wearing thin.

About five minutes later, I heard Bian murmur, "Holy shit."

Phyllis replied with some relief, "Well . . . at last."

Bian held a page in front of her face, staring at it with open amazement.

She slid the page across the table in my direction. It was from Charabi, and opened with one of his recurring themes, bitching about the ineptness of American soldiers as occupiers. Halfway down, I read,

So you will see that my situation has become most tenuous and dangerous. My Iraqi Shiite brothers do not trust me. I am being out-maneuvered by Sadr and Sistani for leadership of the Shia people, because I am seen as a cowardly expatriate who escaped the worst of Saddam's years, and now works for the Americans, without proper loyalty to my country. In the streets, I am called an American puppet, a Pentagon lick-toadie, and other names too abominable to repeat. This is all so unfortunate and so terribly shameful. This is a big problem for me, and you must appreciate how this is also a big problem for you, my brother. America is the country of my second love, and truly, I am your best hope for a leader for my country. You once saw this, and I pray you can still see this, yes? I know I am losing of your trust, but look into your heart and still you must see me as a good friend.

So I have met with my friends I have earlier described for you, these Persian people from Tehran who say they do not like Sistani or Sadr. They have friends in the Iranian intelligence service, and have promised me that possibly there can be a trade of information that would be most beneficial to me, to you, and to them. I want to have back your trust, and I am knowing I must provide you something that will put you back into loving embraces with Thomas and Albert.

I am sorry for this trouble I have caused you. Although you must remember, it was not me who resulted in these terrible embarrassments of false intelligence and promises that have not come true. It was people I trusted, some of who you equally met and just as well trusted.

But my friends in Tehran have information they

can give me that they promise will prove of enormous value to you—valuable to your soldiers here, but also to you personally, and professionally, my dear friend of so many years.

Unfortunately, they insist I must give them something in return, something that in importance is equally great. Alas, this is the land of bazaars—always there must be something given for something received. So I am leaving to you and your brilliant mind to decide what I can offer these Iranian friends. It is bad luck we cannot discuss this on the phone without the big ears of your government overhearing, but you must believe when I tell you what they are offering is bigger than you can imagine.

Bian handed me a few additional pages, essentially more back-and-forth stuff, as the two men argued about the conditions of this trade. Daniels's messages were furious complaints about how Charabi had already screwed him, ruined his professional reputation, destroyed his career, and how his bosses, Tigerman and Hirschfield, were threatening to fire him unless he salvaged the situation. The sum of Daniels's argument was this: Charabi had gotten him into this mess, and he now owed him a big favor, something dramatic, and in the spirit of dues owed, something unconditional.

I thought Daniels was exposing his desperation, and I thought further that Charabi recognized it, and shrewdly exploited it. With each message back, Charabi stubbornly insisted there had to be a trade, and he cleverly sank the hook a little deeper. Essentially, he promised a piece of intelligence that would make Daniels a big hero, a golden bullet that would result in a huge intelligence coup and restore him to good graces.

I looked up and asked Bian, "You're familiar with the conditions over there. When were these—"

"Written? Oh, I would guess"—she appeared thoughtful for a moment—"five . . . at most, six months back. Around the time the Shiite insurgency erupted last spring."

Phyllis stood up and went to her desk, saying, "That's about right." Over her shoulder, she asked us, "Do you understand the full import of this message?" We indicated we did, and she lifted up a piece of paper and informed us, "This message won't be found in either of your stacks." She added, "Several other messages have been extracted as well. In one, Charabi disclosed to Daniels what he's offering." She paused, a little theatrically, then informed us, "He claimed Iranian intelligence had the name and possible location of the key moneyman behind the most lethal wing of the Sunni insurgency. That information would be provided to Daniels only after the Iranians heard what he had to offer. I'm about to show you Daniels's eventual response."

She handed the page to Bian, who read it, and then slid it across the table to me. It was a brief and unambiguous e-mail from Daniels to Charabi:

> Be clear on this—fuck me, and you're dead. This is not an empty threat. I'm going way out on a limb here. This works, or you're fucking dead. Simple as that.
>
> You insisted on something important, something the Iranians desperately want—so here it is. The National Security Agency has broken the Iranian intelligence code. From the beginning of the war, we've been reading their deepest secrets.
>
> I'm sure you recognize how valuable this information is to them. And I'm sure you know what would happen to me, and to you, should anybody find out where this came from.

Somebody had taken a Magic Marker and blacked out, or in Agency terminology, redacted, the next ten or so lines. I wondered about those passages I wasn't seeing. Sometimes that's done when a vital source needs to be protected; more often it means the institution needs to be protected, by hiding an embarrassment or screwup. I wish I could do that with parts of my life.

Bian was staring at the top of the conference table. Sounding deeply stunned, she blurted, "Do you realize what this bastard did?"

Phyllis obviously did. We all did. Treason. To save his sinking career, Cliff Daniels had conveyed a huge and damaging secret to an enemy nation. I wasn't sure I understood everything, nor did I have the expert knowledge or regional expertise to fully analyze it. But I understood this: In exchange for the name of a terrorist, Clifford Daniels had exposed to Charabi, and thereby to the Iranians, the knowledge that we were reading and decoding their most sensitive communications. On top of everything, this wasn't even a good trade. I mean, Cliff Daniels not only was a traitor, he was stupid.

But instead of replying to Bian's question, to me Phyllis said, "Now, give me back that page."

So I did, positive it would never again see the light of day.

Nobody said anything for a moment. We were all three, I think, too stunned and completely consumed in our own thoughts.

Regarding Phyllis, I had no idea what thoughts were running through her mind. But I had a premonition, or, considering the circumstances, a postmonition, that Phyllis knew when she sent me to Daniels's apartment that morning it might lead to something like this.

Maybe not exactly like this. But something.

As for Bian, I was sure she was thinking what I was thinking. Clifford Daniels was lucky; somebody beat us to him. By the time we finished lumping him up, a bullet through his brain would've been an act of leniency.

Phyllis stood and walked toward the door. She said, somewhat ominously, "There is somebody here who can explain all this to you," and then she walked out.

Normally, when you have a crime, through exacting detective work, the miracles of modern forensics, and pathology, you work backward, from the aftermath to the crime itself; you reconstruct, analyze, and reconnect the evidentiary traces, because the parts have to be made whole again, because that whole is a human identity—a name—the person whose fingertips left the telltale stain, whose skin is embedded in the fingernails of the victim he shoved off the balcony and sent caterwauling down twenty floors onto the pavement below.

But when the crime is bureaucratic in nature and origin, you have a different species of criminal, with a different genre of evidence. To get from A to Z, you follow a different arc—less linear—more M to Z, then full circle back to A to M. In place of a corpse, and in place of forensic traces, you have a long trail of paper, words, thoughts, and expressions that, when added together, expose a deed—a crime.

So Bian and I now knew the category of the crime, the identity of the criminal, and we even had a roughed-out portrait of the motive: treason, Clifford Daniels, idiocy fueled by naked ambition. Also a murder remained to be solved, though that suddenly looked like the least of our problems, though it was also, quite possibly, a related one.

Some sins are larger than others, no matter that they violate the same commandment. Thou shalt not kill—all its varying shades and distinctions are defined, parsed, and echeloned in the criminal code; murder in the first degree, murder in the second, murder in the third, criminal manslaughter, and right down the line. Yet when a killing is part of a holocaust, when it is a piece of a whole, one of thousands or one of millions, none of these terms fit—they become too tolerant, too morally shallow, too belittling.

Such appeared to be the case here. Bian knew this, and I, too, knew it; like Alice peering into a rabbit hole, we had just glimpsed the fool in a crazy hat, and clearly somewhere, Tweedledum and Tweedledee and a Cheshire Cat were pounding the drums. I stared at Phyllis's empty chair and wondered about the crazy queen's role in all of this.

Bian shifted in her seat. "Okay, I am starting to feel paranoid."

"Do you want out?"

"No. Do you?"

"Yes. But it's too late."

After a moment, she asked in a whispery voice, "What about Phyllis . . . can I trust her?"

"Absolutely not."

She stared at me. "Do you trust her?"

This was a different question and I replied, "Sometimes."

"Do you trust her this time?"

"Her agenda and ours might not be the same."

"Why?"

"Because there's bad chemistry between this administration and the CIA. You've probably read the gossip and rumors in the newspapers."

"I have." She took a moment to think about this.

I gave her that moment, then said, "You know about the hunt for blame over who failed to prevent 9/11, and you know the White House and the Pentagon laid it on the Agency's doorstep. Now the Hill is investigating how flawed Iraqi intelligence made it through the net.

The administration's already shoving the blame here. So is the Pentagon. Langley is pissed."

"This isn't part of some bureaucratic vendetta, is it?"

"I think everything we've seen is genuine. But now we need to consider *why* we were allowed to see it."

She stared at me without responding.

I continued, "I also think what we do about it, how this is handled—" The door flew open and I stopped talking.

CHAPTER FOURTEEN

Phyllis was back with a gentleman in her wake.

She informed Bian and me, "This is Don." Don seemed to have misplaced his surname.

He walked across the room and shook my hand. Then he shook Bian's hand as well, and I noted he held it a few seconds too long.

He was quite tall, about six foot five, trim, and moved with an athletic bounce in his step. About my age, very fit, with a full head of slicked-back black hair, and fairly good-looking, if you like the type.

Of course, his name wasn't Don.

And of course, this meeting never took place.

I asked Don, "Where do you work?"

He smiled and said, "Same place as you. The Agency. That's all you need to know."

Aside from administrative types and a cadre of appointed political overseers, Agency employees tend to be either analysts or operators. In general, analysts are fairly ordinary in appearance, bookish, intelligent-looking, and—no offense intended—they take their fashion cues from college professors.

Also, analysts have last names.

Don was attired in a blue wool and cashmere suit, severely tailored with a Savile Row cut right down to the Continental fanny flap, glossy black Italian loafers, and a thick, expertly knotted pink silk tie with a matching pink hankie in his breast pocket. Message to Don: Real men don't *have* to wear pink neckties.

That he spent too much on clothes, however, was the second clue. What gave him away was his overall demeanor—cocky and calculating. Also, he had icy brown eyes.

A lot of these operational types think they are irresistible to the ladies, and maybe I was a little piqued at the way his hand lingered in Bian's hand. I mean, this poor girl's fiancé was probably at that moment fighting hand to hand with a bunch of blood-crazed jihadis in some Baghdad back alley, and Randy Don was trying to get into her drawers. Asshole.

Anyway, Don sat at the head of the table, and Phyllis returned to the seat behind her desk. Phyllis mentioned a few things about Don: Ivy League degrees in Arabic studies, career man, able to leap tall buildings with a little help, and so on.

She summed up by telling us, "Don has long and extensive experience with Iraq that dates back before the first Gulf War. He is a highly regarded expert who happens to be personally acquainted with Mahmoud Charabi." She waited a beat before adding, "He worked, occasionally, with Clifford Daniels."

Don acknowledged this introduction with a droll, disaffected smile. Probably, had Phyllis informed us that Don was a dickless idiot with a pea-size brain, his expression would've been identical.

Now it was his turn, and he looked at Bian and then at me. "I don't actually like discussing this with you. Okay? The Director ordered this . . . so . . ." He allowed a long moment to pass, then added, "I'll tell you as much as I think you need to know."

I very reasonably asked, "*How* will you know what we need to know, Don?"

"I'll know."

I smiled at Don. "So, if it's an embarrassment to the Agency, that's off-limits and you won't tell us about it?"

Don, of course, did not reply to this. He stared back with an empty expression and suggested, "Why don't we start with your questions?"

"Okay. Was there a pissing contest between the Agency and the Pentagon over Iraq?"

"There are disagreements between the Agency and the Pentagon over a variety of issues. Who controls intelligence? How much Agency effort should go to supporting soldiers, how much to politicians? That's where it begins." He offered us a reasonable facsimile of a smile. "It never ends."

"You forgot to mention Iraq."

His smile disappeared. "You need to be more specific."

"All right. Specifically, between the CIA and the Defense Department, were there differences of opinion over whether to invade?"

"Yes."

"Would you describe those differences?"

He smiled again, which of course meant, "Fuck you."

I smiled back and asked, "Were there differences over whether Saddam had stockpiles of outlawed weapons?"

"On that topic, even within the Agency . . . yes, there were . . . differences. Our general consensus was that there possibly were weapons, with a caveat of ambiguity."

"Say again."

He replied, "Buyer beware—that's what it means, Mr. Drummond."

"You're not blowing smoke up our ass, Don? According to news reports, the Director personally assured the President there were weapons."

"Maybe he did; maybe not. The Director, however, is not the Agency. Just a temporary figurehead."

"I'm still confused."

"So was he," he said, and he laughed. Don apparently enjoyed his own humor.

I did not laugh. "But the Agency is being blamed for the faulty intelligence?"

"By certain quarters—yes."

"Certain quarters? Like the American public?"

"Well . . . our friends in the press seem to have manufactured the unfortunate impression that the Agency was largely responsible. Then again, they have their own credibility issues, don't they?"

"Where would the press get this idea?"

He did not reply.

"From sources inside the White House? From sources inside the Defense Department?"

Don did not reply to this either. Regarding this line of inquiry, Washington has an amazing cornucopia of more than a dozen different intelligence organizations. To an outsider this might sound superfluous and maybe absurd—an insider *knows* it's insane. But they all are ostensibly indispensable on the basis that each does something different, or employs different collection means, or offers a unique perspective, or serves different masters with differing needs.

It's a little like medieval Venice with all those interlocking families sharing the same cramped turf, warily coexisting, sensitive to slights, and completely paranoid about their own territory, prestige, and existence. Bureaucratic drive-by shootings and political poisonings aren't out of the question.

Yet, despite this excess of riches, before the war, Tigerman and Hirschfield had decided to add one more, their own in-house intelligence hothouse, and Clifford Daniels was brought in from DIA as a founding member. The expressed mission for this small cell was to cull through the raw intelligence provided by other agencies, to question, to reinterpret, to determine if anything vital had been missed, misinterpreted, or overlooked. But there were critics who claimed the reason was to cook, customize, and massage the raw intelligence to justify an invasion, and a war.

Don had known about this, and I now knew about it as well. The policy wonks in the Pentagon had muscled their way into the intelligence business, and a larger bureaucratic war was going on here, a battle for tax dollars, for influence, for reputations—and now a battle over blame—and I wanted to know where Don stood on it. Well, I already knew where he stood; I just wanted him to admit it. Then, when the bullshit flew, we would *all* know where he was coming from.

I looked at Don. "In any event, we all know the Agency has been made the public scapegoat. Does that piss you off?"

"Personally? Why should it, Drummond? Just business."

Bullshit. "How did Charabi end up as the Pentagon's man?"

"That's a long and complicated story."

"You're a clever guy. Come up with an abbreviated version."

"All right." He offered me a strange smile, like he was measuring my coffin size.

As I mentioned, Don was full of himself—arrogant, actually—and that nearly always equates to thin-skinned. Also, he would tell us what *he* wanted us to know unless I pissed him off enough to provoke a few inadvertent truths from his lips. Sizing him up, he was a cool customer, a world-class bullshitter, and he affected a certain imperturbable coyness. He actually seemed to be enjoying this game of cat and mouse, and he obviously liked being the center of attention.

He stopped smiling and said, "Charabi approached us after the first Gulf War." He paused and appeared thoughtful. "Late 1993 . . . maybe early 1994. I, myself, met with him."

"What was the purpose of this meeting?"

"It was in the nature of a negotiation."

"Go on."

"He was offering to provide intelligence about conditions inside Iraq. It sounded attractive. In fact, it sounded great. The truth is, getting and keeping good sources inside Iraq was . . . difficult. Saddam was—surely you've read this—almost insanely paranoid and ruthless. A lot of our sources ended up in graves. This was not helpful for recruitment."

He paused and looked at Bian. She said, "So it sounded good. What happened?"

"His offer came with stipulations. For one, we had to agree to emancipate his people from a monster."

"I thought that was our policy."

"It was. Later. But then—and even later—we were . . . let's just say, *concerned* about Charabi's additional conditions."

Bian suggested, "He wanted you to put him in power."

He nodded. "He wanted to be king." He paused, then said, "He claimed he had hundreds of Iraqis in his pocket, exiles, and also people in country willing to help. And of course these were Iraqis—very cliquish, very clannish. You get one, you get dozens of relatives and tribal members. They would gather intelligence, and after Saddam was gone, they would form the base of his power. Also, he's Shiite, as are about 60 percent of Iraqis. Better yet, he's a secular Shiite, so the Kurds—and maybe even the Sunnis—might find him palatable."

Bian commented, "For the situation, that sounds like an attractive résumé."

"The *perfect* résumé. So, yes . . . I agreed to meet with him." He paused, then added, "I brought along another gentleman. An Agency psychiatrist who specializes in quick profiles of foreign leaders. He's quite good at it. Would you care to hear his assessment?"

I said, "Sure."

"A classic narcissist, compounded by a manipulative personality classification."

I looked at Bian and shrugged. She shrugged back.

Don was amused by our ignorance and with a snotty smile informed us, "Here's language even you'll understand, Drummond. A self-serving asshole with a velvety tongue who will screw you for a nickel."

"Was that you, or Charabi? Or both?"

He gave me a long, hard stare. He turned to Phyllis. "Do I really have to put up with this?"

She advised him with some insight, "He's trying to taunt you. Ignore him and he'll stop."

I smiled at Phyllis. She ignored me, and to humor her, I stopped smiling.

Bian said to Don, "I have no idea how these things work. Presumably this was a vetting process and this snapshot psychoanalysis was part of it. Right?" He nodded, and she asked, "Did this psychiatrist veto an arrangement?"

"That's not how it works. He offers insights; I decide. However, he classified Charabi as a high-risk asset. Specifically, he predicted Charabi would follow his own agenda, guided by his own scruples, which in the doctor's judgment were scarce and very elastic."

Incidentally, every time he spoke, Don's eyes flashed toward Bian. You knew exactly what was going through his filthy mind. Geez—dogs in heat show more savoir faire than this guy.

Bian, for her part, seemed totally oblivious, or perhaps she mistook Don's interest as intellectual flattery. Message to Bian—it's not your mind he wants to get into.

I have known women who live for this kind of attention; others I know do nothing to invite it and are perilously blind to the signals. I don't mean that Bian was naive, or a naif, but she spent four years at West Point, where the boy-to-girl ratio is about ten to one. In such a male-dominated environment, I imagine the female either dampens her antennae or becomes a sexual hypochondriac.

Anyway, I tried to catch Don's eye and said, "I haven't knocked over any foreign governments, so maybe this is going over my head. For replacing Saddam, isn't that a reasonable trade?"

"On first blush, Drummond . . . yes, sure . . . I might agree with you. A duplicitous liar for a pathological mass murderer. Sure. Why not?"

"That's what I asked you—why not?"

"I ran his background and he wasn't . . . credible."

Credible, for most people, concerns integrity and trustworthiness; these people, however, play by different rules, and more often it's about whether they can get a grip on his short hairs.

Having not spent time with Agency types, however, Bian found this concept elusive and asked, "Can you explain that?"

"Well . . . why do you think he fled Iraq in the first place?"

"The newspapers said—"

"I know what the media reported. He experienced some political squabble with Saddam and was forced to flee for his survival. Where do you think they obtained that story, Major?"

"I see. Then what did Charabi forget to include?"

"Charabi was a banker in those years. A midlevel account executive at the Iraqi national bank. A virtual nobody"—he smiled—"for Saddam, a nonentity. The man and his views were irrelevant."

"But Saddam later went through a lot of trouble to have him murdered. There had to be something."

"Over three million Iraqis went into exile during Saddam's rule. Many of these people were politically opposed to Saddam. He would've run out of bullets if he tried to kill all of them." He stared at Bian. "When he went to that much trouble, the motive was always personal."

"I see."

"But you still haven't guessed, have you?" He gave us both one of those triumphant, I-know-something-you-don't little grins and said, "Charabi was an embezzler. He moved about twenty million dollars from one of Saddam's personal accounts to his own personal account in Switzerland. It had nothing to do with politics." He added, "It was, for Saddam, a matter of personal honor, of principle."

Bian remarked, "That principle being that Saddam could loot billions from his own people, and they couldn't steal it back."

Don laughed and awarded her a wink. "Hey, I like that." He said, "Here's another insight I think you'll find fascinating. After the invasion, we found, inside Saddam's palaces, dozens of copies of *The Godfather* videos." He added, "It seems Saddam perceived himself as a godfather figure—that formed his self-image, and that inspired his style of leadership. Pathetic, isn't it? Life imitating art."

This was interesting; also, it was irrelevant. Returning to the topic, I said, "So you told Charabi you weren't interested. What happened next?"

"You never say no in this business. I just let it hang when I left." He stared at me a moment. "But Cliff Daniels, while still on the Iraq desk at DIA, also attended that meeting."

"I'll bite. Why?"

"There is, inevitably, something of a rivalry between our two agencies for good sources. As first among equals, we generally get first pick. Sometimes," he added, smiling, "sources we don't want end up in the arms of our friends across the river. Sloppy seconds."

On a hunch, I asked Don, "Did your shrink friend also assess Daniels?"

He paused, then said, "In fact, he did." It appeared to amuse him that I would pick up on this. He looked at Bian and said, "Pardon my French, it was in the nature of a sport fuck for him. You know how weird those guys are."

Don winked at Bian and with a sort of mocking smile turned back to me and, regarding that assessment, asked, "What do you think?"

I thought Don needed ten pounds of saltpeter pumped up a catheter. But I recalled everything I knew about Daniels, his life background, Theresa's description of their marriage and their life together, his e-mails to his ex, and those to Charabi. "A classic passive-aggressive personality. Right?"

He seemed at first irritated by my guess, but eventually said, "Well, I suppose he's not *that* difficult to figure out." *Up yours, Don.* "In fact," he continued, "Cliff was one of those people who stank of ambition and frustration. He kept trying to impress Charabi—dropping hints about his own importance, his own brilliance, his ability to make things happen."

He turned once again to Bian and asked, "What do you get when you put a passive-aggressive in the same room with a manipulative narcissist?"

Bian replied, "A marriage made in hell."

Again, he laughed. Don had his own metaphors, however, and said, "It was like watching a leech attach itself. You know? Daniels was an accident waiting in the wings, and Charabi a hundred-car pileup in search of a busy intersection."

I liked Bian's metaphor better. Less wordy.

But recalling the letters I had just read from Crusader Two—that mixture of cloying friendliness and ingratiating coercion—any or all of these analogies and/or metaphors seemed to fit what occurred. As they say, no man is more dangerous than he with a will to corrupt. Charabi was that man, and he had skillfully worked his seduction, and Daniels was so absorbed by his own ambitions and his own professional and personal frustrations that deciding between right and wrong meant only what was right for *him*.

"How was this meeting arranged?" Bian asked.

He answered her question with a question. "Why do you think DIA was present?" So we thought about it, before he informed us, "Albert Tigerman—a few months before this meeting, he had met Charabi at a Georgetown cocktail party, was impressed by the possibilities he presented, and thought it would be a smart idea to develop a relationship." He looked pointedly at me and noted, "This is what happens when neophytes dabble in intelligence work."

In fact, Don's suffocating air of superiority was pissing me off. We were discussing, after all, how a manipulative liar weaseled his way into our intelligence system, how he misled us, fed us false intelligence, and caused incalculable damage.

Don should've felt some remorse over this, even been deeply embarrassed. Yet in his mind this was just more proof of his own virtuosity. Don was smart, Cliff was an idiot; this was zero-sum gamesmanship, and Don won.

I knew I shouldn't, but I said, "You know what? I can't believe you still have your job."

"What the—"

"You were there, Don. At the beginning. Did you intervene? Did you keep Charabi and Daniels apart?"

"What are you—"

"You left that room knowing Clifford Daniels was an easy mark for this shyster. You allowed this to happen."

Don was a little put off by this charge, and he stared at me with those flat brown eyes. "That's utter nonsense, Drummond. I'm not the least bit responsible for what happened."

"Bullshit. After that meeting, Charabi turned Daniels into his boy toy. Over the next decade, Charabi got money from the Pentagon and institutional support in Washington. Worse, he got a conduit to feed his lies and deceptions into, a river of lies that flowed straight to the Oval Office."

"You're forgetting something. The Agency made well-known our view that Charabi wasn't credible. On numerous occasions we conveyed this to the White House. We even went to the unusual length of leaking this to the press."

"That's covering your ass, not preventing a disaster. The ass you failed to cover was the country's."

"You don't know what you're talking about." Don was staring at me now with some intensity, I'm sure wishing he had brought a gun to this meeting.

Phyllis snapped, "That's enough. We're not here to affix blame. Right now we need to understand what damage was done, and how it can be fixed." After a moment of reflection, she amended that. "*If* it can be fixed."

Phyllis was right. Don and I exchanged looks. I think we both felt bad about our little display of bad manners, not to mention our failure to keep our eye on the ball. In fact, Don said to me, in a very apologetic tone, "Fuck you."

"Up yours."

What this meeting needed was a commercial break, and on cue, Bian's cell phone began bleeping—it had one of those irritating musical ringtones. She flipped it open. "Major Tran . . . Oh, hi, Barry. You're working late . . . I—Well, hold on . . ."

She looked at me. "Detective Enders." She looked at Phyllis and Don. "Please excuse us a moment." She looked back at me. "It's important. Let's step out to take this."

Which reminded me; in addition to investigating Daniels's crimes, we were also investigating his murder. I got to my feet and reoriented my mind-set back to the A-to-Z mode.

CHAPTER FIFTEEN

We walked out and headed straight to the coffee bar, where we discovered a pot, quarter filled with gooey black tar. It looked like it had been brewing for a week. "Can I pour you a cup?" I asked Bian.

"You can't be serious." She appeared horrified. "It looks poisonous."

My ass was really dragging, and if I didn't get a jolt of caffeine I would pass out. I filled a paper cup for myself, and when it didn't melt the paper, took a long sip. "Ummh . . . good."

"Why do men do such stupid things to prove their manhood?"

"Men don't—"

"Of course they do." She laughed. "You're really funny."

Actually, if it was possible, it tasted worse than it looked. But as Mom always reminded little Sean, waste not, want not. I set aside the cup for later.

Into the phone, Bian said, "I'm back, Barry," then went into listening mode for about two minutes. She made a few verbal nods and once or twice prodded Enders to elaborate on some point, but I had no idea what they were discussing. Eventually she said, "Okay . . . yes, I've got it . . ." Pause. "Yes . . . Colonel Drummond's also here." She looked at me and said to him, "Why don't you repeat this to him directly?"

She handed me the phone. Enders said, "I hope you two are working late, not screwing around."

"You have a filthy mind, Detective."

Bian was looking at me inquisitively.

Enders said, "Give me a break, Drummond. Tell me you're not thinking about it."

I looked at Bian. "My God, you're right. There's a female inside that uniform."

"Who you trying to bullshit? The lady can make cooked spaghetti stiff again."

Bian seemed to be seeking my attention by sort of waving her middle finger.

Well, enough male bonding. In fact, Bian's expression indicated it was beyond enough. "Where are you?" I asked him.

"The lab. The autopsy wrapped up an hour ago, and now I'm here."

"I wish my laundry worked that fast."

"Slow day." He added, "Where were— Oh yeah . . . the autopsy—" Then, as if reading off a page, "Stomach contents: steak, well done, and a baked potato, with a spinach salad. That was probably dinner. Serology results: high alcohol content, point one nine, so Daniels was legally stewed. That's not uncommon with suicides, incidentally. Cause of death: gunshot to the head, fired two to three inches from Daniels's skull. Death: immediate—sometime between midnight and one."

"Okay, that's how it looked."

"Was it? There were no open bottles or empty glasses in Daniels's apartment."

"So he went out and got smashed beforehand. Does it matter *where* he got drunk?"

"Probably not. Now guess what you saw but didn't see?"

"Let me see . . ." I knew this contradiction was coming and answered, matter-of-factly, "Cliff Daniels was right-handed and the entry wound is in his left temple."

A little miffed that I ruined his surprise, for a moment he said nothing. Then he found his inner voice, which was pissed off. "You bastard. You knew . . . and you never mentioned it."

"I recall you saying my views weren't welcome." Which was true, of course, and petty of me to bring up. I added, "Anyway, it's irrelevant. Also, probably misleading."

"The hell it is. This is highly suggestive that a right-handed killer fired the bullet. Then, to cover it up, the killer had to place the gun in the victim's left hand." As if I needed it spelled it out, he added, "In other words, it wasn't suicide—it was murder."

I allowed him a moment to cool off, then asked, "Are you armed?"

"Of course."

"Good. Work with me here." I instructed him, "Remove your pistol from the holster."

"Okay . . . it's out."

"You right- or left-handed?"

"Normal. Right-handed."

"As was Daniels. Switch the pistol to your left hand."

"Okay."

"Now raise the pistol . . . now aim the barrel at your temple . . . just above your left ear."

"There'd better be a point to this, Drummond. People are staring at—"

"Is the pistol there?"

"Yeah . . . okay, it's—"

"Quick—pull the trigger."

He said, after a long moment, "Very fucking funny."

"I didn't hear a bang. I knew you were smart."

"If you were standing here, you'd hear a bang, you son of a bitch."

"How hard would it have been?"

"I got your point. But it's not natural. Unnatural things are always cause for suspicion."

"Not *always*. Sometimes they merely require alternate explanations."

"I'm dying to hear this one."

"Think of what you observed inside Daniels's bedroom. The television was on, a porn flick in the video machine, the victim had an erection, and his right hand was gripped on his doolie." I added, "The term is multitasking."

He did not reply.

I said, "Cliff Daniels, not being ambidextrous, faced a choice. Which takes more strength? Greater deftness? Spanking your donkey or pulling the trigger?"

After a moment, he replied, "I wouldn't know, would I?"

In spite of himself, he laughed, and I, too, laughed. Actually, I liked this guy. No good cop ignores his gut instincts; his were telling him this was wrong, and he was going with it. Well, it *was* wrong; he just didn't know why. He lacked what Bian and I possessed, factual knowledge of Daniels's professional and extracurricular activities, or about the large and growing population who might want him dead, and why.

To tell the truth, I felt a little guilty; he was one of the good guys, diligent, honest, good cop. But his concern was law and order in his county; mine was peace and security throughout the entire United States. Bottom line—you can rationalize just about anything under the guise of "for the good of the country"; it's a slippery slope, and I might have been overstepping that line.

"Back to the autopsy," he said, after a moment. "Other than that, Daniels was missing his tonsils. Twice had his left knee cut on, and—"

"Was there blood splatter on his left hand?"

"Well . . . yeah—there was. Not a lot. Also there was some burnt powder. Blowback."

"And has this blood been tested? Was it his?"

"It's the right blood type, A pos. The DNA test will take longer, of course."

For some reason this did not surprise me. After a moment he added, "One other observation. His liver showed the beginning stages of cirrhosis. Daniels was a big-time boozer."

"It's the family hobby."

"No shit. The Mrs., too? Hey, how'd that go?"

"Different. His ex celebrated with a fresh bottle of gin."

"She want him dead?"

"Yeah . . . but no. She's going to miss him. Busting his balls was the one great joy in her life."

He thought about that a moment, then said, "Tim . . . the forensics guy you spoke with . . . he told you about the hair fibers?"

"Three types as of last count. Why? Were there more?"

"Isn't three enough? Personally, after looking at Daniels, I never would've pictured it. You know?"

I glanced at Bian. "My partner says it's all about size."

"That right?" he replied. "My wife's always telling me it's all about becoming more sensitive, about helping around the house more. Shit—you're saying all I had to do was grow a bigger dick."

I laughed.

"According to his former," I told him, "Clifford had a thing for the ladies. He screwed his way out of the marriage."

"Well . . . that can happen." He informed me, "Anyway, two of these hair specimens turned out to be organic. The redhead and brunette."

"Organic? What does—"

"Straight from the head. That's what it means. The follicles come off with the strands. That's how you tell."

"And the third sample . . . the blonde?"

"Yeah . . . the blonde. The hair was real enough, only the ends were cut at the end, and knotted. Know what that means?"

"A wig."

"Hey, I knew you CIA guys were sharp. Thing is, the cheap ones have synthetic hair—manufactured stuff. Better ones are made from authentic hair, contributed by real people, and knotted into a wig piece." He asked, "What do you think about that?"

"Hold on . . . I'm trying to picture Daniels in a blonde wig . . . Wait, it's coming to me—oh my God . . ."

"What?"

"I went out with her—him."

"Very funny."

"What am I supposed to think, Detective? Maybe he had a lover with premature baldness. Maybe he told the redhead or the brunette he was in a blonde mood, and one or both obliged. Maybe Daniels attended a costume party as Marilyn Monroe. Possibilities abound."

After a pause, he replied, "You left out a possibility."

"Did I?"

"You know you did." He then told me what I left out, saying, "Maybe he had a visitor who wore a disguise because this visitor didn't want to be recognized by the neighbors. And maybe this visitor didn't want to leave DNA traces. Add that up, and once again, maybe he didn't kill himself."

"I didn't want to insult your intelligence." I asked, "Fingerprints?"

"We collected four or five samples. We printed the maid's before we released her, and lifted Daniels's prints off his corpse. Disqualification and isolation will be finished tomorrow."

I was sure that would lead nowhere, but kept the thought to myself. I asked, "As of this moment, what's your thinking on this case?"

"You know what? I was leaning toward suicide. It sure looks like suicide. But some guy from the Defense Department called like six times today. Waterbury?"

"I know him."

"He every bit the tightass he sounds like on the phone?"

"Jam a quarter up his ass and you get a dime."

He laughed. "Who is this guy?"

"Bian's boss."

"I'll bet people are beating down the door to work there." Apparently we had exchanged enough slapstick and insults, because his tone turned serious. "Point is, I've got this corpse, and who shows up and starts nosing around? A CIA guy, an MP, and now I've got this Pentagon jerk looking over my shoulder." He asked, "See my problem here?"

Actually, I saw the problem the instant Bian notified me who was calling. The hour was late and detectives don't put in that much overtime unless they smell something, and what he smelled stank.

Also, supervisors have to authorize overtime—for both the detective and the lab—so Enders wasn't pursuing a private hunch.

Waterbury was an even bigger idiot than I gave him credit for, if that was possible. His idiotic snooping was stirring up the one thing he, and the people he worked for, least wanted or needed—public scrutiny about how Daniels died.

"You're reading too much into this," I insisted.

"I knew you'd say that."

"Okay . . ." I allowed a moment to pass. "You want the full truth?"

"Sure." He laughed. "That's why I called the CIA."

"Don't take my word for it—check the *Post* about two weeks back."

"Why?"

"It will confirm that Cliff Daniels was scheduled to testify before a House investigating subcommittee next week."

"So?"

"So . . . let's just say money was missing from an operational account. A lot of money. You didn't hear this from me, okay? Seriously, this is I'd-have-to-kill-you-if-you-knew stuff. I barely know the half of it—to be honest, the other half I don't want to know."

"All right. Tell me the half you know about."

As he knew I would, I ignored that line of inquiry. I said, "The point is . . . powerful people on the Hill are all over the Pentagon's rear over this." I added, "The White House is now involved. That's why this guy Waterbury is climbing up your back."

"Is that right?"

"What I'm saying is this. Ten tons of crap was about to land on Clifford Daniels's head. He did a bad thing. He was getting caught. He was, as you might imagine, agitated and depressed. We've spoken with his coworkers. They say he'd been acting strangely the past few days, and—"

"I'd like to interview those witnesses."

"Barry, I . . . how far did you say you are from retirement?"

He cleared his throat and said, "I don't appreciate threats."

"No one does, Barry. The federal government entrusts you and your department to handle this . . . with the professional discretion it deserves. Should that faith be lost, an army of truly tightassed people in blue suits will descend upon you and turn your world inside out. Are we clear on this?"

"Make it clearer."

"Suicide, Barry. The guy knew his fanny was swinging in the wind. He chose to spare himself and his family the shame and indignity of public exposure." I paused. "Don't complicate things."

"Maybe he—"

"Gotta go. The White House is on the other line."

I punched off, and Bian, who had obviously been listening closely, commented, "You were rough on him."

"Nonsense. I did him a favor."

"Then don't do me any favors."

"Here's something you should already know. In this case, ignorance *is* bliss."

She asked, "You think he bought it?"

"No. He's smart. But he'll at least make sure all the i's and t's are dotted and crossed before he raises the M-word."

"So you're just buying time."

"Do you have a better idea?"

Apparently not, because she said, "What about the wig?"

"Forget about the wig."

"You've got to be kidding. As evidence, it's extremely pertinent."

I looked at Bian. "We're not communicating."

"About what?"

"Think, Bian. Everything here points to a premeditated act, not something spontaneous, or even situational. Not only did the killer wear a wig to disguise her appearance and avoid DNA traces, she also splattered some of Cliff's blood and a little burnt powder on his shooting hand. What does this tell you?"

She considered my question for a moment and concluded, I thought accurately, "That . . . the killer was a professional."

I nodded at her and added, "She studied her target carefully, and I think it's now fair to conclude that the murder was planned down to the most minute detail."

"Explain that."

"She knew Daniels had a gun in his apartment. His ex told us how much that pistol meant to Cliff, and possibly he bragged about it to his killer. Maybe he showed it off as a talisman of his importance and machismo. Ergo, the killer had been inside his apartment before last night, which we already suspected. And by showing her his gun, maybe Cliff himself planted the idea of using *his* own gun to kill him. It had all the obvious advantages, after all, especially as a prop for a staged suicide. Further, we now know Daniels was a ladies' man—in his ex-wife's words, whatever couldn't outrun him, the man laid wood on it. Plus he was an alcoholic. His killer was familiar with his two obsessions, booze and broads; she, in effect, exploited them as vulnerabilities to arrange his murder. She made sure to get him drunk *before* they went to Cliff's apartment—thus, no saliva traces, nor were her fingerprints on his glassware." I asked, "After print elimination, we're left with two or three unidentified sets. Do you want to bet any of them will be hers?"

"Okay . . . I get it." She sounded irritable, and I realized I had come on a little forcefully, or worse, condescendingly. Commissioned officers in the Military Police Corps aren't savvy beat cops, nor are they detectives. What they are are leaders and supervisors of other cops. Though generally conversant with policing techniques, they don't think like sleuths, and a case like this would stretch the talents of even the best CID agent.

Also, I felt bad about busting Barry's balls and I may have been venting a little. This is when you know you've been around Agency people too long. I was starting to act like *them*.

"I'm sorry," I informed her, and I meant it. "This is a tough one."

"You're a tough one."

Back to the original topic, I said, "Okay. I think it's also fair to assume that our killer was firmly grounded in police work and forensics. She used this knowledge expertly. Does this sound right to you? Daniels's murder was completely cold-blooded, not an act of passion. A premeditated execution. An almost perfect crime."

"Almost? Oh . . . right. The perfect crime would have looked conclusively like a suicide. No doubts."

"Exactly." A fresh thought struck me, and I said, "But why kill him there . . . in his own bed? In that manner?"

"I'm not sure what you're asking. The effort to make it look like suicide was to throw us off the scent. Didn't we already cover this?"

"Let's cover it again."

"I'm confused."

"I think we were both confused." I asked her, "If I told you to kill a man, or if you had your own motives for murder, would you do it like that?"

"I don't think that way."

"Here's my point. Professional killers don't get close to their victims. They pump a bullet through the back of their head, or they murder from a distance. A sniper shot, for instance, or an arranged accident. Less risk of failure, and less possibility of leaving inculpatory evidence."

"Maybe the killer was overconfident."

"Maybe." I suggested, "Knowing what we now know, though, consider this possibility: Maybe this killing wasn't cold-blooded."

"That's not what you've been saying, nor do I think it comports with the evidence."

"The forest and the trees might be telling us contradictory things here, Bian. Consider the indignity . . . the pathetic circumstances of this man's death. I laughed. As did you. Imagine the jokes going around the Arlington police station at this moment."

She thought about this, and I added, "Maybe that was her intent. In fact, for the killer, maybe that was a primary goal. If this gets out to the press—as surely it will—Cliff Daniels will be a laughingstock, stigmatized for eternity."

"And you believe the killer planned that?"

"I don't know. But I'm starting to think that our killer, or whoever sent her, was deliberately arranging a . . . well—a mortal degradation. There are some societies—Ethiopians, for instance—when they took war captives, they castrated them and then sent them home. By turning them into eunuchs, they couldn't bear children bent on revenge. Ancient cultures thought about those things, right?"

"I've met men I'd like to castrate," she noted, staring at me.

"Also on a practical level, it made men think twice before fighting the Ethiopians. Better than nuclear deterrence, right? But on a more primal level, it was meant to shame and dishonor soldiers who surrendered, who violated an ancient code of warrior courage and conduct—no guts, no manhood. Emasculate them, then send them back to their wives and their girlfriends in shame." I looked at her. "Who do you think handled the castrations?"

"Let me guess . . . their women?"

"Not only that, this punishment was *conceived* by Ethiopian women. Forgive me if this sounds sexist, but females do tend to be more creatively vindictive."

"Good point. Remember that." She smiled for a moment, then said, "And you're saying this explains why a woman was sent to handle this? Or at least that it offers insights about how a woman chose to handle it?"

"I'm saying she took great risks and went to considerable lengths to choreograph his murder in a way that is certainly unique. We already concluded that she probably went out with him before last night, partly as a reconnaissance, to get to know her victim, to—forgive the pun—to size him up, and maybe to design his murder." I noted, "The manual calls it staging. In other words, maybe this was more personal, and more stylized, than we assumed."

"Okay . . . that could be. It might even be a lead." She thought about this a moment, then suggested, "We should check his charge-card records. See where he went over the last few weeks. Restaurants, movie theaters, that kind of thing. Maybe somebody will remember seeing them together."

"Yes, we definitely should."

"It sounds like there's a 'but' behind that."

I nodded. "But that would be a careless mistake on her part. Too obvious. I have the sense this lady was neat and tidy."

"As in, maybe she paid? Or they went someplace that didn't require an expenditure of money?"

"There's a novel concept. A woman who doesn't expect an expensive dinner before *amore*."

She pushed a finger into my arm. "Because she intended to kill him."

I smiled back. "I mentioned earlier that the method of a suicide often conveys a message. That can apply as well to murder. Serial killers, for instance, usually employ signature methods. Understand that method, and you have insight into the unique pathology of the individual."

"I've read the literature on it."

"Good. So what message was *she* sending? Re-create."

"I told you, I don't think like that."

"Perversion, cruelty, and lust are your weapons. Think like a pissed-off woman, Bian. This man did something personal, something so infuriating that, for you, or for the person who enlisted you, a simple death isn't satisfying enough. Something more is required. Eternal humiliation."

She looked at me a moment, then said, "Then she really hated him. A burning, passionate hatred."

"Go on."

"Okay. Here's what I think. I don't think she was sent by anyone, I think this was her own vendetta. From the beginning, obviously she was seducing him, not the other way around. The act of seduction was a phase, a necessary act of her revenge. As hateful and repulsive as she found him, she was in control of the situation, and the act of fornication, for her, was just that—compulsory, symbolic, gratifying. They were making love, in his mind; in hers, she was just fucking him."

"A form of betrayal, right?"

"That might be how she thought of it. What creature is it that . . . that mates and . . . you know?" She shrugged.

"The black widow."

"Yes, the black widow—it has sex then slays the male."

"Right. She exterminates her mate from the gene pool, ensuring the male will never cheat on her, will never produce competing offspring."

"But this is obviously different. That's sex as genetic survival. Sex can also be a contest for domination." She went silent for a moment, then suggested, "I would bet she made him beg for it, made him grovel."

"You think?"

"Why not? Some women do it to men they love."

"Why?"

"A primal exertion of power. Men are physically stronger, but women have a counterbalance—a vagina, and permission. The pleading, the degradation restores the balance. A sexual yin and yang. *He's* not in control. *She* is."

"Wow."

"You asked how a woman thinks. I'm telling you some women do think, and do act, that way. I'm not saying I approve of it—I don't—yet it's not uncommon. Is it abnormal or deviant? What *is* normal and healthy when it comes to sex?"

As tempting as it was, I let that one alone and asked, "But there's more, isn't there?"

"Well . . . give me a moment." She looked thoughtful for a while, then said, "Okay, let's deal with the final act. She got him excited . . . erect, actually, and then she killed him, and positioned him to appear like he was engaged in masturbation. Perhaps there's a message there."

"Another act of domination?"

"I . . . I don't think so. I think her need for domination was culminated when they first had sex. This was . . . well, I think she was, as you suggested, choreographing his humiliation. Perhaps she did make him beg a little, but if so, it was no longer for her own enjoyment, her own fantasy fulfillment. Now she was manipulating his lust as a sculptor shapes clay before the carving." She looked at me. "I don't know what he did to her, but in her mind, his final death scene may have equated with that act."

"His nakedness . . . his erection . . . death on a bed . . . the bullet through his head . . . what?"

"Without knowing what he did to deserve this, I have no idea." It was interesting that she used those words—"to deserve this"—yet that went to the heart of the motive, and that was what we needed to focus on. His killer, or whoever sent her, was enacting a retribution. Like the Ethiopian woman lopping off the Mr. Johnsons of their enemies, this was the killer performing her own idea of castration. Bian looked at me and added, "There's really no way of telling, is there?" She asked, "Where do you think she is now?"

It was a good question and I considered it a moment. "If I had to guess, probably she left the country the morning after Cliff's murder. Maybe from Dulles, or maybe she drove to Baltimore or Philly to widen the trail."

Bian concluded, "Then we'll never find her."

"They all make mistakes, Bian. You just have to find that mistake."

"You really believe that?"

"I know it."

CHAPTER SIXTEEN

We reentered the office, and Dandy Don was chatting with Phyllis, something about a trip to Paris and a restaurant on the Avenue de Who-gives-a-shit where he enjoyed something that in his words was exquisite, called *fwa grass*, which apparently is not something you mow; it's something you eat. Why did I not like this guy? I held out the coffee cup to Don. "I thought you might want coffee."

He looked taken back by my generosity, but accepted the cup. "Well . . . uh, sure."

Before Bian could get out a warning, he took a long sip and—"Shit!"—gooey black stuff sprayed out all over the tabletop. He slammed down the cup and stared at me. "You're not as funny as you think, Drummond."

Wanna bet?

An odd sound exploded from Phyllis's throat, a hiccup or maybe a choked laugh. Evidently she didn't like Don either. This was good to know.

After an awkward moment, she explained to Don, "Drummond takes a little getting used to."

This might have been the understatement of the day.

Bian was giving me a look that said, "Grow up." I mean, I'm trying to protect her virtue, to show her what a phony putz Donny Boy is before he starts humping her leg.

I smiled at her. She looked away.

Don, however, had now concluded that Sean Drummond was the class clown, which was what I wanted him to believe. I often do this to witnesses on the stand. I never cease to be amazed at the stupid things people will say when they think you're stupid.

Trying to restore a modicum of seriousness, Bian said to Don, "As an expert on Iraq, what do you make of this exchange of information between Daniels and Charabi?"

Don swallowed a few times and regained his composure. He turned to Bian and said, "Be more specific." *Prick.*

Bian replied, "Were you aware Daniels was giving Charabi this secret?"

"No."

"Was this . . . officially sanctioned?"

"Why ask me? I thought that's what you and Drummond—"

"It was not sanctioned," Phyllis quickly interjected. "The Director alone had authority to bless this release."

I turned to Phyllis. "And you're sure he didn't?"

"Better yet, he's sure."

"Who knew we broke the Iranian code?" Bian asked. "After all, a breakthrough of such vital sensitivity and intelligence value . . . wasn't this compartmentalized?"

"Of course it was." Phyllis explained, "A small team from the National Security Agency handled the deciphering, and from within the Agency we handpicked a small cell to manage the use of the fruits."

Don added, "Decoded interpretations of the transcripts were hand-delivered by an Agency courier to a military exploitation cell in Baghdad. But the military, including this exploitation cell, were kept in the blind about where, or how, this knowledge was obtained. They didn't need to know where it came from to know how to use it."

Don, anticipating our next question, informed us, "And no . . . Daniels was not read on, nor was he part of this operation. Nor did he have the security clearance to be in the loop."

I thought about that a moment. I asked, "Do you know for sure that Charabi revealed this news to the Iranians?"

Don studied me for a moment. Eventually he said, "You think like a lawyer. You're wondering if the cocked pistol was actually fired, if there is a victim, if there was a crime."

He turned to Phyllis, who nodded. He informed us, "About three months back, we saw . . . yes . . . there were definite signs of compromise, that the Iranians knew what we were up to. But frankly, we were in disbelief. At first. We had no idea how this could have happened."

"And now you know. Describe these signs."

"Ask another question."

"All right. These signs—they were irrefutable?"

After a moment, Don replied, "Yes."

"How? Why?"

"You're probing into areas that are . . . Look, for the purpose of your investigation, you don't need to know about this. Okay? It was a huge loss. Leave it at that."

"Got it."

"Good. The point is—"

"Why was it a huge loss?"

"You don't back off, do you?" He looked at Phyllis, who nodded again. He turned back to me and said, "Okay, I'll tell you this much. Because the Iranians had, and still have, their fingers deeply inside Iraq. It's a long, porous border with smugglers' routes that have existed for a thousand years. They've been moving large amounts of money, weapons, and people to various Shiite parties and factions. Put two Army divisions on that border and it wouldn't make a dent. They can't be stopped physically. Just electronically."

"And using these decoded transcripts you were tracking all this?"

"Yes . . . *were.* Once they learned their code was compromised, they've taken the appropriate steps and devised an alternative communications structure that, so far, has been foolproof." He looked at Bian. "You have a combat patch. You were there, right? I think you appreciate firsthand how invaluable this information was, militarily and politically."

Bian leaned back in her chair and thought about this. Eventually, she leaned forward and said, "The timing . . ." She paused. "This disclosure occurred near the start of the Shiite uprising, right?"

Don nodded. "None of Daniels's messages are dated. You know that. However, this message was sandwiched between e-mails that place it within a few weeks—perhaps days—before Muqtada al-Sadr's Shiite uprising. In fact—"

"In fact, that's enough on that topic," Phyllis interrupted.

Don and Phyllis exchanged quick glances. An important piece of this story was being withheld, and I wondered what that part was. More important, why were Bian and I being kept out of the loop?

You can go crazy asking yourself these questions with these people—they won't even tell their own kids where they hid the Easter eggs.

Anyway, Don shifted gears and began speaking extemporaneously, without questions or prompting, which was sort of refreshing. Clearly he was an expert on this subject, and he offered us a rich and fairly informative tutorial about the shifting situation on the ground in Iraq.

Essentially, within a year after the invasion, the country had become embroiled in a civil war—more accurately, several concurrent civil wars—between Shiites and Shiites, between Shiites and Sunnis, between Sunnis who wanted to return to Baathist ways, Sunnis with different designs, and three or four splinter groups that nobody understood, probably including themselves. Tossed into that potpourri were foreigners pouring across Iraq's borders because it was a shooting gallery with American troops as targets. In short, what we had was Uncle Sam trying to put together a jigsaw puzzle with pieces that didn't fit together and that wouldn't sit still.

I interrupted at one point and asked, "So what's the problem between these Shiites and Sunnis? They're all Muslims, right? Don't they believe in the same faith?"

Don looked like he could not believe I asked this. "Yes, they are all Muslims. The theological differences are small, almost irrelevant. For all Muslims, Mohammed is the prophet who received the word of God from the angel Gabriel and gave it to his people. The major differences stem from after Mohammed died, over who should inherit his mantle. His cousin Ali or his best friend, Abu Bakr. The Shiites believe only Mohammed's bloodline can be caliphs, and the Sunnis believe it was Mohammed's intent to pass it to Abu Bakr. Over this issue, the Muslims divided into two opposing sects, each side accusing the other of perverting Islam, of being apostates. Eventually, the first leader of the Shiites, Husayn, and his followers were killed by Sunnis in a battle in Iraq. Clear?"

"No."

"The Shiites believe the twelfth iman, the last iman, will return to earth from a cave to rule a perfect godly society. For the Sunnis their holy city is Mecca, in Saudi Arabia. For the Shiites the most holy shrines are in Najaf and Karbala, in Iraq. In the seventh century, when Husayn and his Shia followers were slain by the Sunnis, the schism became a blood fued. Only a tenth of the world's Muslims are Shia, and embedded in their beliefs is a lot of minority anger, the sense of always being repressed by Sunnis, of being part of a religion shaped from injustice. So it remains."

I looked at him and said, "So this is like a family feud over the old man's inheritance."

Don did not seem impressed by my clever simplification, and he instructed me, "It's no less significant, and no more meaningful, than the feuds that divided Christianity and produced countless wars in Europe. Papal power, the right to divorce, theological interpretations—there are many issues that divide even our faith. Except for one thing: The Muslim schism never subsided, never softened, never healed." He then shifted back to his larger discussion.

Don eventually summarized, saying, "I explain this so you'll understand the meaning . . . the full scope of what Daniels gave Charabi, and the relevance of what the Iranians offered in return. As you might suspect, Iranian intelligence has been keeping a close eye on Iraq's Sunni community. Bear in mind that under Saddam—a Sunni—Iran and Iraq fought a bloody seven-year war. The Iranians do not want another Sunni to rise to the top."

He paused to see if we had any questions. We did not.

He continued, "Also understand that Iranian intelligence has an excellent read on what's happening inside Iraq. It's their primary collection target, they live next door, they're more culturally savvy than we are, *and* they've invested decades developing and refining their sources, particularly among their Iraqi Shia coreligionists. So it's not just losing insights into what Iranian agents were doing inside Iraq, it's also getting their take on what's happening in a country they know better than us." He let that sink in, then said, "Losing that window was . . . well, it still is an intelligence catastrophe."

I mentioned, "Like losing the seat next to the smartest girl in algebra class. How do you pass the final? Right?"

Don's eyes had sort of a patronizing glaze. "I suppose that's a . . . well, an intelligible analogy."

It seemed like we were back to questions and answers, and I looked at Don and asked, "What exactly was the nature of the deal between Daniels and Charabi?"

"I wasn't privy to it, right?"

"Right. So surmise."

"Okay. Here's what I think. As you know from the news, even before the invasion, the Pentagon and the White House were touting and backing Charabi as the future prime minister of a democratic Iraq. You read that, right? And clearly, his godfathers were his controller, Daniels and, obviously, Cliff's bosses, Tigerman and Hirschfield, who had their own long relationships with Charabi and persuaded the White House to make him their man in Baghdad."

"Right."

"So, in the middle of the invasion, Charabi and select members of his Iraqi National Symposium were flown over to and prepositioned inside Kuwait. The idea was to rush them in the instant Baghdad fell and place them in charge of the government."

"So what happened?"

"That *is* what happened. The day Baghdad fell, Charabi was flown in by an Army Black Hawk, where he was met by an Army band and a color guard and given the full pomp and ceremony treatment. And we immediately began screwing up the occupation. It was a big mess, and the administration immediately had reservations about the initial American team sent over to run things, so they replaced it with a new team, and it became an even bigger mess."

Bian, who had been there during that period, commented, "On top of that, Saddam's Iraqi government had crumbled, then disintegrated. There was nothing to put Charabi in charge of. It was utter chaos, for months."

Don smiled and nodded at his prize pupil. He said, "So Charabi was left to sit around Baghdad, cool his heels, and wait for things to settle out. But simultaneously, the prewar intelligence he and his people provided was, piece by piece, being disproven. Search teams fanned out all over the country and checked the sites Charabi and his people had pinpointed—no nukes, no bioweapons sites, no huge stockpiles of chemical weapons. For the White House and for the Defense Department, this was more than embarrassing, this was a strategic fiasco."

"Buyer's remorse," I suggested. "So they all began having second thoughts about Charabi?"

"They began having what should've been first thoughts," commented Don with his typical self-assured arrogance.

Bian smartly observed, "But not Daniels."

"No, you're right," Don replied agreeably. "Mahmoud Charabi, after all, was his creation. He'd been his faithful controller for all those years, and later his conduit into the U.S. government. He could divorce and run away from his wife. But not Charabi."

Don leaned across the table and looked at me. He said, "So . . . we come now to the question of . . . *why*? You asked whether there was a deal or an arrangement between these two. And now you're wondering why Cliff Daniels—a former soldier, a career civil servant—*why* he agreed to betray his country. He was a regional expert, after all. Don't assume he didn't understand the damage he was inflicting. He did." He inched closer and once again repeated, "The question is *why*."

This sounded like one of those revelatory Sherlockian moments, and I had this strong urge to play Sherlock to his Watson and declare, But isn't that elementary, my dear Watson? But Phyllis was reading my thoughts and giving me the Look, so instead I limited myself to the observation, "Yes, that *is* the question."

"Because Daniels was a late-middle-aged civil servant with an undistinguished career, nearing retirement, and his close association with Charabi was about to become the tagline on his professional tombstone. For him, there was one way out, and only one way: Charabi *had* to become prime minister. If that happened, as his closest American confidant, Daniels was looking at a second life, probably a job in the White House, and probably a prestigious title he could eventually carry into retirement." He looked around to be sure we all understood this brilliant insight. He noted, "Implicitly or explicitly, this was always the deal. Success for one meant success for both. Failure, too, was a collective deal."

As much as I did not like Don, it made sense. Theresa had as much as said the same thing, and reflecting back to the messages I had read, all that "good friend" and "my brother" crap was merely Charabi reminding his partner in crime that their fates were inseparable, that if Charabi got his big prize, Daniels would ride his coattails.

Since we were now into hypothesizing, I asked, "This Sunni moneyman, was he, or were the Iranians, offering the genuine article?"

"I . . ." Don glanced at Phyllis with a suddenly constipated expression. "I can't really . . . Phyllis hasn't shown me that page."

We all three glanced at Phyllis, who nodded sympathetically as though he were referring to a different Phyllis.

Don quickly recovered his aplomb and said, "However, it's a good question. Could the Iranians have fed Charabi—and thereby us—a red herring? Possibly . . . sure. That was another amateur mistake by Daniels. This is Tradecraft 101. Due diligence, right? Always force a source to verify *before* the deal. Now we don't really know, do we?"

I noted, "Then Daniels not only was fed lies by Charabi in the lead-up, but maybe the process continued right through."

He winked at Bian. "Excuse my French, but yes . . . this could be the proverbial kiss after the fuck. But by the same token, the Iranians *do* have a strong motive for unmasking such an individual to us. Iraq's future is no trivial matter to any of its neighbors. They all have factions they're clandestinely backing. The Iranians, for example, would love to use us to clean the clocks of the more potent Sunni insurgent groups." By way of comparison he mentioned, "Reverse the situation; imagine if Iraq was Mexico. Would we keep our hands out of it?"

Bian asked, "Where is this Sunni money coming from?"

"That's the billion-dollar question, isn't it?"

He gave us a moment to ponder this, then continued, "Iraq's Sunni neighbors—specifically, Saudi Arabia, Jordan, and Syria—none of them want a Shiite caliphate on their borders. Understand that since 1979, when the Iranian revolution ushered the ayatollahs to power, Tehran has been trying to spread its Shia revolution throughout the region. For the Sunni neighbors, Iraq under Saddam had been an invaluable barrier, a buffer zone, if you will. Excluding Iran, Iraq, and Lebanon, the neighbors are all predominantly Sunni, and they are all ruled by Sunnis. But they also have sizable Shiite minorities, who, in many cases, feel politically and religiously marginalized, if not repressed. Also there are particular tinderboxes that could blow up and destabilize the entire region. Take Lebanon—like Iraq, it's a fragile and unstable melting pot with a large, resentful Shiite population who are aligned with the Iranians, and with the Syrians, who have controlled it for two decades. Ignite problems in Lebanon and those problems spread to Syria, Israel, and Jordan. If Iraq goes Shiite, it . . . well"—he glanced at me—"it will stir up a world of shit."

Long story short, Don had not a clue where the money was coming from.

Bian asked, "But what was Charabi's motive? He had our backing, or at least the Pentagon's support. Why risk betraying us and getting close to the Iranians?"

"We read the same messages. Right?"

Bian nodded.

I wasn't so sure we did, but in the interest of moving things along, I also nodded.

Don said, "Put yourself in Charabi's shoes. You're in Iraq, the Sunnis have put a price on your head, you're in a life-or-death struggle with all these other Iraqi Shiite factions for political power . . . and this guy—your handler—suddenly, he begins threatening to cut you off at the knees." He paused for a moment, then asked, "How would you respond?"

I said, "I'd fly back here and knock his teeth in."

He smiled derisively. "I'll bet you would." He continued, "Daniels was an analyst, not an operator. Handling a field asset is an intricate and demanding art. They're under terrific psychological stress, many are pathetically conflicted, and most are phobic. What I'm suggesting is this: He flipped his own asset into Iran's arms."

Bian had obviously given this some thought and suggested back, "Alternatively, Charabi became worried that he would lose our support and decided to make the Iranians his insurance policy. So he passed along what Daniels gave him, and now, as a quid pro quo, the Iranians owe him a favor. At the very least, they won't actively oppose his rise as a Shia leader." She added, "And with Daniels dead, we would never know."

He replied, "That could be what you're seeing in these messages. Charabi has begun playing both sides against the middle—us against Iran. For him, the best of both worlds."

Bian noted, astutely, "Except it only works as long as the U.S. remains blind to this deal between Daniels and Charabi. After all, he betrayed us."

This seemed like an appropriate moment to ask, and I did. "Do you think Charabi had Daniels murdered?"

Don replied without hesitation, "He would be my number one suspect. As Bian said, with Daniels dead, so was the secret. But don't rule out Hirschfield and/or Tigerman either. They may have been privy to this exchange between Charabi and Daniels—they might even have been behind it—and maybe they were frightened about what Daniels might say before the House investigating subcommittee." As if we needed to be reminded, he said, "They are hyper-ambitious men. Don't underestimate how far they might go to keep his mouth shut."

Once again, Don and I were in agreement. In fact, I was about to ask another question when Phyllis stood and walked around from behind her desk. She approached Don, saying a bit curtly, "Thank you for dropping by. I'll pass on to the Director how helpful you were."

Don looked a little surprised at this abrupt dismissal. He checked his watch. "I have a little more time. If they have more questions—"

"That won't be necessary."

Don's face registered a shifting mixture of bewilderment and frustration, and eventually settled at resentment. He got to his feet and stood a moment. "I'd like to be kept in the loop about this investigation. Actually, I . . . I need to be kept aware. This is important to us . . . to me. You know that."

Phyllis replied, somewhat cruelly, "You'll hear from me at the appropriate moment."

The confidence seemed to drain out of him. For a long moment he maintained eye contact with Phyllis. He opened his mouth and started to say something, thought better of it, and then spun around and left.

Bian and I remained perfectly still as the door closed loudly behind Don, and as Phyllis returned to her seat behind the desk. She folded her hands in front of her and stared at her desktop, sphinxlike.

Eventually she deigned to speak. "Which of you would like to hazard a guess at what this is all about?"

CHAPTER SEVENTEEN

Bian rose to that challenge and replied, "Don is . . . No, he *was* the head of the exploitation cell for the Iranian transcripts."

Phyllis nodded. "Yes. On both counts." She looked at me and said, somewhat crossly, "You shouldn't have taunted and humiliated him that way." She added, "We've put him through hell these past three months. The poor man has virtually walked around with a lie detector connected to his tail."

"I handled him as I would any witness who might be lying, quibbling, and withholding." I added, "People without last names bother me."

"I know *why* you did it. That's why I'm having doubts about you. This is not a criminal case, nor can it be treated in a legalistic manner. I really—"

"Excuse me—it's a murder case."

She gave me one of those looks that suggested I was dancing on thin ice. "Hear me out, Drummond. We are at war. In wars people do stupid things, even venal things, things that very often result in deaths. The lines between stupidity, ineptitude, gullibility, and criminal mischief become very fluid. Do you understand the distinctions?"

"Maybe."

"Maybe won't do." She examined me a moment, and I had the sense the ice was cracking. "You're a soldier, and for various reasons

I would prefer to keep you on this investigation. But for the same reasons I'm now experiencing reservations. Do you understand what I'm talking about?"

"I don't exactly . . ." Care.

She turned to Bian, who apparently was guilty by association. "Do you understand, Major?"

Bian replied noncommittally, "A fuller explanation might clear up any misunderstandings."

"All right." Phyllis studied us both a moment. Her fingers, I noted, were clutched and looked fidgety, for her, the equivalent of a hysterical fit.

I thought I knew why, and also I thought it best to hear her out. She informed us, "I've been in this agency or its predecessor through seven or eight wars. World War II, Korea, Vietnam, Grenada, Panama, two Gulf wars—fill in the blanks. Were you to closely scrutinize any of these wars, were you to look past the sepia-tinted memories and turn over all the rocks in this town, you would discover a dismaying array of bad decisions, mistakes, misimpressions, incompetence, and in a few cases, outright lunacy. Many tens of thousands of lives were wasted. The historians know barely a quarter of it. I was here, I saw it firsthand, and I doubt I know the half of it. But bad things happen in wars, and had those things become exposed to the public *during* those wars, our history books might . . . well, they *would* look quite different."

"I'm still confused."

"Nothing is black and white here."

"I'm a lawyer, Phyllis. We invented moral relativity. I don't need this lecture."

"And I don't need a legal gunslinger," she snapped. "The mission of this agency is not law enforcement, it's intelligence. I'm suggesting a little . . . moral patience."

"Don't need that either."

"Well . . . what do you need?"

I thought I now understood where this was going and replied, "Cliff Daniels committed a very heinous mistake, one that may have crossed over to a crime—possibly several crimes—including espionage and possibly treason. We have the paper trail of his misdeeds. Also, we have two high-level officials, Albert Tigerman and Thomas Hirschfield, who possibly knew about this crime, who possibly ordered or condoned it, and who possibly were coconspirators, or, at the very least, have embarked on a cover-up. Not to be overlooked, there has also been a murder and they are also suspects in that crime. I hope this is not news to you—each of these things have sections and titles dedicated to them in the federal statutes."

She smiled patiently, as if she was humoring me. "That's a lot of possiblys. What would you have us do?"

"What the law *requires*. Call in the FBI. Let them chat with a federal judge, and do what they do best—read people their rights, threaten, bust nuts, kick down doors, cut deals, until somebody squeals. It might surprise you, but regarding federal crimes, there actually are laws and tested procedures that usually get results."

My sarcasm apparently struck a nerve, because she replied, "I believe I have a little experience in these matters, having lived through it three or four dozen times."

"And may I say that this agency has a wonderful record of handling it right every time."

Her eyes narrowed. She took a long breath, then said, "Use your critical faculties as an attorney—how would you describe the evidence?"

"I don't understand the question."

"I think you do."

"Then why ask *me*?"

"Weak and inconclusive, right?"

"Well . . . yes, and—"

"And to compensate for that lack of material evidence, I'm sure you have a long list of willing and credible witnesses."

"You know I—"

"And you should know that the instant anybody calls the FBI, the administration will throw a shield of executive privilege over everything involved in this matter. Of course it will be challenged, and of course the courts—after all, we are at war—will uphold the administration's claim. In twenty-five or fifty years, the classifications will expire and we'll finally get to the bottom of this."

I said, "Maybe."

Phyllis looked annoyed. "Where are the maybes?"

Bian, who had been sitting and listening to us bicker and debate these weighty issues of right versus wrong, of legal procedure versus seat-of-your-pants bullshit, chose this moment to observe, "I think she's right."

This statement annoyed me a lot, coming as it did at such a pivotal moment; no less from a military police officer; no less from a comrade in arms; and last and not least, from my putative partner.

Partners are supposed to back each other up. Right? I was really pissed and I looked at Bian. "I don't remember asking what you think."

"Don't use that tone with me," she snapped. "I told you before, I don't like to be condescended to."

I studied her a moment. Now she was really pissed. I could tell.

"I'm sorry."

"Try it again and you'll be sorrier."

My goodness. But Phyllis quickly swooped down on her new ally and asked Bian, "*Why* am I right?"

Bian looked at me and answered, "Even if you apply the most optimistic standard, there is only one person we could even hope to charge with a crime." She added, "He's dead. Beyond that we have only suspicions that would sound outrageous to any rational person."

Phyllis nodded at her prized pupil. "But do you believe these suspicions are . . . do they hold water?"

Bian stared back at her.

Phyllis said, "This is important. For instance, when was the relationship between Clifford Daniels and Charabi first formed?"

"About ten years ago," Bian replied. "Don mentioned the year . . . 1993 or 1994."

"The fifteenth of December 1994, according to the report he was required to file after that meeting. But until *this* administration came to power, their partnership was meaningless—inane and silly, to tell the truth. The previous President had no intention of invading Iraq. It did not become fully empowered until after Hirschfield and Tigerman returned to the Pentagon, and it really gained legs post-9/11."

She stood up and began quickly pacing around the room. "The information and sources fed us by Charabi were pivotal to the President's decision to go to war. And, of course, they were included in the public justification for the invasion. Believe me, I know. Were it not for this information . . ."

She let that statement drag off, and I nodded. That's what it said in the news reports, and Phyllis, who had been on the inside, had a firsthand view of the decisions that led to war, and now she was confirming the reportage.

Phyllis continued, "Don surmised that Daniels prodded or drove

Charabi into the arms of Iranian intelligence." She looked at me. "What do you think about that?"

"*Inter canem et lupum*," I replied.

For Bian's benefit, Phyllis translated my Latin: "Between the dog and the wolf. The more up-to-date expression is that he placed him between a rock and a hard place." She focused on Bian and asked, "Do you believe that? Is it the only explanation?"

Bian played with her pen for a moment. "I don't . . . There's an unproven assumption here, isn't there?"

Phyllis stopped her pacing and leaned across the table, facing Bian and me. "We're *assuming* that Daniels drove him into Iran's arms. But there's another possibility, isn't there?" I could almost hear the game clock ticking.

So I eliminated that assumption from my logic train, and thought about it . . . and . . .

And holy shit.

Eliminate that assumption and you arrive at a whole new theory—that maybe Charabi didn't need a shove, or even a nudge or nasty threat, because he already worked for Iran. And from there, it was a hop, skip, and a jump to the slightly more expansive proposition that Charabi was—from the beginning—working either with or for Iran's intelligence service. Bian also pieced this together, because she looked at me, her eyes large.

Phyllis said, "Possibly Mahmoud Charabi was . . . well, in the intelligence lexicon, an agent of influence. He may even have been an Iranian plant to feed us disinformation." She started to say something else, thought better of it, and, with a regretful pout, instead suggested, "I'm surprised we never considered this before. It is the oldest gambit in the business."

I thought I had seen everything. But the hypothesis, the idea, the supposition—or whatever it was—that Iran, via its agent Charabi, had recruited first Tigerman, then Daniels, then the entire Pentagon, and then the White House, was almost beyond belief. Almost.

Phyllis understood this. She said, "Hard to digest, isn't it?"

I made no reply to that understatement. I was still caught up in the idea that the whole reason behind a war might be a con job by the Iranians, who wanted Saddam gone and who duped Uncle Sam into handling the dirty work for them. It made sense, and it didn't make sense.

Bian suddenly stood up. "I might be sick."

I looked at her. Her face had gone pale and her legs a little wobbly. She placed her hands on the table and began drawing deep breaths.

Never personalize things—that's the golden rule. But Bian, because of her direct personal investment in this war, was more emotionally upset by this suspicion than Phyllis or I. To learn that it might all have been the result of some geostrategic hustle clearly unnerved her. Or perhaps she was responding as any normal person would to such a shocking theory; maybe I had become more like Phyllis than I pretended, too jaded, too cold-blooded. Whew—there was a frightening thought.

I played it back and forth inside my head a few times. Deductively, Charabi and the Iranians shared a common goal—Saddam gone and a Shiite in his place—and better yet, from Iran's perspective, a malleable Shiite who owed them a big, unspeakable favor. Further, what could be better than having the U.S. take the flack and casualties for a preemptive war most of the world, and a growing percentage of the American populace, regarded as unjustified, unnecessary, and strategically dangerous? This gave a whole new meaning to killing two birds with one stone.

The mullahs in Tehran might even consider this some sort of aesthetic retribution for America helping to install and then propping up the shah. I knew also that most Iranians believe to this day that the United States had somehow instigated and then artificially prolonged their bloody eight-year war with Iraq—a war that ultimately cost half a million Iranian lives. Not entirely true. But nations are free to invent their own histories; they don't have to be fair or accurate, they only have to make people feel good about themselves—even Americans are not above inflating our boogeymen and embellishing our myths.

There was an almost biblical quality here—an eye for an eye, and a tooth for a tooth, so why not a war for a war? Especially with the added sweetener that the victim doesn't even know he just got screwed?

On the other hand, we were making a big leap in judgment. Okay, yes, it did *seem* to fit the facts as we now knew them. But truth, like life, depends on which end of the telescope you're looking through.

Phyllis allowed us a moment to collect our thoughts, then told us, "We three are the only ones who have put these pieces together. Except the Director . . . I informed him about two hours ago." She added, "He nearly had a heart attack."

But this was not exactly so, and I said, "If this is true, Charabi knows, and the Iranians know."

Bian heard what was I saying and commented, accurately, "That would mean they have . . . well, they have the balls of the President of the United States in their hands."

Phyllis took this in and replied, "Perhaps they do. Were they to leak this, there won't be a need for an election here next week. A coronation will suffice."

Which raised the ever-evocative question. I looked at Phyllis. "Why us?"

"I need my best man on this."

"Where is he?"

"That would be you." She smiled.

This was such utter bullshit, I had to smile back.

She said, "I have my reasons."

"I'm sure you do. I'd like to hear them."

But this was not my game, this was Phyllis's game, and she responded, "Tell me what you think."

"Instead I'll tell you what I know. You're worried about your agency."

"It's your agency as well."

Wanta bet? I expanded on this reasoning and continued, "You don't trust your own people. They might leak this to destroy this President, or they might exploit it to intimidate or blackmail the White House."

"I won't claim there's any love around here for this President. And yes . . . there is considerable resentment within the Agency toward this administration," she acknowledged. She then observed, "You appear to have a dim view of Agency people."

"I think Agency people are great. I really do. You're the one who seems to have a problem trusting them. That's why us, right? Military people follow orders."

"That thought had entered my mind."

"In fact," I continued, "you and your boss want to be the dealers. You control the information, you control the investigators, and you control the results."

She neither confirmed nor denied this assertion. She didn't need to. Knowledge is power, more so in Washington than most places, and this knowledge was the equivalent of a hundred-megaton hydrogen bomb tucked in your pocket.

I could picture the Director seated beside that handsome marble fireplace in the Oval Office, smiling pleasantly and saying something like, "Mr. President, the Agency needs the biggest budget increase in its history . . . and yes . . . I know, I know . . ." He would pause to shake his head. "Times are hard . . . what with the national debt exploding . . . yes, yes, it's certainly difficult to justify, and . . . but . . . well, here . . . Browse through this file I'm putting on your lap. Maybe you'll find it in your heart to support me on this."

Phyllis lifted a paper off her desk, which she handed to Bian, who read it before she passed it to me. It was another of the missing messages, this one from Charabi to Daniels, and it read:

> Clifford, my most loyal, truly dearest friend. I am apologizing for this long lapse of time that I have not given you the promised information. Alas, I should have heeded the old Arab saying: To trust a Persian is to trust a snake. Truly, they are the rottenest race of all Allah's followers, dirty beggars, Ali Babas, and thieving miscreants. But they continued to insist, as I have several times repeated to you, that the trail of this bad fellow has been lost, and he needed to be re-found, which now they say has been accomplished. As my Persian friends promised, this is a big fish, the moneyman behind Abu Musab al-Zarqawi, whom you know has killed many of your soldiers and caused much mayhem in this country. This man has the name Ali bin Pacha, a Saudi who stays in the city of Falluja, in a white compound at the end of the Avenue of Ali, near the city center. They say this man can be recognized because he misses his left leg, and they advise you must move swiftly, because a man of such value and cleverness does not grow roots. So you see, my friend, I am not, as you cruelly and unfairly proclaimed in your recent messages, a rotten turd.

Phyllis informed us, "This was the last message in the file." She added, "It was sent only two days ago."

Bian looked at me. "Then this man . . . this Ali bin Pacha—"

"That's correct." Phyllis finished Bian's thought, "Presumably he's still on the loose, still in Falluja, and still ripe for the taking. But for how long . . . ?" She shrugged.

I said nothing. I hoped she wasn't thinking what she seemed to be thinking.

She was studying me, her left eyebrow cocked expectantly.

When I didn't *voluntarily* volunteer, Phyllis prodded, "Well, Drummond . . . ?"

So that was what she was thinking. Did I want in? No, absolutely not—this was nuts, or worse.

For one thing, Ali bin Pacha might already have shifted to a new location, or alternatively, this whole thing might be another con by Charabi, and/or by his Iranian pals.

Second, Phyllis was keeping secrets. An operation of this nature is risky even when you *know* what's happening behind your back and everything is on the up-and-up.

And not insignificantly, now that we were cognizant of criminal activity, if we failed to refer this to the FBI, we were also committing a crime.

I'm not always a stickler for rules and legalities, especially when I think I won't get caught. This was not one of those times.

But before I could answer, Bian leaned forward and responded, "I'm in." After a moment, she added, "Actually, if you think about it, I'm the ideal choice."

"Why would that be?" asked Phyllis, her eyes on me.

"I completed a full tour there. I know the country and culture, I'm fluent in the language, and I have recent operational experience."

I looked at Bian. "Have you ever done an operation like *this*?"

"I . . . I spent six months policing some of the most violent sewers of Baghdad."

"Answer the question I asked."

"I've arrested suspects, and I've planned raids on insurgent compounds." Apparently I looked dubious, because she added, "I don't see a difference."

There was a world of difference—her unawareness of that was the first clue that she was the wrong person for this mission. Clue two, there was no right person.

I tried not to sound patronizing and said, "Well . . . how do I say this? I mean—"

"You don't say it," she snapped. "I'm an MP. You're a lawyer. By training, experience, and inclination, I think I can handle this better than you."

Phyllis cleared her throat and said, "Drummond was in Special Ops before he became a lawyer." She smiled. "He served for five years with a unit that performed operations almost identical to what I have in mind. He might be a little rusty . . . I'm told, however, that it's like riding a bicycle."

Partly true, and in that statement Phyllis revealed a little more of her thinking, about her intentions and about my favorite subject: me.

What wasn't true was her comforting sentiment about easing back into the profession of arms. Perhaps Sean Drummond had once been a lean, mean killing machine, death from the skies, one hundred and eighty pounds of twisted steel and sex appeal. The new Drummond had packed on a few pounds, a new attitude, and had become a creature of the courtroom, with all that implies.

I couldn't recall the last time I was on a firing range, nor had I run more than ten miles in years. As battlefield veterans will tell you, the key to survival is speed—depending on the day you're having, either toward the enemy or away. I recalled the admonition the Army drills into the thick skulls of all new recruits: "There are two kinds of soldiers on the battlefield—the quick and the dead."

Well, I was quick with my tongue, but my footwork and my survival instincts could stand a little work. Maybe a lot of work.

Bian, who required a moment to absorb this new and interesting facet of my professional background, eventually said, "Oh."

"So you see," Phyllis continued, "he has the ideal résumé."

Without the slightest concession of inferiority, Bian replied, "It's irrelevant. I'm offering; he's not."

For a moment nobody said anything.

What could I say? I knew what Phyllis was doing—pitting me against Bian, exploiting my overblown chauvinist instincts, and at the same time engaging in a little emotional blackmail. Phyllis is a world-class manipulator, and usually knows exactly how to push my buttons—but not this time. If Bian wanted a piece of this, she was a big girl. Her life, her call. Welcome to the newly liberated world; equality between the sexes means an equal risk of coming home in a pine box.

I was curious, though, and I looked at Bian, then at Phyllis, and said, "What exactly is it that you intend?"

"I thought that was obvious," Phyllis replied. "Get our hands on the low-hanging fruit, Mr. bin Pacha." She added, "What to do about Charabi is trickier. But he's not going anywhere, whereas bin Pacha could disappear at any moment." She looked at me and said, "Charabi will have to wait."

I couldn't believe what I just heard. "We seem to have a different definition of low-hanging fruit. Ali bin Pacha is in Falluja."

"Yes. I recall reading that from the message."

"Maybe you don't read the newspapers. The Army declared it a no-man's-land six months ago and pulled everybody out. It's a jihadist country club."

"That's what our assessments say. A most unpleasant place."

"Unpleasant? This is the same city where the four contractors were killed and hung from a bridge."

"I know, I know . . . These are very nasty people. All the more reason they have to be stopped, whatever it takes."

"And you know the chances of nabbing this guy and getting back out are nearly impossible?"

"It would have to be a very well-run operation."

"And you know this could be a trap?"

"Yes, that's an important consideration. We'll certainly have to account for it in our plans."

"He's an important figure in the insurgency. He'll be heavily guarded."

"I think he would . . . yes." She looked at me. "But if Charabi told the truth—"

"Or if the Iranians told him the truth . . ."

"All right . . . that's another risk." She was becoming visibly annoyed by my stream of well-reasoned objections and added, "Assuming this bin Pacha is the moneyman behind al-Zarqawi, getting our hands on him would be an incredible blow to the insurgency. Large rewards are worth large risks."

"Here's a no-risk solution. Drop a bomb down his chimney. No more bin Pacha *and* we'll all be alive to talk about it. What's not to like?"

Bian said, "Why are we debating this? Temporarily interrupting Zarqawi's supply of funds accomplishes nothing. He'll replace bin Pacha, who, anyway, surely has an understudy or backup. These are not stupid people—they do not run a sloppy operation. I know. I was there."

"But—"

"But if we capture bin Pacha, who knows what he can reveal?" She looked at me. "You don't understand the nature of this war. It's not about cities captured or terrain held. It's different. It's about people, important people who are key to the enemy's operation. The moneymen, the chief planners, the bomb makers. Take them out of commission, find out what they know, and you strike a crippling blow to the insurgency."

She looked at me to be sure I understood. She said, "Neither his money sources nor Zarqawi will be located if he's dead. That's what we want to accomplish, isn't it? Get Zarqawi. Find out who's providing the funds and terminate their support."

"How about if *we're* terminated?"

She replied, "That's not your problem. You're not going."

"Good point."

She looked at Phyllis and suggested in a tone I found insultingly dismissive, "We don't need him anymore. I can handle this."

Phyllis avoided my eyes. "You're right. Sean, show yourself out. Everything we discuss from here on is need-to-know only." She added, "Needless to say—"

"If word leaks, you'll mount my balls on your wall."

She pointed at a spot on the wall and said, "Right there. Only three of us are in the know. You understand—a leak of any type would be ridiculously easy to narrow down to its source."

"I know my responsibility, Phyllis, and I do it."

I stood. My eyes shifted from Phyllis, who was being her typically inscrutable self, then to Bian, who refused to make eye contact.

Somebody had to say something, and after an awkward pause, Bian said, "It was nice working with you, Sean. If I ever . . ." She smiled weakly. "Well, if I ever need a lawyer, I hope you would agree to represent me."

"Follow through with this, and you *will* need a lawyer."

She did not reply.

I took two steps toward the door and stopped. I didn't like the way this was ending. I knew they wouldn't listen, but I needed to make one more try. I mean, I understood why Phyllis thought this was a good idea; conspiracy, double crosses, and deception are like oxygen to these people. But Bian? What was she thinking?

I spun around and told Bian, "Waterbury isn't going to let you do this. You know that."

Phyllis informed us, "Leave Waterbury to me. I'm sure I can persuade him it's in his, and in the Pentagon's, best interest to loan us Bian."

"You'll blackmail him."

"Whatever."

I said to Bian, "Is this about Mark?"

"What?"

"You heard me."

"Leave him out of this."

We stared at each other a moment. She was giving me that look women give when they wake up beside a complete stranger. "I'm right," I told her. "You believe you owe this to Mark."

"You have no idea what you're talking about."

"You did your tour, Bian. It's his turn in the box. Were he here, I'm sure he'd tell you the same thing."

"How do you know what he would tell me?"

"Because if he's half the man I think he is . . ." Actually, even I couldn't complete that hackneyed cliché. I leaned across the table and got about two inches from her face. "You've already done your part."

"I didn't know there was a limit to how much duty you owe your country."

"Duty, no. Stupidity, yes." I pointed at Phyllis. "She's manipulating you."

"I know what's happening here."

"I don't think you do."

"I . . . yes, I do. Better than you."

"Then you would know there are other ways to handle this. And you know what? Some even make sense."

"That's not even an option," Bian replied. "If Daniels's stupidity is exposed to the public, it will blow the lid off the war. We'll be the laughingstock of the world. The entire coalition will run from Iraq. All those lives wasted . . . I won't let that be on my conscience."

Phyllis stood and approached me. She tapped a finger on her watch and said, "You've had your say. There's a great deal to get done, and not much time to do it. Please see yourself out."

I turned around and headed toward the door. No way was I going to become involved with this. I had had my say, and my conscience was clean. My actions would look good in front of the eventual inquest that would inevitably result from this stupid idea, too.

I turned around again and I sat.

Bian studied me a moment. "I don't need your chivalry."

"How about my idiocy?"

"I mean it, Sean. I'm not some helpless damsel in need of some misguided white knight."

"This isn't about you."

"Then—"

I pointed at Phyllis. "I'm going to keep an eye on her."

Phyllis smiled. I knew she had expected this outcome; I hate being so predictable, and I decided not to give her the satisfaction of knowing how much that pissed me off. I smiled back.

She had obviously thought this through and said, "So here's the way this will work. Drummond, you will get our man in Falluja. Bian, you will employ your expertise in interrogation and language to find out what he knows."

I looked at Phyllis. "And what will you be doing back here?"

"Somebody has to figure out what to do about Charabi."

I said, "So that's the carrot?"

"As long as you're there, we might be able to kill two birds with one stone."

CHAPTER EIGHTEEN

Trips to combat zones normally are preceded by long and extensive buildups, months of exhaustive training, equipment and personal preparation, country orientations, updating of wills, and so forth.

On the plus side, this affords you the knowledge, the mental outlook, and the expert training to survive—with a chance to tidy up a few loose ends in case vice versa happens. On the minus side, it condemns you to months of restless nights filled with anxiety and cold fear.

So in a way I was happy with only seven hours of notice; in a larger way, I was unhappy with any notice. Speed, however, was the ticket. Mr. bin Pacha might be the paranoid type who hops beds every night, or he might feel secure inside Falluja and get sloppy. We were banking on sloppiness and hoping for the best.

So Phyllis allowed me five hours to go back to my apartment, rest, shower, pack some field uniforms and incidentals, and then I returned to the office for two fast hours of briefings. What this entailed was a rough sketch of a plan that, in Phyllis's words, was still "evolving, still being perfected," with an advisory that "an update will be provided upon your arrival."

I thought about this and replied, "Said otherwise, I'm jumping out of a plane without a parachute, hoping the ground moves before my landing."

"Don't worry. Only the good die young."

"You'll live forever."

She smiled, sort of. She then instructed, "Once you arrive in country, we can't risk telephonic contact. You can't imagine the number of collection systems operating inside and over Iraq these days. It is, of course, our number one collection priority, and our friends at NSA are as likely to intercept your emissions as the enemy's. Once you're in country, you're on your own."

I was already on my own, but kept that thought to myself.

Bian, I should mention, did not make an appearance, nor had she left me a short note wishing me good hunting, bon voyage, have a nice funeral, or whatever sentiment applied. Well, it didn't really matter as the plan was for her to join me in Iraq in a day or so, unless she had an onset of common sense in between.

An elderly CIA doctor with quirky bedside manners administered three shots for diseases I've never heard of, issued me a bottle of malaria pills, and warned me to stay away from the local food, which wasn't going to be a problem since, as I mentioned, pickles on hamburgers is for me adventurous gourmandism.

He pressed into my palm a box of prophylactics containing twenty-four rubbers, which I stared at in surprise. I'm as overconfident as the next guy, but I would be in country only two, maybe three days, max.

I asked, "Are these the largest size you have?"

He laughed, and even managed to act like this was the first time he had heard that line. It was a stupid joke, but those about to embark on suicidal missions tend to be humored. He informed me, "Hell, boy, these aren't for your nozzle. Nobody over there gets any poon. These keep dust and rust out of your weapon's nozzle. Ha-ha."

Ha-ha. He was very funny. Seriously.

Phyllis then pulled me aside and offered a few parting words that were brief, yet so emotionally heartfelt and moving that I actually choked up a little. She said, "Don't screw this up, or I'll have your ass."

Anyway, next stop was the parking lot, where an Army Black Hawk helicopter awaited. I climbed aboard, and we lifted off and departed for Delaware, a flight that lasted nearly an hour.

We flew at low altitude, and rather than dwell on the unhappy future, I occupied my mind observing the countryside below. America—truly, it is an amazing land, an inspiring land. The countryside was peppered with massive homes, many with large swimming pools, and what appeared to be outhouses, though probably they were cabanas or artists' studios or secondary residences where the crazy aunts and aging parents are kept.

Like every society, ours is a confounding mixture of rich and poor, of haves and haveth-nots. And yet, I think, what makes us different from most is that here the poor can become rich, and the rich can become stinkingly richer or blow it all and end up cleaning all those swimming pools. This, I think, accounts for why we have so far limited ourselves to one revolution. Yet I also think we take for granted that because America has survived for over two hundred years, it will last another two hundred, ad infinitum. But the foundation is not as sturdy or impervious to harm as we once assumed, as nineteen homicidal maniacs showed us on September 11. That was supposed to be a wake-up call, the klaxons warning that bad people are out there, that they own the night, and we must, by courage, wiles, and force of arms, take it back. And yet here we were only three years after the fact, the lines at the recruiting stations had dwindled, and the sad but vacuous story of an over-the-hill pop star accused of diddling little boys had drowned out what brave men and women were doing in Iraq and Afghanistan.

It struck me, too, that this war has produced no galvanizing heroes, or none the American public has ever heard of—no Audie Murphys, no Doolittles, no Schwarzkopfs. As a nation we no longer glorify war, which, for a society, is probably healthy and good. But when we fail to honor our warriors, I wonder.

Not that Sean Drummond was harboring thoughts of returning a hero. The first time I went off to war, my father offered me one good piece of blunt advice: "A dead hero is still dead. Come home, son."

Well, I was three for three so far, with a few nasty nicks on the last one, which was either a warning or a new lease on life. But every time you push it, you wonder if the fates are thinking, "Hey, this clown thinks he can beat the house odds; let's lower the boom."

There was no need to go through the usual passport or customs nonsense, nor did I require an updated visa or passport. The boarding ticket was my military ID with a set of freshly minted, albeit phony, orders, and the plane was a shiny United Boeing 747 on contract to Uncle Sam's Air Force that was departing from Dover Air Force Base.

The flight was filled with about two hundred soldiers and a few Marines, men for the most part, a few women, nearly all young, most of whom had already endured six months in Iraq, were granted two weeks of stateside R&R—rest and recuperation—and were headed back. Picture two hundred people who had just spent two weeks screwing and drinking their brains out. This was not a happy plane.

I took my assigned seat beside an Army captain with the crossed rifles of the infantry on his collar and a nametag that read Howser. For the first hour, he said not a word—on his lap was a thick photo album he was flipping through, over and over, gazing thoughtfully at pictures of his lovely young wife and two little girls, twins actually, who were as cute as puppies.

With nothing better to do, I ogled the pictures over his shoulder. This intrusion did not appear to bother him, though eventually he did look up and ask, "Not married, sir?"

"Nope."

"Maybe that's better."

"Maybe."

"Nobody to worry about."

"You mean nobody to worry about *you*."

"Yeah . . ." Whereupon Captain Howser launched into a long, rambling discussion about his wife—Sara—his daughters—Lindsey and Anna—and how they had spent their two weeks of peaceful respite together. Very nice. Two guys, side by side on a long international flight, killing time with fond reminiscences and sappy anecdotes: Lindsey's first steps, Anna's first trip to the potty—her first *successful* trip—how Sara never complained about his absence, never lamented how lonely she got, never mentioned the anxiety attacks every time the doorbell rang with the possibility of bad news on the doorstep.

Indeed, this was what distinguished this flight, and certainly what separated these passengers, from any of the other half million international travelers flying over the world's oceans at that moment. These passengers didn't want to be here, weren't looking forward to the destination, and nobody had a guaranteed return ticket.

I sometimes envy guys like Howser; they have somebody to come home to, somebody who wants them home. For some odd reason, Bian and the photograph of her beloved fiancé, Major Mark Kemble, popped to mind.

My gut instincts said that Bian's seemingly illogical enthusiasm for this mission had something to do with him, mixed, perhaps, with a lingering feeling of injustice over her father and Vietnam, a war lost, ultimately, because America lost faith in the cause. These are powerful furies to carry in your heart and your mind—love and ghosts, the living and the dead, the man she loved today, and a war that stole her chance to love her father.

In the words of Tennessee Williams, the heart is the most stubborn organ. About women, that sounds about right. About men, he definitely overlooked a more stubborn organ.

Which opened the question of what motives placed me on this plane, headed off as I was to do something my instincts said was foolhardy, my legal judgment said was wrong, and in my professional judgment, bordered on suicidal.

I recalled my father's favorite admonition: Never let your dick write a check. Good advice, Pop—but like most good advice, the devil is in the details.

In truth, Bian Tran had made a strong impression on me. Were I completely honest, I was a little smitten by her, and maybe a wee bit jealous of Major Mark Kemble. Indeed, this was a unique and spellbinding woman, a personified American dream. Arriving on our shores as a young child, impoverished, confused, homesick, and bereaved by the recent death of her father, she mastered a new language, absorbed a new culture, worked hard, marched through four years at that uniquely American institution, West Point, and, I suspected, were I to check her military file, her officer efficiency reports would be uniformly sterling.

In short, this was an intellectually gifted, forceful, driven lady. Also, as has been my experience with other immigrant children, I suspected that Bian Tran was a little hyperpatriotic regarding the ideals of her adopted land, inebriated by her sense of duty and, maybe, by her willingness to sacrifice for those she loved. It's interesting. Over 10 percent of American soldiers in Iraq weren't even U.S. citizens, just hungry young people trying to earn the dream.

Those of us born with the silver spoon of citizenry in our lips, I think, tend to be more convinced that we deserve our American birthright, particularly its fruits and indulgences over its labors and burdens. I did not think, though, that Bian was a mindless fanatic; in fact, I was sure that something else, something more—perhaps love, perhaps guilt, perhaps both—was driving her. I would have to keep an eye on that.

Also I didn't trust Phyllis. Well, I didn't trust the CIA. In my months in this job, I had found these were good people, patriotic, courageous, and enormously talented, who nearly always do what they think is best for the Republic. The problem is, they do it behind a curtain of smoke and mirrors; this isn't always a temptation to good judgment, or worse, good results.

Anyway, Captain Howser recognized a pal at the front of the plane and excused himself. This apparently required an exchange of seats, as, shortly afterward, a man, large and burly, with the stripes and diamond of a first sergeant on his collar lumbered down the aisle toward me. The name patch on his chest read Jackson, and he looked at me and said, "You mind, Colonel?"

"If you have a photo album, I mind a lot."

He laughed. "Divorced. Twice. How about I tell you what complete bitches they were?" Whereupon he fell into the seat and stretched out.

On his left shoulder, I observed the patch of the First Infantry Division—his current unit of assignment—and on his right shoulder, that of the Third Armored Division, a unit he served with in a previous war, or on a previous tour in this war. He was a combat veteran several times over with that weary, deromanticized, been-there-done-that look of somebody who was too tired to talk about it.

He said to me, "You're JAG." His eyes moved to my shoulder where there was no unit patch. "Where you assigned in Iraq?"

"I'm not."

"Then why—"

"I'm a tourist. Maybe you can recommend a good hotel. A pool and spa would be nice. A good, well-stocked bar would be more than nice."

"You're nuts." He laughed.

"Me? Who's coming back a second time?" I informed him, "It's temporary duty. Just in and out."

"Oh . . ." I thought for a moment he was going to knock me out with his beefy fists and trade uniforms.

"Meeting a client," I told him. That, in fact, was my cover, and should anyone ask, that's also what it said on the phony orders in my breast pocket. Good covers are always based on fact, and in reality, there was a prisoner facing charges, though he hadn't yet been assigned counsel. I had even briefly studied his case file to substantiate my cover; the guy didn't have a prayer.

"What's his tit 'n a ringer for?" Jackson asked.

This seemed like a good chance to practice my cover, and I replied, "Mistreatment of an Iraqi prisoner."

"They're real sensitive about that these days."

"Sure are."

"Ever since that Abu Ghraib thing."

"Yep."

"That was a bunch of wacko idiots, you ask me. What the hell were they thinking?"

"They weren't. They were just doing."

After a moment he asked, "Your guy, he do it?"

"Never touched the guy."

"Uh-huh."

"But I think the seven witnesses and the victim's broken jaw from the rifle butt might prove a little tricky in court."

He laughed. "I can see where that could be a problem."

That about covered everything I knew, so to change the subject I asked him, "So how is it over there?"

He took a moment to contemplate this question. "Sucks."

Any soldier who is happy in a war zone needs his head checked. I asked him, "But is it worth it?"

He understood what I was asking and replied, "Is now."

"Why *now*?"

"You know Tennyson?" After a moment, he clarified. "Alfred . . . the English poet." And then he quoted, "'Ours is not to reason why, ours is but to do or die.'"

"'Charge of the Light Brigade,'" I replied.

"Says it all."

"Bullshit."

He laughed. "Complete bullshit." He twisted sideways and faced me. "A month ago I sent home two of my kids in body bags, and I damn sure give a shit that my soldiers are dead." He soberly contemplated his combat boots. "Now it better be worth it."

I looked out the window at the expansive blue sky, at the marshmallow clouds below, and off in the distance, I noted a jet contrail headed in the direction we had just come from. Possibly that sleek silver container also was filled with soldiers, their year at war over, their minds choked with memories of long, tedious days, of comrades wounded, mangled, and worse.

And it struck me that Bian was right about one thing—we *could* blow the lid off this war—and among some on this plane, I would end up man of the year, and among most, loathed.

First Sergeant Jackson closed his eyes. Field soldiers have the stamina of babies, and within thirty seconds he was comatose and snoring loudly. Time for business. I opened my legal briefcase, withdrew a thick sheath of papers, took a moment to clear my mind, and dug in.

I recalled the old Army saying—a plan lasts until the second it's implemented. I have found this to be generally true, but I think it's important to have one, to have a baseline, and if you've really done your homework, workable options for when the poop flies. What we had in this case was seat-of-your-pants bullshit.

The basic idea—what the Army calls a POW snatch; POW standing for prisoner of war, and snatch implying the goombah in question might not be a willing participant. Such operations are always risky, as bad guys invariably hang around their own neighborhoods, usually in the company of other bad guys, and you have to be quick or *you* end up on the short end of the stick. There are, in fact, times when the roles become reversed, but it's bad luck to dwell on that—and hard not to.

In the interest of airtight secrecy, rather than rely on career Agency types or even uniformed military who might become nosy about Sean Drummond and Mr. Ali bin Pacha, the heavy-lifting stage of this mission was going to be done by private contractors employed by Phyllis.

These were people who had done work for the Agency before, and they passed the entrance exam; they were still alive to do another job. They are not mercenaries, mind you, and they are sure to point that out to you; they are patriotic Americans, mostly former Army and Navy Special Forces types who are still serving their country, and it just happens to be for more money.

And why not? They get one to two hundred grand a year, less Mickey Mouse, bosses they can talk back to, and when they're tired of it, they cash out and walk. This might be a workable option for Drummond's second career.

On the brighter side, they are professionals, usually handpicked, highly experienced, and they don't get jobs unless they produce bang for the buck.

Oh, yes—that unsettling matter of my trust issues with my boss. I wasn't completely paranoid, yet I was aware of another big advantage of private contractors. They aren't accountable to anybody except the name on the paycheck, no questions asked. Not that I expected a bullet in the back of my head. It was a factor to bear in mind, though.

Of course, Phyllis would never do that to me. We were friends. Right?

Anyway, before I departed I was given the name of my contact, Eric Finder—a hopeful surname for this job—the location for our meeting, and even passwords we would exchange to confirm our bona fides. How cool is that?

Inside my legal case were street maps and satellite photos of Falluja—where Ali bin Pacha was in residence—a few thick binders filled with information about that city, and various threat assessments produced by in-country CIA types regarding a man named Ahmad Fadil Nazzal al-Khalayleh, who was a Jordanian by birth, nom de guerre al-Zarqawi, and some of his known associates—Mr. Ali bin Pacha's name, incidentally, was nowhere on that list.

The general thrust was this: Mr. al-Zarqawi ran a rough outfit. The exact size of his organization was unknown, and ditto for its makeup and exact membership. It was presumed to include a small, die-hard, highly trusted cadre, a few hundred warriors and kamikazes, and probably a few thousand sympathizers who provided safe houses, transportation, odd jobs, logistics, intelligence gathering, and whatever.

These people were a mixture of Iraqis and foreign talent, and it was notable that the local Sunni populace were largely on his side, not ours. In fact, Zarqawi was regarded locally as a Robin Hood type, despite taking money from the rich and giving only death to the poor. Lately, however, killing Americans was becoming too risky and difficult, so he had shifted his sights to murdering Iraqis, often indiscriminately, which was wearing thin with some locals.

Here's what was known: The structure of his organization was basically cellular and compartmentalized; small groups, connected vertically, not laterally, so no hands knew what the others were doing. A number of these cells had been captured or infiltrated; yet, to date, nobody had fingered the man himself, which was interesting.

A twenty-five-million-buck warrant was on Zarqawi's head; this in a part of the world where two grand was enough to sell your adorable, beloved daughter to a stinky camel farmer. This suggested that al-Zarqawi was either very good, very feared, very lucky, or very ruthless, none of which are mutually exclusive.

Nothing that I read here was news, of course. As with the rest of the conscious American public, I knew about Mr. al-Zarqawi and about his more flamboyant idiosyncrasies. He liked seeing his masked face on the tube, and he knew how to sweep Nielson ratings, as our broadcaster friends say. His particular form of attention-seeking behavior was making home videos of himself beheading helpless captives, which tells you he has a few big issues with Western civilization. Also, if Sean Drummond fell into his hands, I might be in for a very dramatic, one-act theater career.

Anyway, after two hours of reading and studying, I remembered I had slept only three hours the previous night. I stretched, put my papers away, locked my briefcase, and within seconds was sound asleep.

I would like to say I rested fitfully and experienced pleasant dreams, but when I awoke, here's the dream I remembered: I was kneeling on a small dark mat, three tall figures stood behind me, black masks covered their heads, coarse tape covered my mouth, a hand was tugging my head backward, and I could see a large, crisp blade hovering in front of my throat, moving closer . . . closer . . . and . . .

CHAPTER NINETEEN

What jarred me awake were the wheels of the big 747 bouncing and skidding on hard tarmac. I opened my eyes, looked out the window, and got my first clue of something gone wrong—the airport. It shouldn't be, yet this airport looked familiar, and I knew I had been here before. The cobwebs cleared, and I knew where I was: Kuwait.

The second tip-off was the pilot announcing in that smooth, everything's-just-fucking-fine tone, "Ladies and gentlemen, thank you for flying United. For your safety, we were diverted from Baghdad Airport, which is currently experiencing a serious threat from surface-to-air missiles. I apologize for any inconvenience. When you deplane, you'll be met by representatives from the armed forces who will connect you with ground convoys heading north."

This isn't the kind of announcement you hear on domestic routes. But this guy was so slick, for a moment I thought I was on a normal flight and we were about to be promised free food vouchers to mollify our discontentment, or whatever.

His tone then turned funereal, and he added, "It has been our distinct honor to have you on board and . . . and . . . and from the bottom of my heart, on behalf of the entire crew . . . God bless you all."

You could almost hear a collective gulp from his passengers. A simple good luck would've been sufficient, thank you.

Anyway, he parked his big plane in the middle of a large empty ramp, off to the right of the runway where there were no other aircraft, and neither was there a terminal. The night was pitch-dark, yet the airport was well lit, and I could observe trucks moving around, all of them American military vehicles.

I checked my watch, which I had already preset to local time—4:00 a.m. An elevated stairway was rolled up, and we deplaned and waited in a large gaggle on the tarmac while our duffel bags and personal gear were unloaded down a long rolling ramp and arranged in a long line for pickup.

Several officious-looking types with MP brassards on their arms and clipboards and flashlights in their hands began corralling the troops and loudly directing them to various holding areas, depending on their units and ultimate destinations in Iraq. The Army has a reputation for efficiency that is rarely merited, which is why "Hurry up and wait" is the unofficial Army motto. Except when it's to the Army's advantage; then the anal minds kick in and usually get it right.

First Sergeant Jackson and I shook hands and wished each other good luck. I quietly separated myself from the group, confident that Phyllis had learned about this unexpected diversion and made the proper arrangements.

I wouldn't trust Phyllis with my life. But I definitely trust her to get me where *she* wants me to be.

The weather was nice, incidentally, mid-seventies, without a hint of rain, almost balmy. Definitely nicer than October in Washington. Bermuda was nicer still.

After a moment of wandering around I observed a soldier using a flashlight to brighten a handwritten sign that read, "LTC Drummond."

I approached him and confessed that that would be me; in response, he offered a sloppy salute and informed me that his name was "Carl Smith . . . PFC Smith, Eighteenth Transportation Battalion," and explained he would be my chauffeur for the drive up to Baghdad.

I spent a moment doing the senior officer thing, asking Smith a few shallow, innocuous questions, as he did his respectful subordinate thing, offering brief, perfunctory replies. The senior officer is expected to show a personal interest in his or her subordinates, regardless of how temporary or ephemeral the relationship. On the surface, this translates as concern, and establishes rapport. But neither has it escaped my notice that the normal nature of these inquiries—married status, hometown, family, that kind of thing—correspond to exactly the data an officer needs to know for a next-of-kin letter.

Anyway, Carl Smith. He was dark-haired and dark-skinned, and he informed me that he was thirty-two, yes, a little damned old for his rank, divorced—damned happy about that—an Alabamian—damned proud of that—and, like many of his peers, in a fit of angered idealism had rushed into an Army recruiter's station the day after September 11—a decision he now looked back on as damned impetuous.

He appeared unusually fit for a transportation guy, but probably Carl had a lot of free time to spend in the weight room. Booze is prohibited for soldiers inside the war zone, and Arab women aren't turned on by Christian men. When all else fails, you turn to the worst vice: exercise.

He led me to a dust-coated humvee; I threw my duffel in the back, climbed into the passenger seat, and off we went at a good clip. Military humvees, incidentally, aren't the gaudy gas munchers that are so la-di-da among Hollywood's spoiled and beautiful. They're diesel for one thing, but also they're more primitive and entirely lacking in bling, such as sound muffling, air-conditioning, or entertainment systems of any form, with seats that are ergonomic atrocities. But as our Chinese friends say, a thousand sins can be overcome by one great virtue; I was relieved to see the one accessory that counts in these parts, the newest up-to-date armor.

We drove out of the airport—Smith flashed his military ID to clear us through the checkpoint—then moved at high speed along a black tarmac road for about an hour, connecting with a military convoy headed north, up the infamous Highway 8, to Iraq.

This convoy was a long mixture of fuel tankers, heavy trucks loaded with large green containers, flatbeds carrying replacement Bradley Fighting Vehicles, and, interspersed among these vulnerable noncombatant vehicles, an Armored Cavalry troop with tanks and Bradleys to chase the Indians away.

Carl informed me, "We'll hang at the end. Don't get no better than that."

"Fooled me. We're getting all the dust and fumes."

"Yeah . . . well the IEDs—the roadside explosives—usually they target the front or middle of convoys. Causes a traffic jam with stationary targets to shoot at." He added, "Dust or shrapnel? You're the colonel."

"Which is worse?"

He smiled agreeably, and tossed me goggles for my eyes and a green rag that I tied around my nose and mouth, cowboy style.

Fortunately, Carl Smith proved to be the untalkative type, though—less fortunately—not the silent type. He spent nearly the whole trip whistling country tunes—like many backcountry southern males, he had perfected a loud and penetrating whistle—while I alternated between nodding off, studying the contents of my legal case, sticking my fingers in my ears, and wishing I had a gun to pop this guy, or myself. I hate country music.

Around midafternoon, he handed me lunch; having slept through the meal on the plane, I was lightheaded with hunger. The meal was an Army MRE—Meal, Ready-to-Eat—proof that the Army has a sense of humor, despite what you hear.

One bite, and I remembered what I don't miss about being a field soldier.

Anyway, the drive lasted about thirteen hours, and, aside from passing through one large city early in the trip, for the most part we traveled through terrain that could charitably be described as monotonous and awful—flat desert, a balance between beauty and cruelty, until we were deep inside Iraq proper, at which point we saw more frequent signs of life: palm trees, shabby buildings, caved-in huts, wrecked and abandoned cars on the roadside, and sometimes, in the distance, a remote village presumably built around a well or an oasis, or a Taco Bell. Just kidding about that last one. But why would anybody live here?

I was reminded of those desolate little American towns in the middle of the Mojave Desert, and where once there was a reason for them to exist in such remote and inhospitable settings—gold mines, or borax, or Pony Express stops—they had long since become abandoned, sweltering white elephants. Some have become picturesque ghost towns with tumbleweeds billowing through the streets, though a few still are populated by quirky, eccentric folk—loners, flakes, and hermits—exiles from the hurly-burly of American life, or perhaps perps hiding out from the cops. But what were the people in these isolated little Iraqi villages like?

I could not fathom the gap between people who live like this and the typical young American soldier who would experience a monumental fit were he deprived of his PlayStation, cell phone, chat rooms, cable TV, and fast food. Indeed, all of these things now existed here, on the military bases, and soldiers returning from a day battling insurgents spend their evenings e-mailing their families and one-and-onlys, playing video games, and browsing porn, which is, I suppose, as healthy a mixture as any to put it behind you and get your head straight.

The Vietnam warriors of my father's generation also maintained their connections to their former lives, to the American lifestyle, to what the Army euphemistically terms "creature comforts." Their adversaries lived in jungles and tunnels, exposed to the elements and surviving on rice and raw fish, even as helicopters swooped into the American base camps loaded with cold Budweiser, *Playboy* magazines, pizza, and Bob Hope with alluring ladies in miniskirts, all good reminders of what they were fighting for.

One way to win an insurgency is to melt into the environment and culture—to go native—and beat the locals at their own game. This, of course, just has never been the American way. We rearrange the culture and environment to suit us.

Indeed, the day was coming when this highway would be chock-a-block with fast-food places, minimalls, and Days Inns for the hungry, tired traveler, with the obligatory Koran tucked inside the bedside table, a prayer rug at the foot of the bed, and an arrow pointing at Mecca carved on the bedpost. This, I guess, was what the insurgents were fighting against, just as Hitler, Tojo, Mao, and Stalin had fought against it before them. Good luck. The carpetbaggers are here and change is around the corner. Probably someday their grandchildren would look back and wonder what all the fuss was about.

Occasionally we saw long convoys of slow-moving American military vehicles headed where we had just left, toward Kuwait, and behind them, crawling in long impatient lines, Iraqi cars, buses, and trucks, no doubt entertaining unkind thoughts about their occupiers. Passing a military convoy in this country is nearly as perilous as jaywalking in New York City.

His incessant whistling aside, Smith remained almost supernaturally alert, robotically scanning the roadsides for anything that looked out of place or even innocuously suspicious—dead animals, or wayward barrels, or broken-down cars; the usual costumes for roadside bombs. Whenever he saw something he didn't like, he jerked the humvee off the road to stay on the safe side, bumping and grinding through a few hundred yards of sand.

Increasingly we began to pass ramshackle villages with kids in raggedy clothes who stood by the highway with their hands extended—begging for food, money, or trinkets—a few of whom had obviously learned something from the GIs. By the end of the convoy, when Carl and I passed, the kids were all waving farewell with their middle fingers.

Maybe it was a local gesture meaning good luck and good health. Or maybe not.

Well, enough touristy detail. By late afternoon, we were passing through, or by, larger towns and small cities, and by early evening we entered the outskirts of a large, sprawling city with telltale landmarks that were recognizable from television. I glanced at Smith. "Baghdad?"

He leaned back in his seat and stretched. "Better be."

I mentioned, "I have an appointment in the Green Zone. You know the way, right?"

He nodded.

I glanced at my watch. I was sixteen hours late for my rendezvous with Eric Finder—but if Phyllis had known to send transportation from Kuwait, I assumed she had also reset our meeting.

Then Carl said, "That ain't where yer goin', though." I looked at him, and he added, "The blood-dimmed tide is loosed."

After a surprised pause, I replied, "And everywhere the ceremony of innocence is drowned."

If you're interested, this is Phyllis's eccentric idea of passwords, a passage from a Yeats poem. I guess I understood how this might be sort of a poetic metaphor for this case and all that. But the golden rule of operations is KISS—keep it simple, stupid.

I mean, Carl could have said two, and I could have replied three. Works fine.

Indeed, we were on the same wavelength, because he asked me, "Who thought up that silly shit?"

"My boss."

He stared, obviously wondering if it was contagious.

I stared back. "You're Eric Finder?"

"Nope. Still Carl Smith. I'm taking you to Finder."

"There must be a good reason you lied and didn't identify yourself."

"Must be."

"I'd like to hear it."

" 'Cause you'd of spent the whole drive askin' me dumbass questions." He stared straight ahead. "Don't really like to bullshit."

To confirm his suspicion, I asked, "Tell me about your group."

"Like what?"

"How many?"

"Fifteen. Only ten are involved in this, though. Orders are to keep it small and tight as possible."

Of course. The less witnesses the better. "Who are they?"

"Former Delta or Rangers mostly. There's two ex-SEALs, and one guy who was NYPD SWAT." He commented, "He talks real funny." He glanced at me and remarked, apparently in reference to his own credentials, "Delta. Five years."

"Is there a name to this organization?"

"Nope. Truth is, we don't like to be known. We don't bodyguard or handle facility protection like them other groups."

"What do you do?"

"Wetwork."

He confided this matter-of-factly, as though I was expected to know he and his team specialized in rubbing out human targets. In fact, I was now a little embarrassed that I ever accepted Carl Smith for a simple driver.

His impressive physical fitness aside, the man was intensely wound, and a stone-cold introvert. A man of few words is often a man of few thoughts; or he can be someone whose thoughts are best kept to himself.

There was a time when I recognized dangerous men, which was how I survived three conflicts, albeit the last time the bad guys scored a few points by pumping two rounds into yours truly. But that Sean Drummond had lost his edge; if he wanted to survive this one, he needed to remember that. I asked Smith, "How much do you know about this mission?"

He smiled. "Much as I need to know. Why?"

"You know what it's about?"

He shook his head. "We're paid plenty not to know."

"How much?"

"Fifty thou' apiece. Plus expenses."

I whistled.

He glanced at me and insisted, "Hey, we ain't mercenaries."

"Then how about you guys do this one on the house?"

He did not find this funny. After a moment he asked me, "How much you know 'bout Falluja?"

I pointed at the three thick binders on my lap. "I've read and memorized every detail inside these Agency binders."

He asked a little dubiously, "What do they say?"

"I'm an idiot if I go near the place."

He nodded that this was a good insight. In fact, he said, "That's all you need to know. This here's one of them things where a little knowledge is a dangerous thing. Just do everything we tell you; don't even think you know what the heck's going on." He glanced at me and confided, "We get into Falluja a lot."

"No kidding. Where can I buy some postcards?"

He ignored my nervous sarcasm and informed me, "The Agency hires us to tag buildings."

"Which means what?"

"What we do, we hang around inside the city and sort of watch out for hajis. We see one, we follow 'im back to his nest. We tag the building with an electronic marker, call it in, and wait around to make sure the asshole stays put."

"And then?"

"Then . . . well, 'bout an hour later, an F-16 comes along, launches a big missile, it locks onto the electronic signature from the tag, and boom. No more assholes."

This sounded like an interesting job, and I wanted to know a little more, but he continued, "Point is, Falluja's asshole central. They're Sunnis, right? . . . Only they're Wahhabis, like the Saudis. Big-time fanatics. Got it? They don't even get along with other Sunnis, and even Saddam had trouble with this place. He finally said fuck it, problem too hard. Gave up."

I nodded. Though more concise and picturesque, this accorded with the historical and social synopses I had just perused in the CIA tour guide. Even in America, our cities and regions have their own quirks and idiosyncrasies; so if you're operating there, you need to be sensitive to that and adapt, or you stick out like a zit on the prom queen's nose. I mean, I once wore a Yankees cap and "Nixon's the One" T-shirt in Boston; I barely made it out alive.

As I understood it, the Fallujans were like Iraq's Hatfields and McCoys, ornery, moody, and combustible. They don't like outside interference from any outsiders, and particularly they don't like Christians sticking their noses into their affairs. I recalled that about seven months back the Marines had launched an all-out assault, and the fighting turned so fierce they were ordered to conduct a hasty withdrawal—aka retreat. The Marines claimed it was to spare civilian lives; the jihadis said that it was to spare Marines. Whatever.

Knowing my Marine Corps friends, this probably wasn't a good time to invest in Fallujan real estate or to open a shopping mall. A mortuary, however, had possibilities.

"Jihadis now run the place," Smith continued. "They got their own police, they got spotters and informers everywhere, and they got reaction squads that land on yer ass in a split second."

"Got it." I noted that we had peeled off from the convoy and left the roadway. We were bypassing the city center and now were traveling through side streets in what were essentially middle-class neighborhoods in this part of the world.

From the sun's position, I knew we were traveling west, and from my CIA binders I recalled that this direction was the eye of the storm—Sunni territory, the nexus of discontentment and bad attitudes toward Americans.

The city center, I knew from newsreels, had wide, glorious boulevards lined with palm and date trees, statuesque luxury hotels, magnificent government buildings, and opulent palaces, all in line with Saddam's effusive vision of turning Baghdad into the Paris of the Mideast, though the effect was more of a Babylonian Las Vegas.

But outside of the glitzy pomposity of this Potemkin city center, where we were now traveling, the streets were narrow to the point of claustrophobic, grubbier; in fact, squalid. The buildings and homes were packed closely together, and nowhere did I see trees, grass, or shrubbery, which shows that Iraqi homeowners have more sense than Americans—except for the people, nothing here needs to be watered, fertilized, or manicured.

Speaking of fertilizer, what really got my attention was the smell. The city's sewage system obviously wasn't back up to speed, and this was a windy fall day. I couldn't imagine the effect on a breezeless summer afternoon. Were I in charge of this occupation I would worry about people's innate tendency toward mental association; the Americans are here and it smells like shit.

Also there was a fair amount of pedestrian and street traffic, small trucks laden with goods and vegetables, and various models of Japanese and European cars, most of which looked old, though it's difficult to judge in a part of the world where sun and sand prematurely age paint jobs, and people. We began slowing down and after a few moments, I asked Smith, "Where are you taking me?"

He pointed his finger toward a home at the end of the street, a narrow, one-level house, squat in shape, tan or dirty white in color, constructed of concrete and stucco, with bars on the windows, an orange-tiled roof, and an oversize satellite dish, like a big wart sticking off the side. In the States this would be called a Mediterranean ranch, as would the surrounding homes, which were identical in size and architectural style. The Achmeds had no trouble keeping up with the Bashirs on this block. Usually this is a source of domestic harmony, though apparently not. He explained, "It's a safe house."

A moment later he pulled up to a two-car garage whose double door had been conveniently left open. I deduced from this that our arrival was expected. A squat, ugly, lime green 1980ish Peugeot with Iraqi plates was parked to the right.

I knew that few Iraqi homes have attached garages at all, and a two-car is a very rare indulgence; probably this feature weighed heavily when this house was chosen. Regardless, a military humvee is monstrously wide, and it took Smith a few careful attempts to maneuver it inside the garage without peeling the side off the Peugeot. He parked, turned off the engine, and said, "Get out."

I did, while he bolted behind the car and quickly pulled shut the garage door. He next walked to the Peugeot, opened the rear door, withdrew an armful of clothing, and began separating them.

He withdrew a black chador—a veil—and an abaya—a long, baggy woman's black robe—and tossed them at me.

Without further ado, Smith began stripping off his American Army uniform and then slipped into black jeans, dark sweatshirt, and worn Adidas sneakers. With his jet-black hair and dusky complexion, as he was now dressed, he passed for an Arab. I held up the dress and examined it more closely.

He noted, "For one thing it covers your all-American good looks. For another . . . You speak Arabic?"

I shook my head.

"Well, there you have it. Nobody talks to women 'round here less they're hitched."

Obviously these people had thought this thing through. Carl Smith struck me as competent, meticulous, and well attuned to the local culture; how I struck him was another story.

I pulled the abaya over my head and tried to figure out how to put on the chador. Eventually, Smith grew impatient with my fumbling and reached over, saying, "Like this." He made a few deft adjustments and then tapped my shoulder. "Remember how to do that."

While he placed my duffel and legal briefcase in the car trunk, I regarded myself in the Peugeot's side mirror. Smith could pass for a native, as I said; the problem was me, and even the veil didn't fully hide my whitebread looks. But at least an observer would have to be close to pick up on my blue eyes and untrimmed eyebrows, and if they got that close, probably the jig was up anyway.

He slipped an earphone into his ear, from which extruded a mouthpiece, and spent a moment adjusting a few knobs. He said into the microphone, "Smith here. Ready to roll." I had not a clue whom he was speaking with, though the lack of verbal foreplay suggested the call was expected, and further, that we were under the eye of somebody. He listened for a moment, "Uh-huh . . . okay. Yeah, I'll avoid it."

I said, "Avoid what?"

"None of your business."

"If you want your fifty thousand bucks, make it my business."

He studied my face. "You're not gonna be trouble, are you?"

"Avoid *what*?"

His stare turned cold. "A suicide bomber nailed a bunch of people on our planned route. The Army's got roadblocks up. We don't wanna git caught up in it."

"Right." This wasn't my first clue that Iraq sucks, but it was a potent one.

He continued to stare at me. "From here on, we're operational. Understand? The slightest dick-up, the tiniest mistake . . . and we're dead."

"No problem." I walked around the Peugeot, opened the passenger-side door, and started to get in.

He looked at me, and said, "Hey, pal . . . Arab women don't never ride in the front."

"Right." I climbed into the backseat, he opened the garage door, slid into the driver's seat, and we quickly backed out into the mean streets of Baghdad.

CHAPTER TWENTY

Complete darkness.

We drove north through more suburban streets and ended up traveling west, on Highway 10, which connects Baghdad with Falluja.

The earpiece remained in Smith's ear, and occasionally he conversed with his compatriots, brief little conversations, all business. There appeared to be a car ahead of us, running interference, and another to our rear, securing our tail.

This reinforced my impression that these people had their act together. Somebody better—I didn't.

Athough Falluja is a mere thirty miles from Baghdad, the traffic was fairly dense, principally due to more slow-moving American military convoys that completely clogged up the highway. Smith informed me at one point, "Lots of military traffic tonight. Weird. Most Iraqis and even the Army like to be home when the lights go out. The goblins come out."

A few moments later he pointed to our right and said, "Abu Ghraib prison. Over there . . . See it?"

I looked and saw nothing except a few lights from industrial buildings. Maybe I would come back during daylight when I could view Iraq's most famous landmark in all its splendor. Maybe not.

After we departed Baghdad proper, I noted, the towns and cities looked poorer, run-down, virtual slums. And according to the CIA guide, we were traveling through the more prosperous, better-developed part of Iraq—the Sunni Triangle—where Saddam threw money and favors at his Sunni coreligionists and Tikriti tribesmen. Where the Shiites live, in the towns and cities of the south, must really suck.

I checked my watch: nearly nine. "When does this thing go down?"

I observed him observing me in the rearview. "Thought you knew that."

Not wanting to reveal how grab-ass this was, I replied, "Update me."

"Tonight."

Tonight? "I . . . I meant what *time* tonight?"

"Usually best to go in about two in the morning."

I thought I knew, but asked, "Why?"

" 'Cause by then most of the jihadis are asleep. They're pretty half-assed that way. That gives us an hour to get in, an hour for the snatch, an hour to get out. Maybe thirty minutes of wiggle room in case the shit hits the fan. Understand?"

"What happens if it takes longer?"

"If we're still there by five, best to lay over till tomorrow night. The hajis set up checkpoints, looking for American spies." He added, "Don't worry. We got safe houses inside Falluja."

After a moment, he informed me, "The target could move anytime. Some of these people, they don't never sleep in the same place twice." He looked me in the eye through the rearview mirror. "We expected you fifteen hours ago. That was your prep time. You okay with that?"

"Do I have a choice?" I suggested, "Maybe he moved yesterday."

"Maybe."

"I was sort of hoping he had an attack of conscience and turned himself in while I was en route."

He smiled thinly. "Well, you never know." He said, "We got a two-man team observing the target building."

"And what does this team see?"

"There's jihadis in there, all right. Maybe five. Maybe more. They don't hang about in big groups. Seems somebody keeps tagging their hideouts and blowing them to hell, and now they disperse as best they can. No way to know if your particular asshole's there."

A few minutes later, Smith took a right turn off the highway, and we traveled for another five minutes before he switched off the headlights and we drove for a while in blackout mode. He turned left onto a dirt trail and drove for about a hundred bumpy yards before stopping and turning off the ignition.

He twisted around in his seat and looked at me. "The others will get here in a few hours. You should nap." He slipped night-vision goggles over his head and stepped out of the car, where he began spinning in slow circles on his heel, observing our surroundings.

It required a few moments for my eyes to adjust to the night, and around us, I saw, were flat, open fields with no growth, no stalks or seedlings, though off two to three miles in the distance were several small, dimly lit villages. All in all, a good location for a meeting. Smith could observe anybody approaching from at least a mile away, a range that exceeds even the most sophisticated sniper rifles. You have to think of these things.

I closed my eyes and spent a moment thinking about what was next. Assuming we made it intact into Falluja, assuming bin Pacha was inside the building, and assuming we actually caught him—which, by my count, involved thrice ignoring the old Army dictum that assumptions make asses out of everyone—there was still the vexing matter of what to do with this guy once we had our hands on him. Smith and his team were supposed to transport us back to Baghdad, where I would rendezvous with Bian, who, if all was on schedule, was already cooling her heels in a specially chartered aircraft at Baghdad Airport.

Accompanying her would be an Agency doctor, a totally unnecessary precaution, Phyllis had calmly assured me—though it never hurts to plan for the worst. Knowing Phyllis, the doc was named Mengele and his toolbox was packed with truth serum, electric shocks, pliers, toothpicks for fingernails, et cetera. But maybe my imagination was running away with me. Or maybe you had to know Phyllis.

Anyway, as I had implied to the first sergeant on the plane, Bian was cleared into the airport on the pretense of picking up an American military prisoner, with his lawyer, and then transporting them back to the States. That passenger would of course be Mr. bin Pacha, his esteemed attorney would be yours truly, and the destination would not be America—where bin Pacha would acquire the protective shield of U.S. legal rights—but a location where he would have no rights and might feel more amenable about ratting out his colleagues and betraying his cause.

So the question was, what then? I didn't think bin Pacha was the type of guy who would voluntarily spill the beans. These were hardened terrorists, people who enthusiastically drive cars piled high with explosives into civilian crowds and military convoys.

That wasn't my problem—my job was to deliver bin Pacha to Bian; her job was to make him open up and squeal. But I hoped she and Phyllis had come up with a few better recipes than the ones I heard them tossing around before I departed. With that reassuring thought, I dozed off.

The next thing I knew, somebody was pounding metal on the car window. I must've been jumpy, because Smith said, "Relax. It's Finder."

My rear door was opened and I stepped out. I glanced at my watch and saw I had slept for hours: 1:15. I could sense but not see Finder's eyes examining me in the darkness, then he said, "Welcome to Iraq, Colonel. You've traveled a long way."

"And you've picked a lousy way to make a living."

"Don't kid yourself. The money's damned good."

"But of course that's not why you do it."

He laughed. "Bullshit. Why else would I do it?"

Although it was dark, I could make out a man: short, perhaps five and a half feet in height; age, late thirties; color, black; build, slight; with facial features that looked improbably fine and delicate. On the battlefield, of course, it's not about the size of the man; it's all about the size of the gun. His voice, on the other hand, was deep baritone and commanding.

He informed me, "Your partner beat you here. She linked up with me five hours ago."

"Partner?"

"Yeah, Tran. Major Bian Tran. She's your partner, right? She's in my car."

Maybe she *had* been in his car, but nearby, out of the darkness, Bian's voice said, "Change of plans, Sean. I'm accompanying you."

I looked in her direction. "No, you're going back to the plane."

"It's good to see you, too."

"In seven or eight hours it will be even better. In Baghdad, as we planned."

"Phyllis and I talked it over after you left. And we—"

"Am I or am I not still in charge of the snatch?" I asked.

"Well . . . yes. That hasn't—"

"Good." I looked at Finder. "The lady wants to go back to Baghdad. Now."

She looked at Eric Finder and stated very firmly, "The lady does not." She then turned to me and suggested, even more firmly and less pleasantly, "We should have this discussion alone."

In the darkness, I couldn't observe Finder's expression, but I didn't need to see his face to know what he was thinking: *Here I am on the cusp of a dangerous and difficult mission, and those idiots from Washington send me Lucy and Ricky.*

I took Bian's arm and marched her until we were fifty feet from Finder.

I spun her around and said, "This isn't working for me."

"You're right. It's the abaya. You look ridiculous." I should note here that she also wore an abaya and a chador, and she looked good; actually, she looked great. Her eyes were really beautiful. Mysterious-looking.

"Bian, I'm not in the mood. Okay? I—"

"How do I look?" she interrupted.

"I'll tell Finder—"

"I can't imagine how women wear these all day. They're hot, cumbersome, and unattractive. On the other hand, no need to shave your legs, wear stockings, or bother with your hair. Plus if you put on a few extra few pounds, nobody notices. Maybe they're smarter than we are."

"Stop ignoring me."

"Start acting civil. Maybe I'll consider it."

I took a few breaths and tried to recover my usual nonchalant pleasantry or whatever. I smiled nicely and said, "The outfit becomes you."

"Thank you." She swished around.

"How was your trip?" I asked.

"Better than yours. You'll enjoy the return ticket. A big private jet, comfortable seating, real beds, a well-stocked galley." She smiled and added, "I smuggled aboard a six-pack of Molson. For you. For your return trip."

I said nothing.

"It's in the fridge," she continued. "Nice and cold. Think of me when you drink it."

"Right now I'm thinking of choking you."

"You see? There's the thanks I get."

"Stop it."

"And how was your trip?"

"I ate MREs salted with sand, and my driver was addicted to whistling country music." I said, "I hate country music."

"He could have been a rapper."

"Hey . . . you're right. I had a wonderful trip."

"I came up-country on Highway 8 a few times. The noise didn't appeal to me either, the first time. People were shooting at us. I recall that trip taking twenty-three days, not fourteen hours."

I knew what she was doing—reminding me she was a soldier, and a combat veteran who had tasted battle. I informed her, "I'm going to have enough trouble watching after myself."

"Is this one of those stupid macho things?"

"Let's not go there, Bian."

But she was already there and replied, "You're . . . Okay, maybe you've done this kind of thing in the past, and maybe you think this is no place for a woman. Times have changed, pal. Catch up."

"A bullet through the brain is timeless."

"In your case it wouldn't make a difference."

Bitch. "Bian, listen. This is not a job for any MP—male, female, or anything in between. I was trained for this, I've done it half a dozen times, and I'm out of my league here. Also, Finder and his people are a team. Rule one, the team always looks after the team first."

"Then you should be glad I'm going. I'll watch your back. Promise."

When I made no reply, she observed, "Maybe I *need* to look after you." Anticipating my next thought, she added, "And don't even think about pulling rank. Phyllis approved this."

"Did she?" I looked at her and asked, "Why? What changed?"

"Nothing, per se. You need an interpreter."

"I have an interpreter. Some of Finder's men are fluent in Arabic and—"

"Exactly—*and* we don't really want them to know what's going down."

"That's ridiculous. Even if they find out about bin Pacha, they can't make the connection to Charabi or Daniels."

"What if they find out who we have our hands on? They lack the appropriate security clearances, they haven't been vetted, nor are they accountable. And think about this—a twenty-five-million-dollar bounty is on Zarqawi's head. Should they figure out who bin Pacha is, they might choose the bonus over you." She added, "You're going into Falluja. The perfect place for a perfect murder."

"This sounds like Phyllis talking. People she can't control give her gas."

"It was her brainchild. I'll admit that. But the longer bin Pacha's apprehension is kept under wraps, the more vulnerable his financial network is to exploitation. Hours make a difference. You see that, right?"

In fact, I did see that. Were word of bin Pacha's capture to become public, his contacts in the insurgency would shift locations and his financial sources would head for the hills, or at least cover their tracks.

Bian informed me, "Unless you have a better option, I'm going." She added, "You know what, Sean? *I* need to be there. You don't."

"I'm going," I informed her.

"Why? I see no reason for you to take that risk."

Neither did I. But I hadn't traveled this far to sit on my ass. This wasn't a valid reason but it was a good one. "I need to be there."

"You really don't. Take a moment and think about it."

I took that moment. The easy answer was that despite not doing this my way, destroying Zarqawi's supply of money might shorten the war, might save American lives, and if nothing else, would take one more jihadi asshole off the street. It matters not what branch you wear on your collar, what matters are the words printed on your chest: U.S. Army. Killing bad guys is what soldiers do.

But I knew there was an answer that was more complicated, and probably less noble. Two words: Bian Tran.

She looked at me a moment in the darkness. I couldn't read her thoughts; I didn't need to, to know what she was thinking: *Why isn't this schlub taking this excuse to get off this runaway train?*

She then did something that took me completely by surprise. She leaned forward and kissed me. She backed away, and we stared into each other's eyes a moment. She said, "You're nuts."

I was, indeed, nuts. She took my hand and led me back to Finder, who was conferring with two other men who had materialized out of the night.

Smith, still standing vigil beside the car, continued to spin on his heels and scan our surroundings. This was one paranoid citizen.

Finder introduced the new gentlemen and we shook hands. They were named Ted and Chris, and they looked like inflated balloons from World Wrestling Entertainment, large, immodestly muscular, and unlike their boss, these guys looked like they were manufactured to be here. They also were dressed in dark civilian clothing, which let them blend in with the locals, and also happened to be the right wardrobe for night action.

Chris smiled and said, "Nice to meet you." Ted grunted.

Finder said to Bian and me, "Have you straightened out your . . . difficulties?"

Bian allowed me to do the talking. I replied, "A minor misunderstanding. Here's the deal, Mr. Finder. We go in together."

"No problem."

"Major Tran is fluent in Arabic, and she will be the only one to speak with the prisoners. You need to tell your men this."

He smiled. "You mean we can't tell them to drop their weapons or you're dead, motherfucker?"

"Does that work?"

"Fire a few warning shots into their head first and . . . yeah, usually." He laughed.

Bian clarified, "The colonel is referring to any form of interrogation about their identity. Once the occupants of the house are in your custody, your men will leave us alone with the prisoners. There will be a brief interrogation to confirm their identities, and I'll handle it."

He thought about that a moment. "I'll pass the word." After another moment he announced, "My turn." He looked at me and asked, "Are you really a lawyer?"

"Are you really here voluntarily?"

He shook his head. "I don't understand why you're here, and I won't ask." He continued to shake his head. "A lawyer and an MP. I should've held out for a hundred grand each."

"We can handle ourselves," Bian informed him.

Finder acknowledged the absurdity of this statement with an easy smile. "Let me be blunt. My priority is my people. I will not let you put them at risk. If need be, I'll shoot you, or leave you in Falluja, which is worse. Are we clear?"

His tone sounded perfectly reasonable, which made it a little scary, like he meant every word. Oxymoronically, I was starting to like Finder. He seemed intelligent and businesslike, certainly there was no confusion where he was coming from, and I noted that his men treated him respectfully, if not affectionately. With the best leaders, loyalty up is matched by loyalty down, and the bottom line of loyalty down is to take care of your own first. This would be great if we were only part of his unit.

He allowed us to ponder this warning, then informed us, "You don't need to know how this is going down, and I won't waste an explanation. Here's what you do need to know. If you get separated, you're on your own. The target building is in the industrial section, on the west side." He looked at me. "Carl told me you have maps. Bring them. It's a small city, head due east, and if you walk fast, you'll make the outskirts within twenty minutes. Stay in your costumes till then. But once outside, ditch those Arab clothes. The city's surrounded by Marines, they've lost a lot of people, and this has put them in an ugly mood. They shoot first and sort it out later. It will be good for your health for them to see those American Army uniforms. Understand?"

I looked at Bian and she nodded. He continued, "I told the Agency you need to have compasses and a thousand dollars each in your pockets." He said, "Show me," and we did.

He said, "The money is life insurance. The Fallujans are less bribable than most Iraqis, but you never know. If you run into a terrorist, the money won't help; you're just tipping your own killer. If it's an ordinary citizen, on the other hand, five hundred bucks could buy a few minutes of silence. Start by insisting you're a reporter—they all know that word—then press money into their hands as fast as you can."

"Has this ever worked?" Bian asked.

He looked thoughtful, then said, "Not that I know of." He laughed.

He handed us each napkin-size American flags. "If you see American troops, wave these. It helps." He said, "My people will handle the assault and apprehension. You'll stay with the fire support element. Do you have a problem with that?"

Ordinarily I don't like being told what to do, but one should always make an effort to oblige his host. Also, on a more noble note, the assault element is definitely where the risk is. I said, "No problem."

"We've been told to take everybody alive, and that's what we'll attempt to do," he continued. "No money-back guarantee, however. If they're all asleep, we'll have a good chance. If they have one or two guards, well . . . those we'll have to take out. But if your man is a big shot—you wouldn't be here if he weren't, right?—he won't be pulling guard duty. These Arabs are very hierarchical; leading by example to these people means getting more rest, eating better, and taking less risks than the foot soldiers."

He turned to Carl Smith and ordered, "Trunk of my car. Get their weapons, first aid kits, vests, and night-vision goggles." He turned back to Bian and me. "The goggles and first aid kits are standard Army issue. I assume you know how to use them." We did not contradict that, and he asked, "Are you comfortable with M16s?"

We both nodded.

"Good. The safeties remain on till I tell you otherwise. Once again, until *I* tell you. I don't want either of you accidentally shooting my people . . . or yourselves."

Obviously, Bian and I had a few credibility issues. I said, "Carl mentioned safe houses inside Falluja—why don't you show me their location on the map?"

"Should it come to that, my people will lead you to one."

In other words, were Bian or I separated, incapacitated, or captured, Finder didn't want us possessing the ability to expose his team. As I warned Bian, the team came first. And Drummond and Tran came second. This meant last.

Time to exert the power of the purse, however, and I said, "Okay, now you listen to me, Mr. Finder. If Major Tran or I fail to make it out with our prisoner, no money. Understand? The prisoner, and both of us, alive—that's the deal. Protect us, or this whole thing is a waste of your time."

He smiled and suggested, "I think your problem will be a little bigger than mine."

"Not if one of us survives. Do you understand what I'm telling you?"

We stared at each other a moment.

He said, "I guess I do."

"Point two. The ingress and assault are your show. Neither I nor Major Tran will interfere. But once our target is in custody—once we start the egress—new rules. Your advice will be welcome, but I'm in charge and you'll obey my instructions."

"If they aren't stupid or suicidal."

"They won't be."

He looked at me a moment, unconvinced, then said, "Anything else?"

"The major and I travel in and out together. Who's transporting us?"

"That would be me. I have a few more instructions to pass on, about rally points if we get split up, how we handle casualties, that sort of thing. I'll explain it all during the drive."

So the ground rules were set. He spoke into his microphone and began instructing his team, all of whom began racing to their respective cars. I checked my watch: 1:30.

In another thirty minutes, one way or another, this thing would be starting, or ending unhappily, and I would be traveling home in a bag.

Bian squeezed my hand and whispered, "Thank you." Smith handed us civilian bulletproof vests, weapons, six magazines of ammunition, flashlights, first aid kits, and night-vision goggles.

Bian and I stripped off our abayas, slipped the vests over our heads, hooked the first aid kits to our belts, stuffed the side pockets of our battle dress trousers with spare magazines, and then redressed.

I said to Bian, "What if this guy's not there?"

"Think optimistic."

"I am."

CHAPTER TWENTY-ONE

The car was a red Toyota Corolla, and Bian and I sat, cheek to cheek, in the cramped backseat, Finder and the hulking muscle known as Ted in the front.

Virgin soldiers and virgin girls on the verge of first action tend to respond alike. For the soldier, there is a natural anxiety and a corresponding adrenaline rush, which tends to evoke displays of juvenile bravado, telling silly jokes and laughing too emphatically at the punch lines. A girl tends to react by asking silly questions, like, "Do you *really* love me?" Apparently there were no virgins in this car—so there were no bad jokes—but you could cut the fear and anxiety with a knife.

Now there was no traffic on the road, and Finder drove with his headlights off and his night-vision goggles on. This road was, for the most part, straight, and he drove briskly and confidently; with all the potholes, it made for a bumpy and uncomfortable ride.

After another ten minutes he began pumping the brakes when, directly to our front, four lights flashed on and illuminated our car. He came to a complete stop, and sat perfectly still.

About thirty meters to our front, I noted, two humvees blocked the middle of the road. A nervous voice in English yelled, "Driver . . . out of the car now. Hands up, and step out of the car."

Bian whispered for my benefit, "Nighttime roadblock. They're edgy. Don't even breathe."

I didn't move, but I did breathe.

Finder shifted the car into park, twisted around, and said to us, "Marines. I'll handle it." He opened his door, stepped out, and stood, frenetically windmilling his arms over his head.

An American voice yelled, "Do you speak English?"

Finder replied, "Isn't that a stupid fucking question? Would I be obeying your directions otherwise? Name's Finder. Get Captain Yuknis."

This was not the same as the old World War II drill where the Marine asks, "Who won the '42 World Series?" and the Jap is betrayed by his cultural ignorance and blown to smithereens. Without authorized passwords, however, you have to improvise, and a little colloquial profanity is as American as apple pie. A long moment passed without a response before a voice yelled back, "He's napping."

"Well, hell, boy, roust him. Tell him Finder's here."

I could overhear young American voices debating whether to trifle their captain with this. This appeared to be part of a Marine infantry company—about 180 short-haired hardcocks—and in units such as this, a captain is the commander, and he might not tell God what to do, though God pays close attention when he speaks.

After a moment, Finder yelled, "For Christsakes—would you hurry it up? Wake him up, or I'll have your asses."

A moment later I observed a gentleman, tall and lanky, striding through the trail of lights. As he drew closer, I observed the profile of a helmet and fatigues, which were Marine style, and overheard him inform Finder, "Dammit, Eric, I was having my first wet dream since I got in country. Got a woodie the size of Mount Everest. This better be good."

"Mount Everest? A white boy? Yeah . . . bullshit." Finder laughed. "Hey, better of been your wife in that dream."

" 'Course it was." He laughed also. "Both her sisters, too. Especially that big-tittied one, Elizabeth."

Bian whispered to me, "Pigs."

"Nonsense. Boy talk."

Somebody punched me in the ribs.

Finder informed Captain Yuknis, "Got a job tonight. We'll be coming out between four and five. Appreciate it if you'd pass word to your Marines."

Instead of replying, Captain Yuknis yelled to his men by the humvees, "Sergeant Goins, if you'd be so kind, extinguish those damn headlights before Abdullah the sniper ventilates me."

The lights went out, and Captain Yuknis stepped closer to the car and bent forward at the waist. I observed him observing us through the windows. To Finder, he said, "Who are the Iraqi ladies?"

"You don't want to know."

He was carrying a flashlight. He turned the beam on our faces and examined us more closely. To Finder, he commented, "The one on the left's a looker. That other one . . . whoa, my boner just blew a flat."

They both laughed.

I mentioned to Bian, "You're right—pigs."

Now she laughed.

Yuknis turned around and faced Finder. "About tonight . . . you might want to reconsider."

"Can't. This one's not cancelable. Not even postponable."

"Rethink that, Eric. Trust me on this."

This sounded like an ominous yet unclear warning and Finder did spend a moment thinking about that. "Give me an idea of what you're talking about."

"I can't talk about it, okay? I've already—"

"Just give me an idea of the time, Chris."

"Early."

"How early? Help me out here."

Choosing his words carefully, Yuknis replied, "You didn't get this from me. Okay? By four, I wouldn't be inside Falluja." After a moment he amended that. "By three-thirty I wouldn't even want to try coming out of Falluja. Get my drift?" He then said, "It's big."

Finder glanced in our direction, then said, "Allow us a moment alone. Please."

Captain Yuknis stepped back a few paces. Bian rolled down her window, Finder stuck his head inside, and in a low voice he asked us, "You understand what he's saying?"

"I got it," I assured him. "An attack. The artillery barrage will start around three-thirty."

"Yeah. And by three the whole city will be surrounded and isolated. My guys have been reporting heavy military traffic all day. So now we know why, right? These Marines are royally pissed off about what happened to four contractors a few months back. I knew them. These were good guys. It really sucked what they did to them, and it's payback time."

I looked at Bian. Without hesitating she said, "But not until three-thirty. One and a half hours from now. Plenty of time."

Finder regarded her a moment, wondering, I'm sure, if she had a death wish. He thought about it for a while, then said, "The risk factor on this just jumped through the ceiling. So I'm going to ask you—why do you need to do this?"

Because we're halfwits. But I said, "We can't afford to lose this man."

"He's *that* important?"

"In a word, yes."

He looked at her. "We're private contractors. But we're also Americans, veterans, and we believe in what we do." He leaned in closer until his face was inches from hers. "I'm going to ask once more, and I'd better hear the truth. This guy is *that* important?"

"You can't imagine."

He looked at me. I nodded.

"Okay. At three, we're booking, whether we have him or not. This will not be subject to negotiation. Understand? If you want to stay, that's up to you."

He spun around, walked back to Captain Yuknis, and they held a quick whispered conversation, probably him telling Yuknis what a couple of idiots we were, which corresponded nicely with my own view.

Finder jumped back into the car, saying not a word to us. To be fair, this was more than he bargained for, financially and figuratively. In truth, it was more than I bargained for—or more accurately, it was more than I'd been *told* I bargained for. No good deed goes unpunished.

He jammed his night-vision goggles down onto his head and his foot down on the accelerator. As he drove, he spoke into his microphone and updated his team on this newest twist. I could overhear only his side of these conversations, and it did not sound like he got any guff from his team. Then he informed us, "Two cars are three minutes behind us. Yuknis promised to let them through without any delay or bullshit."

Ten minutes later, I observed through the moon's illumination the looming silhouette of a city, presumably Falluja. I checked my watch—2:00 a.m.—and reminded Bian, "Come three, we're out of here also. That's an order, Major."

She patted my arm. A nice gesture, but it was not a reply.

I recalled from Eric's briefing that we were entering the city on the western side, known on local maps as the industrial section. And indeed, we soon were driving through narrow streets between large warehouses and desolate factories. It had the appearance of a forlorn ghost town—appearances *can* be deceiving, though, and here was a case in point; the intelligence estimates predicted between five to ten thousand armed beings living within these streets, the world's largest gathering of terrorists. Added to this overall aura of spookiness, no lights were on, though here and there I caught glimpses of flickering illumination from candles or warming fires. From my CIA reports I recalled that both the electricity and the sewage had long been on the fritz.

Well, in a few hours, illumination would be provided free of charge, courtesy of the USMC and United States Army Artillery Corps, and on the subject of sewage, the shit was going to fly.

The technical term for this is indirect fire, because the ordnance flung by mortars and artillery arcs through the air, as distinct from ordinary bullets that fly straight from point A to point B. Artillerymen cannot actually observe their targets; they impersonally adjust a few knobs and levers to set the elevation and deflection of their tubes and barrels, and let loose.

The result tends to be indiscriminate and amoral; a 155mm artillery round, for instance, has a killing radius of nearly a hundred yards, and it matters not whether within that circle are enemy soldiers or innocent infants—or gullible idiots sent by their CIA bosses.

Eric turned around in his seat and warned us, "One minute to the dismount point." I wondered if Phyllis had known about the timing of this attack before she dispatched us. You never know what she knows, which is part of her charm, and the vicarious thrill of working under her. I spent a satisfying moment dreaming I had my hands around her throat, she was gasping for breath, begging forgiveness, and . . .

"*Sean*," Bian interrupted. "I said it's time to put on your goggles."

"Oh . . ." I pulled my night-vision goggles over my eyes and the world turned varying shades of green. I looked at Bian, who also wore her goggles. Combined with the veil and chador, she looked spooky. As did I, apparently, because she said, "Haven't we met in a horror movie?"

I laughed. "I'm the creature from the black lagoon. You're from *War of the Worlds*."

Eric glanced back and said, "You two are scaring the shit out of me. Put your magazines in your weapons, but don't chamber a round. And remember—they stay on safe."

He took a sharp left and turned in to a long alleyway between two large warehouses, turned off the ignition, and said, "Let's go."

Bian and I followed him back down the same alleyway we had just come down to the street, which thankfully looked empty of pedestrians. Ted remained beside the car, and I realized his job was to guard our getaway transportation, which showed good attention to detail.

We began to jog, and Eric seemed to know where he was going. Somebody better, because I didn't have a clue. I had studied the city maps, but at night everything looks different, plus the jihadis had taken down the street signs, an indication they knew the Marines were coming and didn't want to make it easy on them.

We jogged about a quarter of a mile, which is not as easy as you'd think in a long black robe that I kept tripping over. How do women survive? The streets were empty, but I had the odd sensation that we were being watched. Actually, I was sure we were being watched. But by whom?

Eric suddenly made a sharp right turn into the entrance of a large, two-story warehouse. This was the back side of the building, and Eric had already informed us that the front side faced the target building. The door we entered was garagelike—presumably this was a loading dock—and we raced through a dark, cavernous empty space and then up a narrow metal stairway that led to the second floor.

As we entered, I scanned the room through my goggles and noted, by a far window, two large green men walking toward us. Eric said to us, "My guys. Relax."

The two men drew closer, and Eric gave them our names and introduced them to us as Jack and Larry.

We were all whispering, which was totally unnecessary. But I have noticed that in moments such as this, everybody lowers their voice a few octaves. Even badasses.

We exchanged pleasantries, and the one named Larry, who had a distinctive Queens accent, said, "Follow me."

We did, walking over to a window that had been punched out, offering an unobstructed view of the street below and the target building across the street. On the floor directly beneath the window, I observed empty cans of pears, a large pile of balled-up candy wrappers, six empty soda bottles, and assorted other nutritional debris. Presumably this was the observation team Carl told me about, and from the evidence, they had been here all day, possibly the preceding night, and were now experiencing severe sugar overload.

Larry seemed to be in charge and he pointed a finger out the window. Speaking to Eric, he said, "Right there—your target building."

We all looked at the two-story rectangular warehouse on a street corner. The narrower side faced us, while the wider side fronted the intersecting road.

He continued, "One goombah on the roof . . . right"—his hand shifted slightly to the left—"there. See 'im? Okay, another slimeball's hiding inside the front entrance. We wouldn't know, right? Only this hump sometimes steps outside to burn one." He chuckled. "Smoking truly can be hazardous for the health. He's mine."

Eric spent a moment visually surveying the building and then, addressing his whole team, said into his microphone, "Target building's two floors in height. Standard construction. Stucco over cinderblock, probably steel girders for the skeleton . . ." And so forth. He had an impressive mastery of architectural detail, and I wondered if he had been a builder before he became a destroyer. He turned to Larry and asked, "Other entrances?"

"Yeah . . . a regular doorway on the far side. Donny can grease whoever comes out that one."

"Okay." Into his microphone, Eric said, "There's an exit—a door—on the far side. That's yours, Donny. Anybody comes out, shoot for the legs." After a moment, Eric instructed Carl, my old driver, "A three-story building's due east of the target. You get up on that roof. When I give the go, take out the roof guard. Repeat that to me."

Eric listened a moment before he said, "Uh-huh." He then said, "This goes down in two minutes. Synchronize with me. Time is two-fifteen."

He glanced at Bian and me for a moment, and seemed to recall that we were extraneous; I can do nothing without being instructed.

Larry, the New Yorker, dragged over a tripod I had not previously noticed from out of the shadows. The three-legged device was a sniper's stand, and on the swivel on top was mounted a wood-stocked specialist European rifle I didn't recognize, with a screw-on silencer and a high-end night-vision scope. These guys had all the bells and whistles. Somebody was deep into the Agency's pocketbook.

Eric checked his watch and said to Jack, "Time to move." He looked at Larry and said, "Don't let these two out of your sight till I give you the signal."

Larry nodded. Eric and Jack disappeared back down the stairs.

Larry turned to us and said, "Wanna watch?"

We did, so we morbidly edged closer to the window as Larry hunched over his weapon and began adjusting a knob I assumed was a brightener for his nightscope.

A moment later, a four-door sedan, silver in color, came rolling down the street, no faster than fifteen miles an hour. It pulled to a stop directly in front of the entrance, a man stepped out, and for a brief moment he looked around and observed his surroundings. The car windows were darkened, making it impossible to tell whether there were other passengers.

Larry concentrated on his task and whispered, "Tommy Barzani. He's Kurdish-American and speaks the local patois. 'Cause of that, he always gets the shit jobs."

The man appeared to be an Arab, and was dressed in Iraqi casual, tan slacks with an open-collared dark shirt with what looked like an AK-47 in his right hand. He moved confidently to the doorway and knocked, yelling loudly in Arabic.

Bian translated, "He says he is carrying an important message and please open the door."

Larry, staring through his nightscope, mentioned, "The jihadis stopped using cell phones and radios months ago. They know we're listening, they know we track the source, and they know it attracts missiles. Now they're low-tech. Mail by messenger." He drew a long breath and held it.

After a pause, the door opened and a head stuck out. I heard Larry's rifle spit, and I saw the head explode, then the body connected to that head tumbled out of the doorway and into the arms of Tommy Barzani.

Almost instantaneously, two men, one carrying what looked like an Uzi, the other hauling what looked like a SWAT battering ram, jumped out of the car, lifted the feet of the corpse, heaved it through the doorway, and barreled inside.

Larry directed a finger at his earpiece and said, "Just got a confirmation from Carl. Rooftop guard's out of the picture."

My goodness—these guys *were* good.

Next, I observed two figures, Eric and Jack, sprinting willy-nilly across the street, then through the now unguarded doorway, into which they disappeared.

"What are they doing?" asked Bian.

"The initial entry team," I told her, "should be clearing the ground floor. Eric and Jack will rush straight upstairs and begin securing rooms." I said to Larry, "Right?"

"Yeah . . . like that. But likely, I just nailed the only goombah on the ground floor. All five should be upstairs by now."

I asked, "The NYPD teach you to shoot like that?"

"I taught them to shoot like that. SWAT instructor. Ten years."

"What takes you from the NYPD to here?"

Larry looked at us and replied, very slowly and very simply, "They fucked with my city. Now I'll fuck with theirs."

Interesting perspective. Interesting guy.

He cupped his hand to an ear. "What? Yeah, yeah . . . okay."

He looked at me. "Eric says you should get over there right away. I stay here, covering the block."

A minute later, Bian and I were crossing the street, and then we were at the entrance to the warehouse. I stopped and stood with my back to the wall by one side of the door; Bian stood by the other side. I whispered to Bian, "Weapons off safe."

"Eric said—"

"Who cares?"

"Right."

I said, "Cover me." She took a crouch, and I announced, "Entering now."

I went in, rolling on the ground, and then, coming to my knees, began scanning the ground floor through my goggles. I noted a lot of heavy machinery. This seemed to be a factory rather than a warehouse, and the nature of the equipment suggested the purpose of this building had once been tool die work. I also observed a line of thirty to forty large artillery shells standing on their bases in neat, orderly rows. These were not an ingredient normally associated with automobiles, unless they are being outfitted for one-way trips.

I continued my sweep. Supposedly this entire floor had been cleared by Eric's men and thus was hypothetically safe. But I'd known guys who walked into "cleared" rooms and were carried out.

Aside from the heavy machinery, the artillery rounds, and a gory corpse with only half a head, I saw no living beings. I made my way to the base of the stairs and whispered to Bian, "All clear."

In two beats she was directly behind me and we went up the stairs, stepping lightly, with our weapons pointed up.

A voice at the top of the stairs challenged, "You're Drummond, right?" I sensed that a weapon was pointed at me.

I had this weird impulse to scream "Allahu Akbar," which was not a good idea, and probably was not really funny anyway. I asked instead, "Where's Eric?"

"Follow me."

We took a left at the top of the stairs and ended up moving swiftly down a narrow, unlit hallway lined with four or five doors on each side. The doors were all open, and several were splintered, presumably the handiwork of the SWAT ram I had watched one man haul inside. At the end of the hallway was the final office, which we entered.

Inside, Eric was seated on the corner of a desk, swinging his legs back and forth, the picture of casual intensity. Two of his men stood behind him with Uzis directed at six Arab gentlemen who were lined up against the wall.

Judging by their states of dress or undress, the prisoners had been caught by surprise, probably asleep. One was completely naked, one wore underpants—boxers with little red roses, actually—and the other four wore trousers and T-shirts. None wore shoes, which was either a weird coincidence or, as I suspected, Eric's people had taken them away to discourage attempts at running away.

I removed my Arab headpiece and night-vision goggles, and withdrew the flashlight from my pocket.

Eric informed us, without apparent regret, "Aside from the two exterior guards, we had to kill one. He made it to his weapon . . . and . . . well . . ." After a brief pause, he gave us a verbal fifty-cent tour, saying, "They all had weapons in their rooms, if you're interested. So they may not look like it at the moment, but these are bad hombres. And maybe you didn't notice the artillery shells downstairs. Also, we collected two laptop computers. I thought you might want us to hold on to them."

"Good thinking."

He pointed at the corner of the room, where I observed a corpse lying on his back, with both hands folded neatly across his chest. His two forefingers were contorted into a small cross. Somebody had a sense of humor.

I moved closer and then examined the corpse. There was a small hole in the center of his forehead, and blood was spreading outward from the back of his skull, creating a small pond. Eric informed me,

"He was rooming with that guy," and pointed at an older man at the end of the line of living prisoners.

The dead man's eyes were frozen open with that look of somebody without a care in the world—at least, not this world. If this was Ali bin Pacha, we had a big problem.

Checking the next block, I asked Eric, "You're sure nobody escaped out the other entrance?"

"This is all of them."

I next walked down the line of six prisoners, pausing briefly in front of each one, and as I did, I directed the beam of my flashlight at their faces. The reaction of freshly detained prisoners can be very revealing. Here we had six men who probably went to sleep feeling completely secure in a city populated by their fellow jihadists, and were rudely awakened by strange American men pointing guns in their faces.

What should follow are a few moments of disorientation, confusion, and fear. At least this is what you hope, because it is also axiomatic that, during this brief period, prisoners are most likely to talk, to divulge valuable information, or to do something incredibly desperate, and often stupid.

And indeed, four of the faces revealed exactly the range of emotions an optimist would hope for. Fright, anxiety, confusion, even hopelessness.

This was definitely not the case, however, with the second guy from the end, who was heavyset and muscular, about six foot two, with a broad face that glared back at me with an expression of anger and scorn. Hardy Hardass. Also, there was a fanatical glow in his eyes, which is never a good sign. So here was one guy to keep an eye on.

The last man in the line was a little older than the others, who all looked to be in their early to mid-twenties. His face was long and thin, and I held the light on it for a long moment, and noted it was crisscrossed with scars, and that one of his eyeballs was milky white. A fairly handsome man, though the scars and eyeball, in this light, looked eerie, and you knew he was no stranger to violence.

He was grinning at me the same way a pretty girl smiles at the cop who has just pulled her over for speeding, confident she is smarter, wilier, and should all else fail, has big enough boobs to fix the problem. I studied his face, and he studied me back with a lurid nonchalance. Joe T. Cool, and here, I thought, was the guy to keep a close eye on.

But these were not trained soldiers, nor did they have a code of conduct for these situations, or even a modicum of training regarding how to handle themselves. If we were lucky, this was bin Pacha and his bodyguards; with less luck, here were six suicide bombers who didn't give a rat's ass whether *they* lived or died; only whether *we* lived or died.

As I moved down the line, Bian was looking over my shoulder and also studying their faces. I had the sense she was processing their deportment and making snap assessments, which, in these situations, you have to do. To Eric, I said, "You and your men take a break downstairs."

He mentioned, "You know we can't transport six prisoners out of here."

"How many?"

"One."

I regarded him a moment. "Two," he said. "That's it."

In any interrogation, it always helps to have a few prisoners to play off each other. Two was fine.

He pointed a finger at his watch. "Ten minutes. I hope you have a magic key to find your guy."

"And you're using up precious time."

He said, "Well . . . one other thing. They were searched. But you'd better keep a weapon on them, unless you'd rather we slap cuffs on them first."

Bian shook her head. I wasn't sure why, nor did I particularly agree, but this wasn't the time or situation to argue. Prisoners look for weaknesses or division in their captors, and this was not the occasion to encourage silly misjudgments.

Besides, this interrogation was her gig, and as she had assured me several times, she had considerable experience with this. A little late, I realized that I had failed to ask whether those were successful experiences.

Anyway, the six prisoners were following our exchange with considerable care and attentiveness, their eyes moving between our faces as we exchanged words. Standard behavior.

I was sure that three questions were going through their minds at that moment: *One, who are these mysterious people who arrived in the night costumed as they are, as Arabs, shoving guns in our faces? Two, why us? And three, since they aren't dressed in American military uniforms, what rules, if any, do they play by?*

Eric and his men stepped out of the room, and the door closed behind them. Bian turned to me, pointed at several candles, and ordered, "Light those. Now."

Her tone was authoritative, even harsh, though I knew it wasn't directed at me; she was now playacting for the audience against the wall.

And what you could see was how very surprised and displeased these men were to hear a woman's voice, and worse, that she appeared to have their collective balls in her hands. They weren't used to what American males had to put up with.

I lit the candles, and Bian removed her veil and then her abaya, and shook out her hair. As the English gentleman said, a rose remains a rose by any other name, and a beautiful woman is still mesmerizing even when holding a loaded gun to your face. Maybe especially then.

Now the six men all had their eyes locked on Bian. Two actually smoothed their hair and stood a little straighter, and the naked man immediately slapped his hands over his groin. Modesty was the least of their problems, all things considered, but it's funny how some people think, their reflexive responses at times of peak stress.

Bian repositioned herself directly front and center of the group, spread her boots about two feet apart, placed her hands on her waist, thrust forward her hips, and elevated her chin. This sudden metamorphosis from demure female to haughty dominatrix was a little theatrical, but also it was very persuasive—even I did a double take. But as with other forms of social interaction, an effective interrogation has to take into account local customs, belief systems, and communal fears. Clearly Bian knew this.

Here we had six Arab gentlemen raised in a culture where women are devalued, obscured behind veils, unable to drive, literally speaking only after being spoken to. And now, on top of the indignity of capture, it turns out an American woman—an infidel slut—would be conducting the interrogation. Bian understood their shame and disorientation, and now she was heating up their humiliation.

She allowed a few tense seconds to pass, long enough for it to sink in that this truly was her show. Eventually, in a very harsh tone, in English, she asked, "Who speaks English?"

No response.

She scanned their faces and announced, "I demand an answer," and she asked again.

Again no response.

"At least one of you speaks English. We know this. Step forward . . . now."

It took a moment for me to realize why she was so confident somebody spoke English, much less why it mattered. The artillery shells downstairs meant bombs, either the car-borne or the roadside variety; ergo, somebody inside this room had the engineering faculty to construct such devices. That meant a high level of education, probably at a foreign university, and probably he spoke English. In the pecking order of terrorists, bomb technologists are just below financiers, so taking one off the streets was like winning second prize in the lotto.

Again, though, no response.

Bian glanced at me. She pointed at Sammy Naked and Captain Underpants, and very coolly said, "Separate these two."

I looked at her a moment. She barked, "You heard me. Now!"

I stepped forward and, covering me, Bian elevated her weapon at the prisoners. I grabbed the poor naked man by his arm and flung him forward, then followed suit with the man in undershorts.

The two men now stood in the middle of the room, looking even more dazed, unfortunate, and confused, wondering what made them special and regretting whatever it was.

Bian ordered me, "Take them downstairs. Tell Finder to execute them."

She looked and sounded completely serious.

I stared at her back a moment, and she sensed my hesitance, because, keeping her weapon on the men against the wall, she glanced backward and winked.

She turned back to the prisoners and began speaking in Arabic, probably apprising them that their fellow jihadists were about to become compost.

I used my M16 to prod both men out of the room, through the doorway, and then down the long dark hallway to the stairwell. You aren't supposed to threaten prisoners with death or bodily harm, of course; but neither are you supposed to send human bombers into the streets to murder civilians. And on a more Zen-like note, if they did not speak English, they did not understand the threat, and it's not a threat. I hoped that circuitous logic would sound as good in court as it sounded to me at that moment. We had reached the top of the stairwell and as a precautionary measure, I called out, "Drummond coming down with two prisoners."

I had the prisoners lead the way down the stairs. They moved like sheep, passive, completely clueless. Neither of these clowns had the slightest idea what was going on.

Finder was standing at the base of the stairs and he asked, "Who are these guys?"

"Object lessons."

He looked at me closely. "Meaning what?"

"She's using the shock treatment. Divide and conquer. We culled these two out to be shot."

"For real?"

"No . . . not for real."

"You're sure? No extra charge."

I stared at him.

He laughed. "That's a joke, Drummond. Lighten up."

I left him with the two prisoners and returned back upstairs. When I reentered the room, Bian was still loudly haranguing the prisoners in Arabic. They were paying rapt attention to her and ignored me.

She halted her monologue and glanced at me.

I told her, "That second guy, the naked one, took three slugs. Boy, was he hard to kill." After a moment, I added, "He kept screaming in Arabic, begging to be put out of his misery."

A bit subtle, maybe, but I could see from her expression that she picked up the message—neither man spoke English.

She glanced again at her prisoners and commented to me, "I'll give you one or two more in a second."

"No hurry." I leaned casually against the wall. "Finder's guys are busy castrating them, and finding a place where their bodies face west. A good hidey place where nobody will ever find their corpses." I laughed.

Bian also laughed.

This coarse allusion referred, of course, to the dual Muslim and extremists' beliefs that a corpse must be cleansed and buried, facing east, soon after death for a suitable entrance to heaven; and those who enter as martyrs are met and pleasured by a flock of beautiful virgins, which, without your equipment, falls into the category of an empty blessing.

And, through the corner of my eye, I noted that the second prisoner from the left registered an expression of mild outrage. He heard, and more important, he clearly *understood,* what we were saying.

Bian picked up on it as well. She pointed at the man. "You . . . step forward."

He stared straight ahead, as if she was talking to somebody else.

Bian stepped directly to his front and positioned herself maybe two feet from his face. Joe Cool stood to the man's right, and the relative complacency and indifference on his face made this man's anxiety all the more palpable: Nervous Nellie.

Bian stared into Nellie's eyes and said, "Well . . . ?"

He shrugged like he was clueless. Then, out of the blue, Bian's weapon went off. In such a confined space, the loud bang sounded like a cannon, and we were all, I think, surprised and stunned.

I took a step toward Bian, but she turned to me and said, "Oh, shit. It was an accident."

"Accident?"

"My weapon . . . it was off safe, and . . . I . . . well, I guess my finger . . . Oh, shit."

Nellie Nervous had crumbled to the floor, and he lay there gripping his left knee, writhing, bleeding, and moaning something in Arabic.

I took a step toward the wounded man, but Bian said, "Sean, please, what's done is done—let me handle this."

I looked at her, and she did appear surprised and shocked that she had shot the man. She looked down at him and pronounced something in Arabic. But her tone sounded a bit harsh for an apology; in fact it sounded like a threat, and he quickly muttered something in reply that resembled a wounded animal mewling.

I said to Bian, "Whatever you're doing . . . stop now."

She ignored me and prodded the man on the ground with her boot. She said something with a harsh undertone in Arabic.

He said, "Okay . . . yes, yes . . . I speak English. Not good, though. Do not shoot me again, please."

Bian stepped back from him and asked, "Which of these men is Ali bin Pacha?"

"Uh, oooh, you have ruined my knee . . . Ow, I am in great pain . . . I—"

"Answer me. Which one?"

"Who . . . who is this name?"

"Ali bin Pacha. Point him out."

The man rocked around a bit, holding his knee and contemplating his pain, which appeared to be considerable. Finally he said to her, "Me. I am this man you search for . . . this Ali bin Pacha."

"Liar."

"No, American lady. This is truth. Please, not to shoot me again. Please—"

"You're *not* bin Pacha. If you don't point him out, I'll blow your brains across the floor."

On the one hand, I should yank her out of the room; on the other hand, I wanted to hear this guy's response. Possibly, his shooting was an accident, and while that act was unfortunate, sometimes good comes from bad. On the other hand, what if it wasn't an accident? Was she really ready to blow this guy's brains out?

She jammed the barrel of her weapon down hard on the man's wounded knee. He cringed and howled with pain.

That answered it. I quickly stepped toward her, intending to take the weapon out of her hands.

But Hardy Hardass had the same idea, and he was closer. He lunged at Bian, who was ignoring him, and had carelessly allowed herself to get too close to the prisoners.

Before I could take a step, his arms were wrapped around Bian, and he had her M16 across her throat.

He was pulling it upward, screaming, "Allah Akbar, Allah Akbar." Bian's feet were off the ground. She was struggling and kicking, but he was large and strong, and she looked a rag doll being shaken in a mad dog's mouth.

I drew back my M16, then shoved it forward, buttstroking the center of his forehead. There was a nasty cracking sound and his head jerked backward, but he did not loosen his grip. Now ugly gurgling sounds were erupting from Bian's mouth.

I once again drew back my weapon, buttstroked him harder, and I knew I had hit the sweet spot, because a loud "Ooof" popped out of his throat. He released Bian and sank to his knees, groaning.

Bian also collapsed to her knees, heaving and coughing.

Now Sean Drummond also had stopped paying attention to the threat in the wings, and I swung around and directed my weapon at the two men against the wall who were edging toward me. "Don't." They seemed to understand, if not my words then Mr. Automatic Rifle, because both froze.

Eventually, Bian pushed herself off the floor, stood, and straightened up. She picked up her weapon and turned her gaze to Hardy

Hardass, who was transfixed by his own problems, such as the torrent of blood flowing down his forehead. She said something short and sharp in Arabic. Slowly he stumbled to his feet and moved back against the wall. I asked Bian, "Are you okay?"

"I'm . . ." That answer stopped in midsentence, and she stared off into space.

"Are you—"

"Yes. I'm fine. A little dazed . . . out of breath . . ."

Before I could say another word, she swung to her right and—bang, bang, bang—first one, then another prisoner crumpled to the floor. I looked at her, and I looked at them. Two of the prisoners, like Nervous Nellie, now lay on the floor holding their hands on their left knees, writhing and howling from pain. The other, Joe Cool, sort of sank to the floor, staring at Bian, in no apparent pain, just mildly surprised.

I, also, stared at Bian. She avoided my eyes.

"What did you just do?"

After a moment without a reply, I told her what she had done. "You just shot unarmed prisoners."

She glanced at me, and for a moment I wondered if I was next.

"Hand me your weapon, Bian."

She did not hand me her weapon but did say, "I didn't kill them."

"Your weapon—now."

"I did what was needed. And it worked."

She straightened up and for a moment seemed to contemplate what she had done. I examined her face, and did not like what I saw; she should have looked shocked, or enraged, but instead she struck me as completely in control of her emotions and senses. Aloof, actually. Finally, she said in a surprisingly calm tone, "Sean, please. Go downstairs. Tell Eric we need him and his men up here right away."

"*You* go downstairs. I'm not leaving you alone with these men."

Instead of addressing that thought, she said, "Give me your chador, please."

I thought she was going to use it to sponge or stem the flow of blood from one of the men she had just shot. So I handed it to her, keeping a spring in my step and an eye on her weapon. Instead she bent over and used it to gag Nervous Nellie, who was making whiny noises and looked ready to empty his bowels into his pants.

Then the door burst open and the argument was settled about

either of us going downstairs. Eric and two of his men came barging through the doorway, weapons directed at us.

"It's safe," I yelled before anyone made a nervous mistake. "We're in control."

Eric lowered his weapon and examined the bodies on the floor. He said, "What the fuck?"

He was not expecting a reply, and continued, in a furious tone, "Didn't I tell you two to keep your weapons on safe? Holy shit—those shots were heard for ten blocks around."

I looked at him, then at Bian, and suddenly I understood what—and more to the point, *why*—she had done what she'd done. The message from Charabi to Daniels had described Ali bin Pacha as having lost his left leg, and therefore Bian had fired into their knees, a field expedient method for determining whose legs were real and whose were not.

I faced Eric and said, "Dress their wounds, and cuff and gag all of them."

"The hell with that. Those shots alerted every jihadi in this sector. Time to leave—now."

"Do it." I pointed at Nervous Nellie, and then at Joe Cool—aka Ali bin Pacha—who was observing me with a look of calculation from the floor. "They're the lucky two getting the all-expenses-paid trip."

"Are you nuts? Listen, in about two minutes the whole city is going to kick our asses."

I stared at him. He stared back.

He shook his head and turned to his two men. "All right. Hurry."

But Ali bin Pacha had other ideas. He suddenly pushed himself to his feet and launched himself at Bian, who was paying too much attention to our conversation and not enough to the guy her back was turned to.

He yanked the M16 from her hands and spun. It happened so suddenly that, before I could move, I was staring down a gun barrel.

I saw that it was pointed at my face, and in the brief instant I had to observe his eyes and face, I saw that his diffidence had disappeared; his lips were curled into a nasty smile, and his dark eyes were blazing with intense hatred.

I squeezed shut my eyes and heard a shot, amazed that I didn't feel my brains fly out the back of my skull.

When I opened my eyes, bin Pacha stood with his weapon pointed at the floor, and he was looking back at me with equal amazement. He sank to his knees and the M16 fell out of his hands.

I was yelling, "Don't shoot him. Shit . . . don't shoot *him*." Well, Eric had already shot him.

I walked over and kicked the M16 out of bin Pacha's reach. He was teetering on his knees, and he stared into my eyes, then down at his stomach at the dark blood leaking out of a small hole in his shirt. He looked a little surprised, and a lot annoyed.

I shoved him on his back and got down on my knees and pressed down hard with my right hand on his wound. I said to nobody and everybody, "Get me a field dressing. Now."

Bian handed me a dressing. She asked, "How bad is it?"

"I don't know. It's not pumping, right? So it's not arterial. That's good. But something vital inside might be punctured." I tore open his T-shirt and examined the location of the wound. He was going into shock, mumbling incoherently, perhaps curses, perhaps prayers.

The hole was about three inches to the left of his navel. I tried to recall from my high school biology days which internal organs were located in this region. Kidneys? Spleen? Intestines, probably, and that meant a high likelihood of infection. Also, I remembered from personal experience that, as wounds go, this one *really* hurt.

I reached a hand underneath him and felt around. No exit wound. So the good news was there was only one exterior wound through which he could bleed to death; the bad news was he almost certainly *was* bleeding to death, internally.

I placed the field dressing over the hole in his stomach and wrapped the tie-offs around his back, then knotted them tightly.

As I did, Eric and his men used green rags to gag the men, field-dressed their wounds, and attached police-style plastic cuffs to their wrists. In less than a minute, everybody was gagged and wrapped, and their bleeding was stemmed, which would put one point back on the board at a war crimes tribunal.

I glanced at Bian, who looked back and nodded. This was neither the time nor the place to discuss it, but we both knew our relationship had just changed.

Eric's men hoisted Nervous Nellie and Ali bin Pacha over their shoulders and hauled them out of the room. We departed directly behind them, leaving behind a corpse, two wounded men, and a bad memory.

Evidently, Eric had already alerted his people that it was time to egress, because two cars—the silver sedan and the cramped red Corolla—were idling curbside by the entrance.

Nervous Nellie was thrown roughly in the trunk of the silver car, and I helped place bin Pacha upright in the backseat of the Corolla, where I could keep a close eye on his vital signs.

We all piled into the cars, and Eric punched the pedal and burned rubber.

Eric had his night-vision goggles on and the car's headlights off. He was pushing at least forty through narrow streets with sharp turns that were unsafe at twenty. I couldn't tell which was the more imminent threat, a bunch of pissed-off jihadis or Eric's lead foot. Then I recalled how jihadis handle prisoners and said to Eric, "Faster."

Bian and I sat on both sides of Ali bin Pacha, and with all the sharp turns, he was being tossed between us like a broken rag doll.

In less than three minutes the buildings thinned out and we were back in the outskirts of the city. I'm usually good at remembering places I've been, and saw no recognizable landmarks, so this wasn't the same way we entered—presumably Eric was following good tradecraft and varying our route. I overheard him conversing with his team, and it sounded like one or two of the other teams were trailing us, guarding our back door to be sure we made it out with our cargo.

Bian said not a word. I felt no need to tell her how I felt. I was pissed; she knew it. Not only had she shot the prisoners, she had compounded her sins with inexcusable carelessness and twice allowed the bad guys to get the drop on her. The second time nearly got my head blown off; I take this personally. Also, our precious prisoner might not live long enough for an interrogation, this whole trip might be a waste of time, and Phyllis and I were going to have a long, one-way conversation.

Anyway, we now were out of the built-up area, bouncing along the same dusty road we took into the city, and I realized that Eric had somehow found a way to take us back through the lines of Captain Yuknis's company. I checked my watch: 3:20. I relaxed. Okay, Ali bin Pacha might expire before we got to Baghdad, but that aside, the worst was behind us. What more could go wrong?

Well, one shouldn't test the fates, because suddenly we were bathed in lights, and Eric hit the brakes hard enough that bin Pacha flew forward and slammed headfirst into a seat back.

The lights shut off nearly as quickly as they'd flashed on, and an American voice yelled, "Driver, out of the car. Hands above your head."

Eric stepped out again. This time, however, rather than the tall, lean silhouette of Captain Yuknis, the figure approaching through the darkness was short and squat, he moved with an affected John Waynish swagger, and he was accompanied by a pair of large Marines pointing M16s at Eric.

I rolled down my window and could overhear Eric and the officer speaking; arguing, actually. A minute passed, and things were not improving. Eric's voice was getting louder, and his interrogator's tone was turning nastier, and more imperious.

Great. I was here because my duplicitous boss outwitted me, my partner had just committed a war crime, my prisoner was probably bleeding to death, and—well, you get the picture.

I needed to vent, and this situation—and this guy—would do nicely.

I threw open the car door. "Sean, don't . . ." Bian insisted. "Please, leave this to Eric."

"Shut up."

I stepped out of the car and began walking toward Eric. In the near distance I heard the sound of M16 charging handles being cocked, and a little late, I recalled my Arab clothing. I stopped, reached into my pocket, withdrew my little American flag, and began frantically waving it, even as I slowly and carefully pulled the abaya over my head and set it on the ground.

The officer was yelling in Eric's face, "I really don't give a shit who you *say* you are, or who you *claim* you coordinated this with. I'm—"

"Captain Yuknis. I told you."

"Yuknis was called to a meeting at the Tactical Operations Center. I'm in charge now, and I'm placing you and that car under military custody. And yes, it will be searched. Explain your story to an interrogator when one becomes available."

"The car can't be searched."

And so on.

I approached the officer and directed the beam of my flashlight first at his chest, then on his collar. His nametag read Berry, and he sported the black bar of a first lieutenant, indicating he was Captain Yuknis's second in command.

I then shifted the beam to the lieutenant's face and was surprised by how youthful, actually baby-faced, he was. The longer I've stayed in, the more I've noticed that lieutenants are becoming younger and younger. But the junior officer in the military is an interesting creature, endowed with powers and responsibilities that far outstrip his experience and wisdom level. Some respond to this gap with intelligent humility, some with a self-destructive insecurity, and others by the silly illusion that it is deserved. Had I not guessed where Lieutenant Berry fell on this spectrum, he barked, "Get that damned light out of my eyes."

I replied, good-naturedly, "Good morning, Lieutenant Berry. Fine day, don't you think?"

"Who are you?" he demanded in a nasty tone.

"You're the executive officer of this company, right?"

"Who the fuck are you?" he repeated.

"If it was your business, don't you think I would've answered the first time?"

"Oh . . . a wiseass," he said, showing surprising perceptiveness. After a moment, he ordered, "Put your hands over your head."

"Why would I want to do that?"

"Because I'm ordering you to."

"Silly reason."

"Is it? I'll have you shot. Is *that* silly?"

When I did not raise my hands, he looked over his shoulder and said to his two Marines, "Search and cuff this asshole. If he resists, use force."

Before either Marine could move, I said to Lieutenant Berry, "Now would be a good time for you to slap your heels together."

"You . . . huh?"

"Heels. The little stumps at the back end of your feet. Assume the position of attention."

"I know what the hell heels are."

"Well, sometimes with Marines, you have to explain these things." I overheard one of his bodyguards chuckle, even as he stepped closer with his M16 pointed at my face. I directed the beam from the flashlight to my own left collar and said to Berry—and indirectly to his bodyguards—"Order that Jarhead to back off before I place you all under arrest for assaulting a superior officer."

I could see the confidence drain out of his face as he stared for a moment at the black leaf of a lieutenant colonel. He seemed unsettled and uncertain what to do next, then like the little martinet he obviously was, he fell back on military instinct, drew himself to attention, and popped off a smart salute.

I did not salute back. "Lieutenant, you have insulted and threatened the life of a senior officer." I turned to Eric. "You witnessed this, did you not?"

"Sure did. He cussed at you. Called you a bad name, too. He even threatened to kill you."

I observed, "Yes, a real snot. Any decent prosecutor will get him at least ten to fifteen in Leavenworth."

"Sir, I didn't know who you were . . . I didn't recognize—"

"I recognized you. We were a mere two feet apart. I see no reason why you couldn't recognize me." I allowed him the necessary few seconds to consider what an unreasonable prick I am, then concluded, "No, I'm afraid that doesn't excuse your behavior."

"Would a Marine apology do, sir?"

"Not even close."

"Well . . . I—"

"Lieutenant, how familiar are you with Article 834?"

He looked at me, then at Eric.

I explained, "To wit, interfering with, blocking, and/or jeopardizing the progress of a vital military operation. Just below treason in the Uniform Code of Military Justice and punishable up to life."

"But sir . . . I didn't know—"

"Ignorance is no excuse, Lieutenant."

"No, sir."

"The proper response is yes, sir."

"Uh . . . yes, sir. What I . . . well, what I meant—"

"If you'd be so kind, you'll speak when I tell you to." After a moment, I asked, "Do you have a radio?"

"Yes, sir."

"Where?"

"In the command vehicle, sir."

Now his voice was audibly quaking. Clearly, Lieutenant Berry was realizing that there are life-threatening dangers on the battlefield other than bullets. I said, "Call your unit. You will tell them that three civilian automobiles will be passing through. They will not be stopped, questioned, or in any way harassed." After I beat, I added, "I want each car saluted as they pass through."

"But, sir, I don't even know who you are."

"Son," I replied, using that awful expression, "I'm the guy who can ruin your life. Two seconds. Decide."

Lieutenant Berry used up his two seconds, then raced to his vehicle to radio his Marines while Eric and I walked back to the car and got inside. Eric slammed it into gear, and we quickly drove through the unit, where, I noted, the Marines were holding their weapons at the position of a military salute.

Eric chuckled and said to me, "And I thought *he* was an asshole."

"He's a bedwetting wimp."

"Are you really a lawyer?"

"Why do you ask?"

"Article 834? There is *no* friggin' Article 834."

"You're sure?"

"Yeah, I'm . . . Oh . . ." We both laughed.

After a few minutes, Bian urged Eric, "Hurry. The prisoner's breathing is getting shallow."

Just at that instant, to our rear, was a series of loud explosions, and the night sky lit up like a lightning storm sent by a very angry God, a God without pity, though this was just the opening omen, a foretaste of what was coming.

I turned around and peered through the rear window. Falluja had just entered the opening stage of the Marine Corps urban renewal project. Sometimes, as idiotic as it sounds, the old adage is tragically true: You have to destroy the village to save it.

CHAPTER TWENTY-TWO

The remainder of the drive to the airport took forty minutes, during which bin Pacha lapsed into unconsciousness and his breathing turned unsteady. We passed through only one more checkpoint at the entrance to the airport, manned by a squad of anxious-looking civilian contractors, who allowed us through without a hitch.

Bian then guided Eric to a covered hangar, inside of which was a large, gleaming Boeing Business Jet. The ramp was down and the door was open, so presumably somebody was inside. I walked up the stairs and stepped inside to begin my search for the doctor. The interior of the aircraft was hot and stuffy, and the crew seemed to be off on crew rest, because they weren't present.

To the right, I entered what appeared to be a large lounge area with walls of burled wood, lush blue carpet, a large video screen, a glass conference table, and a combination of lounge and office chairs, with an oversize plush circular sofa. I continued to work my way to the rear and next entered a dining room that was equally extravagant with a long mahogany table, coordinated mahogany chairs, and an impressive chandelier that looked like crystal but was actually plastic. Then there was a private office, a sort of cubicle with a large desk loaded with all the electronic marvels and goodies.

I could not imagine why the Agency needed this flying *Queen Mary*, much less how it convinced Congress to foot the bill. Well, I guess I had an idea: a sotto voce arrangement with certain members of the Intelligence Oversight Subcommittee who might need to borrow this aircraft for long overseas trips, in the interest of national security, of course.

Anyway, the plane seemed empty, and there were only two doors I hadn't yet opened, both at the rear of the aircraft.

So I opened the first one on the right and stepped into what appeared to be the master suite, a gaudy cage with rococo wallpaper, a mirrored wall, and a small bar, which I absently and unhappily noted was unstocked. Also, on the queen-size bed I saw a gentleman asleep in his underwear. I gave his leg a shake.

He opened his eyes and looked at me, blinking.

He looked fairly intelligent: thick glasses, thoughtful eyes, and all that. I asked, "Are you the doc in the house?"

"It's a plane."

That gift for pedantry nailed it. "And yes . . ." he confirmed as he rubbed his eyes and stuck out a hand. "Bob Enzenauer."

"What kind of doc are you?"

"Well . . . what kind of patient do you have?"

"A gut-shot one."

"Always bad." He sat up. "Allow me a moment. I'll be right out."

I left him and returned through the maze of aeronautic lushness to the hangar.

Bin Pacha now lay prostrate on the cement, and Eric and Bian hovered over him. Also, the silver sedan had arrived and Nervous Nellie was seated on the cement, looking more miserable and emotionally conflicted than ever with Eric's big gun aimed at his head.

Bian had knelt down and was taking bin Pacha's pulse. From Madame de Sade to Ma Barker to Florence Nightingale—this lady changed roles faster than I change underwear.

She looked up at me and said in a concerned tone, "His pulse has dropped. This isn't good. There has to be internal bleeding."

Eric looked at her, then at me, and said, "Sounds like we better conclude this deal quickly."

"The requirement was alive." I handed him the two M16s, and I noted two laptop computers and my legal briefcase and duffel bag piled neatly on the floor beside bin Pacha.

He glanced down at bin Pacha. "This is the very definition of close enough for government work. Works for me. How about you?"

Considering the ugly alternative—a perfectly healthy bin Pacha and a wall in Falluja decorated with my brains—I didn't want to sound ungrateful to the man who saved my life. "Deal." I looked at him and said, "Please pass my compliments to your people."

"I will."

"You do remarkable work." And I meant it.

He stuck out his hand, and we shook. I told him, "I'm doubling your pay."

"You can do that?"

Phyllis was going to go nuts. "I just did."

He smiled and patted my arm.

I mentioned, "About Phyllis, incidentally . . . are you aware she has an unlimited budget?"

"No . . . I—"

"Black money. Totally unaccountable. She can spend like a drunken sailor."

"For real?"

"I only mention this, because . . . well, before I arrived she was telling me . . . bragging, actually . . . all the other contractors get twice what she pays you."

"You're serious?"

"FYI. For next time."

For a moment we stared at each other. He looked like he wanted to say something. Finally I said, "Eric, as soon as you have enough, go home."

"Good advice." He turned around, and he and his people climbed into their cars and departed.

Doc Enzenauer now was hunched over bin Pacha, pinning an IV into his arm. He looked up at me and said, "What about that other man?" He pointed at Nervous Nellie.

"Just knee-shot." I pointed at bin Pacha. "He's your priority. Don't let him die. Do whatever it takes."

He gave me the Look.

I asked, "Am I overstating the obvious?"

"There's a folding bed in the crew's lounge. First door on the right. If you want to be helpful, get it."

Bian accompanied me, and as soon as we were inside the aircraft she pulled my arm and spun me around. She said, "We need to speak."

"Not now."

"You haven't said a word to me since the factory."

"Not true. I told you to shut up. That's a standing order until I rescind it." I looked her in the eye. "Right now, I'm not in the mood."

She was, though, and asked, "Aren't you going to ask me why?"

"You shot unarmed prisoners. Why would I ask or even care why? In fact, anything you say at this point can and probably will be used against you in a court of law."

"I deserve better than that from you."

"Do you?"

"I want you to know *why*. This is important to me, Sean. The truth—are you willing to listen?"

When I did not reply she said, "We were down to two minutes. I knew bin Pacha was missing his left leg, and I assumed he wore a prosthetic. You remember that from the message, don't you? So I . . . I shot them each in the left leg. It worked, didn't it?"

I had already figured that out. "Did it never strike you that all you had to do was lift up their pant legs?"

"Yes, but—"

"But it was just easier to shoot them."

"No, I . . . It was . . . one of the hardest things I've ever done."

"But you made it *look* so easy."

"Also I realized that if we left those men physically intact, they would be available to battle the Marines. These are dangerous men, hardened terrorists, murderers."

"Are you finished?"

"Not yet. I'm not saying what I did was legally right. It wasn't. I know that. Yet I still believe it was the proper thing. If it saves the life of a single U.S. Marine—"

"That's why the Army has its own court-martial system with boards composed of veteran officers."

"What are you talking about?"

"They appreciate the unique strains and stresses that accompany combat, the situational judgments, the rationalizations for questionable conduct, the extenuating matters." I opened a door, but it turned out to be a galley closet. "Save it for them."

"Sean, I'm telling the truth." After a moment she asked, "Why do *you* think I did it?"

"Maybe you snapped. Maybe you have bad memories of your time here, flashbacks, an illogical hatred of Arabs, or battle fatigue, or latent sociopathic tendencies, or PMS. Possibilities abound. I really don't know. I really don't care."

I moved toward the pilot's cabin and stopped at the first door on the right. I opened it and stepped inside.

"You know what I think?" Bian asked.

She doggedly followed me inside what appeared to be the crew's cabin. She said, "This isn't *your* war. How did you phrase it before? Correct me if I misquote you. It's just a news event, a tidbit tucked between the weather and the sports update. That wasn't only the great American public you were describing, it was you."

There were no fold-out beds, but I did see a door that I assumed led to a closet.

She said, "You're just passing through, an impartial observer, a reluctant tourist, emotionally disconnected. I'm not. Nor are the hundred and fifty thousand soldiers and Marines fighting here. It's life, and it's death, and that's how you have to play it."

"Bullshit."

"Is it? You didn't even want to come. You're here only because Phyllis and I shamed and pressured you into it."

True enough. And yes, maybe that did make it, not easy, but at least *easier* to pass judgment. I had *my* wars, *my* battles—Panama, the first Gulf War, and Mogadishu—and as my father likes to say about *his* wars, those were the last *real* wars. No, I had no emotional connection to this one—like empathy and sympathy; I understood, I just didn't emote. I avoided eye contact with her, opened the door, and inside was, in fact, a fold-up bed, which I reached for.

Bian said, "Look at me, Sean."

I looked at her.

"You weren't so judgmental tonight when we threatened those men with execution. That also is a violation of the laws of war. Going all high and mighty now doesn't look good on you."

There was no need to point out the difference between threatening and doing; she understood the distinction. And yes, I had crossed a line; she, on the other hand, had jumped galaxies.

She continued, "Had I been some burned-out, hyperventilating basket case, I would've killed those men. I couldn't . . . and I didn't. I deliberately wounded them. Explain that."

I couldn't explain it. Had it been battlefield rage or simmering racial hatred, those men wouldn't be crippled; they'd be worm meat.

But in the eyes of the law, it mattered not whether her motive was expediency—as she claimed, to separate the chaff from bin Pacha—or, as she further rationalized, to immobilize a future battlefield threat. Shooting unarmed prisoners is, at the very least, an excessive use of force; at worst, it is a method of torture.

"Don't be angry with me."

"I'm disappointed in you. There's a difference."

"That's worse." I looked at her again and noticed that tears were coursing down her cheeks. She said, "I think there's something between us . . . and . . . I . . ."

I grabbed the bed and tried to maneuver it out of the room. It was too large and unwieldy, and I said, "Give me a hand."

"Tell me what you intend to do."

"I'm going to report you."

"To whom?"

"When I decide, you'll be the first to know."

"Am I under arrest?"

"Not yet. But consider yourself under military custody."

"I want to finish this . . . I . . . I *have* to finish this."

"I can't trust you around prisoners, Bian. I'm sure I don't need to explain why."

"Then you're not thinking straight. You can't finish this without me. You know that."

"Do I?"

"Yes. If we can get bin Pacha to talk, how many lives might that save? You have . . . This is very importent to me. Come on, we've come this far."

She had a point. She understood the operating environment and she could converse in Arabic, whereas I couldn't even ask, "Who's handing over the moolah, bin Pacha?"

On the other hand, I could not get past the memory of those men toppling over.

She sensed that I was conflicted and said, "Satisfy your conscience after we're done, okay? Mission first, right? What is it they say about babies and bathwater? What more damage can I accomplish?"

"Are you out of clichés yet?"

"You know I'm not."

I looked at her. Against my better judgment, I said, "Promise you won't shoot anybody."

She smiled and crossed her heart. "Promise."

"No mistreatment of the prisoners."

"I won't even squash a sandfly without your consent."

"You won't even pee without my permission."

"That's what I meant."

"Give me a hand with this bed."

She did and we carried it out to Doc Enzenauer, who in our absence had also hooked up Nervous Nellie to an IV. The doc was hovering over bin Pacha, and he looked up and said, "He's stabilized. But without opening him up, I can't diagnose how serious his wound is. He needs to be on an operating table right away."

We lifted bin Pacha by his arms and feet and gently set him down on the bed. Bian explained to Enzenauer, "This is Ali bin Pacha."

"I thought he might be."

"So you're aware of his importance, and the complications. There are several field hospitals nearby. But you understand the sensitivity of his identity becoming exposed?"

"I'll give him a sedative that will keep him under and shouldn't react badly to whatever the anesthesiologist pumps into him." He added, "But I can't guarantee he won't talk."

Bian looked at me. "Well?"

"We'll move him first. We don't want an ambulance coming and linking him and this airplane."

"I hadn't considered that."

Enzenauer and I lifted up the cot and hauled bin Pacha out of the hangar while Bian trotted off to look for an MP with a radio to request the services of the nearest medevac facility.

I mentioned to Enzenauer, "I'll accompany you. After he's admitted, however, you're on your own. Long night. I need sleep."

"Well . . . that's why I'm here." He then asked me a good question. "How do we explain the victim? I assume you don't want him recuperating in an American military hospital. So, something that justifies a release as soon as he's ambulatory."

An idea was forming inside my head, and I said, "Tell them he's a member of the Saudi royal family. Shot by a terrorist, right? Stress his connection to the Saudi king and he'll get first-class treatment." I craned my neck around and looked back at Enzenauer. "How do we explain you?"

"That's easy. Lots of rich Saudis retain their own personal Western physicians."

I nearly told him I have my own proctologist, named Phyllis. He didn't seem to have much of a sense of humor, though.

He added, "I have a friend who does it. Lives in a monstrous mansion out in Great Falls. The pay is incredible." He chuckled and said, "My wife's always badgering me to get my own royal."

"Now you have one. Your client, Ali al-Saud, was here on a business trip. He didn't explain the purpose to you, because it was none of your business. Right? But he brought you here and asked if you wanted to accompany him to see the local sights. He was walking down the street, a stranger in dark clothing stepped in front of him, and bang. Completely arbitrary. Keep it simple. If they ask about you or your background, tell the truth. Just not the CIA part. The best lies stretch truth."

He nodded.

"So you put your patient in a taxi, rushed him here to the American air base, and asked for help. You ran into me by the front gate . . . I located a medic—somebody from a unit at the airfield—he provided the IV and blood. Right?"

"Exactly how I remember it."

"Don't mess this up, Doc. Getting him out will be Phyllis's problem."

We set down the bed, and about three minutes later, Bian jogged up. She said, "An air medevac's en route. Shouldn't take long. They're only three miles away as the crow flies."

I explained our intentions and she agreed it sounded workable. I told her to remain in the airplane and babysit Nellie Nervous and reminded her not to kill him. I promised I'd be back in two hours and instructed her to call Phyllis from the plane and update her.

We heard the *whack-whack* of helicopter blades.

CHAPTER TWENTY-THREE

Good news/bad news.

A suicide bomber struck near the city center, and our arrival coincided with the victims, a mass of broken, traumatized people streaming into the field hospital. Some walked or limped in; the majority were hauled in on stretchers. The admitting nurses were overwhelmed and rushing from patient to patient, sorting the horribly wounded from the merely wounded from the too far gone to save, a triage situation.

I had never seen anything like this. I had seen dead and wounded soldiers, but here the wounded were all civilians, for the most part women and children, looking bloodied and dazed as they cried out for attention and help. I saw tearful fathers carrying wounded little children, and little children standing with desperate expressions beside horribly mangled parents.

What did the terrorists hope to accomplish by this indiscriminate massacre? Worse, I overheard somebody mention that this was only half the casualties; the rest had been rushed to civilian hospitals, which eventually were overwhelmed and began diverting the overflow to the care of the U.S. military.

At one point, Enzenauer and I exchanged eye contact. The ugly irony of us bringing bin Pacha, here, at this moment in time, caught us both off guard and feeling guilty.

In this cauldron of misery and confusion, the admitting nurse asked only a few cursory questions and showed no curiosity or dubiousness about our responses before Ali bin Pacha was admitted for emergency surgery. In Iraq, it seemed, everybody has the inalienable right to get hurt without explaining why.

Doc Enzenauer dutifully emphasized the diplomatic importance of his patient to the admitting nurse, and a few minutes later repeated it word for word to an Army doctor, along with a few comments about his own credentials, which turned out to be fairly impressive—John Hopkins Med School, internship at Georgetown Hospital, specialties in psychiatry and the heart—and he was allowed to enter the surgery room as an attending physician.

I found a cup of coffee and sat and waited two hours before I could hitch a ride on a military ambulance transporting patients to the airport for evacuation to the hospital in Landstuhl, Germany. Both patients lay on stretchers, one unconscious, the other floating in and out, so dulled by drugs the difference was negligible.

An attractive nurse, who looked mildly Latina and seemed quite pleasant, rode with me in the rear of the ambulance. Her nametag read Foster, and I asked her, "What's your first name?"

"Claudia."

I didn't see a wedding or engagement band, and I asked the question I ask all attractive women. "Married?"

"Five years now. My husband's in New York City. That's where I'm from. The Big Apple, right?"

"Isn't that a suburb of New Jersey?" She did not seem to appreciate this comment, but she smiled a little dryly, and I asked, "Miss it?"

"What I would do for a real tuna ceviche. You know this meal? A Honduran dish. Served in a coconut shell. Muy delicioso. There's a restaurant in the city, Patria. Real Latin food." She laughed. "I still got four months left on this tour. My crazy husband already made a reservation for the day I get back. Is he some kind of nut or what?"

And so we passed the drive for a while; she loved her husband, she missed him, and couldn't wait to get back and make babies by the bushel.

Claudia was Army National Guard—a part-timer—and the last thing she or her husband had expected was a combat tour that interrupted their lives. I eventually asked her, "What happened to these men?"

She pointed at the unconscious patient and said, "Sergeant Elby is a truck driver. National Guard. Like me." She reached over and carefully adjusted his blanket, a gesture as unnecessary as it was telling.

"A roadside bomb, about a month ago. Both legs are gone, his left hip, too. Also his kidneys aren't functioning, so he needs dialysis twice a day. The damage from these bombs is . . ." She looked away for a moment. "He might lose an arm before we're done."

Not they're done, or he's done; *we're* done.

I glanced at Sergeant Elby—he appeared young, about twenty-five, and his face was heavily bandaged except for his nose, which was bruised, scabbed, and apparently broken. His left hand, also covered with scabs, stuck out from beneath the blanket. I noted a thick gold wedding band. I could not imagine this level of damage inflicted on a human body. In fact, I did not want to.

She stroked the hair of the other patient and commented, "Lieutenant Donnie Workman. He graduated from West Point only two years ago. Shot by a sniper during the assault on Karbala. The bullet entered his chest cavity and tumbled and ricocheted around, ripping up a heart valve and perforating a lung and his stomach. He's touch and go."

I watched her face as she stared down at these battered and broken men. I said, "You care deeply about them. I see that. Will you travel to Germany with them?"

"No . . . I . . ." She hesitated. "I'll hand them off . . . to the flight crew. It's a medical flight—good people, very competent, and . . . they don't lose many passengers."

She swallowed heavily and regarded their battered bodies. "We're not supposed to become attached to our patients. But you know what? You do. A lot of them never speak to you. They can't, right? But you learn so much about them. Always their friends stop by to check on them, and always they tell us this man is very special, and they tell us why, and these are the reasons we must save him . . . or her. Pretty soon, you know all about them."

She seemed to be experiencing separation anxiety, and she seemed to want to talk about them. So I asked, "Like what?"

"Well . . . like Andy Elby . . . he has two children. Eloise and Elbert, six and seven. Wife's name is Elma." She smiled and said, "They're from Arkansas, where funny names like that are common. You learn that stuff when you deal with a lot of patients. Anyway . . . Andy was a truck driver in civilian life, too. A simple guy. You know how that is, right? Poor guy, working full-time, doing the National Guard thing to pay for summer camp and braces for the kids. He never expected to be called up. Never expected this."

Again I looked at Andy Elby. If he survived as far as Walter Reed hospital, Elba and the kids would join him there, staying in temporary lodgings, living hand to mouth. Having had several friends who lost limbs, I was aware of the aftermath—a numbing saga of operations as the doctors chase infections and try to cut off dead and infected tissue before it works its way up, like cancer, and destroys the body. Elba would be shocked when she saw him, and she and her kids would go through hell as the docs tried to coax and force Andy's body back to a level where it could function on its own. As for what would come afterward, well . . . life would be different. Sad.

Claudia continued, "Donnie—I know, I know—I'm supposed to call him Lieutenant Workman. Anyway, Donnie was this big lacrosse star at West Point. A few of his classmates stopped by to see him. They told me Donnie was one of the most popular cadets. And academically, top of the class. His classmates all believed he would be the first general officer. Isn't that something? This is some talented guy." She paused before confiding in a low whisper, "I don't think Donnie's going to make it."

I took her hand and held it. "You're an angel. You've done everything you can."

Tears were now flowing freely down her cheeks, and Claudia Foster told me, or perhaps someone much higher than me, "I'm going to miss them. God, I hope they make it."

"Most do."

"And some don't."

We sat in silence for the remainder of the drive, me holding Claudia's hand as I thought about these fine, promising young men, and about the bombing victims at the field station, about Nervous Nellie, who constructed bombs that blew people to bits, about Ali bin Pacha, who gathered the money and wrote the checks that underwrote suicide bombings and street massacres, about Cliff Daniels, whose selfish ambition contributed to this, and about Tigerman and Hirschfield, who held open the door for the dogs of war.

Claudia said nothing, just attentively watched her patients. Her mood had turned reflective, and I had the impression that her thoughts, like mine, had to do with the consequences of evil and incompetence, of stupidity and fanaticism. She had no idea of the precise causes, but every day she saw the result, and every day she and her patients lived, or died, with it. I had a very good idea, and I wanted revenge.

The driver let me off after we had passed through the airport checkpoint, and I stepped out of the ambulance. I took two steps, then turned about and said to Claudia, "Were these men able to talk, they would tell you this: Thank you."

She offered me a faint smile and said, "Don't take this wrong, okay? I hope I never see you again."

I blew her a kiss and walked away.

CHAPTER TWENTY-FOUR

Bian awaited me in the plane's lounge. She looked up when I entered and asked, "How did it go?"

"Don't ask. Why aren't you asleep?"

"Look who's asking. You look like hell." She studied my face and said, "Is something wrong?"

"No, I'm . . . Where's our prisoner?"

"In the guest suite, locked to the bed. I barely nicked his calf. A flesh wound. I soaked it with disinfectant and put on a fresh dressing." She noted, "He doesn't react well to pain."

"Did you interrogate him?"

"I promised, didn't I?" She added, "I'm being good."

"And did you call Phyllis with an update?"

"I did. She sounded pleased. Incidentally, she's flying here."

"On her broomstick?"

Bian smiled and replied, "I'm serious. She's in flight, and the Agency switch connected us." She checked her watch. "Took off five hours ago. She's scheduled to arrive in seven hours."

"Did she mention why?"

"Well . . . no. But I asked. She said something that sounded evasive. She's very cagey, isn't she?" She made a sour face and added, "That was the good news, if you're wondering."

I felt a headache coming on. "I don't want to hear it."

She said it anyway. "Waterbury is accompanying her."

I collapsed into a comfortable lounge chair and thought about this a moment. Among the more agreeable aspects of working for Phyllis Carney—possibly the *only* agreeable thing—is that she tends to be old school. This is to say, she gives you jobs, she generally does not interfere, and if you succeed she treats it as par for the course, no big deal; if not, she fires you, and then goes the extra mile of ruining your career.

She's not vindictive; that would require a level of emotion she does not possess. What she is, is a throwback to an older era, a living time capsule of habits, instincts, and methods that reside now only in history books. And for my generation—the boomers—bred as we were to be unconditionally nurtured and blithely agnostic about personal responsibility, we are a little disoriented by a lady boss with such Calvinist impulses. Also, it strikes me that Phyllis is aware she has become a generational misfit; I actually think she gets a sadistic pleasure from this. Her nickname around the office is Dragon Lady, which I personally find insulting, disgusting, sexist, and dead-on.

Her flying here, however, was a curious deviation from her normal modus operandi, and that Herr Waterbury was accompanying her suggested other problems, and other issues. But what? Well, for one thing, a higher authority, like the White House, finally got its act together and realized the kids at the Agency were playing with matches around political dynamite. Maybe they didn't know everything, yet here we had a case where knowing very little could change the nameplate in the Oval Office.

So Phyllis, or the Director, or both, had been dragged down Pennsylvania Avenue, put on the red carpet, and read the riot act.

Which might explain, as well, her traveling companion. Either Mark Waterbury ratted her out or he was the watchdog dispatched to monitor or control her every move and report back. Those aren't mutually exclusive suspicions.

Or I could have this all wrong. The capture of Ali bin Pacha was a big victory in a war that badly needed a few notches on the success pole. So maybe they were flying here to make sure their mugs were in the victory photo. I could actually see Waterbury doing this, and it wouldn't hurt Phyllis to score a few brownie points either.

So, was it that simple and innocuous? Maybe. But maybe not.

This case just kept getting deeper and more complicated, starting with a corpse in an apartment, and now we had a bomber in the bedroom, a terrorist paymaster in an operating room, and if one or both of them spilled the beans, who knows what else might land on our plate. You like to think of investigations as ordered, a sensible progression of steps guided by a start and headed toward a tangible finish, where the lodestar for the investigator is the illusion that things happen for a reason.

But in truth, sometimes it's day by day, a journey without a map or an exit ramp in sight. In a way, I thought, this case had become a microcosm of this war, having looked so simple at the start and now our troops were sinking deeper and deeper into the muck of every tribal and religious and political mess in the region.

I looked at Bian, who was thumbing through a *TIME* magazine. I asked her, "Did you mention *anything* to Waterbury?"

"Sean, please." She looked up. "I'm not stupid."

"I know that." I bent forward, untied my combat boots, and kicked them off my feet. "Maybe he just misses you."

She commented, "I'll bet he misses you more," and went back to reading. "He doesn't want you out of his sight." Bian looked up from her magazine again. "Whew . . . what's that poisonous smell?"

"You're no petunia yourself."

She laughed. "I do feel icky. Did you notice there are showers on this plane? Two of them." She stood and began unbuttoning her battle dress blouse.

"Is there anything this plane doesn't have?"

"Well . . . the bar's not stocked. Maybe you noticed that." She bent over and began untying her boots. "Speaking of which, why don't I get you a cold beer?"

She wasn't expecting a reply, nor did she get one, and she disappeared in the direction of the forward galley. She reappeared after a few moments, down now to a tiny sports bra and camouflage pants. Part of me admired what a good soldier she was for staying so trim and fit, and another part—the more dominant part—noted that I was in the presence of the ninth wonder of the world, a half-naked woman hauling a six-pack.

She tossed me a cold one, withdrew one for herself, and there was that inspiring symphony of two cans opening simultaneously.

I took a long sip and said, "Ah . . ."

She said, sort of out of the blue, "I hope I'm not being nosy. Why haven't you ever married?"

"Why buy the cow when you can buy milk?"

"Stop being obnoxious. That was a serious question." She leaned her back against the bulkhead and studied me with her curious black eyes. "You're a handsome man. Rough around the edges, maybe, but a lot of women would find you attractive."

I decided I owed her an answer that was honest and forthright, and I gave her one. "Mind your own business."

She laughed. She took a long sip from her beer. "Don't tell me you're one of those relationship-phobic types. The instant the M-word comes up, you put in a request for reassignment."

"Time for my shower."

I got up and walked back to the bedroom at the rear of the plane. Right beside it was another door, which I opened and peeked inside. It was a large stall, basically a green faux-marble cage with six or ten shower heads designed by a sadist and passed off as a yuppie must-have luxury item. There was nowhere to change, so I stripped down to my undies in the hallway and stepped inside.

I turned on the water, slipped off my undershorts, sipped from my beer, and leaned back against the wall. The water was as cold as the beer, and it didn't feel good, though after a moment of acclimation it was refreshing and awakening. The soap was French and smelled like a lady's boudoir—personally, I prefer the odor of stale sweat—and I scrubbed off the dirt, washed my scalp, and was rinsing my hair when I heard a hard knock on the door.

I heard Bian's voice, but it was muffled and I couldn't make out what she was saying. Two thick fluffy white towels hung from a hook and I wrapped one around my waist and opened the door.

Bian, also wrapped in a towel, her hair wet and bedraggled, said, "I turned on the water, and it's . . . it's frigid."

"Maybe the plane has to be turned on for the water heater to operate. Do you have the key to this thing?"

"Then . . . yours is cold also?"

"Yes, it's—" And before I knew it, her towel dropped to the floor and she stepped lightly into my stall. In one fluid motion, she released the towel from my waist, pulled me around by my shoulder, and closed the door as she passed. Wow, she was nimble.

And then . . . well, there we were, a man and a woman, nose to nose in our birthday suits; actually, nipple to nipple. Bian laughed and asked, "Are you shocked?"

I drew upon my legendary self-restraint and averted my eyes.

Well . . . I peeked, of course. And hers was a lovely body indeed, built for comfort and for speed, lean and muscular, broad-shouldered, without an ounce of flab that I could detect. Her skin was a wonderful mocha hue, and all the appropriate plumbing and female esoterica seemed to be present and accounted for.

"Bian . . . what are you doing?"

"Don't you mean what are *we* doing?" She had grabbed the soap bar and began scrubbing my chest. "Hypothermia prevention, straight from the Army cold-weather manual." She laughed. "The doc's gone, the crew's doing their mandatory bed rest and . . . and well . . . the manual stresses that *any* warm body will do."

Her hand had moved down to my stomach and was heading south. I didn't recall that particular technique from the manual, but it was an effective improvisation, because I was warming up. I informed her, "I'm not sure this is a good idea."

She observed, rightfully, "Your little friend seems to feel differently."

"Little?"

"Well . . . bless my stars . . . From an acorn to a mighty oak . . . you're— Oh my . . . Water him and look what happens."

I laughed. I'm a sucker for precoital silliness.

She grabbed my arm, spun me around, and began soaping my back. It felt good. She began kneading and massaging my muscles; that felt even better. After a few moments of this, she mentioned, "You have a lot of scars."

"Well . . . I had an unpopular childhood."

"These look more recent."

"Exactly."

She laughed.

I reminded her, "Hey, aren't you a little engaged?"

She invoked those magical words—"Why don't you let me worry about that?"—and she spun me back around, handed me the bar of soap, and said, "Now do me."

Well, what could I say? No was an option—except reciprocity is the mark of a gentleman, so I spun her around and soaped and scrubbed her back. She arched up like a cat. Her skin was wonderfully smooth. And buttery.

For the next few moments neither of us spoke. The only sounds were water pelting off our bodies, and somebody seemed to be breathing heavily.

She turned around and stepped into me. "Now do my front."

I looked at the soap and then into her dark eyes. There's a big difference between the back and the front, and once we started this, well . . .

Actually, we already were well past the start line, and part of me was urging, very insistently, "Come on, Drummond. Bedwetting wimps quit. *Look* at that finish line—do this, Drummond. You can—you know you can . . ."

Another part of me was halfheartedly pumping the brakes.

Maybe casually tapping the pedal.

Bian sensed my reluctance and she stepped forward, rubbing her body against mine. "It's okay. Really."

I smiled, and she smiled back. She rubbed a little more.

So . . . here we were, headed toward no return.

And then . . . Well, then I did what no man should ever do. I asked myself the entirely irrelevant question: Why?

I knew a shrink would say this was a visceral, even predictable response to a mission that had been tense and dangerous. The human psyche gets wound up, and death and violence breed thoughts of procreation, which has something to do with sex. It's Freudian, or maybe French—inner peace through orgasm.

Also, aside from a few obviously minor idiosyncrasies—my occasional chauvinism, my pigheadedness, my faltering career—I am fairly irresistible. Women, after all, are willing to overlook a lot. Even my brother, who's a selfish, overbearing prick, always has a babe on his arm. I mean, I love the guy. I'm just not sure why.

Of course, he is stinking rich, with a huge house on a glorious bluff overlooking the Pacific Ocean. With women, that helps.

Bian rubbed a little more and said, "Excuse me, but I think I've made my intentions clear. It's your move."

Or was this plain and uncomplicated horniness? Maybe. But such impulsiveness seemed incongruous for a lady whose life and career were the embodiment of self-discipline. No . . . that just didn't wash, if you'll pardon the bad pun.

So, two possibilities. She was using her body to manipulate me, or she was making a huge emotional mistake, which was about to become my mistake.

Sex, in my experience, comes either at the start of a relationship, when intercourse is no more or less meaningful than a handshake—except nobody wakes up in the morning regretting a handshake. Or it is part of a ripening relationship, an acknowledgment of deepening affection, love, and commitment. Bian and I were more than acquaintances, and less than in love. In love and in battle, timing is everything; when the timing is off, what follows usually sucks.

I took a few deep breaths, stepped back, picked up the towel, and carefully draped it around her body. She looked surprised. "This is a joke, right?"

We stared into each other's eyes for a moment. I said, "Would you buy it if I told you I'd keep going if I didn't care about you?"

"That's . . . the stupidest thing I've ever heard."

"Right."

She looked away for a moment. "This is really humiliating. I'm throwing myself at you. I think you owe me a better explanation."

"Okay. I do owe you a better explanation," I agreed, trying to think up that explanation.

"I'm listening."

"This doesn't feel right. Not here, not now. You're engaged, and I particularly don't like the idea of sleeping with a soldier's girl. I think you're emotionally confused, and I'm not the key to resolving it; I'm part of the problem."

"Maybe you're overthinking this."

There was a new one; usually, I underthink these things. "Maybe."

"I—"

I put my finger on her lips. "Bian, don't talk, listen. We're both confused right now. You're beautiful and sexy, I'm very attracted to you, and . . ." I paused, then said, "When this is over, you need to have a word with your fiancé. We'll see where we stand. Sound right?" In keeping with the watery theme, I added, "This is either a rain check or maybe, in a saner moment, it will be rained out."

She threw a towel at me. "Being a noble prick doesn't become you."

"I'm regretting it already."

She was quiet for a moment, then said, "I have to rinse off. Since you're such a gentleman, why don't you get out?"

"If you hear a gunshot, it will be me blowing my brains out."

She smiled. "Oh, please don't."

I smiled back.

She stopped smiling. "Let me pull the trigger."

CHAPTER TWENTY-FIVE

I broke into my duffel bag, shaved, and changed into fresh battle dress. When I emerged from the stately bedroom, Bian had returned to the lounge and had her nose tucked back inside *TIME* magazine.

It's always a little touchy dealing with somebody after you've been naked together, especially when the chemistry failed and it's your fault. I needed a moment to think through my approach.

Well, the proper course would be to sit down and have an honest heart-to-heart discussion about what happened, to expose my inner feelings, to achieve an emotional communion. Men aren't very good at this; we're emotionally awkward, disconnected, and shallow. I can do better than that, and I decided I would. So I told Bian, "Time to interrogate our prisoner. Let's go."

She ignored me and studied her magazine.

"Now, Bian. We need to have this done before Phyllis and Waterbury arrive."

"Fine." She continued reading.

"Also, presumably he knows bin Pacha. A little background will help when we interrogate bin Pacha later. Make sense?"

"Whatever you say."

"You try to untangle whatever he knows about future bombings, and who he was giving his explosives to. You understand that stuff better than I do."

"I imagine I do." Her nose was still inside her stupid magazine.

"Good cop, bad cop—you're the bad cop."

"Naturally."

I stepped toward her and bent forward until my face was two inches from hers. "Put the personal issues aside. Mission first, Major."

She calmly put down her magazine and stood. "I'm not mad at you—okay? I thought about it. You know what? You were right. It would've been a huge mistake."

Boy, was I ever glad we'd had this discussion and got that cleared up. I said, "Come with me."

We went to the guest suite, and as we entered, Nervous Nellie jolted upright and stared at us. I approached him and untied his gag.

He wanted to rub his dry lips, but his hands were manacled to the bedposts, and he had to settle with massaging his lips with his tongue.

He would always be Nervous Nellie to me, but I asked, "What's your name?"

"Please . . . sir . . . my leg, it hurts. Most badly."

I repeated my question.

"Please . . . maybe you have . . . I don't know, aspirin?"

Bian looked at him and said to me, "Dead men don't need aspirin."

This, of course, was not a threat of death, which would be a serious violation of the Geneva Conventions; it was a statement of fact. One could see, however, where it might be misinterpreted.

Apparently this guy misinterpreted Bian, because he said with some enthusiasm, "I am Abdul Almiri."

Bian asked, "From where?"

"Please . . . I am most hungry, sir. Today I have not eaten food. You are required by your laws to offer Abdul food. This is so, yes?"

I nodded at Bian, who left to see what she could scavenge from the galley. Starvation is another violation of the Geneva Conventions, of course, and Abdul clearly knew this. It was ironic that this guy came from a movement that ignores every law of humanity, until the scumbags are caught.

There was intelligence behind those frightened eyes, though, in addition to fear and anxiety, and Abdul was testing to see what the limits were.

I pulled over a chair and sat down beside him. I confided, "I'm going to offer you a little free advice. You need to be careful with the woman."

"Yes . . . I—"

"Abdul, listen—what I'm telling you might save your life. She's a little unhinged."

"I . . . I do not understand this word."

"Crazy, nuts, batty, wacko, sociopathic. The lady goes violent at the snap of a finger. You saw this last night in Falluja. Right? One second she seems perfectly sane and under control . . . and then . . ." I snapped my fingers, and he winced.

Abdul was now staring at me, a little wide-eyed. He said, "But you are soldiers, yes? I am seeing that you and she wear the uniform of the American crusader." True to form, he reminded me, "The Geneva Convention does not permit these things."

"Look around you, Abdul." He had shifty eyes anyway, but they slid around in their sockets a little. I asked him, "Does this *look* like a military aircraft? And these uniforms? They're not real."

"I . . . I do not understand, sir."

"I'm CIA. She's Mossad, Israeli intelligence. A Vietnamese Jew, actually." He looked confused, so I explained, "Even the other Mossad people are scared shitless of them. They have this big chip on their shoulder, always having to prove they're real Jews." While he tried to fit this exotic knowledge into his frame of reference, I added, "And need I really tell you about Mossad? They don't play by any rules. She'll whack you at the drop of a hat."

There is no law against lying to prisoners of war, of course, and in this case, the Arabs have created their own boogeyman. They tell one another so much scary crap about Mossad, they believe anything.

But Abdul was confused. "Whack? This word Abdul does not know, sir."

"Means killing, Abdul." He nodded and I continued, "For her, it's a sport. She has this sick game where she tries to see how many bullets she can pump into a man before he dies." I allowed him a moment to consider that intriguing hobby. I said, "Two hundred and eight."

"I . . . What is this number?"

"Her record. At least, she *claims* that's her record. Personally, I think she's a big fat liar. I once watched her pump seventy-two rounds into a guy, and he was tall and real heavy, and he died. Blood loss . . . too much pain for the heart . . . who knows? But two hundred and eight bullets?—I think that's just bullshit. What do you think?"

"I . . . sir, Abdul does not know."

I thought he did know, but decided to help him reach a clearer understanding. "I mean, you saw her last night. Think back. Everybody got one in the left leg, right? Take yourself—she nicked you. She calls that her chip shot. Don't even ask about her hole in one . . . but it's . . . Well, hey, for a guy, let's just say it's the worst thing that can happen."

Abdul licked his lips and stared at me. "Yes, but you are the good and honorable man. I remember . . . you would not permit her to do this horrible thing to us." He tried a gap-toothed smile and revealed an unpopular childhood. "I am very much thanking you for this, sir."

"Oh, well . . ." I looked into his eyes. "Time was short, Abdul. I could care less, but once she gets started . . ." I leaned back in my chair and coolly informed him, "You're a bomb maker. We've already confirmed this."

"No . . . I am not even knowing these men . . . these men you captured . . ."

"No?"

"No. I was . . . How do I say? I was merely seeking a place to sleep. It is our custom . . . I am of Islam. The Koran requires such hospitality between believers."

Bian reentered the room carrying a plate upon which was a peanut butter and jelly sandwich and four or five small bags of trail mix.

Abdul eyed the plate before his shifty eyes returned to my face, trying to gauge if I was a big enough idiot to buy this. I informed him, "Mr. Almiri . . . there are two insurmountable problems. One, we found the artillery shells on the ground floor. Two, that isn't what Ali bin Pacha informed us about you during the ride to the hospital."

"But that is not the truth. I . . . I do not know why that man would make lies about Abdul."

"He told us you're a maestro at manufacturing bombs from artillery shells."

"I do not know this man."

"He knew you."

"Abdul does not know how to do these things, this . . . this making of bombs. I am swearing to you this."

Bian understood where I was going with this, and said to me, "The tools we found at the factory are being checked for fingerprints. The results will arrive any minute. I'll take his prints, and if they match, he's mine."

Coming from a third world background, Abdul had not anticipated this twist, and his face registered what an unhappy surprise this was. Where he came from, forensic science entails cops bouncing your nuts off the floor until you squeal.

I gave Bian a pissed-off look. "Hey . . . maybe that's how you Mossad people handle these things. The CIA likes to keep them alive . . . at least, long enough to talk. You can't just keep executing them."

She affected a bored posture. "The other ones never bothered you."

"They were different. He might have something valuable to tell us."

"*Him?* Look at him. A stupid mensch. Catch a minnow, and what do you do? I'm tired, and I need a nap. Let's get this over with."

"Well . . . at least give the guy a chance to prove you wrong. Maybe he knows something, maybe not. It's a pain in the ass to dispose of bodies."

"Oh, spare me. Stash him with the other corpses in the city dump. They'll blame it on the terrorists. They always do."

Abdul did not seem to enjoy the way this conversation was progressing, and he decided to join in. "Jordan," he informed us, "Amman, Jordan. Abdul comes from this city."

"How long has Abdul . . . have you been here, in Iraq?" I asked, imitating his third-person usage.

"One year. Perhaps a little more, sir."

"Before that?" Bian demanded.

"I was . . ." He hesitated in midsentence and looked at me. "Sir, please . . . I . . . if I tell you these things . . . I— These people, they will hunt down Abdul. The things they do to traitors, you cannot imagine."

Bian said, "There, you see. Now, will you please give him to me?"

"No, wait . . ." I paused, then asked Abdul, "Have you ever heard of the witness protection program?"

"Ah . . . yes, I believe I have seen about this subject in Hollywood movies."

"Same thing. We build you a fake identity and relocate you. Give you a whole new life. You'd probably prefer someplace warm. Am I right? Southern California, maybe Florida. Babes, beaches, and mosques." I gave him a reassuring smile. "Buy you a nice big house on the shore, give you a million bucks, with a fat monthly payment for expenses. What's not to like?"

Abdul showed some enthusiasm and interest in this subject and asked a few questions, which I answered, though possibly I exaggerated a few details. Finally, I assured him, "The Mafia mooks love this program. They swear that if they knew about this, they never would've been crooks, just hidden witnesses. Have you ever been to America, Abdul?"

"I have . . . yes. For one year. As a high school student. Michigan . . . but Abdul was not liking this place very much. Very cold, sir."

"Got it. Someplace warm. Now listen closely, because I only offer this deal once. Tell us the complete truth, that's rule one. No lies, no fibs, no exaggerations. Rule two, answer everything. Understand? We'll check everything you tell us, and later, we'll probably hook you up to a lie detector. No lies, Abdul."

"Then you are telling me I am in this program?"

I smiled at Mr. Abdul Almiri. "You have the word of the CIA."

He smiled back.

Bian allowed Abdul a brief moment to bask in his good fortune, then asked, "Where were you before Iraq?"

"Afghanistan. I was living at a camp. Teaching."

Bian looked at me. We both understood what this meant.

"Teaching what?" I asked.

"You must understand, sir, that I was . . . I was a simple teacher."

"I do understand." And I did.

"So I was—"

"What? What were you teaching, Abdul?"

"I was, uh . . . telling these students how to make . . . bombs."

"You're an engineer?"

"No . . . well, for two years in university I was studying this subject. In Jordan. But I was making the big mistake of hanging around with some wrong people. Crazy fundamentalists." He looked fearfully at Bian, the bloodthirsty Mossad killer, and explained, "I myself am not very devout, you must understand. Nor do I have great hatred toward Israel. But the Jordanian police accused me . . . What is this American expression? . . . " He paused, then asked, "Guilty by incorporation. Yes?"

Close enough, and I nodded. He continued, "And so, because of this . . . I was made to leave my university."

Bian asked, "So you joined Al Qaeda?"

"I was . . . very angry, you must understand. And—"

"And you joined Al Qaeda?"

"And I was . . . confused. You see, my family wanted—"

I snapped, "Yes or no."

"Yes."

So we went on awhile, and after additional questions we learned how Abdul's talents as a bomb maker were recognized, a little about his job teaching others to shred people into confetti, how he fled after his camp was overrun by the northern Afghan tribes, made his way to Iraq, linked up with some former Al Qaeda compatriots, and opened up shop here.

It was interesting, and at the same time disappointing, trivial, and also dispiriting. What converted this guy into a terrorist was nothing dramatic, no galvanizing grievance, no pulsing psychic need, certainly not the grind of poverty or any particular social injustice. He was an unpopular, slightly brainy kid from a middle-class background, befriended some religious zealots, this led to trouble with the authorities, and the next thing Abdul knew, he was manufacturing explosive devices for an association called Al Qaeda.

I detected undercurrents of self-loathing, mixed with social alienation, boredom, and a bit of an identity crisis. But in fact, his reasoning and his path to terrorism sounded no different from and was no more mysterious than a confused American kid who, out of peer pressure, the need to belong, and because it seems cool, becomes a druggie. But there was a difference, a big one: Abdul didn't blow his own mind, he blew up people. I asked, "How long have you known Ali bin Pacha?"

"Ah, well, I am not . . . not so long, sir. He was not in Afghanistan. Not of Al Qaeda. Also, his duties to the movement cause him to . . . to very often leave Iraq. He must go to meet the people who give us the money."

I repeated my question.

"Maybe . . . I think maybe two or three months. Please, you must understand, sir, we all move about. Even in Falluja, there are people . . . people such as yourselves who . . . who hunt us . . ."

He had no clue that the hunt to end all hunts was under way in Falluja, nor did I see any advantage from informing him.

Bian ordered, "Tell us about him."

He paused to think for a moment. Again he looked at me and said, "Ali bin Pacha is a tough, very fanatical man. You have looked at him in his eyes, yes? He is . . . I would not want Ali to think of me as his enemy. He has no fear . . . no remorse. This is proper saying, yes?"

"Is he married? Does he have children?" Bian asked.

"This I would not know about. We are not supposed to share these things. Some men do. Ali does not."

"How did he lose his leg?"

"I believe in Mogadishu, ten years before. One of your big helicopters fired a missile. Ali now has great hatred to America."

As I mentioned, I also served in Mogadishu, and it was interesting to learn that bin Pacha and I were there together. I recalled intelligence reports at the time describing Arab fighters—including one asshole named Osama bin Laden—who were supporting, advising, and in some cases, fighting alongside Mohammed Aideed, the Somali warlord who had helped manufacture the famine that killed millions of his own people, and who by then had turned his attention to killing our peacekeepers—and me.

Ali bin Pacha, by extrapolation, was one of those men, and by extension, we were dealing here with a man who had spent his entire adulthood trying to kill Americans. "He's Saudi, right?" I asked.

"This is correct, sir. His family is wealthy. And . . . uh . . ." He turned to Bian and enunciated something in Arabic.

"Very connected," Bian translated. "Financially influential."

Abdul nodded, then he then spent a moment thinking about what else he had to offer. He said, "Ali is very educated . . . I do not know his education, but it is said he was once a student at Oxford. He spends much time reading books."

"So he speaks English?"

"Yes, this is so. Better even than Abdul."

"What kind of books?"

"He has many of your American military manuals. He is very smart and he studies these books with great diligence. And he reads thick books about finance."

"The Koran?" Bian asked.

"Ah . . . no. But Ali is, I think, not like me, very devout. But he . . . I believe for him the jihad is political." He reconsidered his words, then corrected himself. "Maybe it is a personal jihad of hate."

I turned to Bian and said, "He wants to talk to you about bombs. Get me when you're finished." I paused, then added, "It would be nice if he was still alive and in one piece."

"No promises."

Ali looked very chagrined by the prospect of being left alone with a homicidal Israeli maniac, but I was hungry. I went to the galley, where I found jars of crunchy peanut butter and strawberry jam, a loaf of Wonder Bread, and a cold Coke. I made four sandwiches, heavy on the jam, and I sat and ate.

From my experience, once a witness steps over the line and becomes a squeal, usually they go from telling you nothing to reciting the entire Yellow Pages, trying to impress you with their newfound good citizenship. Anyway, I heard no howls or slaps and assumed Abdul was behaving and letting it all hang out. Neither did I hear any shots, so Bian also was behaving.

As I ate, I thought about what we were doing, and where this was going.

I had been involved in legal cases that became more and more complicated, one thing leading to another, some related, some not. It is an article of faith in law enforcement that those who commit one serious crime usually exercise a disdain for all laws. So as you investigate deeper, you frequently stumble into a briar patch of criminal behavior, additional crimes, and coconspirators. In those instances you keep plodding forward, putting one foot in front of another, and—if you keep your head screwed on straight—eventually it all makes sense, or it makes absolutely no sense, which can be a revelation in itself.

But this case had turned into one of those Russian Matryoshka dolls, where one thing always leads to another, and you become trapped by never-ending disclosures. So were all these things connected? Were they even related?

What we had here were Abdul Almiri and Ali bin Pacha, tangents, if you will—in Phyllis's words, low-hanging fruit—that, for good and obvious reasons, had to be plucked and squeezed. But they were also a diversion from our original investigation and it was worth pondering whether that was by happenstance or design. I mean, you had to consider the possibility that Phyllis hadn't been totally up-front about her motives for sending us here.

Security and confidentiality, she had stressed. And, okay, yes, certainly I could understand and appreciate how Bian and I fit that bill; good soldiers, discreet, obedient, plus we offered the additional quality of plausible deniability, which people in Washington value a lot. We were also plausibly expendable, since nobody would question two more dead soldiers in Iraq.

And then there was this: Were Phyllis and her boss the lone keepers of the Secret, they would have their own bedrooms at Kennebunkport and bandstand seats at the inaugural parade. Actually, they would pick who was being sworn in. Sounded about right. Were I in Phyllis's shoes, Sean Drummond and Bian Tran would be my first choice.

But considered from another angle, maybe Phyllis was jerking us off. And if so, why? Well, one reason would be to buy time. But time for what?

Or was I being unfairly suspicious? When you work for people who are paid to be underhanded, sneaky, and devious, it does tend to make you paranoid. Suddenly, behind every door lurks a hungry tiger, every order disguises a lie, and the mission that appears perfectly innocent ends with a bullet through the back of your skull. Then again, maybe my imagination was overworking this. But Phyllis does *think* like that.

After ten minutes, Bian joined me in the galley. She informed me, "His job was just logistics—no involvement in planning or execution of the hits. He just built bombs and provided them to others."

"It's a relief to know he's not such a bad guy."

"That was his argument, too. He insisted that he never personally killed or harmed anybody. You know?"

"I know. Did he have anything useful?"

"Not really. Turns out that the man Eric's men shot, he was Abdul's controller. He knew who got the bombs, the chain of supply, and so on." She picked a sandwich off my plate and began eating. "We should turn Abdul over to the military, ASAP. He probably possesses knowledge the Army will find relevant. Technical details about his bombs, for instance. That knowledge is always useful to the disposal units. The sooner the better."

She had been here, and she would know, so I nodded. I put aside the plate, and she accompanied me back to the suite. When we entered, I noted that Bian had positioned Abdul's sandwich about five inches beyond his reach. The man was contorted like a pretzel as he strained to reach it. He looked very annoyed.

I said to Mr. Almiri, "The Central Intelligence Agency thanks you for your cooperation."

He ignored the stupid sandwich for a moment, looked up, and offered me a broad, ingratiating smile.

I informed Mr. Almiri, "About that witness protection offer, after a lot of thought, I've decided on your final destination."

"Ah . . . well, sir, I am certain you will choose well. Abdul can be happy in even a cold place."

"I promised it will be warm. That promise I'll keep." He looked at me expectantly, and I let the shoe drop. "You're going to Abu Ghraib, Mr. Almiri. We're turning you over to the American military. You'll co-operate with them, or we'll tell the entire prison yard that you ratted out your fellow jihadis. Do you understand?"

Abdul looked like a guy on the verge of an orgasm being told to pull it out. "But, sir . . . you were promising Abdul—"

"I lied."

I thought he was going to cry.

I looked him in the eyes. "An hour ago, Mr. Almiri, I was at the American medical facility. Dozens of horribly wounded women and children were being rushed in, the result of a bombing. This might've been from one of your devices, or the handiwork of one of your students. Fry in hell."

I walked out.

Bian followed, and quietly closed the door behind her.

I headed straight to the lounge, removed my boots, stretched out on the comfortable sofa, and within three seconds was deeply asleep.

CHAPTER TWENTY-SIX

The alarm went off at 2:30 p.m. and I awoke from my nap. I walked to the rear of the plane, back to the master suite, where Bian was asleep on the big bed, and I awoke her as well.

We both used the bathrooms to dash cold water on our faces and brush our teeth, and then we reconvened in the galley. We brewed a large pot of coffee, poured peanuts and trail mix into a large bowl, and then moved to the conference room, where we settled in to await the arrival of Phyllis and Adolf Waterbury.

The few hours of sleep seemed to agree with Bian, and her mood had brightened—albiet still a little coolish toward moi. We chewed the fat awhile, the kind of shallow, aimless conversation people have who are just becoming acquainted—or who are working on becoming less acquainted—before she changed the subject and mentioned, "I liked the way you handled Abdul Almiri."

I nodded.

She said, "So you saw the consequences of a street bombing at the field hospital?"

"I did."

"What was your impression?"

"What would anybody think?"

"I don't care about anybody. What do *you* think?"

I put down my coffee and answered her. "These people are savages. They're not making war, they're mass-murdering innocents under the guise of a cause."

"That's it? Nothing deeper?"

"Tell me what I'm supposed to think."

She sipped from her coffee and stared at me a moment. She said, "You can't imagine how many of those things I witnessed during my tour. As an MP, we were often the first responders. I have dreams about it still."

"Dreams or memories?"

"They mix together."

"Tell me about one."

"It . . . it was my first. They all leave an impression, of course. But that first one . . ." She took a long sip from her coffee. "This was before bombings became the tactic du jour. I was in my humvee going to visit one of our roadblocks, and the ops center called on the radio and told me to divert immediately to a neighborhood in Sadr City, the big Shiite slum in the northeastern part of Baghdad. So I directed my driver to the street."

I nodded.

"It was only ten minutes away . . . and we came around the corner, and we turned onto the street, and I . . . Understand, Sean, the ops center had given me no warning—and a blown-up car was there, burning, smoke billowing up . . . and in the street I saw this huge hole and a blackened blast scar. But all around, there were . . . well, body parts . . . scattered like confetti . . . like garbage. Hunks of human flesh and limbs, arms, heads . . . and a lot of them were really tiny, and I realized . . . they were . . . they were pieces of children." She went silent for a moment. "About fifty people were just sitting there, wounded and mangled, waiting to be helped. The dead are dead . . . aren't they? They feel no pain, no misery, but the wounded . . . their wounds are so . . . so horrible." After a moment, she said, "You must've seen that this morning."

"I did see that."

"So . . . okay. How did it affect your view of this war?"

"It pissed me off, Bian. Don't ask me to think deeper or verbalize more than that. I really don't know."

"I see." She looked away and said, slightly dismissively, "At least that's an honest answer."

I squeezed her hand across the table. "I don't know what you want to hear. It's an ugly impression, an image so horrible and contemptible it's almost surreal. It was something ugly that should never have happened, but it did." I looked her in the eye and went on, "You've had time for it to congeal into something else. It takes time. When combat veterans talk about having repressed memories and flashbacks, that's what they mean. Nobody forgets. They just aren't expecting the instant when the carnage rushes back to the surface with full import."

She seemed to understand and seemed disappointed. She said, "I was hoping you would see why we really can't lose this war. Not to these people. Not after all they've done . . ."

Clearly something had happened here, something that had strongly affected Bian's view of this war. I had already suspected that, of course. But now that we were closer, geographically closer, and mentally closer, I was getting a stronger sense of how utterly obsessed she was.

Also, I guess I knew what she was saying. The idea of losing any war is militarily and politically anathema—for soldiers, it is a mark of shame and dishonor; for a nation, a strategic setback; and for the nation's citizenry, a mortifying scar on the psyche that never fully heals.

Like Vietnam. Here we are, thirty years after that last helicopter wobbled off the U.S. embassy roof, and still we haven't come to grips with it. And in the classic military sense that wasn't even a defeat; it was a negotiated withdrawal, a wearied and bloodied boxer refusing to fight to the finish, regardless that the other guy had been stomped almost to death.

But some enemies are worse than others, and the idea of people who are willing to unleash such nihilistic savagery, that we would let them win, that we would cede control of an entire nation to their blood-encrusted hands, clearly this was something we needed to think long and hard about.

These ruminations were interrupted by voices from the front of the plane, and after a moment Phyllis and Waterbury, accompanied by a third gent—Arab in complexion and wearing shimmering white robes with fancy gold embroidery—entered the conference room.

Phyllis was dressed in a smart blue summer dress, and Waterbury in a sort of tropical, crap brown leisure suit with white loafers and a matched belt that were in nauseating taste even two decades ago when they were in fashion.

After we exchanged a few greetings, Phyllis said to Bian and me, "You did a fine job."

"Thank you," said Bian, assuming it was sincere.

She then looked at me, and added pointedly, "I really wish, however, that bin Pacha hadn't been shot. What a botch-up. We now have to wait for him to recover before we can begin an interrogation. If he knew where Zarqawi was, that knowledge might now be too stale to exploit."

I had expected her to say that, and still I found it irritating. I made no reply.

She remembered her good manners and said, "Our guest is Sheik Turki al-Fayef, from Saudi Arabian intelligence. He is here, in an unofficial capacity, to advise us concerning Mr. bin Pacha."

Bian and I exchanged quick looks of surprise. Wow, a lot had sure happened since we left D.C. Unofficial?

Anyway, the sheik neither stuck out his hand nor even acknowledged our existence. He assumed a bored expression with his dark eyes sort of roving around the interior of the plane as if waiting for a salesman to appear.

Waterbury decided he had let too much time pass without making his presence known and said, "Let's all sit. Tran and Drummond, I believe you owe us an after-action report."

Without further ado, the sheik moved immediately to the head of the table, which told you where he placed himself in the pecking order.

Waterbury moved to and then sat at the other end of the table—ditto.

Phyllis pulled out a chair from the middle and seated herself beside Bian.

You have to pay attention to these things. Apparently Phyllis no longer was in charge of this show, and Waterbury was now the man.

Of course, Waterbury couldn't wait to confirm this, looking at me and saying in a commanding tone I found very grating, "Drummond, you lead off. Begin with a brief summary of the operation for Sheik al-Fayef's benefit. Then I'd like to know everything you've learned."

Before I could say, "Up yours," Phyllis interjected, "And Sean, please . . . keep it brief. We've had a long, tiring flight." Which was code for, "Play along with this idiot, and watch what you say in front of our berobed friend. And, yes, and since you didn't ask—traveling five thousand miles in the company of Mark Waterbury *really* did suck."

So I launched into a condensed, highly edited report about my trip, the operation to get bin Pacha, why a bomb maker was grazing on trail mix in one of the bedrooms, and so on. I treated it like a jury summation, which is to say the audience heard a selective, entirely self-serving version of the truth. I'm good at this. But having no idea how much our new Saudi friend knew—and not knowing how much he was *supposed* to know—I omitted all mention of Clifford Daniels, Charabi, and how we learned about bin Pacha in the first place.

Occasionally I turned to Bian to address a few points, a sort of Punch-and-Judy show about how we spent our summer vacation.

I skipped the part about Bian shooting our prisoners. She felt no need bring it up either.

Neither did I mention the shower thing. Why reinforce the sheik's Arab stereotype that all American women are sluts? And of course, Bian was listening. I wanted to make it back from this mission alive.

Nor did I bring up that I had doubled Eric's pay. I really wanted to savor the look on Phyllis's face when I broke that news.

Waterbury listened; to my surprise, he was playing against type, remaining attentive and did not interrupt even once, though he did look like his hemorrhoids were acting up. He was on his best behavior, trying to make a good impression on somebody. Clearly he was not wasting this on me, or Bian, or Phyllis. This sheik, in other words, wasn't just any old sheik. Nor, I was now sure, was he here to "advise" us. But what did unofficial mean?

Phyllis posed a few questions, all of which in one way or another concerned conditions inside Falluja. None seemed to reveal any particular bearing on the issue at hand, and presumably were related to something else on her plate. This lady always had ten balls up in the air, with three more hidden underneath her skirt.

For his part, Sheik Turki al-Fayef looked like he wanted to be anywhere but here. He occasionally yawned, or rolled his head, or drummed his fingers on the table. He chain-smoked four or five really stinky French cigarettes, polluting the entire room.

This being a U.S. government aircraft, I could only imagine the repressed anguish inside Waterbury's manual-riddled mind. I was really tempted to ask the sheik to fire one up for me, and I don't even smoke.

At one point, while Bian handled the talking, I examined our exotic friend more closely. A little fleshy and jowly, late-fortyish, with quick black eyes and one of those dashing, daggerish goatees. For some reason, the descriptive "devilishly handsome" popped to mind, which I found funny. I mean, he really *did* look like the devil. I had this odd thought that the ancient Christians must've framed Arab males as their models for Satan. So what did the Arabs' devil look like? Probably like some chubby whitebread in preppy clothes from Connecticut. And their hell probably resembled New Jersey, which actually isn't all that far from our idea of hell.

Also I suspected his show of diffidence was just that—an act. Beneath that veneer of cool apathy probably lurked a first-class thespian and a sophisticated intellect firing on twelve cylinders. I had known senior Army officers who employ this same technique. It's about power, the power to appear bored, to display bad manners in the presence of underlings. It's all illusion, of course; just like power. Anyway, I ended our spiel by recommending, "We believe Abdul Almiri should be turned over to the military as quickly as possible." I turned to Phyllis and observed, "The Baghdad field station can handle that without exposing our fingerprints."

Waterbury answered for her. He said, "I'll handle it."

"How will you handle it?" I asked.

"That's none of your business."

"Mark, it *is* our business," Phyllis interjected.

"All right, I'll . . . I'll tell the Army one of my people is over here and arrested him."

I exchanged looks with Phyllis. She artfully suggested to Waterbury, "Don't you think they'll wonder why the Pentagon special unit has people over here? You could blow this entire operation."

"Maybe . . . Well, I'll consider it." We all were left with the impression that he might accept that cost as long as he got official credit for capturing a bomber. I had this mental image of Waterbury back home, seated with his pals, smoking a big stogie, rolling a snifter of cognac around his palm, and saying something like, "So let me tell you how I bagged the biggest, baddest bomber in Baghdad . . ."

If this man were any stupider he would have to be watered twice a week.

Phyllis changed topics and informed Bian and me, "Doctor

Enzenauer called about an hour ago. Ali bin Pacha's wound was cleansed and sutured. He's recovering in the post-op."

"So he's going to be okay?" asked Bian.

"The risk now is an internal infection, and that will have to be watched. But in Enzenauer's opinion, he should be ambulatory in about two days."

Bian looked a little relieved, as well she should. Had bin Pacha expired on the operating table, she would've had a few difficult issues to explain.

Everybody was now smiling, and I decided to burst their bubbles, commenting, "I don't think we're going to crack this guy."

"What does that mean?" asked Phyllis.

So I spent a moment regaling her and the others about what we learned from Abdul Almiri regarding Ali bin Pacha, closing with an interesting personal observation I picked up while he was pointing a gun at my head. "There was this moment," I told them, "a millisecond . . . when we just looked into each other's eyes. Melodramatic as this might sound . . . it was like we looked into each other's souls. What I saw in that instant was hatred, a rage that bordered on madness."

Bian smiled and said, "I wonder what he saw in your eyes."

Waterbury cracked, "Were you expecting him to smile, Drummond? He had comrades who were dead or shot. He had just been captured."

Actually, I recalled, bin Pacha had smiled. I said to Waterbury, "How would you know? I don't recall you being there."

He gave me a nasty look.

Phyllis intervened before this turned even nastier and asked, "What's your point, Sean?"

"Breaking bin Pacha will require ingenuity, luck, and time. Months, maybe years. He won't fall for the usual interrogatory tricks and gimmicks, nor will he be goaded into the sloppy mistakes you associate with common criminals." Glancing in the sheik's direction, I added, "In the event anybody *is* considering beating the truth out of him, pain will only fuel his indignation and rage."

Phyllis asked, "Are you inferring bin Pacha has a martyr complex?"

"Well . . ." What was I inferring? "Think of this man like steel. He prefers heat. It tempers him, makes him stronger."

Waterbury regarded me a moment, then said, "You claim to

know a lot about this man. Yet you admitted that you never spoke with him, so that strikes me as . . . absurd."

I smiled back. "I have a strong intuitive sense. For instance, I didn't like you three seconds after we met."

He thought this deserved a serious response and replied, "Yes, but we actually spoke for a while."

Why do I waste my wit on guys like this?

So I ignored him and looked at the other faces around the table. Deciding to treat this like a courtroom summation, I said, "Let's review what we *do* know about Ali bin Pacha. He has been a terrorist his entire adulthood, having survived over a decade in a business we've done our best to make risky. In fact, he was handpicked by al-Zarqawi to represent his movement to outside investors. This is noteworthy. Ali bin Pacha is the chosen face of his organization. This suggests great confidence that he will protect his group's most precious secrets. And further, that he would be viewed by prospective investors as an inspiration, a poster boy for how terrorists look and act. Bottom line, his peers don't underestimate him, and neither should we."

Everybody thought about that for a moment.

Bian nodded at me, signaling her agreement with this assessment.

The sheik said nothing. He was leaning back in his chair, concentrating with great intensity on the glowing tip of his cigarette. Maybe I misjudged this guy, maybe he had a grapefruit for a brain.

Mr. Waterbury broke that silence and informed us, "In my experience, everybody talks." When nobody picked up on that thread, he said, "You just have to find the right approach."

What did he think we were talking about?

The sheik finally looked up and, in surprisingly good English, said, "The colonel has an excellent understanding of this man."

He poked his cigarette at Waterbury. "Ali bin Pacha descends from many generations of Bedouin warriors. He is not like these people from Jordan or Pakistan or Syria. These men, such as your Jordanian prisoner, they are peasants playing at warriors. Ali bin Pacha was bred differently."

"Is that right?" asked Waterbury.

"He is what we call *takfiri*. You know this term? They are worse even than Al Qaeda. Very fanatical, very destructive."

"I suppose you would know," Waterbury replied.

"I do know," he confirmed, which I thought was interesting, if not revealing. "And you will be glad to know I can offer a solution."

Everybody craned forward, anxious to hear this loaded announcement.

"Turn Ali bin Pacha over to me," he told us. "He is of us. We understand him."

Waterbury suggested, "You're referring to rendition?"

"Okay. I am not certain of your precise American expression, but I know it is done." He looked around at our faces and added, "I will of course provide you the fruits of whatever our interrogators obtain."

I leaned forward. "Excuse me."

Waterbury ignored my intrusion and said, "An excellent idea." He looked thoughtful for a moment, which is like watching a beauty contestant tell you she dreams of world peace; even when it's sincere, it's the depth of thought that's scary. Eventually, he said, "Sheik al-Fayef's people have expertise and the resources . . . and well . . . let's be blunt—the Saudis enjoy certain . . . exclusive prerogatives."

By prerogatives he meant the Saudis could electrify his gonads until bin Pacha realized that the truth might not set you free; it can, however, literally save your balls.

The sheik, however, looked annoyed by this innuendo. He said, "It is true that we possess certain . . . resources, and, let me be blunt . . . certain human and cultural insights that American interrogators lack. However, we are not barbarians. We do not resort to torture. I give you my vow that we will not employ such treatment on this man."

I turned to the sheik and noted, "In fact, U.S. law requires a written assurance of humane treatment from the receiving nation before a prisoner can be rendered."

"Is this so?"

"This is so."

"I had no idea."

"It just seemed strange that you phrased it that way."

"Yes," he noted, "of course it was only coincidental."

Apparently, his English wasn't *that* good; he meant rehearsed.

I glanced at Phyllis, who was toying with her pen, as though this discussion had nothing to do with her—what it actually meant was that she didn't need to hear it a second time. I was tempted to walk around the table and inspect her elbow to see how hard it had been twisted. I love conversations where everybody's reading from a script.

I looked at Bian. She raised an eyebrow and stared back. Belatedly, we both were coming to the realization that the powers back in Washington had concluded that bin Pacha was a hot potato best passed to our Saudi friends.

I didn't really have time to analyze this. Parts of it, however, weren't all that complicated: bin Pacha was a potential embarrassment to somebody; Bian and I weren't grown up enough to comprehend or manage the subtleties; and definitely, Turki al-Fayef wasn't here as an advisor.

Anyway, Waterbury, showing his usual finesse, was pushing things along, and he declared, "All right, that's settled." He stood, apparently assuming this meeting was over, and said to his sheik friend, "As soon as you bring in a plane, we'll transfer your prisoner. Questions?"

Phyllis raised no objections, so to help her out, I mentioned, "You can't give what you don't have."

"What are you talking about?" asked Waterbury.

"What are we all talking about, Waterbury? Ali bin Pacha. I'm not releasing him."

"You know what, Drummond?" Waterbury replied. "You're an even dumber son of a bitch than I thought. You work for the United States government."

"And why am I having to remind a former MP of the legal definitions of apprehending officer and current custody? As an officer of the court, until I sign a statement of transfer, Ali bin Pacha is my prisoner."

Bian was just opening her mouth, but only one idiot needed to jump off this cliff. I nudged her shin under the table.

"You'll do as you're ordered, Drummond."

"By whom?"

"By me."

"Let me repeat my favorite phrase. I don't work for you, Waterbury." I looked him in the eye and noted, "Tell me who's ordering you and maybe I'll change my mind." My fingers were crossed, of course.

He chose to ignore my query, as I suspected he might. He turned to Phyllis. "Order him to turn over the prisoner."

I had this weird feeling that I was in the movie *Groundhog Day*, and we were right back where we started, with Waterbury ordering Phyllis to order me to hand over Daniels's computer. This time, though, I did not trust Phyllis to respond appropriately. So before she could comply, I instructed him and her, "I no longer work for Ms. Carney either."

Even Phyllis's jaw dropped an inch over that one, which was a treat.

I withdrew the typed orders from my pocket and held them aloft for everybody to observe. "My boss is the Chief of the JAG Corps. Why don't you call and ask him to order me to turn over my prisoner?"

Waterbury stared at the orders for a moment. "This is preposterous. Jesus H. Christ . . . we all know those orders are phony."

"I don't know that."

"You're pissing me off, Drummond."

Exactly. And so on; around and around we went for a while.

The sheik's head swiveled back and forth, from Waterbury to me, and he stroked his beard and tried to look like he was following this brouhaha between a high official and a lowly functionary. It has been my experience, however, with officials from—how do I express this politely?—from less than democratic nations, that they are laughably clueless about issues that can't be handled through a barked threat or a visit in the night. At least he no longer looked bored or disinterested.

Anyway, it was time to call Waterbury's bluff; unfortunately he was in the middle of a long-winded homily about my duties as a commissioned officer, the constitutional subservience of the uniformed military to civilian authority, and any second, we'd be into the Father, Son, and Holy Ghost.

So the first time he paused to catch his breath, I broke in and said, "Here's another legal reality. Rendition requires a signed authorization by the Department of Justice."

"That's ridiculous."

With lawyer logic, I replied, "Yes, and it's the law."

Waterbury gave me a puzzled stare.

This man was entirely clueless regarding the legal aspects of rendition, which opened the tantalizing question of exactly whose idea this was. Three possibilities. Option A, for an unknown reason, was that somebody in Washington wanted bin Pacha buried forever in a Saudi vault. Option B, somebody in D.C. liked the idea of the Saudis beating the crap out of this guy to make him squeal, which, despite being fairly commonplace these days, also violates the United Nations Convention Against Torture, of which the United States happens to be a treaty signatory. Or Option C, the Saudis wanted Ali bin Pacha and offered us a choice: Hand him over or America will never need another highway bill.

I thought it over for a moment. A, or B, or C each looked plausible. But so did A *and* B *and* C.

Bottom line: Had the White House ordered this, as I suspected it had, I should start worrying about my next assignment, maybe my next career—and maybe my life. But frankly, I was past caring, which is always a danger point for whoever's pissing me off. Also I wasn't completely out on a limb. The golden rule of Washington was on my side: The party with the most to hide always holds the weakest hand.

I knew this. And Mark Waterbury, too, knew this.

So he drew a few breaths and decided the moment was pregnant for a new approach. He dropped his Lear-like act and gave me a friendly smile. "Sean . . . Hey, I'm not out on my own out here. You don't . . . Look, there's strong support for this . . . in Washington."

"*Where* in Washington?"

"At high levels. Leave it at that."

He wished. "Fine. Show me the letter of approval signed by the Attorney General."

"I don't . . ." He looked confused for a moment. "I'm quite confident the Attorney General can be persuaded to issue such an order."

"Well, you never know. Why don't we call him and ask?"

Everyone fell quiet for a moment. Then the sheik looked at me and asked, "What would it require to satisfy you, Colonel?"

I was sure he had heard what I said, and I could only assume that his question was in the nature of a bribe. I was tempted to test his sincerity; I mean, this was the land of genies, and until you rub the bottle a few times you never know. Then again, people who are willing to bribe you are often willing to do other things, too. Like hurt you. Sometimes worse.

So instead, I informed him, "Let me tell you my problem. You people don't share."

He stared back with an icy smile and advised, "You should not believe all the libelous things you read about my country in your newspapers."

"How long have you worked in Saudi intelligence?"

"Over twenty years. This is my career work. Why do you ask?"

I looked him in the eye and said, "In 1996, I worked on the Khobar Towers investigation."

I could see in his eyes that this reference struck home. After Arab terrorists bombed the American military barracks in the Khobar Towers in Saudi Arabia—after nineteen American servicemen were killed and hundreds more wounded—the Saudis quickly rounded up the suspects, and without allowing U.S. investigators a single interview, they were all swiftly beheaded.

As I mentioned, I had a role in that investigation and we smelled Al Qaeda; all we ended up with was two bad smells. I've often wondered how differently the present might look had we interrogated those suspects, had we perhaps gained insights into Al Qaeda and their future plans and plots. That would've been good for America *and* good for the Saudis.

But the Saudis play their own game in this region, and it goes something like this: We cover our own asses and could care less who stuffs a firecracker up yours. Clearly, the Saudis had an under-the-table treaty of some sort with Al Qaeda, probably involving a covert payoff, and the quid pro quo was that Al Qaeda would stay out of the Saudi sandbox and mess up other people, like us.

Nobody could prove this. But the beheading of the Khobar Towers suspects made it impossible to prove anything, except that nineteen American patriots died without justice. The Saudis believe in burying their embarrassments, literally, and we buried ours, quietly.

Predictably, Waterbury was outraged by my impertinence and informed me, "You're way out of line, Drummond. You'll apologize to the sheik."

"If you can convince me why, maybe I will."

"You're pissing me off. Sheik al-Fayef is an honored guest and has very generously offered his valuable assistance."

Maybe I had misjudged Waterbury. Maybe he wasn't such a bad guy; maybe he was *just* stupid.

Phyllis cleared her throat and said, "This finger-pointing isn't helpful. Let's see if we can reason our way through this impasse."

If Waterbury was the heavy hitter, Phyllis apparently was sent as the relief pitcher, because she looked at the sheik, then at me, and suggested, "Maybe an alternative arrangement will satisfy everybody's needs and wants."

Waterbury looked unhappy to be losing control of this thing and began to object, before the sheik raised a hand and said, "Please." He looked at Phyllis, "Describe for me . . . this alternative arrangement?"

I guess I now was calling the shots, because Phyllis bunted that question to me and asked, "What safeguards would satisfy you?"

To tell the truth, I knew from the start that I had no chance of winning this. I could raise obstructions and objections, and make it more painful and time-consuming for all involved. Being a pain in the ass has its satisfactions; in the end, though, I wasn't going to cause any great soul-searching, because the people who ordered this had no souls, just power.

Clearly the big boys in D.C. wanted to avoid taking this case through the Justice Department and up the chain to the Attorney General, because it would eat up time, because actionable intelligence from an interrogation of this nature has a brief shelf life, but mostly because the less people in the know, the less you have to turn into amnesiacs later.

Despite my warning her to stay out of this, Bian butted in. "Why does the rendition have to be genuine?"

Waterbury said, "Shut up."

"But—"

"I said, shut up."

By this point, I think even the sheik seemed to appreciate what the rest of us already knew; Waterbury only opened his mouth to change feet.

The sheik held up a hand and said, "I believe I would prefer to hear about this suggestion."

I thought I understood where Bian was going with this, and on the face of things the idea was very clever; I wished I had thought of it. As I anticipated she would, she said, "I'm suggesting that bin Pacha doesn't need to be rendered. He merely needs to *believe* he's been turned over."

"Yes, and how would this work?"

"We pump him full of drugs. He'll awaken in a Saudi cell, with Saudi guards, and Saudi interrogators. Sean and I prep him beforehand, inform him he's undergoing rendition. I don't care how tough he is. It will scare the crap out of him."

The sheik overlooked this backhanded compliment about his interrogation techniques and nodded thoughtfully.

I slapped on my lawyer hat and quickly offered a few stipulations. "He stays under joint custody. We'll have direct observation and round-the-clock access to his interrogation sessions, and we provide 50 percent of the questions."

Sheik al-Fayef was now stroking his goatee. "And how is this an advantage to me?"

"You know what we know, as we know it," Bian informed him.

I added, "Or you can think of it as avoiding the ugly alternative."

He looked at me. "Alternative?"

I told him, "You can read about it on the front page of the *New York Times*. I'm not sure what bin Pacha knows that scares you, and I'm not sure you know yourself. But your country has enough of an image problem in America after 9/11. Think about it."

So he thought about it, very briefly, and replied, "I'll grant you your wish."

CHAPTER TWENTY-SEVEN

Turki al-Fayef departed the plane to call his superiors in Riyadh with the news that the old deal had just become the new deal.

Phyllis wanted a word with me, alone. So she and I marooned Bian with her boss, who looked a little frustrated and in the mood to browbeat a subordinate.

The inside of the plane was, as I said, a sauna, and my uniform was pasted to my body. Even Phyllis, who has the physiology of a lizard, sported a light coat of dew on her upper lip.

Neither she nor I said a word as we left the plane, or as we walked together through the hangar and out onto the airfield, where there was a brisk breeze, hot yet refreshing.

Eventually, we were far enough away and I said, not softly, "You screwed us and you betrayed us."

"Harsh words. You look tired. So how are you?"

"Didn't you promise to watch my backside?"

"She's a very attractive woman, don't you think?"

"She's a good soldier."

"And very beautiful, too. Do I sense something developing between you two?"

"I didn't even realize she was female until she walked into a ladies' latrine." I wasn't going to let her change the subject, and I asked, "Why, Phyllis? Why did you cave?"

"Incidentally, you handled Turki brilliantly. He's a tough negotiator. You ran a nice bluff, though you nearly drove it off a cliff." She gave me a long stare and added, "Still, you squeezed a better deal out of him than we got."

"Maybe you didn't push hard enough. Who's 'we'?"

She looked away from me. "Powerful people. You don't need to know their names and I wouldn't tell you anyway."

"Tigerman? Hirschfield? Do those names fit?"

She chose not to answer directly, but did say, "Even three years ago, the Agency could have stood up to the whole lot of them. We've lost so much prestige, clout, and influence since 9/11. Did you know the President is considering a new Director?"

"So what? The old Director will make a bundle off corporate boards and speeches and books. The new Director will learn that he needs you more than you need him. The bureaucracy is forever, and the bureaucracy *always* prevails."

"I'm not so sure. Washington is changing. The Agency is due for changes also. It has to . . . and maybe that's not a bad idea."

"Who is Turki al-Fayef?" I asked.

"Turki is the number two or three or four in Saudi intelligence."

"Which one?"

"It depends on how many royal princes decide they want to play spymaster. I've known him for many years, and with Turki around that's all they do: play. It's perfectly harmless."

"But he's not harmless."

"Don't blame him. Turki does what's best for his country, as we do what's best for ours."

"Then hire him. He does it better."

"Stop acting naive, Sean. It doesn't sit well on you."

"Excuse me for thinking we were here to do the right thing."

"How do you know we're *not* doing the right thing?"

Regarding Phyllis, she's not shameless, but she has that annoying Washington syndrome, a stunning inability to blush, no matter how raw the lie or how awful the embarrassment. I asked, "What does Ali bin Pacha know that's scaring everybody?"

"Maybe nothing. Maybe a lot. But he's a Saudi, and his own countrymen can handle this better than we."

"I know you don't believe that."

An Air Force C-130 began sprinting down the runway, and she said something, but it was drowned out by the roar of the noisy engines. We stood, sharing a moment in silence, and watched the big plane lift off, and our eyes stayed on it as the pilot began a series of corkscrew maneuvers intended to elude ground-to-air missiles. This place sucked.

The passengers in the rear of the aircraft were probably tossing their lunch; I was feeling a wave of nausea myself. "What about Charabi?"

"Who?"

I looked at her. "You can't allow this."

"I follow orders." After a moment she observed, "Needless to say, you also will follow orders."

"He betrayed us."

"Do you know that for sure? You have a suspicion based on a flimsy circumstantial foundation. A few e-mails in a computer that belonged to a seriously troubled, contemptible man who perhaps committed suicide. Were you the defense attorney, would you allow that to be entered into evidence? I think not." She didn't need to state the obvious, that her question was as abstract as it was specious, since I would never be allowed within ten miles of that computer or the incriminating e-mails. She did add, however, "You have no tangible proof that Charabi passed any secrets to the Iranians. He's not even a U.S. citizen. That's a requirement for an indictment for treason, is it not?"

"He's a suspect in the murder of Clifford Daniels. That's an extraditable offense."

"You said the murderer was a woman."

"I also told you I believe she was a *hired* assassin. She was the murder weapon, not the murderer."

"There's that 'possibly' word again. I thought the law dealt with facts, and I thought innocence is presumed."

These weasel words had a lawyerly ring, as if Phyllis was parroting the stupid rationale cooked up by the nameless powers that be back in D.C.

You can imagine how much I enjoy legal lectures, and I informed her, "Investigations always begin with vague and uncertain suspicions, you dig a little, and you decide which suspicious assholes need a second look. And, if you're interested, the presumption of innocence pertains to jurors, not investigators. To the cop everybody is a suspect until proven otherwise."

She did not reply.

"He's a suspect. He needs to be questioned."

"He is an Iraqi citizen. This is Iraq. You have neither the legal basis nor the authority, nor the access to question him."

"No problem. I'll just walk into his office and ask a few questions. Perfectly harmless. Man-to-man. See where it goes."

"I was instructed to convey three words: Forget about him."

We locked eyes for a moment.

She said, "The Iraqi people are scheduled to have their first election in January. This is a critical milestone to victory in this war, a necessary step for bringing our troops home. Mahmoud Charabi—maybe you read this in the papers—is a leading contender for future prime minister."

"And that's *why* he needs to be investigated. What if he's elected, and what if he's working for Iran, and what if he's behind the murder of Cliff Daniels? That won't be good for America, and that's not what my comrades in arms are fighting and dying for."

"*Why* is irrelevant. Pay attention. Neither you nor I are allowed to carry this any further." She pointed a finger, daggerlike, into my arm and invoked those sacred words: "That's an order."

"What's going on here?"

There was silence for a moment. Eventually, Phyllis said, "Two words, this time: Martin Lebrowski."

"Who?"

"The man you know as Don."

"Am I going to dislike Martin as much as I dislike Don?"

"More." She added, "The leak of the Iranian operation occurred on his watch. He was responsible for all aspects of that operation. Especially, operational security. Lebrowski was facing a serious career crisis."

"Lebrowski never should have had a career in the first place."

"Whatever. He has more savvy than I gave him credit for. Right after Martin departed our meeting he called a few friends, on the NSC staff and at the Defense Department. He disclosed what we knew." She added, "The details were off, but it didn't matter."

"What happened next?"

"What do you think happened next?"

Her response was as rhetorical as my question. This was Washington—a meeting happened next. The bright boys scrummed around a long mahogany table in a lushly carpeted back room and collectively they realized that, with a seesaw election mere days away, the opposition could begin picking out Secret Service nicknames and contacting their real estate agents. One meeting always begets the next, and this time Phyllis and her boss were invited, not as guests but as factotums to hear their marching orders. I asked her, "And what was Martin's reward?"

"Oh, well . . . he now works in the White House. On the National Security Council staff. A special assistant to the President."

"I love when the good guy wins."

"Martin outsmarted us—"

"Martin outsmarted *you*. Personally, I thought he was an asshole."

"All right . . . me. There's nothing to be done about it now."

She was right, of course. And actually, I felt a pang of guilt for indulging in that bratty told-you-so. I can rise above the vindictive and small-minded stuff. Then again, she doesn't; why should I?

I stared at her for a moment, then said, "Let's make sure I'm clear on all this. In summary: Ali bin Pacha will be interrogated by his homies, Lebrowski has a new desk with job security, Charabi has a papal dispensation, and . . . what have I missed?"

"A few details. Nothing important."

Actually there was something important—me. I asked, "Where does this leave Bian and me?"

"Oh . . . yes. You will complete this leg of the investigation. Actually, the people who redirected this operation are very impressed with both of you."

"Does that mean my plane won't accidentally blow up on the way home?"

She ignored my paranoia. "You've apprehended an important terrorist, Sean. If he talks, it could help change the course of this war. We're all very interested in what he might disclose."

"It sounds like Washington is more interested in suppressing what Charabi might divulge."

"In this business, you rarely achieve all that you want. You have to celebrate what you get." She looked away from me and said, "There's a good chance you'll be rewarded for this impressive accomplishment."

"You can't imagine how good that makes me feel."

"And your personal feelings, as you know, are entirely irrelevant."

"That's what I meant."

"Also I was asked to remind you of the secrecy statements you signed—you remember what that means. As I'm sure you've guessed, this is what Waterbury is discussing with Major Tran back at the plane."

I looked at her a long time, then said, "They're rubbing it in our faces. Yours too, Phyllis. Doesn't this bother you?"

She surprised me and replied, with a rare display of emotion, "You're damned right it does."

We walked on in silence for a few moments before another unnerving thought hit me. "Wait . . ." I asked, "How did the Saudis learn about Ali bin Pacha? Don left before we got to that part."

"That's the question, isn't it?"

I stared at her.

"I'm telling you the truth. Out of the blue, the Saudi ambassador called the White House yesterday. He threw quite a stink."

"Can't anybody in the Agency keep a secret?"

This apparently was funny, because she laughed.

I said, "A very small circle were aware of this operation, Phyllis. How could the Saudis have learned about it?"

"I don't know the answer to that. But the ambassador knew. He wouldn't disclose how, but he knew. So, the Director and I were directed to work out an arrangement with Turki."

"You said yesterday? *Before* we had our hands on bin Pacha?"

"That's right. You might even say that was the decisive factor in our decision."

"I didn't think you made any decisions."

She ignored this sarcastic insight and continued, "We were quite aware that Saudi intelligence could have tipped off bin Pacha's organization. But in the event we didn't figure it out on our own, Turki subtly reminded us."

I said nothing.

"So it became a choice, Sean. A choice between taking bin Pacha out of circulation with the chance of learning what he knows or losing him altogether."

We walked for a distance in silence. A solitary runner in battle dress trousers and brown desert boots, off to our left, was jogging laps around a building on the airfield, and he drew both of our eyes. His brown Army T-shirt was soaked with dark sweat, his chest heaved with exertion, and he continued to place one foot in front of another, running in endless circles. He and I had a lot in common; but he and this war had even more in common. Phyllis dabbed her upper lip with a hankie and commented, "This is such a miserably hot and complicated place for a war, don't you think?"

"I don't recall any wars in good places."

"I recall better wars. Less convoluted ones." In a rare moment of philosophizing, she said a little sadly, "All wars have an ugly underbelly to them. The people who fight those clandestine battles are never invited to the ticker-tape parades, and afterward you won't find them bellying up to the bar of VFW lodges, bragging about their battles."

Moving back to the topic at hand, I observed, "At least we will now know what bin Pacha tells the Saudis."

She smiled. "We would've known anyway."

"What are you talking about?"

"Do you think you're the only smart person in the room? Before bin Pacha's wound was closed, Enzenauer embedded an electronic device beneath his skin. Mr. bin Pacha is already on the air and broadcasting."

I should've been surprised by this revelation, yet for some reason, I wasn't.

I observed the sheik, off in the distance, with his robes aflutter, scurrying across the airfield, back into the hangar and up the airplane steps, without the slightest clue how completely out of his fucking league he was.

I took Phyllis's elbow and guided her back to the hangar. We walked up the steps to the plane and, just at the moment Phyllis stepped through the doorway, I mentioned, "By the way, I doubled the pay for Eric and his team."

If nothing else, I would always have the memory of her expression.

CHAPTER TWENTY-EIGHT

We reconvened and the next few minutes were spent hashing out the logistics, details, and timing of Ali bin Pacha's interrogation. This whole conversation had a rushed and surreal quality, which is usually the case when the room stinks of guilt.

For Bian, and for me, it felt like being rotated on a barbecue spit.

In return for this "small favor you are providing," Turki promised to provide us "a very illuminating file" his intelligence service had on Ali bin Pacha. By inference, bin Pacha had been a target of interest to the Saudis for a long time. I already suspected this, of course, though it was nice to have it confirmed. Then again, the file we received would look like Mom's old coupon book after a busy day at the mall; nothing but holes and ragged edges, a remnant of the mighty file it once had been. He didn't say this; he didn't need to.

Phyllis suggested that since bin Pacha was to remain under joint custody, there was really no need to risk transporting him to Saudi Arabia, that in fact the CIA had a facility south of Baghdad that was perfectly suitable for this kind of legerdemain. She suggested further that "our old friend Turki"—not speaking for me—should fly in guards and interrogators, bin Pacha would be fooled, and we would jointly decide his fate afterward.

Her friend Turki agreed to this suggestion without the slightest hesitation. In fact, I thought he looked relieved.

Maybe the idea of CIA people wandering through a Saudi high-security prison was problematic for him. Who knows? We might bump into his countryman Osama bin Laden tucked away in a cell. With these people, you never know

But since we seemed to be into suggestions, I suggested, "It might be a long time before bin Pacha breaks. I'm sure you're all very busy people. Let Bian and me handle it, and we'll get back to you."

Everybody was impressed by my thoughtfulness, and nobody seemed to think it was a good idea.

But it brought to the surface what we all knew. There were serious trust issues under the table: The sheik trusted nobody, I didn't trust Phyllis, who didn't trust Waterbury, Waterbury couldn't spell "trust," and Bian was playing with an ace up her sleeve. For sure, a lot of phony smiles and false assurances were being passed around, but if this were a poker table, there would be cocked pistols on everybody's laps, and blood would be shed before the pot was claimed.

Also, Phyllis and Turki al-Fayef seemed a bit uneasy in Bian's and my presence. Who could blame them? Rapists don't enjoy hanging around for postcoital chats with their victims.

Waterbury seemed like Waterbury—the man had not the slightest moral clue that this was wrong, nor had he ever read anything in his manuals that suggested otherwise. This didn't make him a bad guy. But it was scary.

At the earliest possible moment, Phyllis departed to visit the station chief at the Baghdad field station to discuss what she vaguely referred to as "important matters."

The sheik followed on her heels, presumably to locate a five-star hotel with air-conditioning that worked and better room service.

Waterbury also left, without informing us where he was going. But my CIA country report had explicitly warned that kidnapping rings were rampant in Baghdad, and, well . . . I crossed my fingers and hoped.

Bian and I were ordered to remain on the plane and guard Abdul while we waited for the military to dispatch a military police team to transport him to Abu Ghraib prison.

She and I shifted to the galley, where we discovered a thick hoard of fresh bologna in the fridge. This struck us both as apropos for the occasion—you know, turkey at Thanksgiving, boiled potatoes for Saint Patty's, bologna after being lied to and fucked. So we made a few sandwiches; I slathered mine with mayonnaise, she loaded hers with mustard, and we adjourned to the big conference table for dinner.

We brought the last four beers with us. It wasn't enough to even get a buzz on, but we already were drunk with powerlessness.

So now we were alone with out first chance to compare notes. Bian kicked it off, asking, "How bad was your lecture?"

"I'll bet yours was worse."

"Waterbury doesn't bother me." She smiled. "He's a big blowhard. Don't let him get under your collar. Do what I always do. Tune him out."

"Seriously, when I told you not to shoot anybody, I didn't mean him."

She held up a forefinger, squeezed the trigger, and laughed.

"They pulled out the rug from under our feet, Bian."

"Why do you sound so surprised? Did you actually believe they'd allow us to take this to full fruition?"

"For all the wrong reasons, yes, I did."

"Well . . . shame on you."

"What am I hearing here?"

"I mean, I'm upset. I'm disappointed. Of course I am. I just . . . Look, once we understood what was happening here, the full import, the total scope, the possibilities . . . I hope this doesn't sound cynical, but I didn't think we'd be allowed to find the full truth."

"Aren't we here because you insisted we had to do this?"

"Was there a choice? You learn that the primary justification behind this war might be a big lie, that the man we sent here to be the next king could be in the pocket of the bad guys, and maybe he exposed to our enemies an invaluable secret. So you have the opportunity to find out and maybe do something about it. Do you say no?" She squeezed my hand and added, "We never had a choice. From the instant we entered Cliff Daniels's apartment, because of who we are, we had to be here, we had to do what we've done, and we had to be told that's enough."

"And you're okay with this?"

"I'm Army. I follow orders."

"That's not what I asked. Are you okay with this?"

"All right . . . I'm depressed. I'm frustrated. I'm disgusted at my own government." After a moment, she confided, "But I'll deal with it. You'll have to find your own way to handle it."

This submissive babble was the last thing I expected from Ms. Gung-ho. Her stubbornness, after all, was what brought us here in the first place. Well, I had made lots of misjudgments during the past few days, nor, like the three billion other males on the planet, have I ever been particularly good at understanding women.

After a long, thoughtful pause, she asked, "What were Phyllis's instructions to you about Charabi?"

"There is no Charabi. Just a figment of my imagination. What did Waterbury say to you?"

"Yeah, like that. And the intelligence leak?"

"You can't get to one without the other. Besides, Phyllis kept all the relevant e-mail messages."

"Good point. Anything about closing out Cliff Daniels's murder investigation?"

I looked at her.

She looked back and observed with pretended innocence, "I ask only because Waterbury mentioned nothing about it to me."

We both sipped from our beers, and out of nowhere we heard the sound of a loud explosion. The chandelier above our heads actually swayed and shook—a little close to home. The highway from Baghdad to the airport was aptly and horribly nicknamed Suicide Alley, and it sounded like a suicide bomber had just nailed somebody. Maybe it was Waterbury; we should be so lucky.

Without speaking, Bian set up the speakerphone in the middle of the conference table. I dialed the Washington switch, gave the nice operator the number, and a few unanswered rings later heard Detective Barry Enders's voice growl, "Jesus H. . . . Look what friggin' time it is. If this isn't about a murder, there's about to be one."

I identified myself and told Enders that Bian was beside me, listening on the speakerphone, then informed him, "We're calling for an update on the investigation."

There was silence for a moment. Enders then said, "What investigation?"

"Barry, it's me," replied Bian. Sounding slightly annoyed, she said, "Don't jerk us off."

"Who's jerkin' who off? A bunch of Feds came in yesterday. They took everything, jurisdiction, the crime scene log . . . my files . . . the lab specimens. They even ripped the pages out of my detective book. Don't even tell me this is a surprise to you."

Bian and I exchanged troubled looks. No wonder Phyllis and Waterbury felt no need to warn us off this venue. Bastards. But smart bastards.

Enders continued, "Now you're calling at this hour to rub it in. What is this, some kind've trap play to see if I'm—"

"Barry," I interrupted, "this is the first we've heard of this."

"Yeah . . . right."

"Who signed the order?"

"Justice Department. I was also ordered to develop a memory lapse. They were real assholes about it, too."

"Yet this is still an open case for you, is it not? A death in your jurisdiction—isn't it *your* responsibility to file cause of death?"

"That's not how it works, Drummond. The Feds give the judgment, I write it down, end of story."

I was, of course, familiar with the proper procedures, and we both knew I was testing the waters. The answer was, screw you.

He asked me, "Why do you care? You insisted it was suicide. And you know what? I have a feeling that's what the Feds will conclude: suicide." He laughed.

Bian recognized I had a credibility problem here and said, "I changed his mind. So did you. Now he . . . actually, we both believe it was something else. Murder."

"Look, I think we're done—"

"What if I offered you insights about *why* Cliff Daniels was murdered?" I asked.

"Great. I'll give you the number to Special Agent Barney Stanowitz. Big ugly asshole with bad manners. His card's in my office. In fact," he confided, "he warned me that if anybody asked about this case I should call him."

Going on instinct about Barry Enders, I said, "Give me a minute, Barry. One minute. Then make up your own mind about what you're going to do."

He hesitated. Not a good sign.

I nodded at Bian, who is much nicer than me, and she said, "Barry, you're a smart guy. I think you know what's going down. A cover-up. Conspiracy. You don't know why, and maybe you don't care. But I suspect you *do* care."

Bian and I looked at each other. No reply.

Bian said, "Barry, please."

"Okay . . . one minute. Drummond, make your case."

This was less than a commitment but more than the phone slamming down.

So I confessed, "Maybe I misled you about the trouble Daniels was in."

"Wow, no shit. Didn't they teach you at law school that it's a crime to lie to the cops?"

"Cut the crap, Barry. One minute. You promised."

"If you want the full minute, speak more clearly."

"Okay. Possibly Cliff Daniels betrayed this country. Possibly he gave enormously sensitive information to the wrong people in Iraq and compromised a very important operation. You wondered why a CIA person and a military policewoman were sent to his apartment. Now you know—espionage."

There was a long, contemplative pause. He said, "My oldest boy—Elton—he's a Marine. First Marine Division. Already been to Iraq once." After another moment he mentioned, "Did my own four years as a Jarhead before I became a cop. Semper Fi."

"Couldn't get into the Army?"

"Hey, I tried. Only the Army recruiter, he said I possessed two irreconcilable issues: My parents were married, and I don't look sufficiently stupid."

"Really? You look stupid enough to me."

We both laughed. He said, "All right, I'll give you more than a minute. Go ahead, blow some more smoke up my ass."

So I gave him part of the story, essentially that Daniels got in over his head and gave a foreign agent some information, though we didn't yet have a clue what that information was, because it was in code, and the code was a ballbuster. Nor did I clarify *how* we learned about this.

He was a smart guy, though. He knew that when dealing with a federal government official, he was not hearing one-third of the story, another third was sprinkled with fairy dust, and the final third was total bullshit. But I fed him enough truth and his cop brain was filling in some of the blanks. I wrapped it up, saying, "Here's the big piece you were missing—motive—*why* somebody wanted to murder Cliff Daniels. In fact, the list of people who *didn't* want Daniels dead would fill a matchbox. There are people in Washington, and here in Baghdad, who would benefit greatly from his death. We're sure his killer was a woman, and possibly she was hired help, but don't exclude the possibility she was working on her own."

For a moment, Barry said nothing. He needed time to process these clues and revelations, and he eventually asked the right and proper question. "What do you want me to do about this?"

Bian had done some thinking on this topic, because she immediately responded, "Now you *know* there was a murder. That simplifies your problem. Focus on the killer."

When he made no reply, Bian added, "Colonel Drummond has a theory that all murderers make mistakes. Is that your theory as well?"

"Yeah, most do. We also have a thick file of cold cases that dates back to 1969. See if you can talk him into examining it. We'd love to know what mistakes they made."

"But this killer may have left trails," Bian insisted. "That high-priced wig. Probably hers. Wigs are no longer fashionable for women—how many stores in the D.C. area sell expensive hairpieces these days? And that triple-X video . . . we assumed it was his and maybe we assumed wrong. Likewise, how many stores in the area sell porn?" I gave Bian a look and she asked Barry, "Am I overstating the obvious?"

"Yeah, I do this stuff for a living. And you're overlooking that people purchase wigs and porno on the Internet these days. I'll check around, though."

Bian looked at me to see if I had anything to add. I suggested, "They had to have gone out together once or twice before. Dated, slept together, whatever. Check his charge-card records. See where he socialized lately. Maybe somebody will remember her."

"Long shot. We already know the guy had a lot of lady friends, right? Who knows which ones people will remember."

"There are no short shots here, Barry."

"You out of bright ideas?"

So I explained my new theory about how the murder was more stylistic than we initially surmised, including a few ideas about the possible symbolism in the staging of his death. On that topic I suggested, "You might spend a little time thinking about what that was intended to convey. If any profilers owe you a favor, call it in. If we get a better idea about how he was killed, maybe we'll get closer to why, and by whom."

"You realize I'll have to do this on my own time."

"You'd better do this on your own time." I added, "And watch your back."

"I figured out that part on my own." He asked, "Say I find something—how do I get in touch with you?"

"You don't. I'll check in with you."

"Got it. So what are you two doing in Baghdad?"

"Vacationing."

"Aw, come on. This has something to do with Daniels's murder. Right?"

"It's the hottest thing in adventure tourism. They advertise it as a safari, only you're the prey. Very exciting."

He laughed. "My boy, Elton, he said it sucks over there."

"Your boy has a good head on his shoulders."

"Let me tell you, he used to be a little asshole. Not all cops' kids are angels. The Corps straightened him out." He chuckled. "The first time he made his bed, his mama wanted to know who manufactured the robot that looks like her kid."

"Barry, listen. If you don't want Elton to spend the rest of his career over here, find something."

"Stay in contact." He hung up.

Bian lifted her beer can and we performed a quiet aerial toast. She said, "They failed to close the back door."

"But they didn't forget. These people aren't stupid, Bian. They won't ignore it."

"I know. What happens if he's caught?"

"He'll be okay. He's a big boy. He understands the risks."

"You're sure about that?"

"He's not a federal employee so they can't screw up his paycheck, or . . . say, reassign him here. You and I, on the other hand, might have a big problem."

"Screw them."

"Why are you doing this, Bian?" I popped that question out of the blue and watched her closely to see how she responded.

She did not bat an eye. "Duty, honor, country. It's that simple."

"Obeying orders is part of duty, and country can be interpreted many ways. You're not telling me something, Bian. I'd like to know what it is."

"Isn't it obvious?"

"With you, nothing is obvious."

"Is that a criticism?"

I took her hand and said, "No, it's not. You're a very exciting, unpredictable, and fun woman to be around. These past three days, despite everything, I've had a great time. I mean that. But from the moment I met you, I've sensed that you have your own agenda."

"This is the second time you've brought this up. It's getting old. What is it you think I'm doing?"

"Something more than truth, justice, and the American way. This is personal for you. I'm just not sure why."

She took a sip of her beer and examined me curiously. "That's hypocritical. You've been with me every step of the way. Has someone put a gun to your head?"

"Well . . . Ali bin Pacha, for one."

"Oh, screw off. Why are you bucking the system? Obviously not to get in my pants."

"Hey, that's below the belt."

To be polite, she smiled at my bad pun. She said, "I told you, I lost friends and soldiers here. I'd blow the whistle on these people in a heartbeat, but the scandal would destroy everything a lot of good soldiers have accomplished through blood and tears. That's something I'm not willing to do. I hope you're not either. But I'm more than willing to trade my career if I can force these people to make it right. Other people are giving their lives and limbs."

"Okay. I believe you."

"You better. And stop trying to psychoanalyze me. It makes me uncomfortable."

I sipped from my beer.

She said, "I know you're the cynical tough-guy type, and I know you'd never confess to doing anything altruistic. And I also know that it's a veneer, and that, underneath, you're maybe even a bigger sucker than I am, and maybe you're as compelled to find the truth here as I am."

Then, out of the blue, she added, "I'm going to take another shower. When I was here, we'd go weeks without them. I hated that almost more than I hated being shot at. It's so nice to feel clean in Iraq for a change."

Women are really into personal cleanliness. Men, on the other hand, think a month without showers and a shave is a cool vacation. But also, that sounded like an invitation. I wasn't sure if it was or not; it sounded like one, though. She stared at me a moment too long, then stood and walked out.

I popped the second can of beer and stared out the plane window. "To feel clean in Iraq for a change"—those words kept gnawing at me. She had meant for it to be taken at face value, and maybe it went no deeper than that. But from cross-examining thousands of criminals and witnesses, I also knew that through skill, luck, or chance, sometimes a Freudian slip lands in your lap, and you need to be receptive. Sometimes it's exactly as it sounded, and you end up spinning your wheels. Other times it's the switch that ends the darkness, or at least lights up a corner of a room.

So. "Clean in Iraq for a change"—what did that mean? Something had happened to her here, something traumatic she didn't want to talk about, but clearly something she felt remorse for, and maybe a deep sadness.

I didn't think Bian was dishonest; to the contrary, I was sure she was highly principled. But as I knew from personal experience, when two or more principles clash, something has to go.

It struck me, further, that she certainly wasn't the naive or overly gung-ho waif she occasionally came across as. With hindsight, what I had taken for gullibility, pliability, and excessive volunteering might have been something more.

Everybody involved in this thing had an agenda—nationalistic or institutional—and for each agenda there was a corresponding motive: passion, folly, obsession, anguish, intrigue, adventure, or, in a few cases, a less complicated matter of personal ambition and CYA. But for Bian—for whatever reason—this was personal. And when you mix personal with professional, you get big problems.

I heard the shower door open, and I heard it close.

This had not been my war, but it had been Bian's from long before we met. As all old soldiers know, what makes it personal for you isn't some galvanizing platitude or geostrategic imperative, or even being shot at. One attends a war because one is ordered to; one puts his heart and soul into it for a different reason. A bond to somebody, a comrade in arms, somebody with whom you share the risk of death, somebody you care about, and hopefully they care about you.

Joining Bian in the shower remained a bad idea, and I was sure she knew this as well; her quest, though, whatever it was, had become mine.

CHAPTER TWENTY-NINE

Bian and I were seated in stiff-backed hospital chairs observing our Arab patient, who remained unconcious. Three days had passed since Doc Enzenauer recommended that we allow bin Pacha a period of recovery before we squeezed his brain like a blackhead. According to the doc, this had more to do with the drugs and anesthetics than the trauma of the operation, and he gave us a long, detailed tutorial explaining why. Don't ask.

Anyway, when Abdul Almiri was picked up by a squad of MPs for delivery to Abu Ghraib, Bian hitched a ride into Baghdad, where she stayed for two days.

She didn't talk about it, and I didn't ask.

I assumed, however, that she went to see her fiancé, Marvelous Mark, which perhaps accounted for why she didn't invite me. I recalled Bian once telling me that Mark and I had a lot in common, the inference being that we'd end up buds, but I wasn't so sure. I mean, we had both seen Bian naked; among guys, that doesn't make for a pleasant bonding experience.

My own two days, if you're interested, were spent in the airplane, monitoring communications and observing the election coverage on cable news; i.e., becoming bored out of my wits.

As before, the polls indicated a dead heat, and an electorate experiencing its usual quadrennial meltdown into terrified indifference. As one pundit put it, the race boiled down to one guy too stupid to spell "principle," yet insisting he had plenty of it, against a guy who spoke a little too much French—if you know what I mean—who had never earned a private-sector buck and now was married to a billionaire with a strange accent, yet was offering himself as the champion of average Joes, underdogs, endangered species, and other people who weren't lucky enough to marry rich. Democracy is great. Iraq should have one, too. Seriously.

If you're still interested, I saw no coverage, or even mention, about the death of Clifford Daniels. A biographer friend of mine likes to say, "When a man dies, the story of his life is no longer his." Apparently the story of this sad little man belonged to people who were working overtime with a big eraser. Ironic, if you think about it. All his life, Cliff had wanted to touch the flame of power and fame; he finally got his wish, and even his ashes were disappearing.

On the second day, the aircrew showed up to turn over the engines. To relieve the monotony, I challenged them to a chess tournament; fortunately, they declined. I had better luck suggesting poker, but they had better luck with the cards, drubbing me for two hundred big ones. The bastards cheated. I cheated, too; they just cheated better.

Anyway, Bian returned early on the third morning without a word about where, or about how, she had spent her days in Baghdad. However, I sensed a new mood of calm contentment with an attitude of cordial reserve toward moi. I assumed this meant she had resolved her internal conflict between Mark or Sean. I won't say I was overly thrilled by this.

Anyway, Bian elbowed my arm and said, "Sean, I think he's waking up."

I looked up and noted that Ali bin Pacha's eyes were blinking repeatedly. Having personally experienced this—twice—I understood what thoughts were passing through his brain.

For starters, you remember your last conscious moments, the images and thoughts playing back like a videotape—you have a bullet inside you, it hurts like hell, you know you might die, you feel a tide of weakness enveloping you, sucking you down into the darkness, and you're thinking . . . This is it. The End.

Now his nerve endings and synapses were crackling with unexpected sensations. He reached with his hands and touched his face, then rubbed his three-day stubble, his nose, and his eyes, confirming that Ali bin Pacha still was encased in a corporeal body, still breathing, still alive.

His one good eye shifted to the IV tube in his arm, and he noticed his surroundings, that he was resting in a bed, his body was covered with clean white sheets, and somebody—Bian—was watching him. From his expression, he realized this woman in an Army uniform was not one of the fabled Stygian virgins waiting to celebrate his martyrdom.

Then the roving black eye discovered me.

I cleared my throat and informed Ali bin Pacha, "You are in an American Army field hospital in Baghdad. I am Colonel Drummond. This is Major Tran."

He stared back wordlessly.

I continued, "We know you work with Zarqawi and we know you are . . . *were* his moneyman. As such, you are not a prisoner of war, you are an international terrorist and will be afforded none of the protections of the Geneva Conventions." I leaned closer and asked, "Do you understand?"

His face remained impassive.

Bian informed him, "You *do* understand. We know you speak English. In fact, we know a great deal about you."

Which was true, courtesy of the file Sheik Turki al-Fayef had promised and actually delivered the day before, albeit a skeleton of the mighty file it had probably once been. It told us a great deal about this man personally, and nothing about him professionally, which was helpful, though not nearly as helpful as it might've been. She allowed bin Pacha a moment to consider her words, then said, "We know you grew up in Jidda in Saudi Arabia. Your father's name is Fahd, your mother is Ayda. Your father is an importer of fine automobiles, which has made him very prosperous. You have six brothers, no sisters."

I added, "From 1990 through 1991, you were a student at Balliol College at Oxford. On your entrance exam, your English was rated as excellent. In fact, you wrote your first-year essay on the poetry of John Milton."

He did not acknowledge this revealing insight either.

I needed to get a rise out of this guy and said, "I read it. Let me be frank. I found it immature, pompous, and presumptuous. You don't know the difference between iambic pentameter and a pizza pie. And you totally misunderstood Milton's intent. About what I expected from an ignorant, backward camel jockey."

I was sure this crude cultural aspersion was irritating for him—it was meant to be—but his expression was immutable.

Bian's turn. She said, "The colonel has lost friends here. He . . . well, he's not a big fan of Arab cultures."

Women have a sixth sense for what gets on a man's nerves, and Bian was cueing me to stay on this path. I said to her, "People who wipe their asses with their hands don't have culture. They can make chemical weapons and bombs, but can't figure out how to produce toilet paper?" I looked down at Ali bin Pacha and asked, "Hey, how do Arabs practice safe sex?" He wasn't going to touch this, and I said, "They put marks on the camels that kick."

A choking sound came from bin Pacha's throat. It sounded like he was trying to clear it, or was pushing words through a dry windpipe. Bian bent forward and said, "Oh . . . you must be parched." She found a glass and a water pitcher by the bed, filled the glass, and held it to his lips. "Here. Drink."

He took a few shallow sips and coughed. Bian placed the glass back to his lips and he drank more heartily. She removed it, bin Pacha turned his eyes to me, and he found his voice. "You will rot in hell."

Now we were getting somewhere.

"Only by the grace of Allah do you still breathe."

"Allah-my-ass. You were too slow on the trigger, pal. Any American kid could've gotten off that shot."

"If there is a second chance, I will kill you. I promise you this."

I laughed. He did not like this, and his eyes sort of narrowed.

Bian said to bin Pacha, "Don't let him goad you. You've just been through a traumatic operation. Don't let him get you worked up."

He ignored her and informed me, "I do not speak with American whores. Do not let her touch me again. Order this infidel bitch to leave my presence."

Bian leaned toward him and said, "Fuck you." Her arm drew back but I grabbed it before she laid one on him.

Well, so much for good cop, bad cop. Now it was bad cop, bad cop, bad prisoner. Obviously, he had a problem with American ladies. This could be a religious or cultural thing, or maybe Ali bin Pacha had some of those icky Freudian issues with his mother, or he liked boys, or girls had never reciprocated his affections because he was a murdering terrorist asshole.

I informed bin Pacha, "American prisons are filled with female guards. They're going to order you around, watch you do potty, and occasionally will strip-search you and do those nasty cavity searches up your butt. Get used to it."

He looked at me. "You are in Arab lands. I will tell you how to behave, and you will conform to my customs. Send her away."

This guy needed to come down a peg and I knew how to do it. I bent toward him and said, "You know what, Ali? You and I, we were in Mogadishu together." This brought a spark of interest to his eyes. "Hey, maybe you and I can join the same veterans' organization. Wear those goofy hats and sit around all day trading bullshit war stories. What do you think?"

He stared at me. I don't think he got the funny hat part.

I continued, "I bring this up . . . only because . . . well, I have this amazing story. Small world and all that. See, a close pal of mine was a helicopter pilot over there. You remember the Apache helicopters? Big ugly things bristling with all those missiles and machine guns that just mess up your day."

Ali bin Pacha was now staring at me with interest bordering on intensity. I continued, "Anyway, one day Mike—that's my buddy's name, Mike—well, one day he came back from this mission and we were sitting around, knocking back brewskis, joking about how many assholes we just killed. And he swore he saw an Arab . . . and he claimed—hey, look, you know how pilots are, okay? Well, maybe you don't. Just trust me, bin Pacha, those guys, they're such bullshitters, they even make up even bigger sins to tell their own priests . . . So, where was I? Oh, yeah, Mike—anyway, he swore he fired a missile and blew off this Arab guy's leg."

I smiled at Bian. "Boy, for a week that's all everybody talked about. Ahab the Arab . . . Ali Baba and the forty one-legged thieves . . . the sheik of where's-a-my-fuckin'-leg."

Bian laughed.

Bin Pacha looked a little upset.

I asked him, "Hey . . . you don't think that was you down there? . . . I mean, Mike amputated this Arab jerkoff, and you're missing a leg, and . . . What are the odds, huh?" I smiled at him.

With typical Arab nonchalance, he replied, "Allah arranges our fates as he wishes."

"Allah-schmalla. He didn't cripple you, pal. It was the United States Army. Come on, how about a little credit?"

He examined my face a moment. "When my leg was injured, I knew it had to be cut off. I ordered my men, saw it off, no anesthetics.

Listen, American—I wanted to feel this pain, to savor this feeling, to remember it always."

"Believe me, I understand. We were drinking *warm* beer over there. That sucked, too."

He smiled. "And am I incorrect in recalling that we drove the American crusaders out of Somalia, that you ran home after we killed your soldiers? I think maybe you should not be boasting about Mogadishu." His smiled widened. "I personally killed one American soldier, and . . . I enjoyed it so much I decided to kill more."

Asshole.

He turned and looked at Bian. He asked, "You are Vietnamese, yes?"

"I'm an American soldier."

"No, you are Vietnamese. From the south, I am sure. So I think that makes you twice the whore. You give yourself to American men, and you serve the American Army that betrayed your people."

"I serve the American Constitution. And who I sleep with is none of your fucking business."

"You spread your filthy legs for these white men who murdered your people. Our Arab women would never do this."

I could feel Bian heating up beside me. I squeezed her hand.

"I have studied this Vietnam War," he continued, sounding just like an arrogant college professor. "Millions of your people died. Your country was bombed, your forests poisoned, your rice fields mined, your cities obliterated. And once the Americans lost too many soldiers, they ran like cowards and left your people to suffer and despair. So it will happen here. *Inshallah.* You will see."

After a moment, Bian replied, "Have you been to Vietnam lately?"

"I have no interest in visiting infidel lands."

"That explains your ignorance. Today, the streets of Vietnam are lined with McDonald's, American luxury hotels, American movies, and American businesses. Guns, dollars . . . whatever it takes, we always win in the end." She smirked at him. "Always."

Whatever he thought about this, he kept it to himself. He turned to me and observed, "You wear the collar insignia of a lawyer."

"Hey, very good. I understand that you study our military manuals." I pointed at the crossed dueling pistols on Bian's collar. "Crossed spoons. She's a cook."

Somebody kicked my leg.

He replied, "I find it curious that your army sends women and lawyers into battle."

"Really? Is it more curious than your movement using one-eyed cripples?"

"I have read your newspapers on the Internet. I think your army can no longer attract young men to become soldiers. Here we have no trouble finding mujahideen willing to martyr for the jihad. Your young are spoiled, decadent, cowardly. They play their video war games and have no interest in real battles where they might die." He added, "Your President lied, and now he cannot find enough new soldiers to come to Iraq to die."

"Don't believe everything you read in our newspapers," I replied, or maybe anything you read. "We can send cooks and lawyers against you with a hand tied behind their backs. Look who's the prisoner."

"I think not. I think your hired mercenaries caused this."

"Who? Oh . . . them . . . the Bowery Boys' Choir. They were here on a USO tour, got a little bored, so we gave them a night off for a little fun." I winked.

"You are a filthy liar."

"No, I'm a lawyer."

He missed the inside humor. He said, "We study everything about you. The longer you remain in our lands, the more we learn about you, and the more dead you will count. We are willing to die for our cause, you are not."

We locked eyes, and I said, "That's why we're here. To help *you* die."

"Yes, but you *are* dying. Your President loses popularity with each coffin. I think you have a lovely American expression for this—you have bitten off more than you can swallow . . . in the corpses of your soldiers."

This was going nowhere. We had all taken our best shots, and now we were merely stoking our mutual resentments. So I changed the tone, and the subject, and told him, "We're here to ask for your cooperation. We want Zarqawi. You're going to help us find him."

He laughed.

As we had discussed beforehand, Bian chipped in to remind him, "There's a twenty-five-million-dollar reward on Zarqawi's head. You've given an eye and a leg to the cause. There's no shame in cashing out now. Surely he considers you expendable and will not mourn your loss. You should return the sentiment."

"I told you to shut up, whore."

I warned him, "There's the nice way, or the hard way."

"Yes?" He looked amused. "Explain for me this hard way. Maybe Abu Ghraib, where your whores will ply their sex perversions and your soldiers will march me around in a hood? Or maybe you will send me to your Guantanamo prison and flush my Koran down the toilet?"

"Do you have a preference?"

"I think not. I think the world knows about the disgusting things your soldiers have done to mujahideen in these places. I think you no longer have a hard way left."

"You can't imagine how much a morality lecture means from somebody who blows up innocent people and slits the throats of helpless prisoners."

"You know of what I am referring, I think."

In fact, I did. I quietly reached down and turned a knob; instantly, a small vial of colorless fluid began squirting into his IV tube.

Ali bin Pacha was every bit the overbaked fanatic Abdul had warned us he would be. Like many extremists, he was emotionally limited, those emotions ranging between fury, hate, and chronic self-righteousness. But he wasn't stupid, and surely he was cognizant that under enough torture, everybody breaks. I recalled a former client who had been beaten to a pulp by a dumb, sadistic southern deputy sheriff until he confessed to being a bank robber, a child molester, and a serial killer, ending with the astonishing revelation that he was the second man on the knoll at JFK's assassination.

Even the sheriff, who was a few quarts low of IQ juice, had trouble with that after learning the confessor wasn't born until 1973. In fact, my client was guilty of nothing except diddling the deputy sheriff's wife. It was criminally stupid, but it was not criminal behavior. The point: Coerced statements introduce reliability issues. That is, unless you begin the process with a man you *know* is guilty; usually then you'll get something more credible and useful.

As an attorney, I am of course philosophically opposed to torture under any circumstances, though men like Abdul Almiri and Ali bin Pacha are tempting. On more practical grounds, however, an interrogation ultimately is a form of negotiation—to succeed, there has to be a carrot, and there has to be a stick. Ali bin Pacha was telling me where I could put the stick.

He informed me, "My comrades will know I am a prisoner of your army. You cannot hide or disguise this. They will post my capture on a Web site, and they will notify Aljazeera, and so the world will hear of this. I think your press will be very interested about me."

"Is there a point to this?"

"I think you know my point. Mistreat me, and your press will create for you another big public problem—another embarrassment your idiot President cannot explain."

The Army advises that one should never underestimate the enemy, and here, I thought, was a case in point. Bin Pacha's people had planned for this eventuality, the capture of their moneyman, they were sensitive to the need to shield him from coercive tactics, and they were sure they knew how to do it.

In truth, on any other day it might even have been a workable plan. I turned to Bian. "These people are smart, aren't they?"

"I guess so."

"I mean . . . this is . . . you know . . . ?"

"I know. This guy so much as gets an infected pimple, and the whole world will scream that we're Nazis."

"That seems to be the general idea."

"Very clever."

"Would you ever have—?"

"Nope. Not in a million years."

Bin Pacha's smile now looked a little less certain; it looked wobbly, actually.

Bian grabbed my arm. "Well, he has been unconscious for three days."

Bin Pacha had not a clue what we were talking about, but he was reading our body language and picking up the sarcasm in our voices. I looked at him and said, "Which do you want first, pal? The merely bad news or the crap-in-your-drawers news?"

The smile disappeared. But maybe he didn't understand the question.

"Well . . . why don't we ease into it?" I continued, "Bad news first. The morning you were captured, the Army and Marines kicked off a big-time assault on Falluja. Last report I heard—this was two hours ago—about three hundred of your fellow terrorists are dead, many dozens more are buried in the rubble, and who knows how many have been turned into mist or paste by tank and artillery shells."

In case he didn't get the message, Bian added, "Your compatriots will never know whether you've been captured, blown to pieces, or just buried in the rubble."

He had asked for it and it was time for the kicker. I said, "Last chance—will you cooperate or not?"

"Rot in hell."

I turned to Bian. "Can't say we didn't try."

"Sure did." She glanced at bin Pacha. "Poor soul."

Bin Pacha now looked very interested in this exchange, dealing as it did with his fate. He insisted, "I am more than willing to live the rest of my life in your prisons. You are fools to think I am fearful of this."

"I'm sure you are not." And I was sure it was true.

Bian had endured this guy's abuse with commendable stoicism—well, but for that one minor incident—and it seemed only fair for her to be the bearer of the worst tidings. I glanced at her, and she nodded.

She faced Ali bin Pacha. "You're being turned over to Saudi intelligence. I've never seen them so anxious to get their hands on a prisoner."

I added, "Your countrymen play by different rules. You're aware of this." I added, "If you're interested, they already have your family in custody."

His eyes went a little wide, but he didn't look as upset as I expected. In fact, I thought I saw a faint smile. This guy had more bullshit bravado than an Army Ranger, which is saying something.

Bian advised him, "Some parting advice." She may have been an infidel slut, but she now had his undivided attention. "Don't hold on to it too long. I've seen prisoners who tried. They were missing body parts, and in some cases, missing family members. And you know what? They all talked."

I assured him, "You'll talk as well."

Bian added, "How much agony and how many parents and brothers are a few hours or days of silence worth?"

Ali bin Pacha's eyelids were fluttering. You could see he was fighting to maintain consciousness, and you could also see that Doc Enzenauer's magical mickey had already coursed through the IV tube, through his veins, and straight to his evil brain.

He tried to say something and what came out was, "Oh . . . I . . . ugh . . ."

To send him off on the right note, I said, "Ali, you're going home."

His eyes closed.

CHAPTER THIRTY

In a convoy escorted by a platoon of detached military police, we drove for more than an hour from the Army field hospital and ended up at the entrance of a small military base. A metal sign by the entrance read, "Forward Operating Base Alpha"—in military jargon, FOB Alpha.

The base was entirely encased within ten-foot-high concrete blast walls and concertina wire, and if, say, you had forgotten you were in a war zone, this forbidding exterior reminded you that there were two worlds here—the violent, hazardous one outside the gates, and these highly fortified bases, like Old West cavalry forts.

Directly outside the gate on the roadway were five oversize speed bumps and a series of oil barrels filled with sand or concrete, arrayed in a winding maze so you had to slow to a crawl and make about ten short-angled turns. Also there were two twenty-foot concrete towers, from each of which the worrying snouts of big .50 caliber barrels followed our progress.

This reminded me, as I said, of an old cavalry fort, though the occupation of Iraq wasn't supposed to look like this: I recalled the stories Grandpa told me about *his* occupation after Germany surrendered—of round-heeled frauleins, of beery nights in gasthauses, of a fortune in black-market cigarettes and silk stockings—the uniquely American version of rape, pillage, and plunder. Better still, his natives accepted their defeat. Occupations are supposed to be the fun part of war, but I suspected no one would return from this occupation feeling nostalgic.

A pair of soldiers cautiously approached the lead SUV, and apparently Phyllis handled the entry requirements. Whatever she said, both guards snapped to attention and banged off crisp salutes, ordinarily a sign of respect—not in a combat zone, though. Might as well hang a fluorescent sign around the neck of the recipient for enemy snipers that announces, "NOT ME, IDIOT—SHOOT HER."

During my own combat tours, we actually used to make a point of saluting senior officers we didn't like. We thought this was very hilarious; they looked very aggravated. Maybe you had to be there, though.

Anyway, the guards signaled for us to enter the compound, and our convoy drove at slow speed over the bumps, through the winding path of barrels, and entered the gate.

I rode in the rear of the trailing vehicle, a military ambulance, with bin Pacha, who remained unconscious, and beside me sat Doc Enzenauer, who occupied himself monitoring his patient's vital signs, adjusting IV fluids, and doing doctorly things.

I looked out the side window as we progressed through the base, which pretty much was what you could infer from the title: a small, temporary encampment located in close proximity to the enemy. Inside Iraq, of course, this would be *any* base flying the Stars and Stripes. As it was, the weapons clearing barrels outside each building and the sandbags covering the roofs dispelled any illusion of an R&R center.

To most civilian eyes, all soldiers appear alike, androgynous beings wrapped in camouflage, with their hair closely cropped and an iron rod stuffed up their rear. But here the troopers mostly looked a little older, they sported the most up-to-date body armor, were carrying the coolest, latest gadgetry, and definitely swaggered more than your run-of-the-mill GIs, who generally look like confused high school kids stumbling around in oversize uniforms.

So this was a base for Special Operations warriors, which made sense because the CIA and Special Forces, which have always been close, after 9/11 have become as inseparable as a hunter and his favorite fetching dog.

After about a quarter of a mile, we stopped in front of a small compound within the compound—also surrounded by concertina barbed wire, and containing five small squarish buildings, each constructed of rough, reinforced gray concrete, ugly and utilitarian. I saw no signs, no windows, and definitely no smiling people standing by the stoop waving welcome signs.

The Army has an umbilical addiction to signs—even the uniform is a billboard of data—so this was not an Army facility, and the absence of windows suggested that these airless dwellings were either ammunition storage facilities or jails. If you were wondering, by the way, only a fool would place an ammo dump in the middle of a troop compound.

As I dismounted from the rear of the ambulance, Bian approached me and said, "When I was stationed here, I heard stories about this place."

"Tell me about those stories."

"Whenever we got our hands on high-value detainees—HVDs, we called them—we of course reported that up the chain. Often, that same night, a group of serious gentlemen in civilian clothes would show up with transfer orders and spirit them away. We jokingly called this the Ministry of Truth."

As Bian explained this, I kept the corner of my eye on Phyllis, who was leading the sheik and Waterbury past the concertina wire and straight to the first building. She opened the door and the group disappeared inside. She appeared to be at home, and something about the sheik's movements and gestures suggested this wasn't his maiden visit either. Why did this not surprise me? I asked Bian, "CIA operation?"

"I believe the FBI is here as well."

"Are they the prisoners?"

She laughed.

I looked around for a moment, then said, "I'll bet one of these buildings has a bar."

"You know what, Sean? You're like one of those guys marooned in a desert. There's no oasis and there's no f-ing alcohol in a combat zone. Get used to it."

"Wanna bet?" Smart as she was, she was a slow learner—Agency people create their own rules, and I couldn't imagine them spending a year, anywhere, without a gin mill. I said, "First round?"

"You're on." She stuck out a hand and we shook.

I looked around again and asked, "Did you ever see any prisoners return from here?"

"That's part of the rep. Once you land here, you disappear into a black hole. Except Saddam. Word is he spent time at Alpha being wrung dry before he was transferred to Camp Cropper in Baghdad. A lot of the prisoners who come here, I think, eventually end up at Gitmo or are renditioned to their own countries."

Supposedly, prisoners apprehended in Iraq are not subject to rendition. But as I was learning with Ali bin Pacha, exceptions are made, especially when they think nobody's looking.

Also the buildings did not appear expansive enough to hold more than one or, at most, two prisoners apiece. I didn't see a graveyard or a large incinerator, so maybe Bian was right. I said, "We'd better go inside before Phyllis cuts a deal and we end up in cells."

We followed the same path Phyllis took, through the concertina wire and the same doorway into the same building, and ended up inside a cramped, rectangular room with a receptionist behind a gray metal desk, but otherwise devoid of furniture and, more mysteriously, of Phyllis and her playmates. I looked around for another door. None. I wondered if we had entered the malicious lair of Dr. No, and at any moment the sly villain behind the desk would break into an evil cackle, push a button, and the floor would drop out beneath us, revealing a pit of snapping alligators.

The receptionist did not look particularly demonic, but you never know. Actually, he was a nice, earnest-looking sort in a white short-sleeved dress shirt, without tie, who very pleasantly asked, "Can I help you?"

I gave him our names, flashed my Agency ID, and informed him we were part of Ms. Carney's party.

He smiled. "Oh . . . right." The floor did not drop, and he said, "She instructed me to tell you to wait here. She'll be back up in a minute."

So Bian and I leaned our butts against the wall and cooled our heels. The room was hot and stale, with that pungent, unpleasant odor of damp earth. The young man behind the desk had said "back up"—ergo, there was a hidden stairwell or elevator that led to a subterranean facility, and probably there was a control device on his desk, and for sure there was a gun under the desk for unwelcome visitors. I smiled at him and tried to look welcome.

It was all coming together—an underground jailhouse. Actually, it made sense. No visible footprint, the noise and activity would be muffled, belowground facilities are fairly secure from breakout, or from break-in, and better yet, are largely bombproof. Ironically, the prisoners here were probably in the safest place inside a country they had made incredibly unsafe. I mentioned to Bian, "I'll bet there's a camera inside that light fixture."

She pushed a lock of hair into place. She said, "Smile for the viewing audience."

Why not? I smiled. A by-product of this shadowy war against terrorism has been the emergence of these clandestine detention and interrogation facilities, about which my reaction can best be described as Jekyllish and Hydey. My lawyer side regards them as an abomination of all that the American legal establishment holds dear—transparency, rights of the accused, timely representation and trial, due process, and so forth. And in my soldier's heart, I have absolutely no problem with them.

The truth is, the people incarcerated in these hidden prisons aren't ordinary criminals; in fact, they aren't criminals at all. Nor, in my personal view, are they prisoners of war, because terrorism is not war, it is the incoherent slaughter of innocents. No, these perps are something else entirely, a conspiracy of assassins and mass murderers who obey no rules, who respect no boundaries, neither moral or geographic, in an age when technology affords them the ability to really bring down the house. New games, new stakes—new rules.

I mean, nobody squawked when the tools of law enforcement were fudged and expanded to handle the Mafia, who, comparatively, are just a bunch of quaint fat guys who never got the message about gold chains and leisure suits. At least they have a code of behavior, and the awareness that they can whack themselves to their heart's content, but when they kill cops or innocents, the gloves really come off. For the terrorist, innocence is the target, and deterrence is the need to look around for a softer target.

No, the nature of this war wasn't of our making; it was theirs, and in a conflict such as this, you win or you lose on intelligence. As Bian noted, this isn't a battle for the enemy capital, or for the decisive terrain, or to capture enemy guidons, the traditional measures of victory in war as we knew it; it is a struggle to locate and get the worst assholes off the street, then climb inside their heads and learn who their friends are, and what nefarious schemes are afoot *before* you learn about it on the evening news.

This doesn't mean the wardens get carte blanche; however, a little isolation and secrecy and some imaginative mind-bending can be worth their weight in human lives.

Anyway, reverting to my lawyer half, I stared into the light fixture and waved my middle finger. Bian laughed.

"Excuse me," I asked the nice young man, "Is there a bar in this compound?"

He looked up and gave me the best news of the day. "Yep."

I smiled at Bian. She gave me the middle finger and said, "I'm shocked."

"And I like scotch." I turned back to him and asked, "Where?"

"Third building back."

After a moment, I mentioned to him, "I don't drink myself. But the lady's a lush."

His smile widened. "Well, it's off-limits to military personnel. Tough luck, huh?"

The nice young man in the white shirt wasn't so nice after all. I asked, "Does your mom know you're here?"

He stared at me a moment. "I can let you go downstairs, but I don't have to let you back up." He laughed.

Sometimes it pays to be polite, and I joined him.

Bian asked him, "What's downstairs?"

"A state-of-the-art interrogation and detention center. Constructed right after the war. The prisoners call it the dungeon. We call it the toilet." He laughed. "Get it? This is where we flush the biggest shits."

Got it. And I'll bet this wasn't the line he used with visiting Red Cross delegations. His phone rang and he answered it. "What? . . . Yeah . . . okay, they're here." Pause. "Sure, I'll tell them." He then pressed his left forefinger on a pad on his desk and, after a long moment, a plate in the wall slid open and revealed a cargo elevator. Unbelievable.

He looked at me and said, "Pretty cool, huh? Ms. Carney says to come down. I'll tell your people to bring in the detainee."

Bian and I walked to and then entered the elevator. He pressed another button, the door closed, and we were flushed downstairs. After about ten seconds it reopened and we stepped out into a small operations center, a warren of interlocked cubes where thirty or so people were performing activities that ranged from sitting on their asses, to resting their derrieres, to loafing on their butts, all functions they could as easily do back in the good ol' USA.

A middle-aged gent in civilian khakis was waiting for us, and he introduced himself as Jim Tirey. He had clean-cut, all-American good looks, serious eyes, and he offered me a firm, businesslike handshake and said, "That will be your last obscene gesture into our cameras. Understand?"

"You must be FBI," I concluded.

"I must be," he replied coolly. "The Special Agent in Charge in country. Follow me."

So we did, down a short hallway, where we hooked a left, and then down a far longer hallway, at the end of which was a conference room that we entered. The air down here was damp and cool, with yellow fluorescent lighting that was intermittently spaced, as though the contractor had overlooked certain sections—but probably generators powered everything and energy conservation was at a premium. The prevailing ambiance, however, was a little spooky, as were our hosts, if you'll pardon the pun.

The conference room itself was small and stuffy, about ten by twelve, with a scarred, worn mahogany dining room table, unupholstered metal chairs, and hanging on the wall, a huge plasma-screen television with wires running octopus-like to a wall-mounted surround sound system. The room smelled of cigarettes and stale sweat, frustration and desperation. Actually I'm making that up; it smelled like lemon Pledge. But on the screen was a top-down view of a cramped prison cell containing only a metal bunk, no blanket, no sheets, and the proverbial pot to piss in.

My CIA friends call this a surveillance room, and my naval friends an observation deck. Same thing, though there's a world of difference in the mind-set.

Phyllis and the sheik stood in front of the plasma screen, slurping coffee from foam cups. Waterbury leaned against a wall on the far side of the room, and at the moment we entered he was regaling them with a tale about his time as an MP, something about how he single-handedly cleaned up the nastiest post in the Army.

Retired soldiers manufacture more bullshit than cows, but considering the source, it sounded about right.

Phyllis had endured this guy on the drive down and her face now had the fixed look she gets in the presence of insufferable assholes, so I cut in by pointing at the screen. "Nice room. Is it mine?"

She smiled at me. "Don't give me ideas."

Tirey took that as a cue and said, "What you're seeing is a one-way cable feed from bin Pacha's cell. Agents from Turki's service are already there and set up." He went on for our benefit, "The only people in this facility with knowledge of the detainee's identity are inside this room or inside that cellblock. That's it. Hermetic containment. We employed identical arrangements when Saddam was our guest."

He paused to see if we had any questions. We did not, and he pointed a finger at the screen and continued, "That entire cellblock is isolated, and the interrogation room we'll use is on the same wing. The two cells next to bin Pacha's contain Saudi intelligence agents who will impersonate prisoners, attempt to befriend him, and coax him into sharing confidences. Old trick, but a reliable one. It works more than you would believe. The guards in the wing are all Saudi intelligence."

He looked at Sheik al-Fayef and added, "Due to the sensitivity of this investigation, the video feed from this cell—in fact from the entire cellblock to the main control room down the hall—has been rerouted to this room. Only from here can you observe or overhear the interrogations."

He went on awhile with this nickel tour, about how the prisoner would be fed, given medical care, showers, and so forth.

It sounded like these people really had their stuff together—a foolproof charade, supertight security, all the electronic bells and whistles, and the object of this drill was about to be put into play. What was there not to like?

I interrupted his spiel and asked, "Are there any Americans in the cellblock?"

"No. Why?"

"Why not?"

Tirey chuckled like that was a dumb question, which annoyed me a little. He said, "A number of our staff speak Arabic—none, however, are *from* Saudi Arabia. I'm told the dialect is distinct to the ears of native speakers and . . . Look, don't worry about it. Everything that occurs in that wing can be seen and can be heard from this room. If a fly bats its wings, we'll hear it. Everything."

The sheik looked happy but not surprised to hear this, and nodded approvingly. One of his French cigarettes was already dangling between his lips and the ashes fell off and left a big mark on his white robe. He asked me, "You spoke with bin Pacha in the hospital?"

"I did. Major Tran and I prepped him."

Bian chipped in, "He'll believe he's awakening in a Saudi prison."

"Yes, yes, this is important." He studied my eyes a moment. Despite, or perhaps because of, our earlier unpleasantness, he seemed to regard me as interesting. He asked me, "And now that you have spoken together, what are your thoughts about him?"

"A tough guy. He enjoys his work, he hates America, and has no fear of spending his life in jail." After a moment, I noted, "I wouldn't want my career hanging on whether he'll talk."

"So you do not believe he will confess his sources?"

"I do not." We locked eyes and I couldn't tell what he thought about this.

Bian helpfully informed him, "I spent six months interrogating suspects and captured mujahideen. Typically, the higher-level ones are superbly trained and conditioned for counterinterrogation. Many proved very difficult to break. Some, impossible."

"Is this so?"

"Well, there are the lucky few who immediately blurt everything. But there are others, prisoners at Guantanamo, for instance, who required over a year of exhaustive effort. Some of those we have broken, we suspect their testimony was planted disinformation."

He offered her a faint smile. "We have never experienced this problem."

Waterbury announced, "There he is," and we all turned and observed the video screen. Doc Enzenauer led a pair of gentlemen in civilian khakis who carried bin Pacha on a stretcher into the cell. They gently hoisted him by his feet and shoulders off the stretcher and onto the metal cot. Enzenauer then bent down and efficiently withdrew the IV from the prisoner's arm, a necessary precaution against suicide.

Enzenauer straightened up and stared up into the camera, which, like the one on the top floor, was apparently planted in the light fixture. After a moment he asked uncertainly, "Can you hear me?"

The sound was locked on full blast and it sounded like he was howling through a megaphone; it was a one-way feed, though, and there was no answer. After a long hesitation, he informed us, "He should remain unconscious for perhaps another hour." He stared awkwardly into the camera, like a stagestruck actor wondering if the scene was over.

Then he and the two men backed out of the room and closed and locked the cell door behind them. We all stared for a moment at the unconscious prisoner resting on the bed, and we shared the same unspoken thought—inside that skull was knowledge that could change the course of this war, that could lead us to the architect of countless killings, that could expose the names of people and groups who were funding the wholesale destruction of an entire society. Unlock those secrets and a world of invaluable knowledge would land in our laps.

Bian whispered to me, "You realize the only thing you and I might've accomplished here depends on whether he talks."

I whispered back, "And it will be worth it."

She nodded and we shared an unspoken agreement: We were going home empty-handed.

CHAPTER THIRTY-ONE

Phyllis and party left to grab dinner in the dining facility, leaving Bian and me to observe Ali bin Pacha.

To kill the boredom, Bian and I made small talk for a while before I very suavely inched into what really interested me. I said, "So, how was Baghdad?"

"You stayed in Baghdad also."

"Airports aren't *in* countries. They're all part of the Twilight Zone."

She smiled. "Baghdad was wonderful. The jihadis took a breather. Very few bombings and I heard gunshots only half the time."

I smiled back. "And did you see Mark?"

"Why do you ask?"

"Am I being too personal?"

"It's . . ." After a long pause, she informed me, "Yes."

"Yes, it's too personal, or yes, you saw Mark?"

"Yes . . . I saw Mark. We got a room at the Visiting Officers' Quarters inside the Green Zone. We spent two wonderful days together."

"Good . . . I'm glad . . . really . . . it's . . . Hey, did you catch the Redskins game?"

"Do you want to talk about this or not?"

"I . . ." *Not.*

She looked at me.

I started to say something, but she beat me to it. She said, "I've made this awkward for both of us, haven't I? Are you mad at me for leading you on? Don't answer that. I know it's my fault . . . and my . . . my responsibility to clear the air. So I'll just say it—I do now, and I will always love Mark. I remembered that the instant I laid eyes on him. I'm sorry if I became confused." She added, in a quiet voice, "I'm even sorrier if I confused you."

"I understand."

"Good. Because I don't." She gave me a sad smile.

"Bian, what happened . . . This is a war zone, a lot of bad memories are flooding back for you, this case is tapping into your emotions, and—"

"Okay, I've got it. What I did . . . in the shower . . . it was a careless lapse, an excusable stupidity."

"Well . . ."

"I . . . That came out wrong, didn't it? I didn't mean it that way, Sean. Seriously . . . I'm incredibly fond of you." She was struggling to find the right words, and eventually said, "If there was anybody in the world I would enjoy cheating on Mark with, it would be you."

"That's—"

"I know. I did it again. I'm a little tongue-tied here. I haven't experienced this before."

"I hope not." I looked at her and asked, "Did you tell Mark about us?"

"I did not. What was there to tell? Nothing really happened, did it? I owe that to you. I doubt many men would've . . . you know."

"Don't remind me."

She smiled. "Believe it or not, I appreciate it."

Mercifully, our little *Days of Our Lives* episode came to an abrupt end, because the door opened and in stepped Jim Tirey, the FBI SAC. I mean, in my line of work, I can and do talk freely and intelligently with hardened killers, pissed-off judges, skeptical juries—but when it comes to heart-to-heart discussions with women . . .

Anyway, for about ten seconds Tirey casually watched bin Pacha on the screen, then he informed us, "We're about to start the treatment. Our welcome concert for all new internees. Thought I'd better alert you."

He turned around, looked at us, and almost as an afterthought asked, "May I join you?"

Bian said, "Please do . . . uh—"

"Jim . . . please." He moved to the table, sat across from us, and took a moment getting comfortable. He said, "I'm told you two went into Falluja and made the apprehension."

Bian nodded.

He shook his head. "That was . . . incredibly brave. The same morning the attack started, right?"

"Somebody forgot to warn us," I informed him truthfully.

"Glad you explained that." He smiled. "I was worried that you're complete idiots."

Bian pointed at me and commented, "He told me he was taking me to Vegas. So you can imagine my surprise when . . ."

Jim chuckled. We all laughed. Ha-ha. Baghdad humor. He said, "Well, for the record, it was worth it. We get a lot of the old regime here, and their testimonies and confessions will be helpful when the Iraqis get around to prosecuting Saddam and the old guard. But their value is historical at this point. Old business. Current operational guys are more rare, and definitely more interesting."

I didn't really want to talk about this, so to divert the conversation, I mentioned, "I didn't even realize the FBI was here."

"The American public doesn't know we're here."

The publicity machine of the besainted Bureau makes Madison Avenue look like pikers, so I was surprised to hear this. "Why are you here?"

He lit a cigarette and spent a moment considering his response. "A little of this, some of that. We give investigations training to the Iraqi police. For a high-value investigation—say, a particularly nasty bombing or VIP assassination—we handle the more demanding criminology work, forensic collection, residue analysis, technical analysis. Also, there are a lot of American firms here—sometimes we investigate them." He smiled. "Believe it or not, there's a lot of graft over here. Uncle Sam is spending over a billion bucks a month, and it brings out everybody's best instincts. Bribery, overbilling, kickbacks, the usual funny business." He stopped smiling. "My detachment's not that big, so sometimes it's just liaison work with the labs at Quantico or referral work with stateside offices."

"This must be a career-enhancing assignment."

He forced a tight smile. "Sure is. If you survive." He added, "But the Bureau *does* look kindly on overseas hardship assignments. If you're interested, we're all volunteers here. This is where the action is—great training, great experience, and great tax benefits."

This sounded like the standard recruiting spiel, and as with Army recruiters, one thing was not emphasized, and that was the great odds of a premature funeral.

But frankly I was having trouble picturing boys and girls in blue suits and starched white shirts running around Baghdad. Tirey apparently read my thoughts, because he remarked, frowning, "It takes a little adjustment. The hours suck. And the working conditions are almost indescribable." He said, "Also, the cops here are a joke. They're lazy, crooked, corrupt, on the take, infiltrated, or scared shitless of the insurgents."

"Maybe the fact that the insurgents are targeting them has something to do with it."

"Tell me about it. It's just that you can't trust them. They destroy evidence, pollute crime scenes, and feed us false leads. I used to think the stateside cops are a pain in the ass . . . You know what? I actually look forward to working with the NYPD."

I could've told him that a lot of foreign armies we work with are worse; instead, I nodded.

He continued, "The Bureau has opened a lot of these overseas stations in the past ten years. In the old days, if you wanted fast track, the New York office was the place to be. Now it's pissholes like this." He shook his head.

Truly it was a new world, and the FBI, like the Army, was struggling to find its footing, and its people, trained and bred as they were to fight American crime in American cities, were having to learn new tricks and new angles, with different rules. He mentioned, "You might be interested to know that we flew in a team of financial forensics specialists. Assuming bin Pacha spills, they'll follow the money."

Bian was just responding to that statement when, out of the blue, our conversation was drowned out by an earsplitting noise, the sound of people shrieking and howling, that was really awful. The surround sound system was set at full blast and it sounded like a live concert from Dante's Inferno. I nearly jumped out of my shorts, and Bian actually did jump out of her chair and grabbed and squeezed my arm.

Jim mouthed the word "Relax." He got up, walked to the video screen, grabbed the remote, and pushed the mute button, which brought instant silence. He smiled at us in an amused way. "I tried to warn you. And don't get your pants on fire. It's a tape. Speakers are mounted outside of bin Pacha's cell. A little mood music to put new detainees in the right frame of mind."

And indeed, on the screen you could see bin Pacha's eyes pop open, and then he bolted upright and made a swift visual survey of his new environment. Doc Enzenauer had cautioned us that the aftereffects of the drugs and anesthetics would leave him groggy and possibly would impair his judgment for a day or two. But on his face I saw no sign of confusion or disorientation—he *knew* he was in the shithole of the universe.

Jim had apparently seen this movie before, and wasn't interested in the rerun. He lit another cigarette and, through the billows of smoke, studied Bian and me. He said, "How did you know bin Pacha was in Falluja? And *where* to find him?"

I mean, it was hard not to admire the sneaky way he'd worked up to this question—this guy was smooth. It was none of his business, of course. But when you say that to a cop they make your business their business. Without pausing, Bian replied, "An informer. A member of his own network, if you can believe it."

"An inside informer? Wow."

"I know. Almost unheard of." After a moment, she added, "You'll enjoy this delicious irony. Zarqawi's people accidently blew up their own man's family with a car bomb. It's about revenge."

Sounded good to me.

But Tirey replied, "What are the odds of *that*, huh?"

My eyes were intermittently weaving between Tirey, Bian, and the video screen. I saw bin Pacha push off the cot and get to his feet. For a moment he swayed back and forth like an unsteady, one-legged drunk, but eventually he achieved his sea legs and steadied himself. His head turned sharply toward the door, then he stumbled, sort of dragging his fake leg, across the small cell.

Bian was telling Tirey, "When I took prob and stats at West Point, we had case studies like this. You know . . . assume a country of twenty-three million people, with ten thousand terrorists, who have fifty thousand direct family members, and who detonate two thousand bombs indiscriminately . . . what's the probability they'll blow up their own families?"

Bian was elaborating too much, which, with a cop or a lawyer, is like slicing your wrist in a shark-filled tank.

"Interesting way to look at it," remarked Tirey, but not all that sincerely. He pulled a drag on his cigarette and said, "Well, here's another curious thing. I was told you two flew into the country for this operation. Why? What's wrong with the local talent?"

Not only was this guy smooth, he was sharp.

On the screen, I observed bin Pacha now gesticulating with his hands. Because our viewing angle was a top-down, you couldn't see his lips moving, though it sure *looked* like he was conversing with somebody. I really wished I'd paid more attention when Enzenauer explained the aftereffects from the drugs and anesthetics. Maybe he mentioned hallucinations during the period when I tuned him out, meaning most of the conversation. I'm not paid enough for medical lectures.

"Don't read anything into it," Bian was instructing Tirey. "Our source is still embedded in the insurgency. You know the mantra—extraordinary sources, extraordinary precautions."

Bin Pacha had crossed the cell and was leaning against the cell door. Now I was sure he was conversing with somebody.

I interrupted their conversation to mention, "Ali bin Pacha's awake. He seems to be talking. Maybe we should turn up the sound."

But Tirey was preoccupied with his interrogation and I think he suspected I was trying to divert him, which I was. Clearly, Bian had underestimated this guy, and was digging herself deeper into what law schools call "the liar's grave."

Also, I *did* want to know who bin Pacha was addressing, and about what. I mentioned it again, and Tirey answered, "In a minute." To Bian, he said, "I don't mean to get into your business." But of course he did, and he leaned closer to her face. "I'm used to being treated like a mushroom around here—fed shit and kept in the dark. But it helps to know the background before we begin an interrogation. Exactly *how* did you learn about his location?"

She asked, "Why would I lie about this?"

Now bin Pacha was waving his arms and gesturing emphatically with his hands. Whatever he was saying looked insistent and emotional, and he placed his head against the door, moving his ear against what must've been an opening.

Tirey was saying, "That's what I'm asking myself. Why would—" when on the screen I saw a cloud of red mist suddenly materialize from the side of bin Pacha's skull. In the same instant, his head flew sharply sideways, followed by his body, which landed in a heap on the floor. I yelled, "Oh shit!"

Tirey looked at me, then he turned to the screen, as did Bian, and their eyes shot wide open as they observed bin Pacha lying prostrate, and the arc of blood and gray stuff splattered across the floor. The TV had amazing picture quality, incidentally; you could even see where the tiniest dots of blood had stuck on the far wall.

"Jesus!" Tirey yelled. "What the fuck . . . ?"

There wasn't time for an explanation. I stood and ran for the door, yelling at Tirey, "Where's his cell?"

He followed behind me, his gun drawn, with Bian sprinting behind him. We made it down the long hallway in about ten seconds, and fortunately the elevator default setting was on the operations floor. We stepped inside, he pushed the proper button, the doors slid closed, and we began our descent.

Tirey drew a few deep breaths then asked, "Now tell me—what the hell happened down there?"

"He was speaking with somebody. Through the cell door, I think. He moved his ear closer—there must be an opening, right?—and his brains blew out."

"Shit."

There was no way to improve on that sentiment and nobody tried. Clearly Special Agent Tirey now knew it had been a big mistake to leave the Saudis in control of the wing. I wasn't sure if he was in charge of this show or Phyllis. But if his name was on the blameline, the brief picture he had just observed on the video screen was his career flushing down the toilet.

The door slid open and we rushed out, then hooked a left and sprinted down a long hallway. We took another left and ended up moving down a short, poorly lit wing with cell doors on each side.

Five armed men in Saudi uniforms were gathered at the end of the hallway, standing casually, chatting, a few smoking cigarettes as if nothing had happened. Appropriately, Tirey raised his weapon and said, "Put down your weapons. Hands over your heads."

About fifteen yards separated us; they had five guns, we had one. The space was narrow and enclosed, and if this was a shooting gallery, the Kewpie doll was theirs for the taking.

None of the Saudis replied; but nobody made a threatening gesture either, which was a relief. Bian said, "Let me try." She unreeled something in rapid-fire Arabic and the five men stared back without responding. Bian repeated herself, louder, more slowly, and more emphatically. One of the Saudis replied, in Arabic, and what ensued was a conversation, brief and sharp, and nobody put down their weapons and nobody raised their hands.

Bian informed us, "The man is telling us to relax. He says they're the good guys. He says we're on the same side."

"We're *not* on the same side," I told her.

"No shit."

"Tell them they're under arrest."

"Don't," said Tirey, who pointed out, "They're not American nationals. I don't have the legal authority to arrest them." He whispered, more ardently, "For Godsakes, don't put them in a corner. We're outnumbered."

Good point. But I don't like impasses, unless I'm the source and it's to my advantage. The man who had spoken with Bian seemed to be in charge and I approached him with my palms extended. This was *my* prisoner they murdered. Bian and I had risked our lives to get this guy, now for nothing. I was pissed, but I wasn't armed, and as Tirey pointed out, there were more of them than us. Clearly, here was a situation that called for adroit diplomacy.

He watched me approach and edged backward a few steps, away from me and toward his group. I stopped about two feet short of him, near enough that I could smell menthol cigarettes on his breath, and near enough that I could be on him before he squeezed the trigger. I gave him a friendly smile. He smiled back. I laid a chummy hand on his shoulder and squeezed, very gently. He sort of relaxed. I landed a hard punch in his solar plexus, a popping sound came from his throat, his weapon dropped to the floor, and he fell to this knees, gasping for breath—as a prelude to diplomacy I thought it was important to clarify that we weren't on the same side.

I took a step back and regarded the faces of the other men, and I noted that they shared this insight, because now four pistols were directed at me. Well . . . so much for diplomacy. I said, "Lay down your weapons. Now."

This is what's called a tense moment. All it took was one misjudgment, and studying their faces, I detected at least two guys who looked mistake-prone.

But at that instant, five Americans, guns drawn, came sprinting around the corner. We must've passed a panic button on our way down here, and Tirey had apparently exercised good foresight and punched it. Sounding relieved, Tirey said to Bian, "Tell them it's over," and he ordered his people, "Take their weapons and cuff them."

Bian said something in Arabic, the Saudi guards saw that the jig was up, and one by one they lowered their weapons and placed them on the floor. This was good, because they had all been pointed at me.

But clearly, the hermetic seal around this operation was now blown. In the next few minutes everybody inside this facility was going to know about Ali bin Pacha, and his death would be the topic du jour for weeks. Murder—it upsets even the best-laid plans. Bian asked Tirey, "Where's bin Pacha's cell?"

"Over here."

We rushed to the cell, though there was no real need to hurry, and Tirey poked a button on the wall that electronically unlocked the metal door, which he threw open. We entered a room that felt immediately claustrophobic, and on the door at about head height I noted a three-inch barred opening—this would be the aperture through which bin Pacha had his brains blown out. Already, the pungent, metallic smell of fresh blood filled the air and our nostrils.

A dark hole was in bin Pacha's temple, and as I looked around at the flesh and blood spattered on the floor, my first instinct was to get medical assistance, though obviously a janitor made more sense.

Bian's first reaction was to bend over, check his pulse, and then verbalize what had occurred. She said, "He's dead. Those bastards assassinated him. They didn't want us to hear what he had to say."

Tirey, now gawking at bin Pacha's corpse, observed, "This . . . this Saudi arrangement . . . this was . . . you know, the CIA's bright idea." He looked at me, and it dawned on him that I was part of the Agency brotherhood. "It did . . . it originated with your people. I . . . I merely followed orders and . . ." He drifted off to a corner of the cell.

His first instinct was to cover his butt, and at the same time to get his beloved Bureau off the blameline. Somebody was going to be held accountable for this, either the CIA or the FBI, and the early bird was already humping the worm.

Actually, he looked badly shaken—I didn't blame him—and I approached him, squeezed his arm, and reminded him, "This is a crime scene. Treat it as one."

"Uh . . ." He looked around the cell, trying to decide his next move.

I asked, "Was the killing recorded?"

He stared back and did not reply.

I repeated the question.

"Uh . . . no. As I mentioned, the video feed from the cell . . . it was, well . . . disconnected from the central control room. The sessions in the interrogation room . . . we only intended to record those."

He looked unhappy to confess this, and I looked even unhappier to hear it. I said, "All right. This was a close-range shooting, right? Probably there's blood splatter on the weapon, probably fingerprints on the trigger, and definitely there will be powder residue on the hand of the shooter." I squeezed his arm again. "Jim . . . Find the killer."

He looked at me, and in true Bureau spirit said, "I . . . This is going to be really sensitive. I have no legal authority over the Saudis."

"Do you think you're building a case for an American court? Screw the legal niceties." I pointed at bin Pacha's corpse. "They did."

"Okay, yeah." He stepped back into the hallway and fell into the groove, ordering his people to separate the prisoners, even as he dispatched a man upstairs to retrieve a crime kit.

Bian started to say something, but I placed a finger on her lips. I pointed up at the light fixture.

I removed my finger from her lips. She took a deep breath and exhaled, "It was all for nothing, Sean. Everything . . . for nothing."

CHAPTER THIRTY-TWO

Here's a sad fact about a land where death by violence is ubiquitous: The aftermath machinery works with stunning efficiency.

Ali bin Pacha's body was bagged, tagged, and deposited in the base morgue—a long metal shelf in a refrigeration van sequestered from the dining facility. The Saudi weapons were all collected, dusted, and tested for powder residue. Simultaneously, the five Saudi guards and the two agents planted in the bordering cells were interrogated by linguists, fingerprinted, swabbed for powder traces, and then locked, individually, into separate cells.

All of which is SOP whenever conspiracy is a factor, and in this case it was a waste of effort, time, and cell space. We had to assume this was a coordinated conspiracy run by professionals; ergo, the Saudis had been prepped and rehearsed long before we laid eyes on them. Still, after a big screwup everybody pays painstaking attention to procedures they should've obeyed before. Human nature. I do it.

Regarding me, for nearly forty minutes, Tirey's people forced me to recount, over and over, what I had observed. This also is SOP, having the witness repeat the story as you look for flaws, deviations, omissions—anything that indicates the witness isn't reliable, or overlooked an important detail, or isn't credible. There were no deviations—bin Pacha was dead, we had been caught with our pants down, and now everybody was scrambling to figure out how, and why. But the subtext here was who should be blamed, rather than who did the crime.

Solving a closed-room mystery, after all—especially with abundant forensic evidence—is no more challenging than tying a hangman's knot. But putting a name to the killer would look good on paper, at least. Everybody was regretful, embarrassed, and uptight. A high-value detainee had been whacked under their noses, in their own ultra-high-security prison. This isn't supposed to happen.

When the Feds were finally bored with taking my statement, Tirey informed me that Phyllis wanted to see me in the observation room.

I shut the door behind me as I entered, and I found Phyllis and Bian alone, seated side by side at the conference table, sipping pale Iraqi tea and enjoying an amiable chat, the topic of which was not bin Pacha, not this case, not even Iraq. At the moment I entered, in fact, Phyllis was informing Bian, ". . . incredible shoe sale, twice a year at Nordstrom. The best brands. Usually about half off."

To which Bian had replied, "I'll be sure to watch for it."

I mean, you forget these are women, with a life outside of spying and soldiering, with feminine interests, quotidian things like shopping, cooking, knitting. Somebody get me a gun.

I said, "Excuse me," before we were all sharing recipes and trading reviews of Danielle Steel's lastest novel.

Phyllis shot me an annoyed look. "In a moment." She handed Bian a wallet-size photograph. "I appreciate your sharing this with me. He's a most attractive young officer."

The picture was Magnificent Mark, of course. I watched Bian tuck it gingerly inside her wallet. She smiled at Phyllis. "He's a great guy. I'm very lucky."

I cleared my throat. "Is this an inconvenient moment? I mean, our prisoner was just murdered, this case is completely blown, and I want to go home."

Phyllis massaged her temples. "We're all upset, Sean. Outrage won't help."

"What will help? New shoes?"

"We were waiting for you, so Bian and I decided to use the opportunity to become better acquainted."

Bian said to me, "Besides, it's not complicated—al-Fayef played us for idiots."

"We are idiots."

Phyllis awarded me a hard stare, no doubt regretting her stupid "maverick and misfit" management theory. Despite losing arguably the most valuable prisoner of the war since Saddam, she appeared cool and collected, another day at the office, another blown operation. But, after all, the Agency had suffered so many setbacks and embarrassments since September 10, 2001, that I suppose you either respond with studied indifference or you eat a bullet. She said to me very quietly, "We are not idiots. But in retrospect, yes . . . we should perhaps have been more vigilant when he was so agreeable about forgoing rendition."

No *perhaps* about it, lady.

She looked at me and said, "You were the only one who asked why there were no Americans on the cellblock. Why? Did you anticipate something like this?"

She did not add, "Because we all were blind to this possibility, including a guy named Drummond." But that was understood. "No," I admitted, and added, "I was operating on my general distrust of Saudis."

"We all let down our guard," commented Bian. "In my view, we were all fooled . . . and we all share responsibility."

Right. But the board of review wasn't going to see it that way—when it's pin-the-tail-on-the-donkey time, there's only one dart, and they shove it up only one ass. But why bring that up?

Phyllis, to her credit, did say, "It's my responsibility."

I asked, "Are you the senior officer in the facility?"

"Technically, that would be Tirey. But this was my operation."

"I thought Waterbury was in charge. Speaking of which, where is the golden boy?"

"Gone." She gave me a faint smile. "A few minutes after bin Pacha was shot, he remembered he had an urgent appointment with somebody in Baghdad."

I smiled back. In other words, the moment the poop hit the fan, his feet hit the floor. And by now I was sure he had called his buds back in Washington and pointed the finger for this screwup at Phyllis. To err is indeed human, but to blame others is the mark of a promising political appointee.

We all knew, though, that the parties who ultimately were responsible were the power brokers back in D.C. who ordered Phyllis to cooperate with the Saudis in the first place and, de facto, set this chain of events in motion. But if you believe any blame was going to fall in their exalted direction you've never held a job in the federal government.

Of course, the guiltiest party was whoever tipped off the Saudis to bin Pacha's impending capture in the first place. This was the name on Ali bin Pacha's death warrant, and this was the guy I *really* wanted to meet.

I asked, "What was al-Fayef keeping us from finding out?"

Bian looked at Phyllis and suggested, "Maybe bin Pacha and/or Zarqawi have an arrangement with his intelligence service? Maybe he's protecting Zarqawi?"

So Phyllis spent a few moments verbally hashing this idea, essentially giving it short shrift, because Zarqawi now was hooked up with Al Qaeda, and Osama had already added the Saudi royal family to his list of people to fuck with. I wasn't so sure about this, but she concluded, "The Saudis may once have entertained notions that they could accommodate bin Laden, but now they know he's a mortal enemy. And I'm sure they've figured out that after Zarqawi's work in Iraq is done, he and his people are coming after them next."

This made sense, but who knows? There were so many players with their fingers in Iraq, I wasn't even sure all the players even knew they were players. Like some huge sex orgy in a dark room, it was impossible to know who was screwing whom, who was being screwed by whom, and who wanted to screw whom—but it doesn't matter anyway because it all changes every few minutes.

Shifting to a topic we could get our arms around, I asked Phyllis, "Was the killer identified?"

"Yes. A sergeant in the security service. Abu Habbibi by name. Acting alone."

"All five of those guards were pointing weapons at us. He wasn't *alone*."

"Tell me something I don't know, Sean."

"That's the problem. I don't know what you don't know."

She smiled, but it had a hard edge.

I said with some understatement, "I hope you confronted al-Fayef about this."

"We talked."

"And . . . ?"

"He was shocked. He claimed ignorance. He swore he had no inkling this would happen."

"He's lying."

"I know he's lying. At least he had the good manners to make it a well-constructed lie."

"Meaning what?"

"He called his headquarters for a background check on Sergeant Habbibi. It turns out the man's parents died in an Al Qaeda streetside bombing about six months ago. This offers a compelling motive for murder—revenge."

Bian and I exchanged amazed looks. This was the same cooked-up pretense she had contrived and tried out on Tirey only an hour earlier. It hadn't worked then, and was even less persuasive now. Bian remarked, "What a coincidence."

This irony sailed over Phyllis's head, and she replied, "I called our station chief in Jidda. The story was in the Saudi newspapers. Habbibi's parents went out shopping, they parked in the wrong place at the wrong time, and their body parts were scattered across two city blocks."

Bian conceded, "Even if it *is* true, it only explains *why* he was chosen as the executioner."

Phyllis smiled. "Now you're getting it." She looked at me and said, "Tell me everything you saw. *Everything*."

I was beginning to feel like a *M*A*S*H* rerun. But I pushed mental rewind and went through everything, from the moment bin Pacha awoke, through the mist of red spray that blew out the side of his head.

I finished my account and Phyllis considered it a moment. She remarked, "A conversation? You're *sure*?"

I nodded. "I'm sure. He may have been talking to himself, but it looked like he was conversing with somebody. The sound from the video was muted, as you know. No recording was made."

She turned to Bian and without explanation said, "Please get Enzenauer. You'll find him in the ambulance." She added, "Tell him to bring his special equipment."

Bian left. Phyllis and I sat and uncomfortably ignored each other for the next five minutes. I was not happy with her; she was not happy with me. Why discuss it?

Eventually, the door opened and Bian entered, followed by Bob Enzenauer, carrying a mechanical device of some undetermined nature. He placed it in the middle of the conference table, where I examined it more closely—I thought at first that Phyllis must be experiencing a cold-blooded, slow-motion heart attack, and this was a defibrillator—before I realized the pole sticking off it wasn't a shock stem but a fat antenna.

I had completely forgotten about the transmitter sewn into bin Pacha's stomach. So this odd device was the receiver, and maybe everything wasn't lost. Maybe.

Phyllis gave him a welcoming smile and said, "Have a seat, Bob."

He did, and for a moment he studied our faces, which betrayed our apprehension, because he asked, "Is something wrong?"

"Very much so," replied Phyllis. "Ali bin Pacha's dead."

"Oh . . . well . . ." An expression of real concern crossed his face, as he apparently assumed this was a result of his medical advice or skill.

And characteristic of her profession, Phyllis was screwing with his head, she knew it, and she let his agony brew for about ten seconds before she clarified, "By assassination. The Saudi guards."

"Ah . . ."

Phyllis continued, "Unfortunately, our Bureau friends failed to record the events inside his cell. So my questions for you are these: Was he transmitting and was he recorded?"

And characteristic of his profession, Enzenauer spent about thirty seconds looking profoundly thoughtful, as if Phyllis had asked him to solve the mystery of the universe. "Well . . ." he eventually said, "the device is noise-activated. So"—he looked at each of our faces—"yes . . . if he emitted noise, he transmitted. As to whether it was recorded, I frankly don't have a clue."

We all stared with deep fascination at the contraption on the desk. I cleared my throat and asked, "Can you make that thing work?"

"Of course." He pushed a few buttons, and we heard the first optimistic whirring sound of a tape rewinding. For the first time that day, it *looked* like something was going right; we stared at one another in disbelief. The tape stopped and Enzenauer pushed start.

As he had warned, the transmitter was noise-activated, and the first sound came through clear as a bell—Ali bin Pacha let loose a terrifically long and loud fart, which he repeated a few times, followed by satisfied grunts. Nobody laughed or even smiled. Such was the mood that even I resisted the impulse to offer a crude comment.

Doc Enzenauer, however, feeling the need to offer a medical diagnosis, pushed pause and said, "After three days of unconsciousness, it's natural for the body to purge itself."

Well, now it was almost irresistible. But Bian read my mind and was giving me a look.

The doc pushed play, and next came the noise of people screaming and howling from pain.

To Phyllis and Enzenauer, I noted, "A tape. To scare the new prisoners."

Phyllis nodded like she already knew this.

Next a voice, yelling, and then the bed creaking as bin Pacha got up. Then, very distinctly, voices—two different voices—and they *were* speaking to one another. There was some back-and-forth between bin Pacha and an unidentified party, in Arabic, and I understood nothing. The conversation was brief, lasted for perhaps a minute, and ended with a loud bang.

Next, Bian's voice, on tape. "He's dead. Those bastards assassinated him. They didn't want us to hear what he had to say."

Tirey. "This . . . this Saudi arrangement . . . this was . . . you know, the CIA's bright idea. It did . . . it originated with your people. I . . . I merely followed orders and . . ."

Me. "This is a crime scene. Treat it as one."

"Uh . . ."

Me again. "Was the killing recorded?"

I reached forward and pushed stop. Phyllis remarked, "Tirey wasted no time, did he?"

"Wait till the official inquiry. That was only the first rehearsal." I looked at Bian. "Translate."

"I'll need to hear it again. All that noise from the torture tape . . . it's . . ." She shrugged.

So the doc took it backward and forward for her a few times, and now Bian was concentrating fiercely and jotting notes. A few phrases—actually, names—were decipherable even to me.

Bian glanced up from her notepad and said to Enzenauer, "Once again, please. I think"—she scribbled something—"I nearly have it."

Enzenauer played it again as Bian tracked the dialogue on her page. "All right," she said, and then read, "After bin Pacha's . . . after the flatulence . . . the first voice is a guard. He yells, 'Are you awake yet?' Bin Pacha replies, 'Yes,' and he asks the guard, 'Why are they playing that stupid recording? Only fools would try a trick of such obvious ignorance. It sounds like something Americans would try.' The guard laughs, and yells back that the tape might be phony, but bin Pacha's pain will soon be real enough."

Bian looked up and explained, "Words to that effect. Arabic is structured differently than English. More formal. Also the verbs and nouns are displaced. I'm converting to the vernacular."

I told her, "You're doing great."

She looked down at her pad and continued, "Bin Pacha asks the guard's name. The guard replies that he is named Abu Habbibi. Then bin Pacha warns him, 'You are making a big mistake that will be poor for your personal health.' Again, Habbibi laughs. He asks, 'Why is that?' "

Bian paused, then said, "Bin Pacha told him that to learn the answer to this riddle, Habbibi must make only two phone calls." She looked up for a moment and explained, "Because the tape is noise-activated, there are no breaks in the conversation. I think here, though . . . from the change in their tone, there was a pause."

Recalling what I had observed on the video, I suggested, "This must be when bin Pacha walked to the cell door."

She nodded—"Makes sense"—and continued, "Again, he tells Habbibi, 'Just make two phone calls—all will become clear. If you fail to make these calls, now I know your name, and you and your family will suffer horrible deaths. But there is a big reward you will be very happy with, if you call and do what these men tell you to do.' Habbibi replies, 'I can barely hear you. The noise from the tape is in the way. Come closer. Move to the opening. Tell me what you have in mind.' "

"And then . . ." Bian had been looking at our faces, and she looked back down at her notepad and continued, "Then bin Pacha said, 'Call Prince Faud ibn al-Souk, or Prince Ali ibn al-Sayyed. They will tell you what to do with me.' Habbibi answered, 'I can't hear you—' "

Phyllis interrupted, "You're sure of this?"

"Positive."

"I'm referring to the names. He named the two princes?"

"I know what you're asking. Listen to the tape yourself. Both names are easily distinguishable."

Phyllis nodded. "Please continue."

"There's not much after that. Bin Pacha recites the phone numbers to Habbibi. I'm not sure I heard them right—he had repositioned closer to the door and the speaker noise was overwhelming."

"Do your best," I told her.

"Well . . . Habbibi had trouble hearing him also—or he *pretended* to have trouble—because his last words to bin Pacha were, 'I need to hear the phone numbers again. Come closer. Move your head against the opening.' " Bian looked up and added, "Then bang—the gun went off."

We all sat back in our chairs. Nobody said a word. Unlike the others, I had a mental visualization to accompany the soundtrack, and as I replayed the scene in my mind, matching words with deeds, it all became clear: a double cross trumped by a double cross.

In retrospect, Ali bin Pacha had thought he was playing us; I recalled that curious smile back in the hospital bed when Bian and I notified him he was being turned over to the Saudis. A smile. We believed we were telling him the last thing he wanted to hear; he believed he was hearing the sound of salvation.

It was, in fact, a death sentence. Neither Ali bin Pacha nor we understood that, though. This man, responsible for countless deaths, believed we had just pulled the ace from his sleeve for him, even as Habbibi maneuvered him, like a big stupid fish, into the perfect position to blow his evil brains out. It was funny, and it was very sad.

Eventually, I looked at Phyllis and asked, "These two princes, who are they?"

She shook her head. "There are five or six thousand princes. The men of the royal family marry many women, and are atrociously fertile. It's the national curse."

I moved on to the next logical questions, which were more in the nature of Socratic statements. "Why would bin Pacha have their phone numbers memorized? And why would he refer Habbibi to them?"

"Protection. He obviously expected some form of intervention."

"But *why* would they protect him?"

Without answering, she stood and paced to the phone. She lifted it up, punched a number, and after a moment ordered somebody to track down Sheik Turki al-Fayef and escort him to the conference room.

She hung up and said to us, "I will do the talking. You will both remain quiet and polite. Don't challenge or harass him."

"I promise," I told her. I might rip off his head and crap down his throat, but I would neither challenge nor harass him.

Phyllis stared at Bian, who replied with obvious reluctance, "I understand."

We sat in silence.

A few moments later, there was a knock at the door.

CHAPTER THIRTY-THREE

The sheik swept into the room. In his hand was a thin valise constructed of buttery leather, on his body the same ash-stained robe, and on his face his customary visage of complacent boredom.

What his expression did not convey was the slightest trace of regret, worry, guilt, or anxiety. Give the man credit, he had panache, which usually I admire; just not this time. I wanted to get my hands around his throat and throttle him.

Phyllis looked lost in thought for a moment, but finally she looked up and said, "Have a seat. We have something you need to hear."

His quick black eyes took us all in, and settled briefly on the receiver/recorder, which he then made a point of ignoring. I was sure he sensed that he had just entered the lion's den, that the animals were hungry, and that this mysterious device was part of the seasoning. He coolly lit a cigarette, set his valise on the table, and sat. Phyllis nodded at Doc Enzenauer, who nodded back and pushed play.

The sheik puffed on his cigarette and listened. To his professional credit, not when the princes were named, nor even when the shot exploded through the speakers, did he flinch or show the slightest emotional reaction.

Enzenauer wisely shut it down before Tirey launched into his CYA soliloquy.

So there it was.

We all sat quietly, uncertain who was supposed to make the next move. But for Bian, for Doc Enzenauer, and for me, there were no doubts; this was way over our heads. Whatever happened next was between the bosses.

The sheik suddenly clapped his hands together and erupted in a delighted belly laugh. "Ha-ha. Oh, Phyllis . . . you have, I think, outsmarted me. How did you . . . No, no—let me guess." He furrowed his brow and playfully stroked his goatee. "A transmitter, yes? Where was it? Sewn into his pants?"

"His body," Phyllis replied, playing the game.

He looked thoughtful. "Ah . . . yes." He offered a complimentary nod at Enzenauer. "Ingenious." He laughed. "Very excellent work, Doctor."

I had to admit, not only did this guy have balls he had charm. Phyllis, however, was neither warmed nor laughing. She said to Enzenauer, "Would you care to leave now?" which obviously wasn't a suggestion, and he dutifully stood and left.

"Who are the princes?" she asked al-Fayef.

"Why does it matter?"

"It matters. Tell me."

"Inconsequential men. Minor figures in the family. You know how our royals are. A big, horny rabbit farm."

Phyllis stared at him a long time, then asked, "But bin Pacha expected their protection—why?"

Until this moment, I think, al-Fayef had been testing the waters to see if Phyllis had put this together. Well, she had—obviously, we all had—and now the brain behind those clever black eyes was flailing for an angle, a ruse, a bluff. He tried to stall for time with another of those charming chuckles, and said, "Phyllis . . . Phyllis . . . how long have we known each other?"

Phyllis's left nostril flared and she hissed, "Be clear on this, Turki. You exploited my hospitality, and you humiliated me. You came into my facility and murdered my prisoner. You—"

"Please," he cut in. "I—"

"I speak, you listen, until I finish," she snapped. She drew a long breath, then continued, "The Director's at the White House as we speak, trying to explain this disaster. When I notify him that bin Pacha's dying words implicate the royal family, you will have problems you cannot begin to fathom. A nightmare for your country. A nightmare for you . . . for you, *personally*."

He stared at her, a little stunned. Until this moment, Phyllis and the sheik had been operating on spy-to-spy protocols, a sort of feint-and-parry interaction, almost like diplomacy, where the real meanings are cloaked behind tight smiles and evasive wording. The sand had suddenly shifted beneath his feet, now the topic was out in the open, and it was his personal health.

She leaned closer, a mere few inches from his face. "We are at war, fifteen hundred Americans are dead, an election is at stake, and the last thing you want or need is for us to misinterpret where your country stands." She added more menacingly, "The last thing you personally want is me as your enemy."

Phyllis had clipped about twenty degrees from the room's temperature. Even I—for once not the target of her anger, which was a relief—felt a shiver go down my spine. Her fury was real and red-hot, and were I the sheik, I would definitely consider the joys of life in Brazil under an assumed identity after a brief stop-off in Sweden for a sex change, because with Phyllis after you, there are no excessive precautions, only reasonable ones.

Al-Fayef tried his best to maintain his composure, but he lost it. He broke eye contact, he stared at the tabletop, and—perhaps I imagined this—he sucked half his cigarette with one draw.

Phyllis said, "You have one chance to explain what's on that tape. One brief shining moment. Don't miss it, Turki."

I thought of all the times Phyllis had lectured me about tact and diplomacy. I might have mentioned her hypocrisy, but I survived the night in Falluja and wasn't going to push my luck.

For his part, Turki no longer looked bored, flip, or charming, just seriously introspective. The man was obviously weighing the trade-off between exposing a sensitive intelligence operation and pissing off his royals, or keeping his mouth shut and pissing off Phyllis.

This seemed like a ripe moment for a little lawyerly advice, and I interrupted the sheik's troubled thoughts to inform him, "Seven members of your intelligence service are now in custody. They are charged with murder and conspiracy to commit murder. Eventually, there will be more charges—espionage, obstruction of justice, probably others."

"You *must* turn them over to me," he responded. "They are Saudi. They must face Saudi justice."

"No . . . I'm afraid this crime occurred in a U.S. facility, they lack diplomatic credentials, and we must follow our laws and try them in our own courts. So, they have the right to a public trial, and I promise you, it will be . . . an unusually public trial."

Spymasters are allergic to public scrutiny, of course, and the idea of having this murder explicitly exposed and detailed to the American public would cause a world of damage. I was sure he now regretted his abdication from rendition, and it was dawning on him as well that murdering bin Pacha here, in an American facility, was a huge mistake—a public relations mistake, a legal mistake, and a professional misjudgment his bosses would never forgive.

He started to object and I cut him off. "We will, of course, indict you as a coconspirator and an accessory."

"You cannot arrest me. I do have a diplomatic passport."

"I know. And certainly, it is your right not to submit yourself to voluntary custody. So, later, you'll be subpoenaed and we'll request extradition. Should you refuse to appear in an American court, you'll be tried in absentia, and on the front pages of every newspaper in America. If convicted, the next time you set foot outside Saudia Arabia, we'll be waiting." We locked eyes and I noted, "If we don't get you today, we'll get you tomorrow. I think you know this."

"You do not want to do this."

"Can I recommend a good lawyer? You really should consider my cousin. She's expensive and bitchy, and worth every penny."

"This is . . . You would seriously damage . . . you would destroy the friendship between our countries."

"I think not," I replied. "Our people need to buy oil and your people need to sell oil. Adam Smith's hidden hand—anybody in the way gets splattered on the windshield of greed and commerce." Again we locked eyes. "Do you really believe the Saud clan will trade their summers at St. Moritz and all those glitzy palaces to protect you? I don't."

To make sure he was clear on this point, I added, "We're expendable, you and me. Says so in our contracts."

This point struck home and he looked away. When he focused again, it was on Phyllis, and he said, "Surely, *you* know better. This is not professional, Phyllis. It would be . . . a grave mistake."

She brushed some lint off her shoulder and replied, "I think you should get the name of Drummond's cousin."

A guy with his background and experience, you would think he'd understand this little duet. And on some level, I was sure he did understand it. When it's you on the hot seat, however, counterintuitive thinking is the first thing to go. Between Phyllis's threat to his personal health, my threat to his country's reputation, and his own understanding of the royal family, his inhibitions had just turned very heavy. He growled, "You will not like the truth."

"Perhaps," replied Phyllis. "And if it's not the truth, you won't like the consequences."

The sheik ground out his cigarette on the floor, then announced, "What has happened here . . . today . . . this is all America's fault."

I decided to treat al-Fayef as a hostile witness—I mean, he was a hostile witness—and I replied, "Our only fault was trusting you. Why did you order his execution?"

"To the contrary, our mistake was trusting you. By that, I mean America." He looked at me. "Do you know who our main enemy is?"

"Yourselves?"

In spite of the tension, he regained a little of his charm and laughed. He said, "This is not entirely untrue." But this effort did not find a welcome audience, and he stopped smiling. "I will tell you then—the Shia. For thirteen hundred years, the Shia. You in the West believe this is some quaint and irrational quarrel. A shadow of history that will disappear once exposed to the sunlight of democracy. It is not. The Shia are apostates, desecrators of the true faith. How many Americans even know the difference between a Shia and a Sunni? Am I right?"

He looked at our faces to gauge our reactions, and apparently decided to start at the beginning. "You come here, into our region, thinking you can rearrange everything. Fix everything. Mix everything up, make a big happy Arab omelet."

"We brought an invitation this time." I looked him in the eye and said, "Three thousand Americans are dead. Fifteen of the murderers were Saudis. Your unhappiness has become our unhappiness."

He did not want to be reminded of this inconvenient truth. "You know," he continued, "I attended George Washington University. Undergrad and master's. Many Saudis attend school in your country." He looked pointedly at me. "Perhaps you attended a Saudi school?"

"I have not."

"Has your President, the grand architect of our Arab future?"

That required no answer.

He continued, "How many Americans attend Saudi universities?" He paused theatrically, as though we should consider this a serious question, where obviously it was not. "You do not know our culture, our people, our ways. You do not care to know. You prefer your Hollywood stereotypes to true knowledge. Yet you believe you possess the cures to our problems, how to shape our futures."

Bian mentioned, accurately, "If a Christian wears a cross in your country, it's a crime. If a woman drives a car or fails to hide her face, or flashes a little bare leg, she's arrested by your religious Nazis. Your schools and universities are known for nothing but teaching religious intolerance and chauvinism. If you want Americans at your universities, accommodate us."

"When I was in your country, I wore your clothes, I ate your foods, and I sent my children to your schools."

I mentioned, "And probably also, you drank like a virtuoso, screwed lots of American ladies, and engaged in all the other fun and liberating activities you don't dare do at home. Acting like an American is a blast. You had the time of your life."

He wisely chose not to confess his sins and indulgences, and instead insisted, "If you want to live among us, live like us. To understand our ways, walk in our shoes. Did not Jesus Christ say something like this?"

"He said sandals. What's your point?"

"My point. You have started this war and made it into an unholy mess. Saddam was a bad man . . . yes, yes, we all knew this—I admit we do not mind seeing him gone. A barbarian. A stain to our Arab reputation. There is a thing, however, worse than Saddam. A Shiite-ruled Iraq, a puppet, or an ally of Iran."

"Go on."

"Who brought the Shia to power in Iran in the first place?"

"The Shiites?"

"No, your President Jimmy Carter caused this. In 1979 he drove Shah Pahlavi from power in Iran, and he opened the door for Khomeini, his ayatollahs, and their Shia revolution. An act of principled moralism, your President called it. America no longer would soil itself by aligning with a despot, he swore. For his moral convenience and ignorant naiveté, he destabilized our entire region."

"Maybe he thought he couldn't screw it up worse than you screwed it up yourselves," I replied.

"Instability of our own making is one thing. Instability from foreign meddling is another."

While I tried to think through this piece of Arab reasoning, he continued, "Afterward came the eight-year Iran-Iraqi war, the Shiite terrorism in Lebanon, and the Iranian threat to carry their revolution into all our countries. Millions of deaths, because of your President, because of America."

He sort of smiled at me and said, "In your vernacular, this sucked." The smile was nasty and short-lived, and he continued, "Now the Iranians are developing a nuclear bomb, and if their Shia allies in Iraq win power, you will have left a mortal threat on our doorstep. Do you not understand this?"

I recalled what we had learned about Cliff Daniels and Mahmoud Charabi, and a light flashed on. I glanced at Phyllis. If this guy became privy to our suspicions about Charabi's flimflammery vis-à-vis America and Iran, the result would be a geopolitical earthquake. I glanced at Bian. She glanced back with silent understanding. I replied noncommittally, "Explain it better."

"Why? You Americans never listen. You are the most insensitive, self-indulgent, self-righteous people on earth."

"Well . . . it is hard being great."

This pissed him off, as it was meant to. He said, "You think the world is your big playground. Your ignorance is awesome. There is an Arab saying that translates something like this—the big man can never see through the eyes of the small man."

"Maybe the big man has a better view."

He stared at me a long time, then he turned to Bian. "I am sure you understand. Look what American power and arrogance did for your homeland, your people."

Bian replied, very wisely, "Stick to the here and now."

"Yes . . . as you wish. Here—we Saudis opened our soil for your military bases, we gave you our diplomatic support, and for decades we have fed your insatiable worship of big cars and big homes with cheap oil. Which brings us to now—how does your President repay our gifts, our generosity, our friendship?"

I suspected he would tell us, and in fact he said, "Now he openly declares the inferiority of our government. Now he preaches about spreading democracy to our kingdom. Because you have found no nuclear or chemical weapons in Iraq, now he shifts his reason for this war, and now it is about spreading democracy. Who does this fool think his democracy would replace? Is he so blind and stupid he does not know he is threatening our royal family?"

Phyllis was visibly tiring of this sidetrack into political dialectics. She interrupted and said, "Come to the point, Turki."

He stared at her a moment. "This is the point. There are factions in the royal family—growing factions—who believe we have made a terrible blunder befriending America. And they believe America is manufacturing an astounding disaster in Iraq, a mistake that will be our ruin. The Shiites are coming to power, and already you are tired of this war, and you cannot wait for your soldiers to pull out, to depart. Who do you think the Iraqi Shiites will turn to for protection from the Sunnis?"

He was on a roll, relishing this chance to lecture ignorant Americans, and once again he answered his own question. "The Persians. Iran. All of the Gulf States—all of the great oil-producing states—we all will face destruction. Imagine over half the world's oil in the hands of the mullahs in Tehran. America is committing economic suicide." He paused then added, more ominously, "You are committing suicide for all of us."

Phyllis had had enough of his commentary and asked, "These two princes, Ali and Faud, were they giving money and aid to Zarqawi?"

He drew a few breaths and said, "This . . . I cannot say this for sure."

"What can you say?"

"It is possible, maybe, that they, and maybe others . . . maybe they have decided that the Shiites cannot be allowed to rule Iraq."

Arabs rarely answer a question directly, especially an embarrassing one. You have to listen closely, cut through the elliptical bullshit, and apply the rule of opposites; no means yes, yes means maybe, and maybe can mean maybe, or it might mean none of your business. Phyllis asked, "Others?"

"Maybe."

"Who are these others?"

"I have no idea." Translation—for him to know, and us not to find out.

"Who are these two princes?"

Here was a question he didn't want to hear and he couldn't evade. But since we already knew their names, we could, and obviously, we would, find out through our own sources. So for once he answered directly and unequivocally. "Prince Faud is the third son of the defense minister. Prince Ali is the second son of the oil minister."

He watched our faces, studying our reactions. He had previously asserted that the princes were themselves insignificant figures—which might or might not be true—but their daddies were two of the most powerful and influential men in the kingdom, and in a land where lucky sperm is the ticket, this made their kids very important indeed.

In response to our silence, he assured us, "I can handle this. And I will handle this."

I was about to ask what he meant by that when Bian leaned across the table. She said, "You had an intelligence file on bin Pacha. Why? Why was bin Pacha under an intelligence watch?"

He treated her question as irrelevant. "We observe all returning mujahideen. Nothing is suspicious about this. These men who have come back from Afghanistan, Somalia, Bosnia, and Chechnya, they pick up . . . strange ideas."

In other words, the Saudis had no problem exporting jihadis, but big issues when jihadis came home.

"How long were you watching bin Pacha?" asked Bian.

"It began, I believe, after his return from jihad in Somalia."

Bian's fingers were tapping the table, and she said sarcastically, "You *believe*?"

"My bureau handles external security, not internal . . . and so I cannot say this for sure. As I said, it was routine."

"Ten years?"

"Perhaps. Not continuously, though, or even very thoroughly. He was merely one of thousands of our returned mujahideen." The irony of this statement eluded him, and after a moment he added, "You saw his file. He raised no particular concerns or alarms."

This statement was so blatantly disingenuous I had to laugh.

He did not like this and gave me a nasty look.

"Yet," Bian noted, "when you learned he was about to be apprehended, your ambassador rushed to the White House and intervened. If this . . . if Ali bin Pacha was beneath your radar, why go to such extraordinary trouble?"

Another question he didn't want to hear. In fact, I had not put this piece together, and Bian's analysis caught me by surprise—not the fact that the Saudis wanted to hide bin Pacha's secrets, per se; something else. It caught him by surprise as well, and he simply stared at her.

Since he was no longer answering, Bian answered for him. "You were aware bin Pacha was part of a terrorist cell and you knew rich

Saudis were giving him money. Until he was about to be captured, you didn't care, or . . . you did care, and approved of his activities."

"This is speculation. Completely absurd."

She kept her eyes on his face.

I also was studying al-Fayef's face. He was too much the veteran professional to do something stupid, like look guilty, or even more stupidly, confess. But he did lick his lips a few times, and with a shaky hand he fumbled out a fresh cigarette and lit it.

He turned to Phyllis and insisted, "I have nothing more to say. Now you must tell me what you intend to do."

Actually, he'd told us as minimal truth he could get away with: a careful mixture of what we could learn on our own, what was intuitively obvious, and what any intelligent regional expert could divine from the facts. The problem for us, and the bigger problem for him, was what he didn't tell us, but that Bian had just surmised.

Regarding Phyllis, as usual her eyes conveyed one emotion, her lips another, and neither betrayed what probably was in her heart, or in her head. I was sure she was angry, frustrated, and worried. But for Phyllis, emotion and logic were never at war; it just never occurred to her that reason has a peer, or that emotion should incubate action. She announced unequivocally and, I thought, predictably, "What's done is done. We move forward."

Bian asked, "What does that mean?"

"It means what it means."

"What about justice?"

"For who?" Phyllis asked.

"For the soldiers who are fighting. For those who are dead. For their families, for their loved ones. For America."

"There is no justice for dead soldiers," Phyllis replied with typically chilling logic. "They are not murder victims—they're casualties of war."

"The Saudis have been feeding money, people, and who knows what to their killers. We now have the names of two princes." Bian looked in al-Fayef's direction and added, "It sounds like there are more names, and possibly the Saudi government's implicated as well. You can't ignore or paste over that."

Wrong, because Phyllis turned to al-Fayef and said, "It's not in our interest to expose the royal family to . . . embarrassment."

He smiled, though I saw no hint of pleasure or even contentment in his eyes; I saw relief. He said, "Good choice. It would be, you know, a disaster for both our countries." He looked around the room, at each of our faces, then added agreeably, "A war is going on, after all. We must remain friends. Good allies."

After all he had just said, about America, about our arrogance, about our incompetence, I was amazed that a bolt of lightning didn't strike. Apparently, while Bian and I missed the cues, the sheik and Phyllis had moved to a new song, this one titled "Row, row, row the boat gently down the stream."

And, in fact, Phyllis gave a cool nod to her sheik friend.

He said, "I recognize, however, that we have caused you certain difficulties." He waved his cigarette in small circles through the air. "Embarrassments. Inconveniences."

"Your sensitivity is greatly appreciated."

He leaned back into his chair and exhaled a long stream of smoke. "Two names, Phyllis. This is all I have been authorized to offer."

Phyllis shuffled her hands and replied noncommittally, "If they're the *right* names."

"Yes, yes . . . of course." He watched her face. "There is a man in Syria, a man who arranges the shipment of weapons and jihadists into Iraq. A smuggler of considerable talent and cleverness." Phyllis looked unimpressed, and he quickly emphasized, "He is big. Very big. Perhaps a third of the mujahideen entering Iraq flow through his channels."

Phyllis stared at him, then nodded. "We're halfway there."

"And I have heard of another man, a Saudi expatriate, who recruits jihadists in Jordan. He—"

Phyllis interrupted. "Forget about him. Recruiters are too easily replaced."

"Ah . . ." A pained expression came to the sheik's face, and he hesitated before he said, "There is another man, in Iraq, who decides the targets the mujahideen strike in the city of Karbala."

Phyllis bent forward with intensified interest.

"Alas, he also is Saudi, from a prominent family—his father is a dear friend of many years—and it . . . I am greatly pained to betray him."

This guy was a real craftsman, and probably he threw that in to make us all feel better. After a moment, Phyllis observed, "You know, of course, that names without addresses are of no use."

"And you know, of course, that my guards will depart with me. Also that infernal machine," he said, pointing at the recorder, with its incriminating recording. He quickly added, "And I'll give you the man in Jordan for free. We have no use for him."

"The recorder and guards are yours. I have no use for them."

As I said, Bian and I were not clued in to the rules here, but the flesh trading was apparently over, because the sheik rose from his seat and began casually brushing ashes off his white robes, even as he nonchalantly took a final pull from his stinky cigarette and crushed it beneath his foot. After about three seconds, he opened his valise, rummaged inside, fished out three manila folders, and slid them inelegantly across the table. He said to Phyllis, "Their names and where they can be found. Also background information that I am sure will be helpful when you interrogate them."

Phyllis grabbed the folders and, one by one, opened them and inspected the contents while the sheik picked up the recorder and inspected it to be sure the damning tape was still inside. They had just sold their souls to each other, and still did not trust each other.

The sheik said to Phyllis, "My sincerest apologies to the Director." There was an awkward pause, and then with a pained expression he confided, "I had no option, Phyllis. It was this, or my job."

She nodded.

"If not me, it would have been somebody else."

"I'm sure."

He looked at Bian and said, "It was a pleasure meeting you." He turned to me and could not help smiling. "Better luck next time, Colonel."

I smiled back. "Count on it."

I knew what Bian was going to say, and she said it. "Go to hell." My sentiments exactly.

The sheik shrugged his robes and left, gently closing the door behind him.

Phyllis quietly read the files and, more to the point, quietly ignored Bian and me. She did not want to have this discussion, and seemed to be silently hoping the problem—us—would go away.

But we did not go away, and she finally looked up at us and asked, "What did you expect?"

"We didn't *expect* anything," I replied. "Just definitely not this." I asked, "Was this little charade prearranged?"

"What does that mean?"

"It means he walked in here with those folders, and you just allowed him to walk out of here with everything he wanted."

"This is how our business works. Turki is a professional, and professionals come prepared." She looked at Bian. "You don't have to like it, but this is how you have to play it."

"I don't like it," Bian responded.

"No? Well . . . try thinking about what will save the most American lives, what will help win this war. Compromises are necessary evils."

"What else would I be thinking about?"

Phyllis studied her face, then said, "He told us who these two princes are. Whatever they did, they're gold-plated, and it doesn't matter—we weren't getting them." She added, "Nor is antagonizing the Saudis in our interest. For all the obvious reasons, we need them."

Bian said, "The calculus doesn't confuse me. But what you just did . . . it was no different than the pact Cliff Daniels made with Charabi, and we're doing nothing about that either. Guilty men walk, and everybody gets to avoid a scandal. That's what I question."

Phyllis's finger was tapping the table, a less than subtle warning that her patience was wearing thin. But Bian was beyond impatience; she was in a slow rage, and being scolded with cold reason not only failed to douse her inner fires it was an aphrodisiac.

Phyllis said, "Welcome to a world where every choice is flawed and you have to pick the one that least stinks. We lost bin Pacha. Nothing will change that. But at least we now have three new names, three fresh chances to pick up key figures, to find out what they know, and who they know."

I heard what Phyllis was saying, and on one level it made sense. I also understood that Bian, a military cop, was taught to reason and was trained to act on another level—good guys versus bad guys; do the crime, do the time. The mind of a police officer is not simple, but the job is morally not all that complex: guilt or innocence, black or white, without any ethical vagaries. But for the lawyer, guilt and innocence are parsed into many shades, crime is subjective, and punishment is merely a commodity you negotiate with a prosecutor, a judge, or a jury. We call this justice, and we say it is evenhanded, and if you can afford a five-hundred-buck-an-hour attorney, you might even believe that. As lawyer friends of mine say, in America you get all the justice you can afford.

So I wasn't really shocked that this applies to espionage as well. And neither should Bian have been appalled, or even surprised. She was, though. And Phyllis, who usually exerts a more deft touch when she shoves around her subordinates, this time appeared surprisingly tone-deaf and clumsy.

I knew it would do no good, but I advised Bian, "I don't like it either. It *is*, though, the best deal we're going to get."

She replied, "That man ordered an assassination to keep us from knowledge that was invaluable to us and embarrassing to him. That same man just bartered his country's way out of a black eye it has definitely earned. That's wrong—we all know it's wrong. Pretend otherwise and you're as bad as her." She stood and left the room.

Phyllis watched her leave and drew a long breath, then turned her eyes to me and said, "You need to get her under control."

I stood and moved toward the door, but then I stopped and turned around. I said, "I understand your decision. I really do, Phyllis. And, you know what? Were I in your shoes, I might've made the same deal."

"Thank you."

For a moment I stood quietly. I then said, "But that doesn't make it any more morally excusable, or even right. So she's disgusted and disillusioned. Frankly, if you and I had souls, we would be, too."

Phyllis started to say something, and I kept talking. "And that's the problem. At the beginning of this case, we had lots of chances to do the right thing. The chance to find out about and expose Charabi. The chance to expose Daniels and his bosses, to expose the truth about the cooked intelligence, about a possible betrayal, and along the way, we stumble into a money scheme that implicates a government that is a titular ally. Instead, we settle for a few garden-variety terrorists. I think you can see where that might turn the stomach of a good soldier."

"She's obsessed with justice and honor. We're doing what's best for the country."

"I won't argue what's best or not. I really don't know anymore, and that bothers me more than anything." I added after a long moment, "Fire me or transfer me; I really don't care. I'm through with this job."

Phyllis did not look surprised but neither did she look ready to fire me. She picked up another folder. "I'll consider this as a sentiment expressed in a moment of haste, anger, and frustration. You have nothing to feel guilty or ashamed about. Nor do I. We handled the cards we were dealt as best we could. If there are moral shortcomings, they lie with others."

I said nothing.

"Sleep on it." She stuck her nose inside the folder. "Make your decision later, with a clear head."

She read. I walked out.

CHAPTER THIRTY-FOUR

Just when you think it's over, you get jerked through a new knothole.

Two matters needed to be resolved before we returned home—and Phyllis made it clear that nobody was leaving until both jobs were finished. Probably, after all that happened, she needed to notch a few victories on her belt before she flew home into a shitstorm. A thousand successes do not wipe clean one screwup, but neither is it a good idea to appear empty-handed before a review board.

Problem one was the apprehension of the smuggler of arms and jihadists into Iraq. As he was operating across the border in Syria, his capture offered what Phyllis politely referred to as "delicate diplomatic and extralegal issues." Under the proper protocol, the American ambassador in Damascus would lodge a formal request to the Syrian government to arrest the perp, followed by a speedy and efficient extradition process. Given Syrian hostility to America, the name of this option was "pissing into the wind."

So when Phyllis said extralegal, she meant illegal, and when she said diplomatic, she meant violating Syria's sovereignty with a kidnapping. Delicate, of course, meant a black bag job by Agency operatives.

As long as it didn't mean Sean Drummond; my fun, travel, and adventure quotient was pegged out.

So Phyllis worked the phones, coordinating his apprehension, and

I was dispatched to handle problem two: to wit, the terrorist master planner in Karbala. As this guy operated inside Iraq proper, his apprehension required neither finesse nor skullduggery, which meant the blunt power of the U.S. Army, and this meant Drummond and Tran were designated to be the mail carriers.

Bian was in the mess hall when I found her, seated alone, and wearing a desultory expression as she picked at her food. I fell into the chair across from her, cleared my throat a few times, and noisily shifted my chair.

She sawed off a piece of steak, put it in her mouth, and chewed.

I smiled at her and asked, "How's the chow, soldier?"

Her mouth must've been full, because she did not get a word out.

The famous Drummond charm obviously wasn't doing it. I cut to the chase and said, "You have one last mission."

"Is this an order?"

"No. You're involuntarily volunteering."

She laughed. Not nicely.

"The Saudi planner in Karbala is being referred to the Army for apprehension. You served on the corps intelligence staff, so I assume you know who to bring this to."

She continued eating.

I informed her, "You and I will together deliver the Saudi file on this man, and then go straight to the airport for the flight home."

"Go to hell."

"Bian, look at me."

She studied her steak.

"You're directing your anger at the wrong person."

"I don't think so."

"Don't hate the players, hate the game."

"Oh . . . now it's a *game*."

"You know what I mean."

"And you know what I mean."

She was being unreasonable, and I guess it was no mystery why. She was furious at the powers that be in Washington, disgusted by their decisions, their machinations, their cover-ups, their bullshit—and she needed to lash out. Sean Drummond wasn't responsible for that, of course. But the idiots in Washington weren't seated across from her, they were five thousand miles away, and not likely to take her calls. Still, this was starting to piss me off.

I said very sharply, "Finish your meal. We'll go to the motor pool together and sign out a vehicle."

She pushed away her tray and focused on me for the first time. "You're right. I still have friends in the corps intel staff. So . . . yes, I do know who to refer this to. In fact, my old office handles these matters."

"Good. Everything should—"

"But if I do this, I do it alone."

"Wrong. We do this—"

"*Alone*. Also, I'll fly home alone," she continued. "Actually, I'd prefer a military flight. The company of real soldiers will be refreshing."

That really hurt. I responded, "How you get back is your business. I don't really care. You are not, however, driving *alone* to Baghdad."

"Why not? I know the way."

"The buddy system. It's—"

"You're not my buddy," she pointed out.

"—it's theater policy. Nobody travels through Indian country without a buddy," I continued. "Also this is a very sensitive and important mission. It requires an armed shotgun."

She looked at me and said, "Suit yourself."

"I always do."

She glanced at her watch. "You know, depending on traffic, this could be your last chance to eat. Go ahead. The food was wonderful, since you asked. I need to freshen up and get my equipment together."

"Fine. Motor pool. One hour." I went to the chow line, loaded my tray, and when I returned to the table, Bian was gone. The dining facility, incidentally, was managed by civilian contractors, and the servers and waiters were all Iraqi nationals, which smacks a little of colonialism—natives waiting hand and foot on their occupiers and all that. Though to be truthful, nobody looked unhappy to have jobs. Contractors might get a bad rap back in the States, but the food, however, was amazing, better than anything I'd eaten in any Army facility, which is not the faint praise it sounds like. I relaxed, savored my first decent meal in days, went back for seconds—twice—and made a pig of myself.

For the first time in years, I even read the *Stars and Stripes*, which reminded me why I stopped reading it in the first place. If the *New York Times*'s motto is "All the news fit to print," the motto here is "There is no bad news fit to print." I particularly enjoyed the article headlined, "Recruiting Riots in Six States: President Orders Lottery System to Decide Which of Millions of Desperate Applicants Get Chance to Serve in Iraq." Okay, I'm making that up.

Anyway, fifty minutes later, with my bags and my tummy packed, I stood before Phyllis's desk waiting to pick up the file. She was on the phone, and it took five minutes before she hung up and asked, "Well?"

"I need the file."

"Don't you two communicate?"

"What are you talking about?"

"Bian picked it up. About forty minutes ago. She said she was meeting you in the motor pool."

I must've looked surprised, because Phyllis asked, "Is something wrong?"

"No. I'm . . . Be back in a minute."

I had a wave of bad feeling in my stomach and I walked as fast my feet could carry me to the motor pool, where my wave of bad feeling immediately turned into a tsunami. Yes, Major Tran had been here, the motor sergeant informed me, and she had signed out a Toyota Land Cruiser, the fancy model reserved for Special Ops, and departed about thirty minutes before. I asked him if the vehicle had a radio; no—no radio, no armor plating, and worse, no Drummond in the passenger seat.

However, the major had left a note, which the motor sergeant withdrew from his pocket with a greasy hand that left black smudges on the paper. It was handwritten and read, "*Sean, don't be angry with me. I don't blame you for anything that's happened. I've been a complete bitch. Sorry. And I mean it. But I need to think this through, and for some reason, you distract me. I'll call as soon as I arrive. Don't worry. You know by now I can handle it. Bian.*"

The sergeant was watching my face and said, "Anything wrong, sir?"

"What? No . . . I— How long is the drive to the Green Zone?"

"An hour, maybe. Hour and a half when the traffic sucks. Usually does suck at this hour."

I should have been furious with her, but I wasn't. Truthfully, she'd been acting strangely ever since her two days in Baghdad—or, on second thought, earlier, as I recalled the shower episode—and I knew the incident with bin Pacha had really pushed her over an edge. When the head isn't in the right place, the body follows. I should have kept a better eye on her.

I returned to the subterranean jail and updated Phyllis that Bian was en route and would call and notify us as soon as she landed. I further informed her that Bian had left alone, which caused a raised eyebrow and a chilly admonition to stay on top of this.

I asked the man on the switch to put through any calls from Major Tran, then found an empty desk and parked myself beside the phone. After two hours of spinning my wheels, when Bian still had not called, I had the switch put me through to the corps G2—the intel staff—inside the Green Zone.

A very polite captain came on the line, I offered him the abbreviated version of my problem, and then asked with great politeness if Major Tran had checked in.

He replied, "Gee, sir, your guess is as good as mine. This is a large staff, with many offices on several floors." He then hypothesized, "Maybe your major got lost, or maybe she ran into an old friend in the hallways. There's a bazaar in the compound, so maybe she's shopping. You know how the ladies are." He laughed.

To which I politely replied, "Captain, I didn't ask you to guess."

"Uh . . ."

"I need to *know* whether she's arrived."

"Uh-huh . . . do you know who she's supposed to see?"

"If I knew, why would I be calling you?"

There was a long pause. "Well, sir . . . that could take a while. There are about three dozen offices here."

"Fine. After you check them all, ring me back."

I gave him my number, and he promised to call. He never did. Petty prick.

After another hour, I returned to Phyllis's makeshift office. I knocked and entered. I updated her and noted that, in my view, Bian was too good an officer, too reliable, and too responsible for the explanation to be innocent. Phyllis promised she would make some calls, and she did; Bian had never showed, but the moment she arrived—*if* she arrived—Phyllis would get a call.

Unfortunately, Baghdad is a big city, and it was already dark and too late to do anything, even if something could be done—which it couldn't. In a city filled with murder, bombings, and kidnappings, a tardy woman is the least of anybody's problems.

So I sat next to the phone all night and into the morning, thinking, waiting, and worrying. I tend to do nothing badly under the best of circumstances, and after thirty minutes people were avoiding me, which was fine. I finished two pots of coffee, and with each passing hour, I became more convinced that something terrible had happened. This was Iraq, after all, so the list of possibilities was endless and frightening, and I ruminated on every one of them.

The call I dreaded came at 7:30 a.m. from a sergeant in the operations shop of the 2/18th Military Police Battalion. His voice was gruff, his manner professional, and the news was bad.

In an alleyway in Sadr City, in the northeastern part of Baghdad, an abandoned silver Toyota Land Cruiser with U.S. military plates had been found by an MP patrol.

In the rear of the vehicle, the MPs discovered a green Army duffel bag. Neatly stenciled upon it was Major Tran's name and partial social security number—from which they deduced she was an occupant—and in the front seat was a leather briefcase in which they found a form from Camp Alpha with the phone number for this facility—which explained the call here, to confirm the major's provenance.

Regarding Major Tran, no trace of her or her body was found.

There were, however, six bullet holes through the driver's door and bloodstains on the seat and windshield.

CHAPTER THIRTY-FIVE

We all walked out of the Camp Alpha compound as a military police detachment pulled up. A two-and-a-half-ton Army truck towed the silver Land Cruiser behind it, which was necessary, as the Toyota's front tires had been blown out by bullets. I did not like the look of that, but for the moment I withheld judgment.

The MPs began unhooking the tow shackles, and Jim Tirey, accompanied by four agents, waited until they finished before approaching the Toyota. They did a quick visual survey around the perimeter of the vehicle, and then dove in, dusting for prints and taking blood samples from the driver's seat—for once, they weren't developing a forensic portrait of the perpetrator, but of the victim. I walked to the driver's side.

As the ops sergeant had indicated over the phone, there were bullet holes in the driver's door, though not six, as he had stipulated—more like ten. Also the driver's window was blown out, with safety glass littering the inside. I studied the number and spacing of the holes; no way could the driver have emerged unscathed from such a fusillade.

An MP sergeant approached on my right and informed me, "We found it about 0600 hours, parked in an alleyway. It was, you know, a part of the city where you don't find expensive autos."

I looked at him but made no reply.

"An anonymous local called it in. Nobody gives you their names here," he continued. "Our Arabic guy took the message and dispatched us." He confided, "We were thinking VED, vehicular explosive device—you know?"

I nodded.

He said, "Ask me, it was a drive-by."

When I made no reply to his hypothesis, he explained, "There's gangs that rove around the city, day and night, hunting for vulnerable targets." After a pause, he asked, "She in uniform?"

Again, I nodded.

"Plain daylight, too," he commented with a disapproving frown. After a moment, he asked, "And she was alone, right?"

"Yes, alone."

"Uh-huh . . . I mean, Jesus H. Christ, that's how you spell stupid. Ask me, she was begging for it."

I turned to him and said, "If you offer one more stupid opinion, it will take ten strong men to pull my boot out of your ass."

He gave me an alarmed look, then wandered away. I continued to stare at the SUV.

I felt somebody take my arm, and when I turned around, it was Phyllis, staring at the bullet holes. She said, "Sean, I am truly, truly sorry."

I didn't trust myself to reply, and pulled my arm away. I moved to the rear of the vehicle, where Tirey's people had now withdrawn Bian's duffel bag and briefcase and laid them on the ground. The contents had been emptied and two agents were surveying the materials, spare uniforms, makeup kit, clean underwear, and so forth. Whatever they were looking for wasn't going to be found in Bian's bags.

An MP hovered over their shoulders, compiling a written inventory of her belongings on a clipboard. This I knew to be SOP whenever a service member is deceased or MIA—missing in action. And I knew also that it's one step short from a bugler blowing taps over a quiet grave.

Tirey said to me, "What do you think?"

I ignored the MP and looked at him. "She's alive."

"You saw the bullet holes? And the blood?" he asked, tiptoeing around what was so clearly indicated by the evidence.

"What don't we see, Jim? A body, a corpse. Bian. Were she dead, she would've been left in the car. They have no use for a corpse, do they?" He seemed to mull that over, and I added, "Also the front tires are blown out. Were it a drive-by, as our MP friends are suggesting, why shoot out the tires? Also the line of bullets in the door was a straight line, yet the window was also blown out. Think about that. If the driver's door was locked and they needed to get inside, they would break it in to get at the prisoner."

We both knew an immediate death was preferable to the conclusion I was drawing. He nodded slowly and contemplated this logic. He said, "I'm sure you've heard about the kidnapping gangs in the city. A lot of times, they call and demand ransom."

"Have they ever kidnapped an American soldier?"

"Well . . . not that I know of. But like all criminal enterprises, these people evolve. For instance, a few foreign contractors have been kidnapped by these gangs."

"And what happened to the victims?"

He paused for a moment. "I don't want to offer false optimism, or pessimism."

"Tell me."

He said, avoiding my eyes, "They were sold to terrorists." He continued to look away. "This happened twice that I'm aware of. Both victims ended up in Zarqawi's beheading videos."

I had spent the whole night preparing for this, and now it was actually happening, the finality of what I had hitherto only imagined. My chest felt like an airplane in a crash descent.

I stared at the two agents going through Bian's stuff, and at the MP listing her possessions. I thought of Bian lying, possibly, in a room not far from where we stood, surrounded, perhaps, by Zarqawi's people, who were sharpening their knives and rehearsing her death. This was a very courageous and resourceful lady, but she was not self-delusional; she was a realist, and she would appreciate the denouement of this story.

I left Tirey and returned to the driver's door. I stuck my head inside the SUV for no particular reason except I really didn't want to converse with anybody. Not with Phyllis and her guilty sympathizing, not with the MPs and their idiotic theorizing, and definitely not with Tirey, who was pulling no punches.

I stared at the dried blood inside the car. Bian's blood. The driver's seat was stained with it, more had splattered on the steering wheel, and some had even splashed onto the windshield and dashboard. She had bled profusely. And while I was sure she was alive when they pulled her out, that did not mean she was alive now.

Indeed, this was the Army's worst nightmare, and for the terrorists, a dream come true; an Army major, a female soldier, a West Point graduate, a beautiful and intelligent young woman whose beheading promised a telegenic horror that would sear itself into the psyche of the American public.

Terrorism thrives or dies on shock and hype, and in their corrupted version of Hollywood, truly a star was about to be born.

"Did you see it?" asked a voice from behind me.

I turned around. A military police buck sergeant, short, black, and female, was pointing at something inside the Toyota.

"See what?"

She stepped closer. "The letters," she replied. She leaned closer and stuck her arm inside the vehicle. "*There* . . . see it? Looks like letters . . . like she was writing something. You know?" She stepped back and commented, "In her own blood."

I followed her finger, and on the dashboard I observed what appeared at first to be squiggles of dried blood, but on closer examination had shape and form.

"Didn't notice it myself, at first," she told me. "Really, not till we hooked up the vehicle to the deuce and a half," she continued, referring to the Army truck that had towed the Land Cruiser. She explained, "Had to climb inside and put it in neutral . . . for the tow, sir. Took about fifteen minutes. Left me a lot of time to look around."

I had leaned closer and tried to read the letters. I said, "The first one looks like . . . what—C?"

"Yes, sir, sure does. And I think . . . the second's either a 'd' or a sloppy 'h.' "

"Followed by an 'a.' Right?"

"Or a sloppy 'o,' " she agreed. "But could be a 'q.' That last letter sort of drags off, sir. Maybe like she was yanked out of the cab as she was writing." She added, "I tol' my lieutenant might be she was still alive. Only he looked at all that blood and said uh-uh." She looked around and said, "Don't tell him I mentioned this. Please. Okay? He's sort of a prick. He don't like to be contradicted."

Was this a message? A clue? Or was the explanation more innocuous? I mean, it was equally possible that, as she writhed in pain, Bian's fingers had been convulsing on the dashboard.

I leaned forward and looked more closely. No—definitely this was neither arbitrary nor accidental. I yelled for Tirey, who rushed over and stuck his head inside the driver's compartment. I pointed at the dash and asked what he read, and more important, what he thought.

He slipped on reading glasses, then read off C, and H, and A, or maybe O. He stepped back and suggested, "It looks like a message. That's what it looks like. Too bad, though, because it also appears that she ran out of time."

The MP sergeant offered the opinion, "Might be they're the first letters of a license plate. You know, the plates of her attackers."

I kept replaying the combinations inside my head: CHO, CDO, CHA, CHQ, CDQ, and then again, CHA—for some reason that combination popped back into my brain. But why CHA? Think, Drummond. As the sergeant suggested, a license plate? Possibly. Then, out of nowhere, it hit me—CHA, CHArabi.

Tirey was explaining to the MP, "If they are from a license plate . . . well, too bad. If they weren't stolen, the attackers will change them and . . ."

He and she continued to chew the wrong possibilities, and I wandered away. I saw Phyllis hanging around by the entrance to the facility, alone. I approached and explained my theory that Bian was still alive—and why—and then in a hushed voice I told her, "In blood, Bian wrote three letters on the dashboard. C-H-A. Name something, or somebody, that starts with those letters."

She pondered this question for a long moment. "I'm not in the mood for games."

"Neither am I. Charabi—Mahmoud Charabi. And the fact that she could write confirms she was wounded, not dead, and now we know who took her."

"Do we? You're *sure* about the letters?"

"Am I positive? . . . No."

"And you're sure she wrote them?"

"Handwriting authentication is tough when the victim fingerpaints in her own blood." I told her, "The letters, however, are not Arabic, they're Roman."

"Okay . . . I would agree that is suggestive."

"You shouldn't argue with anything, Phyllis. Nothing else makes sense."

"No, it's the only explanation you've thought of. But it's still speculative, isn't it?"

"Interpreting evidence *is* always speculation. Footprints, fingerprints, DNA samples—until you ID the criminal, you're guessing what they mean and how they relate to a crime." I said, "Bian was writing something we could interpret. Something she knew we would understand." I added, "She wasn't a random victim. She was hunted down and kidnapped."

"Explain that."

I put my hand on her shoulder and said, "Somebody tipped Charabi about this investigation, and about Bian, and probably about me. That doesn't surprise me, nor should it surprise you—from the start of this thing, *everything* has leaked." She acknowledged that grim reality with an unhappy nod, and I continued, "The moment Bian drove out the gate yesterday, his people were waiting, they recognized her, and they ambushed her."

"How did they know she was here? At Camp Alpha?"

"How did they learn she was investigating Charabi?"

"You're implying an inside source." She then asked in a skeptical tone, "And who would that source be?"

"I have no idea." Though we both knew I was lying, and we both knew who the prime candidates were: Waterbury, and via him, Tigerman and Hirschfield. I recalled how Waterbury had fled Camp Alpha the day before. I had assumed he was gaining bureaucratic traction from a failure, but there was an equally plausible reason: As a former cop, he knew absence of presence nearly always equals absence of suspicion.

Clarior e tenebris—literally, the surrounding darkness emphasizes the light. Waterbury, and by extension, his cronies, were worried. About how much Bian and I knew and how much of a problem we were. And about how close we were to the truth. There was only one way to find that out: They needed either Bian or me—alive. And why not? This was the one place in the world where a kidnapped American raised no particular suspicion.

Nothing else made sense. But if I verbalized that connection, Phyllis would terminate this conversation immediately. So I ignored that mystery and continued, "Charabi's people followed her, and as she drove through a Shiite neighborhood, they struck."

"I see. And why would Charabi care about her?"

"How would I know?"

"For an accusation of this scale and repercussion, you had better know." She thought for a moment, then asked, "Do you know what I think?"

I was sure I did, but she told me anyway. "Guilt, Sean. She left without you and you feel responsible. That's natural, and it's wrong. She made a foolish, irresponsible choice, and probably a mortal one.

It was not your fault." She added, "To take it a step further, you're obsessed with Charabi. I warned you about this several times, and that's what worried me from the beginning. Now you're seeing Charabi everywhere you look."

"Where I'm seeing his name is in blood on the dashboard of Bian's car. That's not obsession, that's physical evidence. Were I to present it to any disinterested jury, I assure you they would be persuaded."

"Implying that I am not disinterested?"

"You have to answer that yourself, Phyllis."

She did not reply to my innuendo, but stared at the Toyota with a thoughtful expression. Eventually, she asked, "Were you to take this to a judge, is there sufficient evidence for a search warrant?"

"We're in Iraq. The occupiers make the rules."

"Answer my question."

"It would depend on the judge, and on the lawyer making the argument."

She looked at me a moment and said, "Get Tirey."

I did, and a few moments later the three of us were huddled about a hundred yards from the nearest prying ears. Phyllis looked at him and said, "Jim, I'm about to tell you an explosive story. This is probably the most dangerous secret you've ever heard, and it must remain that way. It involves very powerful people, and if anybody finds out about it, I won't have to destroy you. Because they will."

Jim did not look shocked by this preamble, though he did look concerned. Phyllis then launched into a quick-fire version of Clifford Daniels's death, the relationship between him and Mahmoud Charabi, the investigation we had pursued, and she then made the possible connection to the disappearance of Bian Tran.

When she finished, Tirey did look shocked, surprised, and a little frightened. Frightened for Bian, frightened about this case, and frightened for himself. He asked, "Why are you telling me this?"

"I think you know why," she replied.

"Okay . . . maybe I do." He looked at her, and then at me. He said, "You understand that Mahmoud Charabi stands a very good chance of becoming the next prime minister. At the very least, he'll be a very senior government minister. This is not a man to mess with."

"Worry less about him," I advised, "than the President of the United States. You now have his balls in your hands. If he finds out, he'll want your balls in his pocket."

Phyllis looked at him and asked, "What do you think about Drummond's assertion regarding Charabi?"

"I think it's an interesting story and a compelling suspicion. Were this the States, I would be talking to a federal judge instead of you."

"About what?"

"About probable cause. About a search warrant. Of course that's never a sure bet—but when the victim leaves such a strong lead . . ." He let that trail off.

Phyllis looked at me and asked a lawyerly question. "Charabi's office is located inside the Green Zone. It's an international zone, but his office is on U.S. property. Who can authorize a search warrant?"

I replied, "For an Army search, the commander. But the FBI doesn't report to the military. I would guess Jim authorizes himself."

"That's correct," Jim said and then asked, "Shouldn't we . . . Hey, look . . . maybe I should contact headquarters. Get a proper clearance. Or . . . at least notify the embassy. They'll throw a conniption if we do what I think you're asking."

Phyllis said, "Absolutely not. They're not cleared to know."

I added, "This is an in extremis hostage situation, Jim. They could be torturing Bian as we speak. In such situations, as you and I know, the law allows you certain latitude for independent judgment."

"I understand . . . but . . ."

"Speed, Jim. The diplomats will write a thousand position papers and hold a hundred meetings, and the answer—if there ever is one—will be yes, no, and maybe."

"Then Bureau headquarters. That can't be—"

"Wrong. In D.C. there are possible coconspirators, some of whom might be involved in the decision. We don't know how far this goes, or how wide. If word leaks to Charabi, Bian's body will be carried out with the morning garbage."

Jim Tirey had suddenly become a visibly conflicted man. He wanted to do the right thing—save an American citizen in distress—and he wanted to do the right and proper bureaucratic thing—save his own ass.

Phyllis took his arm and said, "Under no circumstances will this search leak out. That's best for Charabi and that's best for the U.S. government. Charabi will not be publicly embarrassed, and if offered the option, I am sure he'll want this kept quiet. The embassy and Washington will never know about it." She looked at him and emphasized, "I think that's best for us." She asked, "What do you think?"

This arrangement seemed to assuage his professional and other concerns, and he and Phyllis began hatching a plan for a clandestine raid on Charabi's office, which essentially involved Jim handpicking four or five trusted federal agents, then threatening professional castration if they whispered a word about this to anyone.

I said, "One other condition. I get ten minutes with Charabi. Alone. I have more familiarity with the evidence against him, and thus I have the highest likelihood of convincing him to voluntarily answer a few questions." I noted, "Also, my name will be the only one he remembers."

Jim liked this idea even better.

But it wasn't exactly accurate, since Phyllis probably knew more about Charabi than Charabi knew about himself. But she did not correct my misstatement; in fact she noted, "That makes good sense." Then she said, very seriously, "Don't leave any scars or bruises."

"Fine." I would kill him without scars or bruises.

CHAPTER THIRTY-SIX

The receptionist was a gentleman of Arab descent, heavyset, wearing a black Western suit and a skinny black necktie, who looked up with a naive smile as Tirey and I entered the office.

The smile evaporated after five more agents pushed through the doorway and began fanning out around his office—this seemed to clear up any misunderstanding that we were welcome guests. Sounding suddenly anxious, he asked, "How may I help you?"

Tirey stopped about a foot from his desk and flashed a phony piece of paper and a real shield in his face. He identified himself and said very forcefully, "I have reason to suspect that somebody in this office is involved with a kidnapping. This warrant authorizes my agents to conduct a search."

The space we had entered was a large anteroom that was messy and disorganized, with about seven desks, behind each of which sat an Arab gentleman, dressed, as was the receptionist, in severe business attire. It smelled of stale cigarettes and old teabags, and looked like a cross between a ward politician's back room and a busy mortuary. Tirey instructed the receptionist, "Tell your people to leave their desks and stand against that wall." He pointed at a wall. "If anybody touches anything, they'll be cuffed and arrested."

Apparently they all spoke English, or they knew the drill, because they began standing, hanging up phones, dropping pens, and stepping away from their desks.

I asked the receptionist, "Is Mahmoud Charabi in?"

We had checked beforehand and confirmed that indeed, he was at that moment in his office. Still, it was instructive to see the look on this poor man's face. Unlike his boss, this guy must've hung around during Saddam's reign, because the sudden appearance of armed men bearing legal papers and threats put a very worried expression on his face. He replied hesitantly, "I . . . I do not know this."

I pointed at the phone on the desk. "Tell him Colonel Drummond from the American Army wants a word with him. Now."

He lifted up the phone and punched a number. He spoke in Arabic, but whatever he said took a lot longer than what I said. For all I knew, Charabi's office had a fire escape, and this guy was telling his boss to make tracks.

It was time to make my move; there were two doors on the far side of the room and I walked swiftly toward them. I opened the first door, which turned out to be a toilet, and then I threw open the second door, which turned out to be the devil's lair, and I entered. The door had a switch lock, and to ensure I wasn't disturbed, I shut the door gently behind me, turned the switch, and then turned around and faced my enemy.

A man sat behind a medium-size wooden desk in an office that was neither large nor even well-furnished—it contained only the aforementioned desk, a metal file cabinet, a badly stained wall-to-wall carpet, and Mahmoud Charabi sipping a cup of tea. This was hardly what he had schemed and plotted for decades to end up in, but that was the whole point; this room was a way station, and if things worked out, his next office would be palatial in size and decor, he would have an army at his beck and call, and a nation at his feet.

He stared at me a moment, hung up the phone, started to stand, then changed his mind and fell back into his chair. That moment of indecision aside, he had enough presence of mind to demand, "Why do you wish to see me? You have no appointment."

I moved toward his desk. A rotating chair was positioned in the middle of the floor that looked like, and probably was, U.S. Army property, which I interpreted as permission to sit, and I did.

He suggested, "I think you should leave." After a moment in which I did not leave, he informed me, "Now I am calling the American ambassador to protest." He lifted up the phone and began hitting numbers with angry little punches.

There are two ways to approach a delicate situation such as this;

diplomacy is the recommended course for all the obvious advantages that it avoids nasty confrontations, often gets results, and leaves no ugly feelings. And to be fair, the man to my front was perhaps weeks away from becoming the most powerful man in this country, and as such, he deserved my respect and courtesy, if not for himself, then for the office within his grasp. Also he had powerful friends in Washington who could screw up my paycheck, my career, or worse.

That, however, has never been my way and I said, "Put down that phone."

He continued dialing.

I said, "Go ahead, then. It's your funeral."

He stopped dialing. I seemed to have his attention and he asked, "What are you talking about?"

"Well . . . for starters, who murdered Clifford Daniels? Then, who told the Iranians that we broke their intelligence code? And finally, who shot and kidnapped an American Army major? There's more, but I think that's a good beginning. Don't you?"

Somewhere in there I struck a chord, or several chords. His face went white. He said, "I . . . I have no idea what you're talking about. W-who are you . . . and w-who sent you?"

I ignored his questions and said, "Ordinarily, at moments like this, I would read you your rights and advise you to get a lawyer. But today, I'm your lawyer. And today, you have no rights, only options." I paused, then briefly explained why he should pay attention to these options. "I can destroy you with one phone call."

Mahmoud Charabi, incidentally, was in his late fifties, medium height, and a bit on the plump side—pampered and soft-looking, actually—which did not reinforce the tough-guy expression he was trying to give me. He had graying hair around a bald dome, waxy flesh around a formless face, thick lips around a tight mouth, and full cheeks around small brown eyes that were staring at me a little incredulously. The overall impression was a sort of roundness and flabbiness, which might be why people underestimated this man.

Also he possessed excellent English and was fairly well-spoken, but with a discernible accent, and I detected a slight stutter, perhaps a nervous affliction. To tell the truth, nothing about him looked powerful, charismatic, or even slightly imposing. He looked more like an overweight insurance adjustor than the George Washington of this country. Probably this accounted for why he was trying to lie, scheme, and murder his way into power.

Also he had the unfortunate Nixonian reflex of squeezing his hands together at moments of high stress—at that moment, he looked like he was pressing coal into diamonds.

Lest he harbored any doubts, I informed him, "I have Clifford Daniels's laptop computer." His eyes widened, and to confirm his worst fears, I continued, "You're Crusader Two. And yes—Clifford was both stupid and sloppy. Because, yes, he failed to eliminate the e-mail messages. And yes, Mr. Charabi, they were decoded, and they are very . . . incriminating. Message after message."

"But they—"

Not allowing him to get a word in, I continued, "Imagine, if you will, how those messages will look on the front page of the *New York Times*." He began contemplating the empty blotter on his desk, and in case he forgot, I reminded him what he had written, saying, "Those unflattering assessments of your fellow leaders here in Iraq. Your whiny complaints about the American Army and the American ambassador—'dickhead'? . . . Do you think he'll be flattered by that nickname? I don't. And best for last: You and Cliff cooking up that deal to tell the Iranians we had broken their code."

When he made no response, I said, "Wow. I mean, wow. How is that going to look?"

If his face had looked white before, he now was on the verge of disappearing into thin air. He never imagined he would hear these words; he thought Daniels was dead, that his secrets went to the grave. He said, "Uh . . . w-who . . . please, who are you?"

"It doesn't matter. Major Bian Tran will be brought to this office immediately. You have ten minutes, or . . ." I allowed that thought to drag off.

He looked up at me, very surprised. "I . . . I . . . w-what? I have never heard of this . . . major . . . what did you say is her name?"

I stood up and leaned over his desk. "On your orders, her vehicle was ambushed yesterday evening. She was wounded and kidnapped." We locked eyes. "If she's dead, you're dead. I'll kill you myself." I pointed at my watch. "Nine minutes."

"I have told you the truth. I do not know her . . . and d-definitely . . . I have not kidnapped her. Whoever told you this . . . It is a d-despicable l-lie."

I maintained eye contact and informed him, "Major Tran wrote your name in blood on the dashboard before she was dragged out of her car."

"Oh . . ." He glanced around his office, tried to compose himself, and a modicum of color returned to his face. He said with surprising coolness, "Why don't you sit? Let us talk this over without further threats."

"Here's a better idea. Why don't you pick up the phone and order your people to get Tran over here. Chop-chop."

"Because I can't. You are wrong." He drew a few breaths, then said, "You come into my office—*my* office—accusing me of murder and kidnapping. You cannot blackmail me into confessing things that are such big, terrible lies." He had found his voice, apparently, because he then ordered imperiously, "Sit down."

This guy needed a pop in the nose and I leaned forward to give him one, but he did something that slightly upset my plan. His right hand came up from underneath his desk and in it was a Glock with the barrel about six inches from my groin. He repeated himself, saying, "Sit down," more emphatically and, given that the pistol was threatening man's best friend, more persuasively.

I did not sit, but I did back off a few steps. I said, "Half a dozen FBI agents are in your outer office. Listen . . ." We both took a moment, and you could hear through the walls Tirey's Feds noisily trashing his outer office. "Hand me that pistol and I promise I won't beat the crap out of you."

"I think not. You broke into my office, you threatened me, went crazy, and attacked me. Self-defense—I have justification to kill you."

At moments like this, you have to ask yourself, is he serious or is he bluffing? Well, I had just threatened everything he had schemed for decades to get, I knew he was ruthless, and I had no doubt he was capable of murder. Also he was right; when there are only two witnesses to a murder, the living one has a monopoly on the truth.

But given all that, he hadn't fired yet—that meant I had something he wanted. His curiosity was the only reason I was alive. As long I didn't cure that problem, I had a chance.

You should never take your focus from a man's eyes at a moment like this, but I looked at his gun. "Hey, you know what?" I told him what. "Clifford Daniels died of a gunshot from an identical pistol. A Glock 17 Pro. Right?"

"Is this so? Well . . . I had no idea."

"I just thought it was, you know, odd. A quirky coincidence."

"Perhaps not such a coincidence. I purchased one for me, and one for Cliff. Matching pistols. Brothers in arms." He smiled at me. "A fitting gift—for all he was doing for my poor, miserable country."

"You give America phony intelligence, and now over a thousand of our soldiers are dead. You give Clifford a present and he dies by that gun. Does anybody ever get gifts from you and live?"

He waved the pistol. "You will not be alive to hear me say this again. *Sit down.*"

I saw that his trigger finger had turned white. I sat.

He came right to the point and demanded, "Where is Cliff's computer?"

Clearly, this was part of what was keeping me alive—probably the only thing. I was sure that if I told him the computer was the property of the CIA, and that I alone did not hold the key to his political survival, I was dead. In summary, he needed me alive long enough to learn how to contain this thing, and I needed to stay alive long enough to get my hands around his throat. So I lied. "Hidden. Major Tran and I, well . . . once we saw what was on the hard drive . . . frankly, it was impossible to resist."

"Why?"

"Because there are enough powerful names in those messages to make sure we'll both retire as general officers."

He appreciated my self-serving logic and asked, "So you hid it?"

"I put it in a safe place. Someplace only the major and I know about."

He regarded me a moment, then said, "Who are you?"

"You know who I am."

He repeated his question with his pistol pointed between my eyes, this time adding, "You won't hear me ask again."

"Major Tran's partner. She and I are investigating the death of Clifford Daniels."

"Ah . . . well, then I am confused. I was informed that my old friend took his own life. So, Colonel . . ." He apparently had a politician's vanity about glasses, without the politician's gift for name recall, because he had to lean forward and study my nametag. "Colonel Drummond . . . suicide or murder? Which was it?"

"You don't know me?"

"Why? Have we met before?"

He did look clueless, as if he was totally unfamiliar with my name. But if somebody in Washington had informed him about Bian Tran, surely they had also informed him about me. I found it curious that he felt a need to play games; *he* had the gun, after all. But, since he was being selective, I decided to be selective, too, and instead addressed his first question. "Cliff's death looked like suicide. Certainly, he had ample motive—a nasty divorce, a disappointing life, and as you know, an order to appear before a congressional investigating committee. He was already professionally ruined; next stop was public disgrace."

"So then . . . it was suicide?"

"It was murder. A hired female assassin. It was staged to replicate suicide, and you know what? But for a few sloppy mistakes and contradictions, that might've been our ruling."

I quickly recounted those mistakes, and he listened, but it looked like his mind was on other matters, and he did not seem all that focused or bothered. I concluded, "Were she my employee, I'd cancel her Christmas bonus."

Charabi's expression had now turned to suspicion. He studied me a moment and asked, "Are you wired?" He did not wait for an answer. "Stand up. Remove your shirt."

I did not stand. I had had enough. A murderer, a betrayer, a kidnapper—no way was I going to indulge this man by stripping.

"Your shirt—now," he barked, and once again directed the pistol at my groin. His hand was shaking and his trigger knuckle was white.

Well, why not? I unbuttoned and threw my Army blouse on the floor. I stood and pulled my trousers down to my ankles and did a slow pirouette so he could see I was not wired. He said, "The T-shirt, also," and I pulled it off as well. He informed me, "There is a wonderful Kurdish saying that predates modern electronics. A naked man tells no lies."

"If you think my underpants are coming off, shoot me now."

He laughed, then said, "You can put them back on," and I took a moment and redressed.

Everybody watches cop shows these days, and they presume you can visually detect a listening device, though frankly that perception has long been outmoded by the miracle of miniaturization. My Bureau friends, I knew from personal experience, actually have a bug in a suppository, which gives a whole new meaning to the phrase "talking out your ass." But, to be blunt, yours truly is not *that* dedicated. Had I been wired, though, Tirey's people would already have busted down the door, I would be pointing the pistol at his head, and he would be answering *my* questions. On second thought, a suppository up your ass is not that bad.

Anyway, while I buttoned my blouse, I sat and considered my options and he toyed with his Glock and appeared to consider his. Letting me go seemed out of the question, but shooting me and claiming self-defense clearly wasn't off the table. I had something he wanted—information—and he had something I wanted—the gun. I saw no way that we could meet each other halfway; I don't think he did either.

He eventually said, "Listen to me. I did not kill Cliff—he was my friend—nor did I have him killed." He leaned closer and added, "Nor have I kidnapped this major you keep talking about."

Involuntary sounds sometimes escape from my throat, and I heard somebody say, "Bullshit."

This annoyed him and he reminded me, "I have a gun and you do not. A man in my position has no need to lie."

"You know what? You're right. Boy, I'm glad we've cleared the air, and . . . well . . . I'm sure you're very busy." I stood and got about two steps toward the door.

"Sit! Or I shoot."

"A bullet in my back won't help your self-defense claim," I informed him. I did not like the tone in his voice, and I did stop walking.

"The real issue, Colonel, is what a hole in the back of your head will do for your health."

Good point. I turned around and sat. He waved his pistol. "I do not think the Army sent you here. Who do you work for?"

I decided to tell him the truth. "The CIA." I think he had already put this together, though, because he did not appear surprised or shocked. I told him, "So, this is great. I know you work for Iran, and now you know who I work for." I smiled at him. "Naked men tell no lies, right?"

He asked, "But you are in the Army also? This uniform is real?"

"Yes."

He waved his weapon at my shoulder and said, "You have a combat patch. This means you have been in battle, yes?"

I nodded.

"Have you killed for your country?"

I did not respond.

"How many have you killed?"

"I didn't count."

"This means you lost count. Am I correct?"

I didn't like his questions and said, "What's your point?"

"Do you consider yourself a patriot?"

"I'm a soldier."

"And you have killed for your country—for your people." He looked at me thoughtfully, and asked, "Do you know how many Shiites Saddam Hussein murdered?"

"A lot."

"Is a million a lot? How about two million?" he asked in a mocking tone. "Murdered, Colonel—poison gas, bullets in the back of the head, torture, rape, starvation. Men, women, children, the aged—nobody was given mercy. And I do not even include in this number the four hundred thousand Shia who were forced to fight and die in Saddam's idiotic wars with Iran and America."

"I read the newspapers."

"When so many Jews died at the hands of Nazis, the whole world condemned this. It even was given a name—the Holocaust—as if mass extermination pertains only to Jews. Why does the mass murder of my people not have a name?"

"The murder of your people was a tragedy. And you know we did our best to end it, with food and medical programs, and no-fly zones over southern Iraq to keep Saddam from using his aircraft to slaughter Shiites."

"Your *best*? I think not. Did the murders ever stop? You knew they did not. In the most merciful years, it was only tens of thousands."

"It was not our fight."

He had made his point, he knew it, and he returned to his smaller point, saying, "So you have killed for your country. Would you also lie for your country? Surely a liar has less need for shame than a killer."

"Killing in defense of your country is no sin."

He relaxed back into his chair and gave me a little smile, or a nasty smirk—his lips were fat and it was hard to tell. He said, "Neither, I think, is lying to save your own people a sin. *Taqiyya* . . . are you familiar with this Arab word? This concept?"

"In fact, I think I ordered some yesterday. Means burnt goat meat, right?"

He ignored my sarcasm and explained, "It is a Shia concept. It sanctions lying in defense of our poor, persecuted faith. If I perhaps passed on some untruths to your government, if, before this war, I perhaps exaggerated a few claims, I have no qualms or regret for this."

"When you lie at the behest of your Iranian bosses, and to further your own rise to power, that doesn't make you noble, Mr. Charabi. It makes you a liar and a cheat."

A surprised pout creased his face. "My bosses? Surely, you do not believe I work for Iran?"

I looked at him a long time, then told him a few things he already knew. "You've met with Iranian intelligence, you passed vital intelligence to Iran, and I have no doubt that if we dig deep enough, we'll find you're also implicated in shipping Iranian weapons and agents into Iraq." I told him, "If we dig deeper still, I suspect we'll also find that you were talking to the Iranians long before the war."

"Look all you want."

"Thanks for your permission."

"In fact," he said, smiling, "I will save you some trouble. Yes, you are right." He stopped smiling. "Well, you are *partly* right. I have been talking to . . . certain friends in Iran. And yes, since long before your invasion. And yes, now I am helping them expand their influence among my Shia people inside Iraq. And do you know why?"

"Because you would pimp your own mother for a throne?"

He chose not to respond to this.

So I took another stab. "Because they want their hands around the nuts of whoever's running Iraq, and you've volunteered your balls?" I looked him in the eye and asked, "Yes? No? Am I warm?"

He knew I was trying to piss him off, and his eyes narrowed. He was shrewd, though, and to piss me off, he did not rise to the bait. He gave me a cool gaze and answered himself. He said, "Because it helps me . . . and it helps my people. And because those who I now find myself vying with for leadership of the Iraqi Shia, and for leadership of Iraq—the clerics Sistani, Sadr, and others—they have their own long relationships with the Iranians."

He paused and looked at me.

He said, "Like your government in Washington, Tehran also has many views, many factions. Not everybody there is happy with Sistani, or with Sadr. So I give this gift of great intelligence significance to certain friends in Iran's government, they pass this along to the appropriate people, and now—wallah!"—his chubby hands flew through the air and he performed a silly pantomime of pulling a rabbit out of a hat—"Mahmoud Charabi has his own very powerful supporters in Tehran—and here, in Iraq."

Amazing. Basically, he had found Iranian doppelgängers of Cliff Daniels, and just as he had exploited Daniels, he now was using these "friends" to make deeper inroads inside Iran's government. Then again, maybe it wasn't so amazing. Every con man has his favorite swindle and the conviction that what works once, can work again and again. I should tell his new Iranian friends how well it had worked out for Cliff.

In that light, I said, "When you play so many sides against the middle, sometimes you forget where the middle is."

He interpreted this literally and replied, "Washington is seven thousand miles away. Iran is next door." He got a sort of thin smile on his lips and added, "In the long run it will make no considerable difference. Do you know why?"

"I have the feeling you're going to tell me why."

"Because it is entirely irrelevant. Frankly, the Iranians have as little control over me as you, as America. I am Iraqi, Colonel. I do not even *like* the Iranians."

"That's not a good enough why, Charabi. Tell me more."

"Because what I have is fear of the Sunnis who, you might have noticed, receive considerable support from our Sunni neighbors. These people, they are savages. Murderers. For decades, they have slaughtered and crushed my people, the Shia, while they lived regally off the oil wealth that rightfully belonged to all of us. If saving my people means partnership with the Iranians . . . What was that priceless phrase of Churchill's? That one about Stalin? The one about sleeping with the devil . . . ?"

"I think, Mr. Charabi, it was we who slept with the devil. And you should worry deeply about what happens when America learns about your betrayal, about what an asshole you are. We've lost many lives and spent a fortune trying to liberate your country."

"Betrayal? Ah, I think not, Colonel. I merely passed along a gift. The selection of this gift was not mine, was it? You have read these messages. You know this choice was Cliff's." Shaking his head at me, he added, "Your problem, I think, is not with Mahmoud Charabi . . . it is with Cliff, who, after all, is now well beyond your reach."

This apparently jogged his mind, because after a moment he complained, "Americans are too impatient. They do not like long wars and struggles. You have this maddening obsession for instant gratification."

He thoughtfully played with his lower lip, then added, "If your army departs prematurely, my people will be slaughtered. So what was for us a big dilemma, by bringing in my Iranian friends, I have now helped turn into your big problem. Now you dare not leave for fear that the Iranians will fill the vacuum, and you will have fought this war only to turn Iraq over to them. Yet if you do leave, Iran will rush in, and my Iranian friends will save us. So, Mr. Drummond, your people face a strategic checkmate, and the Shia, my people—Allah be praised—win either way. Either the Americans or the Iranians, or both of you, will save us. It is a nice position for us, don't you think?"

What I thought, as I looked at this man, was that he was about ten steps ahead of anybody in Washington. He was right, we are a nation addicted to instant gratification—instant food, instant sex, instant victories. Also, we never think deeper than tomorrow. Here, he had not only helped lure us into Iraq, he had already devised a trap play to keep us there. It *was* amazing, I thought—and very troubling.

I changed subjects and asked, "What was Clifford Daniels to you?"

"A friend when I needed a friend."

"I find it interesting that you would describe him that way. And I'll bet he would find it interesting. Because now you're here, and he's in the morgue."

And it *was* interesting. I could call this man a liar, a schemer, a thief, a murderer, and a traitor—but accusing him of bad friendship really got under his bonnet. He flew into a long and indignant harangue regarding his "most dearest friend," admitting that Cliff was, yes, an ordinary human being with warts and blemishes—with an excessive professional appetite, perhaps, and yes, that off-putting self-importance some people found obnoxious—but also he was noble and dedicated, a flawed saint, and so forth. Arabs have a real flair for flowery bullshit, and by the time he anointed Daniels the Lafayette of Iraq, I was ready to blow lunch.

When my host has a gun, however, I tend to listen patiently and behave. For some reason, Charabi felt a need to expiate about Daniels, so I nodded agreeably as he spoke. I actually let him finish before I said, "Cliff Daniels was an idiot. When that became clear—even to himself—he went to pieces. A blowhard, a drunk, a womanizer, a man who went psychotic over his career."

"No, he was—"

"He was a small, weak man with unhealthy appetites. A man with elephantine ambitions and pygmy talents on a pathetic quest for power and fame. Unfortunately for him, he chose the wrong meal ticket—you."

"I did not say Cliff was perfect."

"No, you didn't. From the moment you met, you recognized exactly how stupid, how vain, and how vulnerable he was. You exploited those ambitions and vanities. By persuading him to support you and your lies about Iraq, you made a fool out of him, and later, as his world began imploding, you exploited his despondency and made a traitor out of him. With a friend like you, a man has more enemies than he can handle."

"Well . . ." he replied, suddenly uncomfortable. Then he found the bright side, and confessed, "It is a big relief for me to learn this was not suicide, but murder. I was feeling . . . a little guilt."

"You're not off the hook. His murder was the direct consequence of your relationship."

"But I did not kill him." This topic obviously bothered him, and he had the gun, so he changed it and asked, "Tell me about this major. Why do you believe I kidnapped her?"

He had rested his Glock about two feet away on the desktop, I noticed. About twelve feet from me, and I began inching my chair in short, noiseless scoots across the carpet.

Actually, I was somewhat surprised that Mr. Charabi was revealing so much of his thinking to me. Of course, this did not mean he trusted me or enjoyed my company—this meant I was dead.

Instead of answering his question, I asked him, "Did Cliff ever tell you how *he* learned we broke Iran's code?"

"Why do you ask?"

"It was a tightly controlled CIA program. He wasn't supposed to know about it. It's . . . well . . . something of an embarrassment."

He laughed.

"To be truthful, a friend of mine has his ass in a sling over it," I told him with a wink. "I owe him a favor."

"You're saying your agency still does not understand how this occurred?"

Another short scoot. "Why are you surprised? These are the same people who never noticed Aldrich Ames's shiny new green Jaguar sedan in the Langley parking lot."

He seemed to relish this analogy, as well as the irony that Cliff—and by extension, he as well—had picked the Agency's pocket. If I had to guess, he still harbored a grudge that the CIA had rejected his early overtures for a partnership, and later, that Agency people trashed his reputation around Washington and in the press. He obviously had a big ego; now he was being petty. He said, "Why don't I give you a hint? The CIA courier for this cell was a woman."

"Oh . . . and—"

He nodded. "And . . . yes. She was not especially attractive, but as Cliff liked to say, all ladies look the same in the dark." He shrugged. "Theirs was a most brief affair." He smiled and added, "I was given the impression from Cliff that her pillow talk was more intriguing to him than the lady herself."

I took a moment and considered this. The prewar intelligence circle of Iraqi experts in Washington was small, so it was not surprising that Cliff and this courier, whoever she was, were acquainted. And I recalled again what his ex-wife said about Cliff: If it couldn't outrun him, he laid wood on it. So in the end, this lady was both literally and figuratively screwed by Cliff. But that left a big open question: Why did she tell Cliff about the program?

But maybe it wasn't all that hard to figure out. It could have been as innocuous as her justifying her frequent absences to Baghdad, or as mundane as her bragging to her lover about her important work, or she mumbled in her sleep, or she sloppily dropped enough clues that Cliff put it together on his own.

Any or all of these explained *how* the leak occurred. They did not, however, answer how this courier got past her polygraph sessions. Because, if I believed Phyllis, anybody and everybody involved in this fiasco had been lie-tested so many times that the Agency would know the names of everybody this lady played doctor with in kindergarten, and everybody who hid the pickle in her thereafter. Money, sex, and drugs/booze—these sins are the source of most betrayals, and also these are the things Agency inquisitors show great interest in and never fail to ask about.

Well, also, there are ego, ambition, and power—consider Cliff Daniels and Don, aka Lebrowski—but if those were disqualifying evils, the only people left in D.C. would be janitors. Maybe.

Charabi broke into my thoughts and insisted, "I have answered your question. You will now answer mine."

"Okay. The major and I were investigating everything about Cliff Daniels, including his bosses, and including you. Plus we have Cliff's computer, and that's known inside the Pentagon. So Tigerman or Hirschfield contacted you and told you to find out what Major Tran and I know, and maybe to stop us. Damage control. Right?"

He laughed; I scooted another few inches forward. He seemed

amused by my logic, and he leaned back in his chair and said, "No, this is not right. This is very stupid. Tigerman and Hirschfield stopped talking to me months ago. I am a pariah in Washington." He laughed again.

"All right. If you didn't kidnap the major, who did?"

"I believe that is your problem, Colonel."

"Is it? Then why did she write your name in her blood?" Another short scoot.

"I really have no idea," he replied, and we stared at each other a moment.

I knew this man was a liar and a cheat, and I shouldn't believe a word that came from his fat lips. Not his denial about murdering Cliff Daniels, or about kidnapping Bian, but I did. That left open the issues of who did kill Cliff and who took Bian, but as he said, that was not his problem; it was mine.

I mean, he had already confessed he was a liar, that he had betrayed his pals in Washington, and that he was willfully consorting with Iran, our presumptive enemy. On second thought, confession was the wrong word; he was bragging. He was enjoying himself, looking an American officer in the eye and boasting openly and freely about how smart he was, and how deeply and easily he screwed the big, powerful USA, and his enemies in the CIA.

And why not? He thought he was talking to a dead man. Which reminded me, and I took another short scoot closer to his desk, and to his gun. But he quickly picked up the pistol and asked in a coldly reasonable tone, "Do you really think I am so stupid I haven't noticed you doing that? Back away."

Whoops. I backed away.

But it seemed our conversation was drawing to a close, because he sort of summarized our situation, saying, "So, you and I, we seem to be at a crossroad. I do not have this major you want, and you have this computer that is very troubling to me."

"And you have the gun."

"Yes, that also." He leaned toward me and asked, "If I asked you where this computer is, can I trust you to tell me the truth?"

"Can I trust you not to shoot me afterward?"

I saw that his finger was back inside the trigger guard. He was too preoccupied with his own thinking to answer my question—actually, I knew the answer—and he leaned farther forward and began sharing his own thoughts. He said, "Of course, only you and this missing major know where Cliff's computer is located. Now she has been kidnapped, and of course, this is Iraq—forgive me if this sounds cruel—she is as good as dead." He paused very briefly and then said, "So . . . if you are dead, too, nobody will find this computer."

I was afraid he would put that together. Looking like a man who was happy with his own reasoning, he aimed the pistol at my chest, and his finger began to squeeze.

I quickly said, "Well . . . maybe I wasn't completely forthcoming about the computer."

The pistol didn't go down, but neither did it go off.

I told him, "When I said I have the computer, I meant the *Agency* has the computer."

"So you lied. It is not . . . hidden?"

"That depends on your definition of hidden." Actually, it was hidden from me; that's a pretty good definition.

He asked, "And what is your definition?"

"It's in the possession of my boss, who works directly for the Director. Only three or four people have read the messages, or know about them, including the Director."

I was telling the truth, of course, but he looked a little surprised, and also a lot dubious. He asked, "If you lied to me once, why should I believe you now?" Then he answered his own question and said, "I think I will just kill you and take my chances."

"I thought you were smarter than that. You know, for instance, that your e-mails were professionally encoded. Do you really believe a couple of Army officers broke that code? It was a real ballbuster." I tried to remember some of John's technogibberish, and sort of mumbled, "VPN, and ISP protocols . . . firewalls layered upon firewalls . . ."

While he mulled this over, I said, "Kill me, and the deal will be off."

"You have never mentioned a deal."

"Well . . . the idea was that you and I would have a confidential discussion. This whole thing would be kept under wraps, and nobody would be the wiser."

He stared at me very intently with his finger caressing the trigger.

I said, "Why do you think you and I are in here alone? Why did I lock your door? Talk with the agents searching your office—they've been told they're investigating a kidnapping, period. So I go out, tell them you're free and clear, we go away, and you resume your rise to power."

"And why would the CIA consider this a good outcome?"

"We regard it as a terrible outcome."

"Then—"

"You outsmarted us, Mr. Charabi. We recognize reality."

I could see that it made him happy to hear this, and he asked, "And what is this . . . reality?"

"Discretion is best for you, best for us, and best for Iraq." I told him the truth, saying, "The Agency and this administration have taken more than enough black eyes over Iraq. The last thing Washington wants is another public scandal. This scandal in particular." I added, after a beat, "Unless you kill me."

"And then?"

"Good question. Because then . . . well . . ." Because then, well, what? Well, then Sean Drummond would be dead, and who cares what happened afterward? I didn't say that, of course. As persuasively as I could, I said, "Because the CIA does not like it when you kill one of its own. Right now, it's professional. You don't want to make it personal."

He needed a moment to reconsider the situation in light of this new variable. Mahmoud Charabi was indeed sly, and also, I thought, a more complex individual than I had been led to believe. As Don—aka Martin Lebrowski—had described, the man was an inveterate schemer, and a brutal and habitual manipulator of truth and people, as well as nations. But what Don missed—what you would expect an egocentric, careerist prick like Don to miss—was that Charabi could self-justify these behaviors as necessary means to a good end, a moral end, a righteous purpose.

I thought, too, that Charabi truly believed he was the anointed savior of his people, just as he now genuinely believed that he, and he alone, could lead them to the Promised Land. He wasn't the first man to mix selfless impulses with his own greed for fame and power, and he wouldn't be the last. And depending on how things worked out, Mahmoud Charabi would have a place in his country's history books, either as a cherished hero or as a miserable flop who overreached and delivered only more death and misery to a land that already had suffered more than enough of both.

He asked for a war, and he had gotten his wish; I was sure, though, that this wasn't the war he anticipated—or wanted. I looked at his face as he contemplated what to do with me, and it struck me that, like America, he had assumed that the war would be swift, the victory complete, and with the Pentagon's backing, he would already be on the throne. As they say, man plans, and God laughs. Now he was jukin' and jivin', caught up in a civil war partly of his making, playing one side off the other, dividing powerful governments against each other, dancing on powerful cracks, and praying the tectonic plates did not shift and squash him in the middle.

This squat, unimpressive-looking man had grabbed a hungry wolf by the ears. And I was sure I did not need to explain to him what would happen if the wolf got loose.

No, I could not really condemn Mahmoud Charabi for his deceptions, his lies, and his plots; but I could and I did blame those in Washington who wrapped his lies into a nation's justification for war, and in so doing, allowed his machinations to become ours.

I looked up and saw that the pistol still was pointed at me. I could almost hear his thoughts—kill me, or not? I was sure Charabi could, and without remorse, if he believed that was best for his people—and best for himself. Just as I would snap his neck if I could only get close enough. He eventually asked, "How do I know I can trust *you*?"

If he was smart, he wouldn't. But I decided to appeal to his kind of logic. "Because we all have dirt we want kept under the rug. Because this administration trusted you, it used your lies to justify this war, and it flew you over here to become the next prime minister. And because now it turns out you played them like gullible idiots, you were and you are working with Iran, and you betrayed us. In the midst of an election, this administration would be destroyed if the public became fully aware of what utter fools they've been. Our coalition partners might take a walk, and American public support for this war might evaporate." I told him, "We would lose, and *you* would lose."

"Ah, but I have already prepared for this."

It was my turn to smile, and I said, "Were I you, I wouldn't be so smug."

"What does this mean?"

"Perhaps your Iranian friends might step up and save the day, or maybe a raging conflict in Iraq is more than they want to bite off, and they'll take a pass. Then there will be a bloody civil war, and possibly a Sunni victory and another Saddam, in which case I wouldn't want to be you." It was time to force the issue and I stood up and said, "Make your choice."

This made sense to him; it should, because it *was* true.

The pistol came down and he said, "Tell your CIA bosses I have embarrassing secrets about them also. We can burn each other's houses down."

"I understand," I assured him. "And they understand."

I got up and took a few steps toward the door, and he said somewhat weirdly, "You know, Cliff really was my dear friend. I liked him."

I turned around. We stared at each other a really long time, then I said, "What you like, Mr. Charabi, you seem to destroy. You killed Cliff as surely as if you had pulled the trigger yourself. And your scheming, lying, and manipulations have done the same thing for your people. They are still being slaughtered by Sunnis, and you are not the man to save them. That said, I truly do wish you good luck."

I walked out and closed his office door quietly behind me. I approached Jim Tirey and informed him that this was a bust, that Charabi was not in any way implicated in Bian's kidnapping, or in the murder of Clifford Daniels, and it was time to clear out. He gave me a look that combined surprise and confusion with annoyance and said, "You told me it was conclusive."

"I was wrong."

"Wrong . . . ?"

"He had nothing to do with Bian, or with Daniels's murder. Sorry."

"You're . . . *sorry*?" He asked, "And just how do you know this?"

"Because he had a gun, the perfect legal justification to kill me, and I'm alive."

He stared at me for a long time. Eventually, he called his agents into a knot and informed them, "We had bad information. Time to get out of here—now."

He opened the door and we began quickly filing out.

To our common surprise, however, awaiting us in the hallway was an attractive blonde female reporter with a man beside her holding a reflective light, and a second man hefting a camera on his shoulder.

The reporter was staring at me, though I was sure we'd never met. But in her eyes I was sure I saw recognition, which was odd. Jim Tirey also caught her look, and he stared at me a moment inquisitively.

Then the light flashed on and the lovely female reporter completely ignored me and stepped forward, directly in the path of Jim Tirey. She stuffed her mike into his face and said, "Inside sources tell us that Mahmoud Charabi is under suspicion of passing vital secrets to the Iranians. Specifically, that we had broken their intelligence code. Could you comment on what your search turned up?"

Tirey looked at me, and we shared an unspoken thought. He then did something unfortunate and shared that thinking. "Oh . . . shit."

So in the interest of getting a more family-friendly comment, the reporter and Tirey tried again, and in true Bureau form, he told her, "No comment."

He shoved the mike out of his face and began walking as fast as his feet could carry him down the hallway and out of the building.

We all walked behind him. The reporter, true to her profession—i.e., a big pain in the ass—jogged along beside us and persisted in peppering us with relevant questions like, "Is Charabi under arrest? . . . Did you find a smoking gun? . . . Who ordered this search?"

Nobody commented. We all looked like idiots.

CHAPTER THIRTY-SEVEN

Bad news always has company.

Actually, bad thing number one, the story about how Mahmoud Charabi was suspected of exposing American secrets to the Iranians—including Jim Tirey's awkward screen debut—was not even the lead event in the news trailers.

It was almost totally eclipsed by bad thing number two: the shocking tale about the two Saudi princes who were named as financiers for al-Zarqawi, with an interesting sideline about how the Saudi government might be complicitous, and what this might mean for our already troubled relationship. Obviously there had been another leak, and I was sure people in Washington were very unhappy about that. Maybe this wasn't such a bad thing for the American public to know, but it was profoundly bad news for the two princes, and for Saudi Arabia, and for those in the American government who had colluded in the attempt to cover it up. And, too, it could be very bad for my favorite guy—me. I mean, were I the one searching for the source of these leaks, Sean Drummond would be my number one suspect.

I caught a little of this second story on one of those obnoxious cable news scream shows in my room in the Visiting Officers' Quarters. The anchor was interviewing a pissed-off, loudmouth expert on things Middle Eastern, who was haranguing some slick-looking bullshitter sent over from the Department of State to try to defuse this thing. Middle East expert was screaming, "The Saudis are *not* our friends. Never been our friends. We buy their oil, they buy our terrorists."

Anchorman says to Middle East expert, "Aren't you overstating things?"

State Department guy answers for him, suggesting, "I would say he definitely is. This is not the occasion for histrionics. Our relationship with Saudi Arabia is very complicated."

Middle East expert guy stares with disbelief into the screen. "Complicated? If you pay a whore to bite off your own . . . uh . . . your thing off . . . what's complicated about that? That's stupid!"

Pompous news anchor says, "Please . . . be careful here. Families are watching, and—"

"We are not ignoring this," State Department guy interrupts. "The Secretary is in discussions about this with the Saudi ambassador. We're requesting the immediate extradition of the two princes."

Middle East expert guy laughs and says, "Blah, blah, blah. You know what your Secretary should tell them. We changed our minds. We invaded the wrong pissant—now we're gonna turn Jidda into a big Wal-Mart."

Both guys disappear, and anchorman looks gravely into camera, goes on a bit about what a big deal this is, then closes by noting, "But the big question is . . . what effect these newest revelations will have on the President's poll ratings in this neck-and-neck race."

Which brought up bad thing three. Phyllis was gone, disappeared. She had, however, left behind a brief, perfunctory note addressed to me, that read, "*I've been called back to Washington. Close out here, then be on the most ASAP flight. Go straight to Langley, and straight to Marcus Harvey of the Office of Professional Ethics, who will brief you about your rights (nonexistent) and then usher you downstairs for your polygraph appointment. Caveat Emptor; sinners fare better than liars.*" That could be an excellent new Agency motto, I thought, and below her signature was a brief afterthought: "*PS, Truly sorry about Bian.*"

As I mentioned earlier, you have to read between the lines. Since somebody had leaked and blown the whistle on the princes, somebody needed to be screwed, and a screwee—aka, scapegoat—was needed. Since Bian was kidnapped and beyond suspicion, since neither Phyllis nor Tirey had leaked, and since the Saudis hadn't ratted themselves out, by process of elimination, that left moi. Nor did it matter if they could prove I was guilty or not—I was guilty.

If blowing your cover is the cardinal sin of this business, exposing nasty secrets to the press is the mortal sin. I had no idea how the Agency handles these things. I know the Army policy, however, and it goes like this: What you can't kill, you eat. But maybe the Agency had a different approach. Maybe it just killed you.

Bad thing number four: still no word on the fate of Bian Tran. I had struck out and was out of reasonable suspicions, sensible leads, or even idiotic guesses. It didn't matter anyway. My name was mud with Phyllis. And because of me, Jim Tirey was on a wanted poster back at Hoover City, and his tour had gone from career-enhancing to career-ending.

But since it wasn't Charabi, I was down to the usual suspects: terrorists, people who sell captives to terrorists, or garden-variety assholes who kipnap and kill at random, just for kicks. Maybe the MP sergeant was right. Maybe "CHA" referred to letters on a license plate. Or maybe Bian, out of her mind with pain and fear, had been doodling gibberish in her own blood.

I felt as bad as I had ever felt. I had missed something, a clue, a brilliant revelation, a magical key that could unlock the truth and save her life. Yet, irrational and superstitious as it sounds, a feeling, an instinct, some primitive premonition was telling me that Bian was still alive.

But if I couldn't save her, it was time for the last thing I wanted to do, and the one thing I had to do. Somebody needed to notify her loved ones, and that kind of bad news is best delivered by someone who knows and cares for her. So I walked to the office of the corps G1—the head personnel weenie—where a staff sergeant sat behind a short desk directly inside the door.

Personnel clerks have more power in a single finger than all the generals and colonels in the Army. With a single keystroke they can have your paycheck sent to Timbuktu, or *you* sent to Timbuktu, or alter the religious preference in your personnel file to Muslim, which is not the best faith to have before a promotion board these days. So I smiled courteously and said, "Good afternoon, Sergeant. Major Mark Kemble, First Armored Division. Can you please tell me how to get hold of him?"

"Professional or personal?" he asked. "Sorry. Gotta ask."

"Both. His fiancée was kidnapped."

"I'm on it, sir," he replied, and began punching buttons and at the same time eyeing his computer screen. After a few seconds, he articulated, "Kemble . . . Kimble? An 'e' or an 'i'?"

"Why do you think the Army sewed this nametag on my uniform?"

"Uh . . ."

"So I can remember how to spell it."

Old joke—bad joke—but he laughed anyway. "I'll try both," he suggested, then did a few more keyboard punches, and he asked, "The rank and unit . . . you're sure?"

"Why?"

"Well . . ." He bent forward and pressed his nose an inch from his screen, "I've got three Kembles with 'e's . . . and wow, one with an 'i' . . . you know . . . same as that guy with the missing arm in that old TV series, and . . . hey. Look at that . . ."

I leaned forward. *"What?"*

"He's a Richard also. Personal hobby . . . sorry. You know we got two William Clintons in theater? A George Bush, too. How'd you like to be that poor schlub? I'll bet he takes a world of shit, and—" He saw my face and said, "Sorry. I get carried away." He added, "Our Kembles and Kimbles are all enlisted—no Marks, no majors."

"Is your system inclusive?"

"It's connected directly to unit SIDPERS," he explained, referring to the Army's computerized personnel system, which I knew was updated daily. "But maybe your guy DEROSed," he hypothesized, meaning he rotated back to the States. "Or," he suggested, frowning, "could be he's in a classified assignment. I've run into this before. These black unit types—Delta Force, Task Force 160, various snake-eaters—they think they're too good for the theater database."

I could see that this upset his clerkish sensibilities. I said, "So those are the possibilities. What do we do?"

"What I always do." He giggled. "Kick it downhill." He picked up the phone, read off the number for his counterpart in the First Armored Division from a sheet on his desk, dialed, and then we waited. He identified himself to whoever answered, and handed me the phone. I explained to whomever I was talking to who I was looking for. After a few moments, the voice said, "There's no Mark Kemble in the division."

"This is a notification issue. Help me out here."

He said, "Let me talk to my boss. Hold on."

A new voice came on, a major named Hardy, who said, "Sir, could you tell me what this is about?"

"As I informed your sergeant, notification. Major Mark Kemble's fiancée was kidnapped in Badhdad yesterday."

There was a long pause. Mention the word "notification" and even the most bloodless military bureaucrat turns into a human being. As military people, we are all sensitive to, and sympathetic toward, the need for speedy notification, not for the soldier, who is beyond caring, but for the families left behind. The Army tends to treat living soldiers like dirt—it may screw up their pay, short them on body and vehicular armor, force them to spend their careers in places they don't want to live, working for bosses they hate, abusing their families with pay and housing that are a joke—but die, and the Army turns on a dime into the most sensitive, caring organization on earth.

I have often wondered if the Army doesn't have it backward—treat the living well and short-shrift the deceased—but honoring our dead is part of our tradition, and in an eerie way, it is a comfort for the living soldiers as well. "You know what . . ." he finally said. "You got bad info."

"Do I?"

"Yes. Mark Kemble was KIA five months ago."

"I think you're mistaken."

"I think not. We lost only two majors this year. I personally handled the corpse evacuation for both officers." He added, "Karbala. That's where Kemble bought it. Bullet through the heart."

I suppose I must've been in shock, because the next thing I knew the major was asking, "Sir . . . *sir* . . . Are you still with me?"

"Uh . . . yes. An administrative glitch, I'm sure and—" I hung up. All I could do was stare at the floor. Mark Kemble . . . dead. For the past five months . . . dead.

Bian had lied. But, *why*? Further, if her two days in Baghdad weren't spent in the loving arms of her fiancé, where had she been, and what had she been doing? The sergeant was staring at me, and I composed myself enough to ask him where the corps G2's office was located—meaning the chief intelligence officer and staff for the ground war in Iraq.

He gave me the directions, and I walked as quickly as my feet would carry me, first out of the building, and then toward the skiff he had described. It was a controlled facility with a buzzer by the door, which I pushed, and there was a camera over the entrance into which I smiled.

Somebody inside electronically unlocked the door and I entered a square building, specifically into a small anteroom that was sparsely furnished. This time, the receptionist was a female buck sergeant who was studying a men's fitness magazine with considerable intensity, for the articles, I'm sure.

I interrupted her education and told her I needed to speak with any senior officer who had been here for six months or longer, and who remembered an officer named Major Tran. She told me she would see who she could find, and left.

She returned about two minutes later, accompanied by a good-looking lieutenant colonel with the emblem of military intelligence on his collar. I introduced myself, he stuck out his hand, and we shook. He said, "Kemp Chester. How can I help you?"

"Do you have an office?"

He shook his head. "Only generals have offices. I have a carrel. That okay?"

"Not okay. Let's walk."

He gave me an odd look, but out of courtesy or curiosity he followed me, first out of the skiff, and then we began walking slowly around the Green Zone compound. There were a lot of ways to get into this, but I needed to cover my tracks, and without preamble I asked, "You knew Major Bian Tran?"

"Yeah. We worked together. She left . . . oh, two, three months back." He asked, "Why?"

"I'm part of the investigating staff for a 15-6 investigation." He understood that this was a pre-court-martial investigation, the Army equivalent of a grand jury. In response to his raised eyebrows, I assured him, "Relax. She's not the accused."

He seemed relieved to hear this and nodded.

I continued, in my most lawyerly, officious tone, "Major Tran now works in an investigatory agency in the Pentagon. She's a critical witness for what looks likely to turn into a court-martial. The questions I'll be asking are in the nature of a background check." At least this last part was true.

"I see. Well . . . would a few general observations help?"

"They would. Please proceed."

"All-round great officer. Brilliant. Competent. Honest and hard-working, and—"

"*Excuse me* . . . Kemp, I can read her efficiency ratings myself. What did you think about her personally?"

"Well . . . everybody liked her. Ask around. You won't find a soul with a bad word to say." He smiled at me. "But if you do, give me his name, so I can lump him up."

People get nervous about legal investigations, and I purposely made no response, which usually has the effect of making witnesses nervous and more talkative.

After a moment, he said, "I don't know if you've seen her. Absolute knockout. Incredible body, gorgeous face, and—" He stopped in midsentence and cleared his throat. "That sounds sexist, doesn't it? I'm just saying—"

I offered him a manly smile—"She's hot"—and we ended up manly smiling at each other. I make-believe jotted in a make-believe notebook, and intoned, "Under physical description, the colonel stated, without the slightest innuendo, that the major maintained her body and fitness at Army standards."

"Hah . . . that's a good one."

So much for guy bonding. I asked Colonel Chester, "What was Major Tran's assignment here?"

"She was assigned to a special cell. Part of G2, the theater intelligence office, but not, if you get my drift."

"Sensitive stuff?"

"Oh . . . very."

"Like what?"

By his expression, you'd think I had just told him I slept with his mother and then bragged to everybody at school about it. "That's none of your business."

"Unless I have a Top Secret clearance, which I do. And unless it's directly relevant to my investigation, which it is. Please answer my question."

LTC Chester, however, was nobody's fool, and replied, "After I see the written authorization, and after you're read on. I'm not some cherry second lieutenant, Drummond. Don't blow smoke up my butt." He asked, "What's this 15-6 about, anyway?"

"None of your business."

"Typical lawyer. All take, no give."

We did not seem to be bonding, so I took a swing in the dark that wasn't entirely from the dark. "The cell you referred to was an exploitation unit. She was on the receiving end of CIA messages that pinpointed Iranian movements and activities inside Iraq. Her job was to translate those tips into operational requirements and targets, to look for ways to exploit those insights."

He turned and stared at me a moment. He said, "Why did you ask?"

"Confirmation," I replied—and now I had confirmation. "Old trick. We often use throwaway questions to ascertain the veracity of our witness."

"How am I doing?"

"Not good, Kemp. Not good at all." I asked, "How long was she in that job?"

"Can't really say. She was already on the staff when I arrived."

Bullshit. "Colonel, I can just as easily obtain this information from her personnel file."

"Fine. Why don't you do just that?"

I ignored his suggestion and said, "Correct me if I'm wrong. She was the operations officer of an MP battalion during the invasion, then she remained in that assignment a few months after Baghdad fell, then was reassigned here, to G2."

"More like five months in her battalion. It was the G2 himself who pulled her up, if you're interested." He explained, "General Bentson heard she was fluent in Arabic, had operational experience, and she had a great rep. She cleaned up a very violent section of Baghdad at a time when the rest of city was descending into chaos. Great credentials."

"But as an MP."

"*And* she had a secondary specialty in military intelligence. Look . . . frankly—I hope this doesn't alarm you—most of us full-time MI types, we don't know squat about this place, about these people, or about this kind of war." He continued, "Myself, I'm a satellite interpretation guy and this terrestrial stuff is a whole new world." He enjoyed his own bad pun and chuckled. He then added, "My first months in country, I felt like I was just dropped into Oz—just no happy, dancing little munchkins, and in this case, the Wizard's a homicidal asshole."

This jogged something in my mind, and I asked, "So you would say the major was professionally competent?"

"I would say she was incredible . . . extraordinary . . . insert whatever superlative you like. She's a cop and she's military intelligence—she was the *perfect* combination."

"And there's no personal bias in your assessment?"

"Maybe." He thought about it a few seconds, then said, "Terrorism, if you think about it, is closer to crime than war. Typical intel officers can talk for hours about how an Iraqi division arrays itself on the battlefield, and they stare blankly if asked to explain how an insurgent cell infiltrates a city, chooses its targets, and operates." He paused then added, with clear admiration, "Bian knew this stuff. She had . . . a sense . . . an intuition for situations. A hunter's instinct, I guess you'd call it. Every morning, a long line formed in front of her carrel, guys like me, seeking advice."

"Plus, she was hot."

"Well . . . yeah . . ." He laughed. "Get at the end of that line, though, and it could be ten, eleven o'clock before you got a minute with her."

We walked in silence for a few moments among the buildings of the Green Zone. Something wasn't adding up. Well, actually a lot wasn't adding up, but what exactly? Everything Kemp Chester said had confirmed my own high estimation of Bian Tran: an impressive officer, bright, resourceful, courageous, and . . . yes, hot. But if I looked back critically over the course of the investigation Bian and I had conducted, nothing she had said, done, or ever advised had been particularly insightful, illuminating, or to borrow Kemp Chester's more elevated adjective, *intuitive*. I had ascribed this to her professional limitations as an MP officer—more overseer than sleuth. But if Kemp was right, it was time to consider another cause. Because in those rare instances where the hunter also happens to be the hunted, there's a big conflict of interest.

I recalled as well, how eager, how insistent Bian was to come here, to Iraq, in pursuit of bin Pacha and Charabi. Well, this was *her* war, I had reasoned. She was thinking with her heart instead of her head. In fact, that might still be on the mark, but I now had to consider that her motives were more complicated and darker than I had imagined. Because, not incidentally, coming here also diverted us from finding Clifford Daniels's murderer.

Nor, so far, had Kemp Chester contradicted anything Bian herself had told me. There were, however, those troubling things she hadn't said. Like having been part of the G2 exploitation cell. Possibly it was a matter of her secrecy vows. This might sound redundant, but military intelligence people and secrecy are like Donald Trump with narcissistic bullshit; you can't believe how far they take it. But no matter how much benefit of the doubt I gave her, even I had trouble with that one.

And, of course, there was Mark Kemble. Poor, dead Mark Kemble. Why had Bian lied about that? Why keep it hidden? Also, if her two days in Baghdad were not spent in Mark's company, what had she been doing? And more to the point, why lie about that?

I must've reflected too long, because Kemp Chester was engaged in his own reflections and asked, "Hey, what the hell does this have to do with a 15-6? Isn't this supposed to be about an officer's credibility and judgment? What's going on here?"

I took a moment and sized him up, as I would any witness on the stand. A good guy, levelheaded, articulate, smart. But clearly he felt a strong affection for Bian, which I understood, because, like nearly any man who met her, I was at least half in love with her. He was trying to be protective, which raises the ever-provocative question of why he felt Bian *needed* protection. As they say, where there's smoke, there's fire. Not always, but when smoke's being blown up your butt, you'd better be sure.

On one hand, I admired and appreciated his loyalty to Bian, and I liked him for it. The occasion, however, called for the other hand, and I gave him a hard stare and asked, "Have I told you how to do your job?"

"No, but—"

"Because I would really fucking appreciate it if you reciprocated that professional courtesy." I allowed him a moment to contemplate the shift in the tenor of our conversation. I said, "Maybe I've made this too friendly, too informal. Maybe we should reconvene to an interrogation cell at the MP station."

"Okay, okay. Relax . . ."

I now knew what was really bothering me, and asked, "When Bian was reassigned from her battalion to the corps staff, it was supposed to be for a full year—right?"

"I have no idea."

"You're really starting to piss me off."

"Uh . . . okay, a full year. Her fiancé had just begun his one-year tour in Iraq. Bian wanted to stay for the duration of his tour."

"But she rotated stateside after what . . . six, seven, eight months?"

"Yeah . . . maybe."

I offered him another cold stare and he quickly amended his statement. "About seven and a half months . . . She got an early drop. Why is this important?"

"Why was it curtailed?"

Kemp now looked restive and a little unhappy. He said, "Why don't you ask her former boss? Bian and I were friends, and . . . Look, you're making me very uncomfortable."

"And you well know that the personal comfort or discomfort of a professional officer is irrelevant. I asked you a question. Answer it."

"Because . . . well, because it was . . . a hardship transfer. Because her fiancé, he died . . . here in Iraq. His death was very rough on her." He added after a moment, "The general was sympathetic. He personally intervened to arrange a transfer stateside."

I gave it a moment, then said, "Kemp, because this is the Army, I don't have to swear you in or read you your rights, or any of that nonsense. I'm an officer of the court pursuing an official investigation. Lying, quibbling, or misleading statements can and will result in charges. Don't make things any worse for yourself."

Kemp started to say something, and I cut him off. "We're now on the record. Are we clear?"

He stared at me a long time.

I said, "According to the manual, Army criteria for hardship transfers and discharges pertain only to deaths in the *immediate* family. Reconsider your reply."

It looked like he was giving himself a root canal, but he said, "It was . . . just a situational transfer. After her fiancé's death . . . she . . . she went to pieces. She took it very, very hard."

This still didn't sound like the Army I know and love. Unhappy or mentally depressed soldiers, ordinarily, are sent to the unit chaplain, or in these more Zen-like times, to a unit counselor, they get their "give-a-shit" ticket punched, and are returned to duty. In extreme cases, the soldier can be awarded a thirty-day leave for mental convalescence—i.e., a month to drink and screw him/herself silly—which typically fixes the mood rings of most soldiers. If neither of these tried-and-true methods fails to produce a mentally stable soldier who is willing and able to kill at the drop of a hat, next step is a discharge—not a transfer—and their issues become the problems of the VA—the Veterans Administration.

Clearly, my threats and cajolements weren't doing the trick. As somebody knowing once said, stupidity is trying the same thing over and over and watching it not work. What I needed was a new approach, i.e., a bigger lie. I informed him, "I don't understand why you're being antagonistic. Bian Tran is a witness *for* the Army. I am not her enemy."

He seemed to weigh this.

I informed him, "On the stand, where she'll likely end up, she will be cross-examined by a vicious, mean-spirited defense attorney. The defense will of course access her personnel and medical records and, naturally, her mental stability will be at issue. Always is. And if, as you've led me to suspect, there is some damaging revelation, the defense attorney will exploit it to humiliate her in a courtroom before her fellow officers. You can't protect her, Kemp." I took his arm and warned, "Don't try."

He mulled this over. "All right."

"All right, I'll answer truthfully? Or all right, fuck you?"

"Both."

Now we were getting somewhere. I gave him a moment to settle his nerves before I asked, "What happened to Bian Tran? I'm guessing something traumatic."

"Yes, it was . . . very traumatic. Her transfer was psychiatric. Bian felt responsible. She was crushed. She couldn't stop crying. And she couldn't function, professionally or personally. A complete mental breakdown."

It still wasn't adding up. I said, "She lost a loved one. Sad, but this is war, and as a professional soldier, she surely was mentally prepared for this eventuality. A West Pointer, a battle-tested officer who led troops into combat and who suffered the loss of soldiers. Others have described her as tough, resilient, a cool customer. Why did she take it so hard, Kemp?"

"Guilt, Drummond. Plain guilt. So heavy, so overbearing, so painful, it simply shattered her into pieces." He looked away for a moment and said, "Imagine, if you will, how it must feel to be responsible for the death of the person you loved. What this would do to your insides?"

"Why did she feel responsible?"

"I didn't say she *felt* responsible. She *was* responsible."

"How? Why?"

"The CIA courier brought us a message that tipped us off to a large load of weapons and trainers coming from Iran into Karbala. This was during the midst of the Shiite uprising . . . you might remember . . . Sadr's Shiite militia had taken over the city, his people were killing our soldiers, and we all knew a major operation would have to be mounted to restore control. So preventing those weapons and trainers from linking up with Sadr's people . . . well, that would be a real coup. Less guns, less bombs, less American deaths."

"And Bian was in charge of this operation?"

"That's not how it worked."

"Okay. How did it work?"

"Bian was the analyst assigned to shape a response. As I said, the CIA never told us how they knew, or about their sources, but they informed us that the Iranian shipment and trainers were going into the city of Karbala, in a sector assigned to the First Armored Division. Bian provided the division operations shop with an order. A description of what was coming, when, and where to intercept it."

The lights were now coming on. I said, "And the division assigned this mission to her fiancé's . . . to Mark Kemble's battalion."

He stared at the ground a moment, and the man was clearly in pain. Finally, he mumbled, "It was the worst coincidence I've ever seen or heard."

"Because Mark Kemble, being the battalion operations officer, decided he would personally oversee this high-value operation."

He nodded. "Great officer, I was told. Real hoo-ah, lead-from-the-front type. Highly decorated, loved by his men . . . all-around great guy. But something went wrong, tragically wrong—the shit hit the fan, three soldiers were killed, and obviously, Mark was one."

"What went wrong?"

"If you ever learn that, be sure to let me know. Understand that the CIA, they kept our entire exploitation unit completely in the dark about the source of these intelligence insights. Every week or two, some lady courier flew over from D.C., she'd drop off some cryptic crap, she'd leave, and we had to run with it." He added, "I have no idea."

I thought about this. It did not compute. After all, these were military intelligence people, and I said, "But you had suspicions, right?"

After a brief silence, he said, "Of course we had suspicions. Pretty obvious what the Agency had, right? A mole in Iranian intelligence or inside Sadr's movement. Somebody very high up."

Close, Kemp. But not close enough. I asked, "Is that what you thought? What Bian thought?"

"We all thought that. This stuff we were getting was dead-on. Priceless."

"Except this time."

"Yeah. There was no weapons shipment. No Iranian trainers either."

I paused to consider my next question, which was a big mistake. Because, suddenly, it all came together—Bian had literally been turned into the instrument for her lover's death. Kemp did not have the details just right, but he was close enough. Daniels had informed his pal Charabi about the compromised code, Charabi passed it to his friends in Tehran, and they, in turn, decided to be vindictive, sending disinformation they knew was being intercepted, decoded, and read, offering the Americans a target that was too tempting to pass up; in effect, luring an American unit into a trap. Bian ended up near the end of that long chain, and her fiancé ended up in a coffin.

War is filled with ugly twists and bitter ironies, but this cruelty was almost incomprehensible. And before I knew it, something heavy was stuck in the back of my throat. Poor Mark. Poor Bian. I swallowed a few times and tried to dislodge the lump, but it only moved higher until it lodged behind my eyes. Chester was looking at me strangely. "Hey . . . you okay?"

"I'm . . . uh . . . getting over a cold." I coughed a few times and, after a moment, said, "Last question. What do *you* think went wrong?"

"You know what? I've thought about that a lot. We all did. Mark's unit, what they ran into, that was a prepared kill zone, an ambush. I don't know, maybe the CIA's source was a double agent. Or maybe the Iranians caught on to him and used him to plant false information. Whichever . . . Sadr and the Iranians knew we were coming, and they decided to make us pay."

A knot of staff officers carrying briefing folders crossed paths with us and we both fell silent. After they were out of earshot Chester said to me, "There was an investigation. Afterward. But by the CIA, not us. We were even forced to take polygraph tests. But you know what? If there was a compromise, those bastards never shared anything." He paused and then said, very unhappily, "A month after Bian left, the whole exploitation cell was disbanded."

"You're a smart guy, Kemp. What's your best guess?"

"My best guess?"—he stopped walking—"All right, sure." He turned and faced me. "You're not here about any damned 15-6 investigation."

I started to deny this, then thought better of it.

He said, "I have no idea why you're lying to me, Drummond, or what trouble Bian is in. But I promise you"—he looked me in the eye—"if you hurt her, I'll find you, and I'll hurt you."

We stared at each other a long moment. I put out my hand and said, "It's not my intention to harm her, Kemp. That's a promise."

He stared at my hand, but never shook it. "Leave her alone. She's been through enough."

I did not say, "More than you'll ever know," though, in truth, I now knew more about Bian's problems than I wanted to. I felt a deep, deep sadness for her. At the same time, an alarm bell was making loud dings in the back of my head.

I left Kemp Chester standing in a courtyard, fuming. I walked back to the office of the G1, where I ordered the same clerk to find me a private office with a phone, which he did.

I called Phyllis's cell phone and didn't get an answer, so I chose the message option.

I left a brief and unexplained message to immediately place bodyguards around Hirschfield and Tigerman, or better yet, get them both out of town, or barring that, make arrangements for two funerals. I hung up and thought about my next move.

It was time to go home.

CHAPTER THIRTY-EIGHT

Jim Tirey kindly gave me a lift to the airport.

As I mentioned earlier, the route from the Green Zone to the airport includes Iraq's deadliest roadway—known with grim unaffection as Suicide Alley—so Jim's favor wasn't in the true spirit of generosity. He wanted to see me climb on the plane, and be 100 percent sure I ended up seven thousand miles out of his hair. Really, who could blame him?

We pulled up before the terminal, and Jim pulled up to the curb and slammed the SUV into park. I went around to the rear, withdrew my duffel, and looked around for a moment. The hour was late, yet the terminal was crowded and bustling with soldiers; from their gleeful expressions, they all were outgoing, not incoming. This was the first place I'd been inside this troubled land where people looked happy, and maybe the only place where they were sure tomorrow would be a rosier day. Tirey came around and we ended up, face-to-face, on the road.

He said, "Enjoy the flight."

I said, "Enjoy Iraq."

"Hey, my bags are already packed. Any day now, the long arm of OPR—that's the Office of Professional Responsibility, our Gestapo—will have me on a plane back to D.C. for a long discussion about how this shit went down."

"D.C. is filled with idiots," I told him. He gave me a blank stare and I explained, "They think it's a punishment to boot you out of here."

He laughed.

During the drive, we had stuck to the kind of aimless chatter that did not distract us from identifying vehicular bombers who wanted to send us home in a box. There are no leisurely drives in Iraq, incidentally. If I haven't mentioned it, the place sucks. But we both knew there was a big piece of unfinished business, and I asked, "What have you heard from the Bureau?"

"Not a word . . . officially. I've got a pal in the Director's office, though."

"And?"

"He says I'll love Omaha, and Omaha will love me. Lots of free time, very quiet, very law-abiding citizens. It's impossible to screw up there."

"Hey, maybe there's a CIA station in Omaha. We'll get together. You know, prove them wrong." This prospect for some reason did not seem to excite him, so I offered him a synopsis of Drummond's Law. "Somebody else will screw up soon, and you'll be forgotten."

"Hey, I'm a big boy. I don't need—"

"Seriously. They'll send you someplace else that really sucks before you know it."

"I don't think so." He added, miserably, "That video of me with the reporter . . . they've sent it to the FBI Academy as a training aid for new agents. I'm famous."

I smiled at him, and he smiled back. A few seconds late.

Then came an awkward moment, and we stared into each other's eyes. He finally asked, "Did you do it?"

"Did you?"

He stared at me. "I saw that look the reporter gave you. I told Phyllis about it, too."

"No, I did not leak," I told him. He looked skeptical, however, and I told him, "I have an appointment with the inquisitor the moment I land—thumbscrews, rack, lie detector, the works. I'll be sure they send you the results."

"Do that." He smiled and said, "Tell them to ask what you really think of me."

"You . . . you don't really want them to ask that."

"Right . . . well . . ." He stuck out his hand and we shook.

I told him, "Keep looking for Tran."

"I'll do better than that. I'll even leave a memo for my replacement."

"Look me up when you get to town."

He laughed. "You know what, Drummond? I like you. I don't know why, but I really do. And if I ever see you again, I'll shoot you."

Leaving him at the curb, I carried my duffel inside and went straight to the Military Air Transport counter, where a young Air Force enlisted person, cute and perky, stood buffing her nails. I said, "Good evening, Airman Johnson. I need a small favor."

Air Force people are actually misplaced civilians, loose, jocular, with manners more befitting a college fraternity than an armed service. Army people, on the other hand, tend to exemplify the military mind-set, totally tightassed about trivial minutiae, and really into the yes sir/no sir funny business. So, as much as Air Force types grate on Army people, I can only imagine how they view us. Anyway, the young lady in question stopped swiping her nails for a moment and offered me one of those synthetic airline smiles. "Sure."

"I'm supposed to meet a friend here. We seem to have misplaced each other."

"Well . . . that can happen."

"Her name's Bian Tran . . . T-R-A-N. I was wondering if she caught an earlier flight."

"Hold on." She shifted her attention back to the computer, and I held my breath as she punched in Bian's name, and then said, "Wow . . . did you two get your signals crossed."

If only she knew.

"She flew out at eleven this morning," she continued. "She's long gone."

Gone, perhaps. But not abducted. Not dead. And not forgotten—at least not by me. What had been a suspicion, an ugly theory, now was a confirmed fact. Not a surprise, though.

The right and proper thing to do was immediately notify Phyllis about my suspicions and seek her instructions. But Sean Drummond wasn't in the mood to do that. Phyllis was playing her own game, and I still wasn't sure what that game was called. No, I did not trust her, and I definitely did not want to appoint her judge and jury. Besides, what could she, or what could the Agency do that Sean Drummond could not do?

Well, an all-out manhunt was one possibility. Except the law enforcement community would never move on that without first demanding a valid legal justification from the Agency. And Phyllis would never do that, because exposing what Bian had been doing would also expose what the Agency had been doing, which would be like grabbing a shark's fin to save yourself from drowning—only the shark goes home happy.

Which left option two, termination, which with these people means losing a little more than just your job. Certainly, the stakes were high enough. Plus, Bian already was listed on Army rolls as missing in action and presumed to be in the hands of murderous terrorists, so it was really convenient for everybody. But would Phyllis do that? Phrased differently, why wouldn't Phyllis do that? Could I live with myself if I gambled no and yes happened?

Besides, for me this had become personal. I still had no idea what was really going on, but I knew this: Phyllis and Bian had both used me as a pawn for their own ends. Right now they both thought I was still Stupid Sean, totally clueless and in the dark. Wrong. I was now Totally Pissed-Off Sean. I was going to get to the bottom of this if it killed me—which it might.

So I thought back to what the young airman had just told me. Bian had caught an eleven o'clock flight. Tirey, his handpicked crew, and I had entered Charabi's Green Zone office at nine, and we exited with our tails between our legs some thirty minutes later. An hour and a half after that, Bian climbed on an airplane and blew town. Was there a coincidence? Or if I asked the same question differently, was there a connection between our raid on Charabi's office and Bian's decision to fly the coop? I don't particularly believe in coincidences, incidentally.

What I needed to do now was to reconstruct her actions, to work backward and consider what had occurred, to start at Z and find my way back to A. Because my only hope of finding Bian, and of stopping her, was by understanding what she had done. And from there, with a fertile imagination and a little mental elbow grease, how and why.

So, what was Z? Well, that would be the odd look the blonde female reporter gave me as we exited Charabi's office. I had never seen her before—I was sure of it—so it wasn't that she recognized my face, per se; it was the Drummond on my nametag that was familiar to her, because whoever had tipped her off about our raid on Mahmoud Charabi's office had also informed her that I would be there.

And I would bet that if I could go back and have a word with that reporter—if I could make her breach her journalistic *omertà* code—she would confirm that her source was Bian Tran.

And if I stepped back from that moment a few hours more in time, to earlier that morning, I would bet as well that Bian was that mysterious voice who, speaking Arabic, had called and anonymously alerted the MP Operations Center to the location of an abandoned and bloodstained Toyota SUV.

And earlier, there was that moment in the dining facility when Bian had insisted on driving alone to Baghdad, and then, despite orders, chose to depart without me.

Right. She had to be alone to stage her own ambush and kidnapping, and then to disappear into the streets she knew so well. She was a military cop, and she knew how abandoned U.S. military vehicles are processed and handled. So she deliberately planted the necessary documents to lead the MPs to Camp Alpha, as well as a bloody clue on the dashboard that would lead Sean Drummond straight to Mahmoud Charabi.

I wondered if she had found a concealed spot to observe us as we entered Charabi's office. Probably she did. I would.

But everything—her plan and her escape—depended on first creating, then sustaining and shielding the misbelief that she had been kidnapped. Which explained, I thought, what she *had* been doing during the days she supposedly was trysting with Mark in Baghdad—locating an AK-47 automatic rifle to shoot holes in her SUV, filling a medic's bag with her own blood, which she could splatter around the cab of the SUV, and scoping out where she would leave the ambushed SUV—arranging both the pantomime of her disappearance and the logistics for her escape.

"*Excuse me* . . ." the airman said, "I asked, is there something else?"

"Uh . . . where will she land?"

"Went to—" she again examined the screen, "—Dover Air Force Base."

"Thanks." I picked up my bag and shoved off to Gate 6 for my flight.

Not only had Bian taken a military flight, she had even used her own name on the manifest. This was so in-your-face, I should've been amazed. I wasn't, though—that's why I had asked. She was confident that she had fooled us all, and she knew that nobody was going to cross-check the flight manifest for a soldier who only that morning was listed on Army rolls as MIA. But this suggested more than confidence, this suggested a lady in a hurry.

As the MP at the terminal gate checked my orders I checked my watch. My partner had a ten-hour head start on me. But she would land at Dover Air Force Base in Delaware, from where it would require two or, with luck and/or typical Washington traffic, possibly three more hours to drive to D.C. My flight would land at Andrews Air Force Base in Maryland, only thirty minutes from D.C.

I would cut her lead by at least two hours. No longer would I mischaracterize Bian Tran, nor would I underestimate her. Still, I had only a dim idea what was going on here, and I wasn't sure what she had planned next, or even if she had more plans.

I knew where to look, though.

CHAPTER THIRTY-NINE

We arrived at Andrews Air Force Base without my plane experiencing a mysterious and unfortunate midair mishap. Nor did I see a CIA welcoming committee to help me find my way to Langley. Phyllis was slipping.

Getting a taxi, even with two hundred unruly and ambitious soldiers in competition, was faster than you can say abuse of rank.

The instant the first cab pulled up to the guest terminal, I stepped forward and bullied a poor private out of the back, leaving two hundred mutinous soldiers in my wake.

A helpful steward on the plane had kindly recharged my cell phone, and I made two quick calls, first to a person who confirmed what I had already guessed, and second to a person who answered a few simple questions regarding my hypothesis. Then I told the driver where to take me.

As soon as we were outside the air base gate, I rolled the windows all the way down on both my left and right sides and relaxed back into my seat. The wind and air were freezing and, dressed as I was in thin desert battle dress uniform, I might as well have been naked. The pleasure, though, was indescribable—to breathe fresh air, American air, air that didn't smell like human dung, to be freezing rather than sweating, to drive without worrying about snipers or bombs. Have I mentioned yet that Iraq sucks?

The cabbie caught my eye in the rearview mirror. He mentioned, "Back from Iraq, huh?"

"What gave me away?"

"A lot of them do that," he replied, referring, I guess, to my silliness with the windows.

I could observe only the rear of his head: an older gentleman, pockmarked neck, gray hair, my father's age or thereabouts. "You fooled me . . . at first," he continued. "Most guys head for the nearest bar."

"Well, I'm stuck with pleasure before business."

"How about a woman?" he charitably suggested. "Hey, I know a place, in Bethesda. Real patriotic ladies. They got welcome-home specials for vets that'll turn your pecker red, white, and blue. Yeah?"

"No. Thank you."

"Suit yourself."

"I was there only a few days," I informed him.

"That right?"

"I almost lost the war," I explained, truthfully. "They sent me home."

"Good for you. You still don't look tan enough."

"Office job. Lucky me."

"No kidding?" he asked, sounding slightly disappointed.

"It wasn't all milk and cookies. I picked up some nasty paper cuts and fell off my chair a few times. Want to see my scars?"

This got a chuckle out of him. He said, "Y'know, we really believe in what you boys are doing over there."

"That's why we do it."

"Yeah, horseshit. Saw some action myself. 'Nam, '68 through '69."

"Bad war."

"Name a good war."

"The one you make it home from."

"Hey, that's a good one." He started a long riff about *his* war, which I didn't really want to talk about. I interrupted and asked, "Which idiot are you voting for?"

"Neither guy. I'm a Nothingican. Like I said, I went to 'Nam. Politicians suck. All of 'em." He laughed.

He went on a bit, while I tried my best not to hold up my end of the discussion. Unfortunately, he was a conversation in search of a passenger and he wouldn't shut up. He eventually said, "Unbelievable about them Saudi princes. Know what I'm saying?"

"Sure do," I replied absently. If I had a gun, I would've shot him, or myself.

"We should form our own charities and send terrorists to kill Saudis. What's good for the goose, make it suck for the gander." He added, "Lord Limbaugh said that. Good one, ain't it?"

"Good one," I said agreeably. I had an important call to make and it really was time to pull the plug on this guy. I said, "Excuse me, but—"

He cut me off. "I mean . . . do those Saudi assholes really expect us to believe that coincidence crap?"

"Coincidence?"

"Yeah . . . them *supposed* accidents."

"Accidents?"

"You didn't hear? That first guy, Prince Faud, having a car wreck. And that other guy—Ali? . . . Abdul? . . . whoever—the same day skiing off a cliff in Switzerland. My ass. That jerkoff got an involuntary flying lesson."

Goodness. I leaned back in the seat. "Where did you hear this?"

"Radio. The Saudi day-night massacre—that's what the shock jocks are calling it." He asked, "Hey, you don't think our government finally got some balls and whacked them two?"

"Balls? Our government?"

"Yeah . . . what was I thinking?" He laughed.

"Both dead?" I asked.

"Well, when a sixteen wheeler head-ons your ass, or you forget to pack a parachute for your skiing lesson, dead is the usual result. Haha. Those lousy Saudis, though . . . claiming it was just a coincidence. Bullshit. That's what it is—bullshit."

I needed to mull this over, so I sat back, flipped open my cell phone, and pretended to speak into it.

The first thing that struck me was how far behind the power curve I still was. I had spent a lot of time on the plane trying to piece together what Bian had done, and why, and I should've seen this coming. Obviously, I hadn't.

Said otherwise, I was closing in on Bian geographically, and yet mentally we weren't even on the same planet.

Because, second, I now understood who had given the exposé to the press about these two rotten princes, but, more important, now I understood why. As a matter of fact, the Saudis would never turn this pair of princes over to the United States. But neither did they want or need the diplomatic heat or image problem from harboring members of the ruling family known to be funding the deaths of American soldiers and Iraqi civilians. In effect, for the princes, public exposure was tantamount to an execution order.

It occurred to me, too, that Bian's fingerprints were all over another leak. I recalled the moment on the plane in Baghdad, back when Phyllis, Waterbury, and the sheik had first shown up, and Bian and I were informed that somebody had tipped off the Saudis about our impending capture of Ali bin Pacha.

It was interesting that everybody, including Sean Drummond, assumed that that disclosure was the handiwork of some anonymous person back in D.C. And why wouldn't we? That *is* where the disclosures and intelligence compromises usually occur. Bian's camouflage, in other words, was our own cynical preconception regarding Washington and its appalling laxity with secrets, about which nobody was more brutally conscious than she. A sweet irony, if you think about it. I'm sure she did think about it.

But was this Saudi angle part of her plan from the beginning, from point A? No, I thought not. I was sure that Bian was genuinely surprised, as were we all, to learn what Charabi and his Iranian pals had offered Cliff Daniels in exchange for his betrayal: Ali bin Pacha. But, experienced as she was in the shadowy politics of Arab terrorism, Bian was very quick to understand the opportunities bin Pacha posed, for us and for her.

Ultimately, Daniels and Charabi were her real targets, but chance had thrown this promising new opportunity into her lap and she went with it. So while we all sat in Phyllis's office trying to unravel and understand Daniels's betrayal, Bian's mind was on other matters, spontaneously devising a plan to exploit our own worst impulses. And the plan she devised was both brilliant and corrupting, because what she set in motion rested on two possibilities of dishonorable conduct.

One, she strongly suspected that Saudi intelligence was well aware that Ali bin Pacha, himself a Saudi national—and thereby his boss, al-Zarqawi—were getting contributions and assistance from important Saudi citizens, and was desperately trying to keep it hidden. She was a veteran intelligence officer with regional experience, after all. Wherever there's naughtiness in the world of Islam, Saudi money usually is involved. Usually, it's the motor.

Also, I recalled the private conversation Bian and I shared on the plane after Phyllis and Waterbury had delivered the new directive from Washington; to wit, the Saudis were getting bin Pacha and we weren't getting within a thousand yards of Charabi. I was hot as a pistol, and ready to rumble. Bian's mood had been one of casual acceptance, a pessimistic surrender, and that had surprised me. I had expected anger and disillusionment from her, not resignation.

With the view of hindsight, I now understood, because Bian's moment of disillusionment, her journey from idealism to cynicism, had happened long before, in a back alley in Sadr City.

For this play, however, there was no script. All the actors had a free choice because Bian designed it that way—do the right and honorable thing, pursue truth and justice. It was interesting that nobody did.

So even before she flew to Baghdad, she had thrown the dice and notified the Saudis about our impending capture of bin Pacha. Maybe her time in Iraq left her with some low-level contacts in the Saudi intelligence service, or maybe she just placed a direct call to the Saudi embassy in D.C. How she sent up the red flag to the Saudis about bin Pacha didn't matter then, and it didn't really matter now—it was merely the bait that lured the actors onto the stage.

Which led to assumption two: She was betting that Washington would succumb to Saudi pressure and join into what my Italian lawyer friends call *insabbiatura*—burying an inconvenient case in the sand. It was Bian who had suggested the joint interrogation of Ali bin Pacha, a solution that seemed to assuage everybody's concerns.

But I did not believe she understood or even guessed that the Saudis would ultimately murder Ali bin Pacha. How could she? I don't believe she minded, though.

And by eliminating Ali bin Pacha, the sheik and his royal masters thought they had taken care of the problem . . . except for one nasty detail—that hidden recording. This was big trouble for the Saudis, because it was incontrovertible physical evidence of murder and conspiracy. Phyllis saw it as troublesome as well, but she also saw it as an opportunity, a device to squeeze a few new terrorist names from our Saudi friends.

So Sheik Turki al-Fayef made his deal with Phyllis and walked smugly out of that conference room, pleased that he had purchased silence for his country, and pleased for himself, because the ruling family owed him a big favor for saving two royal asses.

And then there was Bian's impassioned tantrum afterward—her display of anger, frustration, and disillusionment that in retrospect was as effective as it was affected. And I understood why. She was offering Phyllis one last chance, the chance to choose principle over practicality—the chance to do the right thing.

And Sean Drummond, too, had been offered that choice.

In fact, Bian was a brilliant seductress who preyed upon everybody's worst instincts and impulses—the Saudi predilection for buying or burying their way out of trouble, and America's susceptibility to make stupid deals in the name of diplomacy, oil, and political expediency. I have no idea how she kept a smile off her face. I could not have pulled it off. Nobody had the slightest clue what fools we were making of ourselves.

Then, later, probably with the same tip Bian had given her blonde reporter friend about Charabi, for good measure she threw in the tale about the two rotten princes. This time, Washington no longer had a choice; as it eventually did, it was forced to publicly request their extradition.

The Saudis had a choice, but they had already tried option A—buying off the problem—so they defaulted to option B—burying it.

For Mahmoud Charabi, public exposure of his lies and his treachery meant embarrassment, and big complications for his future ambitions; for the two princes, it meant death.

So I had worked my way from Z back to M. I knew enough now to speculate about Bian's motive, MO, and intent. Yet, a key piece—maybe *the* key piece—was still missing. So I punched a number into my cell phone, and Barry Enders answered. After I identified myself, he replied sarcastically, "Drummond? . . . Drummond? Sorry . . . can't seem to place you."

"I was busy, Barry. Somebody had to win the war."

"Oh . . . we won?" He laughed, not nicely. "Where are you?"

"Back. Any breakthroughs?"

"A few, yeah." He said, "Hold on. I need to relocate." A few seconds later, he said, "Where was I?" After a pause, he said, "Oh, yeah—Daniels's phone records. Sprint handled his home service, so I got the numbers and names of his recent girlfriends and paid them a visit."

"And . . . ?"

"Let me say first, two of those ladies won't have sex lives without him. Know what I'm saying?"

"He was generous with his attentions."

"Don't you have a way with the words?" He said, "The third lady's named Joan Carruthers. Said she suspected him of cheating on her. Said she was thinking of breaking it off."

"Jealousy. Possible motive, right?"

"Well . . . here's another thing. There was no cell phone in Daniels's apartment. Right? And neither was there a cell phone account at his home carrier, Sprint, so we never considered he had one. You following this?"

"Okay."

"I got to thinking, though—a guy who works in an important Pentagon office . . . this day and age, and no cell phone?" He said, "So I checked around, and turns out he used a different service. Cingular."

"And what did that reveal?"

"More calls to the same three ladies, but, well . . . there were calls to and from another lady."

I knew where this was going, and to save him the trouble said, "Bian Tran." And I knew, further, why the cell phone was missing from his apartment. Here again, the name was Bian Tran. Aware that she had made calls to that phone, probably minutes after Daniels died she had lifted it to throw us off an easy lead. Very slick.

He asked, "What's going on here, Drummond?"

What was going on was that I neither needed nor wanted Barry and the police to pursue this investigation any further. For one thing, as I said, this had become personal, and I wanted to take care of it myself. But also, if everything I now suspected panned out, a thousand tons of shit was going to land on anybody involved with this. Though I knew he wouldn't see it this way, I decided to do Barry a big favor.

"What's going on is not what you think," I lied. "Daniels was suspected of espionage—I told you that. And Bian was a lead investigator. So, yes, they were acquainted before his death. And yes, they spoke over the phone."

"About something as sensitive as espionage? Over an insecure airwave? Do I look that stupid to you?"

Actually, Barry Enders was the farthest thing from stupid. Of all the people I had met in this case, he was the smartest, and he had come closest to uncovering the truth.

Well, on second thought, that made him the second smartest. Bian was the smartest. And Sean Drummond, who had looked over her shoulder every step of the way, was the biggest halfwit.

Because, here again, Bian had cynically gambled on the government's worst instincts—the institutional infatuation with covering up failures and embarrassments. And, here again, the government came through with flying colors; the Feds were dispatched to quash Enders's investigation and Bian got more of the one thing she desperately needed—time. Time to pursue more leads, time to get to Iraq, time to place the noose around the necks of her targets.

"Are you out of answers, Drummond?"

Not yet. I explained, "Bian's assignment was to establish a social connection, to create trust, and see what she could learn about his activities." I added, "They not only spoke over open airwaves, they even met in public places a few times."

"She never mentioned that she even *knew* Daniels."

To me either, Barry. "What can I say? It was a highly classified government investigation."

"Yeah?" There was a long, dubious pause. Reaffirming my high estimation of him, he said, "I also accessed *her* phone records and *her* charge card."

"So what?"

"Well . . . they went on two dates. September 20, a nice dinner at Morton's steakhouse, she had lobster, he had steak, and somebody slurped five scotches and two very expensive bottles of red wine. That came to three hundred big ones. October 15, they attended a ballet at the Kennedy Center—tickets at two hundred a pop." He added, "You know what's really interesting? She booked the reservations on her phone, and *she* paid both bills. And with cash, not charge."

"Tell me something I don't know. It's in her expense reports."

"As a taxpayer, I'm incensed. I saw Daniels's other lady friends. She didn't have to spend a nickel to get this guy."

"Welcome to our new, kinder, gentler federal policy. We try to send them upriver with a nice memory." I said, "Barry, she's not a suspect."

He said, with real steel in his voice, "I'm the cop. I say who's a suspect, and I say *she's* a suspect."

"Forget about her."

"Where is she?"

"Someplace you can't touch her. She's—"

"The hell I can't. Watch me."

" . . . in Iraq and—"

"A subpoena will fix that. Have her ass on the next—"

"Shut up . . . just listen, Barry." He quieted down. "Bian was shot and kidnapped by terrorists two days ago."

He went quiet.

I reminded him, "They don't respond to subpoenas."

He stayed quiet.

"We all feel bad, Barry. She's a fallen hero. You'll look like an unpatriotic shit if you push this."

This, obviously, was not what he expected to hear, and for a moment there was a stunned silence. Eventually, he said, "Well, I'm . . ." Whatever it was he was going to say, he changed his mind and told me, "You know what? If I had a buck for every time you've lied to me, *I'd* be eating at Morton's."

"Call the public affairs office in the Pentagon. They'll confirm that she's listed as MIA."

He promised or, considering the circumstances, threatened to do just that. On that distrustful note we both punched off.

There was one more loose end, and Phyllis was dangling at the end of it. So I dialed her next and, when she answered on the second ring, I said, "Drummond here."

She replied, with a note of impatience, "Where's here?"

"Back." I told her very nicely, "And by the way, thank you for not blowing up my plane. It meant a lot to me. Seriously." I asked, "Did you get my message about Hirschfield and Tigerman?"

She did not respond to my paranoia, yet could not resist reproaching me about procedural minutiae. She said, "You know better than to leave an electronic message. What if I misplaced the phone, or if I hadn't checked my messages?"

"They'd be dead. So what? I never liked them anyway. Neither do you."

"You wouldn't be so cavalier if they *were* dead."

"Wouldn't I? There are more where they came from. Arrogant eggheads are a dime a dozen."

"I don't think I like your attitude." That was the whole point. Phyllis had decided there were things she didn't want me to know that turned out to be things I needed to know. As a lawyer, I expect clients to mislead me and withhold important information, because they are guilty and they want to hide it. So now it was time to learn the source of Phyllis's guilt. She said, "Tell me what that message was about. What exactly is the threat to Tigerman and Hirschfield?"

"I'm not in the mood." I changed subjects and asked, "Hey, how about those two dead princes? Did your sheik friend freak out or what?"

"It's very . . . unfortunate. Turki won't even take my calls. In our business, these deals are supposedly sacred." She added in a tone suggesting I should be very concerned, "The White House is ordering a full investigation."

"So now we're investigating our investigations. Do you realize how stupid that sounds?" I added after a moment, "You should remind them that investigations don't always turn up results they like. Consider this one."

She now sensed that Sean Drummond was a problem employee whom she was mishandling. She said in a far friendlier tone, "Sean, come straight to Langley. We're all waiting for you."

"I don't think so. I'm now the spy out in the cold. Isn't that how you people phrase it?" I added, "I told you to get rid of me. You should've listened."

"Don't be foolish."

"I know about it, Phyllis. About the leak, about the soldiers who were killed, and about the Agency's effort to keep a lid on it. I'm not sure it need ever have been hidden. But it shouldn't *stay* hidden."

For a moment she said nothing. I had just moved the conversation from the abstract to the specific, and she needed a moment to think about this. She took that moment.

She asked, "What do you want?"

Smart lady. "A name. The courier for your exploitation cell."

"I don't know what you're talking about."

I remained silent.

She asked, "How do you know it was a *she*?"

"You're wasting time with stupid questions. I'm three minutes from the *Washington Post* building—that's two minutes longer than you have to answer. Are we on the same wavelength yet?"

Long pause again. "Diane Andrews."

"What happened to Diane Andrews?"

"Why did anything have to happen to her?"

"Who's your favorite *Post* reporter?"

"Sean, please, let's—"

"Personally, I'm torn over where the Pulitzer should land—Mideast desk or national desk? Hey, what do you think?"

"She's dead."

"Dead how? Heart attack? Another fake suicide? Another skiing accident? What made her heart stop ticking, Phyllis?"

"No . . . it was murder. Open and shut."

"Tell me about the murder."

"About seven weeks ago, jogging in a park, at night, not far from here, somebody drove a hatchet through her forehead. No fingerprints, and no forensic evidence. Even the footprints were swept clean with a broom. There were some bruises on her arms, suggestive of a slight struggle, and her killer was right-handed."

"And obviously her killer wasn't caught. Who are the suspects?"

"There are no suspects. Just theories."

No suspects? I thought about this. "But you knew it was premeditated and planned, and the killer understood enough about police procedure to clean up the trace evidence. You knew she wasn't an arbitrary victim and you knew it probably was related to her work."

"Those were our assumptions, yes."

Except that the killer had made no effort to mislead about the cause of death, this smelled a lot like the murder of Cliff Daniels. But before I made that leap, I needed to know more. I took a stab in the dark and asked, "Had she been tortured?"

"Yes . . . no." She said, "Two fingers had been cut off. Her right pinkie and ring finger." She added, "Possibly it was torture. Or, just as possibly, she tried to use her hand to fend off the blow."

"What did she look like? Physically?"

"I don't believe this is getting us anywhere."

"Wow, nice building. I'm cruising the block around the *Washington Post*. Do you think they'll run my picture? I didn't have time to shave."

"Stop threatening me."

"Start telling the truth."

"All right . . . she wasn't . . . she was not overly attractive. Short, about five foot one, chubby, dark-haired, and . . . Is there a point to this?"

This was my turn to ask questions, so I ignored her and asked, "So you became worried when you learned she was murdered?"

"We became . . . concerned. Sad. Diane was one of our own, Sean. She was a nice person and well liked. Nearly twenty years of good and honorable service."

"You know what I'm implying."

"Yes . . . we considered it. Of course we did. But we weren't married to any particular theories."

"Tell me about your other theories."

"Andrews had worked other things, been involved in other sensitive operations. The monsters that haunt us often have long shadows."

As she had from the start of this thing, Phyllis was parsing and limiting information. Had I known about Diane Andrews in the beginning, I would've understood we were dealing with two connected murders, I would've approached the investigation differently, I would've flipped over different rocks, and maybe I would've found Bian lurking beneath one. But Phyllis had put secrecy above effectiveness, and institutional ass-covering over truth. When you get your priorities wrong, you get bad results, and a pissed-off subordinate.

I couldn't resist. "Speaking of long, guess who her boyfriend was?"

Her not having observed Daniels's one memorable anatomical feature, this clue sailed by her.

"Here's another hint," I told her. "She and her lover are now forever together. In heaven—maybe that other place."

This clue struck home, because she promptly said, "There was zero indication of that. Mating habits are *always* probed during polygraphs. Cliff Daniels never came up."

Interesting phrasing. But during my plane ride, I had given some thought to this mystery, and I asked, "Her murder, did it happen before or after you initiated your leak investigation?"

"It was . . . the exact dates, I can't remember . . . but I think, nearly coincident. Why?"

"I'll lay you even money the affair occurred after her last polygraph session, and that she didn't live long enough for another one. Check it out."

"Who told you about this affair?"

"Does it matter?"

"Sean, stop acting paranoid."

"*Stop?* I should've been this way from the beginning."

She took a moment to clear her throat, or to turn off the recording machine. "Please come in, Sean. Now. We all want the same thing."

But that wasn't exactly true. What Phyllis and her boss wanted was to get the Agency off the blameline for the lousy prewar intelligence, with enough ammunition to screw the Pentagon, and enough clout to remain first among beltway equals at a time when Congress was considering a new national intelligence apparatus that might knock their beloved Agency down a few pegs. At least, that was what they wanted *at first.*

But once she and her boss learned the scale and breadth of this thing, their appetites swelled. And why not? Handled properly, the President and his political people, who for four years had treated the Agency like a bureaucratic piñata, would be made to see the error of their ways. In exchange for four more years, the President would have to do a little penance, his people would have to kiss a lot of Langley butt, and in return, the Director would keep a special file locked in his office safe, labeled "For Emergency Use Only."

Or alternatively, this President was already so high on Langley's shit list that a contract extension was out of the question—and his competitor would be awakened in the dead of the night by a dark man in a trench coat and handed a packet of interesting information, and Phyllis and the new President would share a victory waltz at his inauguration ball.

Either way, the Agency couldn't lose. Perfect. What could go wrong?

Bian Tran could go wrong. Neither Phyllis nor her boss had factored her into the equation. They missed what people in Washington usually miss: the human factor.

With that thought in mind, I told her, "If you and I wanted the same thing, we wouldn't be where we are." You can't slam down a cellular, so I settled for punching off with my middle finger.

Now I had another important piece I needed to consider. After Mark's death, Bian had returned from Iraq, mad with pain, grief, and guilt; not emotionally mad, not metaphysically mad—literally mad. And as it so often goes, pain bred anger, fury begat revenge, and revenge meant murder.

But where to start? That was Bian's question.

Kemp Chester had said that everybody in the G2 exploitation cell assumed that compromised intelligence—however it had occurred—had caused the death of Mark Kemble. Chester also described Bian as a hunter by both training and natural instinct. For her, finding the betrayer would be child's play because, unlike the jihadis in Iraq, her prey had not a clue they were prey.

So, Diane Andrews. That was the one name Bian knew—that was where she would enter the trail.

And as would later happen with Cliff Daniels, Bian tracked down Ms. Andrews, studied her habits, and like a couturier of death, she designed the kill around the victim's lifestyle and vulnerabilities. For Cliff Daniels, this would mean his seedier traits—his drinking, his brazen womanizing, his susceptibility to a fatal seduction. Ironically for Diane, her healthier impulses would be her ticket to hell.

So, one dark night, while chubby Diane was out jogging, shedding a few of those unattractive extra pounds, in some isolated spot Bian showed up with a hatchet. Nobody uses a hatchet for murder in this day and age. Too savage. Too messy. Plus, from a forensic angle, you get splattered with your victim's blood and brain matter. Bian, a cop, would know this. But on a different level, what could be more primatively satisfying than bashing in your enemy's brains? As an instrument of primal rage, it was the *perfect* weapon. And if Bian had thought to bring along a broom in her murder kit, surely she included a flashlight to help brush away her tracks, fresh clothing, baby wipes, and a shovel to bury the DNA-enriched evidence in some nearby woods.

I tried to picture it. Alone together on a dark path, Bian accused her, and Diane desperately denied everything. So strong, quick, athletic Bian pounced, wrestled Diane to the ground—chop—off went one finger—chop—off went a second, and then, with the hatchet hovering, Diane chose confession over further mutilation. So she explained about Iran's broken code, and about her affair with Daniels, and how she might—innocently or not—have exposed this secret to her lover.

So Bian now had the name of her next kill, Cliff Daniels. And poor Diane had confessed to a crime for which neither tolerance nor leniency were ever in the picture. Plus, for Bian, Diane had become a liability—from her trips to Baghdad, Diane recognized her, Diane would report this terrifying assault to the cops, and Cliff Daniels would evade his retribution.

Whack—the hatchet in the head took care of that problem.

So there it was. Open and shut.

Was it persuasive? Yes. Was I convinced? No. Not exactly. But maybe.

What disturbed me was that image of Bian ruthlessly torturing her suspect. Sweet, funny Bian Tran? Did such a soulless monster lurk behind those warm and intelligent eyes?

Well, I had watched her shoot four terrorists in the leg without a hint of remorse—that also surprised and shocked me. There's a big difference, though, between squeezing a trigger to wound four men and the close-in, more personal work of lopping off body parts.

Well, a little difference. Maybe.

The cabbie was performing an extended monologue, about the weather, about his daughter in college, about college bills, about life, about politics. I tuned him out as, inside my head, I conducted the summary court-martial of Bian Tran, soldier, patriot, almost-lover, and, very possibly, the most ballsy and clever murderer I had ever met.

I must've been thinking long and hard, because before I knew it, I felt the cab come to a stop and the cabbie said, "Here we are."

I looked out the window and saw that we were underneath the epic overarch of Dulles International Airport. I paid the cabbie one hundred and twenty bucks, threw in a twenty-dollar tip, and stepped out onto the curb, slinging my duffel over my shoulder.

It was time to confront Bian Tran and her monsters.

CHAPTER FORTY

I passed through the revolving doors and checked the nearest overhead monitor, which showed United Airlines Flight 837 as departing from Gate 48 in Concourse B. From the second cell phone call I had made in the cab, I knew this to be the day's final direct flight for Asia—nonstop to Incheon Airport in Seoul—where, were one so inclined, one could transfer to Asiana Airlines for another destination: Vietnam.

In fact, my first call from the cab had been to Happy Vietnamese Cuisine, whose proprietor was Bian's mother. I was not surprised when the lady who answered informed me that Mrs. Tran was not in, would not be in tomorrow, and would never be in again. The woman had then confided that Mrs. Tran decided to become Viet Kieu—a Vietnamese member of the diaspora repatriating to her birth country—and that Happy Vietnamese Cuisine had fallen under new management.

I wasn't surprised, because, for Bian, it was both the perfect escape and the perfect sanctuary. I suspected it had been part of her plan from the start. She spoke the language, her mother missed the old country and would happily live out her days there, and Bian would be impossible to find in a nation of eighty million where every fourth citizen was named Tran. Also, America had no extradition treaty with Vietnam. And Bian liked fish.

I jogged to the boarding gate for the transporter to Concourse B, where the gate guard politely requested the boarding pass I did not have. Instead, I flashed my Langley building pass and mumbled something vague and not overly alarming about national security, the need to check a passenger manifest, and whatever. Civilians are easily cowed by the letters "CIA," and I was allowed to proceed without even passing through the metal detector, which even the guards at Langley won't let you do these days.

I stepped onto the land transporter and squeezed past the travelers, who seemed mostly to be part of a tour group from someplace where everybody was short and addicted to snapping pictures of tall guys in dirty, wrinkled uniforms.

I leaned against a window and checked my watch: 5:10. The flight was scheduled for departure at 5:55 and was listed on the monitor as on time, so boarding should begin around 5:30.

Seven minutes later, the transporter docked and I pushed my way through the height-challenged people into Concourse B—essentially a long corridor extending off to my left and right. A sign showed that Gate 48 was to my left and I began jogging in that direction through the crowds, working my way down.

Bian was either going to be here or not. If she was here, that meant one thing; if not, something else. I wasn't really clear on what either meant except I knew that it was important.

I was more conflicted than I had ever been in my life. In spite of everything, I was still at least half in love with Bian Tran, and more jealous than ever of Mark Kemble. I recalled Bian once telling me that love has no past tense. And also, I remembered how Sean Drummond had skeptically and cynically dismissed this as naive, syrupy mush. Yet, for Bian, it wasn't. She was sacrificing everything she had accomplished—her career, her citizenship, and possibly even her life—all for a man who no longer was even alive to appreciate it. Every guy should be so lucky. And every government should be scared out of its wits.

For the truth was, much of what Bian had done I approved of; parts of it I admired; some of it I even envied. Washington had taken from Bian something she loved, and in return she had robbed Washington of something it loved, the false arrogance that you can fool most of the people most of the time.

And, indeed, much of what she had done was morally ambiguous: treachery in some eyes, justice in others.

Murder—that's where the line stopped. Evil does not correct evil;

nor does it bring back the dead; nor does it heal the pain. I could forgive her for killing in the heat of the moment, and the law, as well, makes mitigating exceptions when passion collides with reason. That wasn't what happened here, though.

Directly ahead of me was the sign for Gate 48. I slowed to a walk and looked around a bit. Bian would be dressed in civilian clothing, whereas I was in uniform, so I was ceding a big advantage: She was blending into the crowd and would spot me before I saw her. Also, a lot of short people seemed to be gathering around Gate 48, and I felt as self-conscious as Gulliver wading through a flock of Lilliputians.

So I moved to the corner wall beside the gate waiting area, leaned casually against it, and peered around the corner. This flight was crowded, and all the seats in the waiting area were filled, with some people lounging on the floor, and others clustered in small knots, chatting or reading. No Bian, though.

Recalling her thing for disguises, I surveyed the crowd again, trying to imagine Bian as a blonde, a brunette, a schoolgirl, an arthritic grandmother. Still no good. The passengers were mostly Asians, and if she was wearing a costume, I was unable to debunk it.

I decamped from my hiding place and approached the ticket counter, where a few people were lined up, rearranging their seats or whatever. People are respectful of uniforms these days, and I butted ahead of an old lady who was in discussion with the counter person, a uniformed lady who looked a little harried and overburdened. I said, "Excuse me, ma'am," to her, and to the counter lady, "Could you please check if Bian Tran is booked on this flight?"

She replied a little frostily, "That information's confidential."

"Of course it is. Could you please step away from the counter?"

She wasn't sure what she was dealing with here and looked apprehensively at the guard, who was loitering beside the entrance to the boardwalk. I smiled reassuringly and said, "Government business. Please. This will take only a moment."

"Oh . . . all right."

She joined me by the window. I withdrew my Agency ID and allowed her a few seconds to study it. Airline people are understandably paranoid about terrorists these days, and before she freaked out, I reassured her, "Ms. Tran works for us."

"Oh . . ."

"I hope I can confide this. We suspect Miss Tran of cheating on her expense accounts and billing us for her boyfriend's travel, who might also be on this flight." I smiled nicely and added, "The government can screw you, but it doesn't like to pay you to screw."

She smiled at my little joke. Nor did she inquire why an Agency person was wearing a military uniform, which was good, because I was winging it and didn't really have a good alibi.

"So"—I pointed at her counter—"if you could quietly check . . ."

We returned to the counter, she punched Bian's name into her computer, and said, "Yes . . . she's booked. Seat number 34B."

"Who's in 34A?"

She looked again. "Mr. Arthur Clyde."

"And 34C?"

"Mrs. Lan Tran."

Bingo. "Has Ms. Tran checked in yet?"

Again she studied the screen, and she shook her head. "She has an electronic ticket. Not required to."

I winked and said, "Your government thanks you."

She winked back and replied, "Put that in a tax rebate and I'll know you mean it. Now, if you'll excuse me . . . I have to begin boarding." She picked up her microphone and went through her announcement, which got the crowd excited and moving.

I walked directly across the aisle to the waiting area for Gate 47 and stood behind a thick pillar from where I could observe without being observed. An elderly lady in a wheelchair, a middle-aged guy on crutches, and a well-dressed couple who looked perfectly robust and healthy—impatient pricks from first class, probably—were lined up, fingering their boarding passes and IDs.

Despite Bian's reservation on this flight, I was still concerned, because now I had an idea how her mind worked. I knew she was smart and cunning and, most important, diabolically evasive. I mean, this could be another ruse. In other words, it was time to consider whether this reservation was a diversion to draw me away from something else. That was a stretch, but I no longer underestimated this lady.

The first-class passengers now were queuing up, an interesting mixture of mostly Asians, who were old and looked overdressed, and a few occidentals, all of whom were young and attired almost impossibly badly—an interesting snapshot in international contradictions.

I had another thought. If Bian was Captain Ahab, oozing hatred and obsession, there still were two white whales she hadn't bagged, Tigerman and Hirschfield.

While Clifford Daniels was most *directly* responsible for Mark's death, Tigerman and Hirschfield were directly responsible for Clifford Daniels's. If you thought about it hard enough, as surely Bian had, these were the two officials who authored the circumstances that put Mark in a killer's crosshairs—by placing a small, weak subaltern into the position where he could do so much harm, by fostering his relationship with Charabi, and afterward, once Charabi's lies were exposed and made them all look like idiots, by twisting Daniels's arm into doing something stupid and hysterically desperate to restore a little luster to their disintegrating reputations.

Also, I *was* having difficulty with the Diane Andrews angle. I mean, in almost every way, it made sense. Andrews definitely had earned a high place on Bian's hit list, and clearly the MOs in her murder and Daniels's were similar. Not identical, but similar. Further, if not from the lips of Diane Andrews, where else did Bian learn about Cliff?

Except . . . well, there *were* those troubling differences. The hand that tortured and killed Diane Andrews was enraged, brutal, and the manner of her execution abrupt and perfunctory. Cliff's killer seemed cooler and, I thought, less impulsive. And then there were those interesting staging aspects that suggested passions more byzantine than rage. But what did that mean? Two different minds? Or a single mind clever enough about police investigations to avoid a signature method? Whenever the killer is a veteran cop, you have a real problem on your hands.

But when two plus two equals five, you have to go back to the beginning and recompute. So I asked myself, had Sean Drummond been the first responder on the scene of both murders, what would have been his impressions?

I thought he would've hypothesized that Diane's killer was a male—somebody with big-time macho problems, a bad attitude toward women in general, and some fairly serious anger control issues. No finesse, no subtlety, just whack—down she went. Plus the killer used a hatchet, hardly a feminine tool. And the amputated fingers, maybe that was indicative of torture. But maybe it wasn't. Because maybe, as Phyllis had theorized, Diane's hand had merely been in the path of the deathblow.

And by comparison, he would've observed that Daniels's murder was more artful, more complexly dramatic, and in its sexually peculiar way, more vindictive. And that would reinforce something he already well knew: In matters of life, and of death, men are shallow. Women think of the little things—the birthday gift wrapped in colorful paper with a fancy bow, or the naked corpse with his hand gripped around his woodie—the special touches that make life or, in this case, death, more interesting.

And, if I carried that logic a step further, had Bian been Diane's assassin, for her this was all or nothing. Everybody with a hand in Mark's death was going to atone; maybe, or especially, Tigerman and Hirschfield.

So if Bian was in the airport, she wasn't killing Tigerman and Hirschfield. And maybe she had killed Cliff, but maybe not Diane. Did it matter? Technically, no. Murder is murder—says so in the Uniform Code of Military Justice. It was irrelevant how many she killed; just that she did commit murder. And Sean Drummond, sworn officer of the law, was supposed to do his duty and help apprehend the perp. Right?

Damn it, no. It *did* matter.

The counter person was calling for seat numbers 50 through 25, and a fresh crop of people began lining up. I no longer had a good view, so I left my hiding place and shifted to the middle of the aisle for a closer look.

And ten people back from the front of the line, with her back turned, stood an elderly Vietnamese lady with stooped shoulders, and directly to her rear, a thin, broad-shouldered young Vietnamese male, short-haired, wearing baggy black dress slacks and a shapeless white office shirt, with a red knapsack slung casually over the left shoulder. At that moment, the elderly lady turned around and exchanged words with the slender boy to her rear, and I recognized her—Bian's mother.

Except for that look, I never would've recognized Bian. She stood like a male, erect, with her shoulders perfectly squared, just as she had been trained and molded in her first month at West Point.

So now all that stood between Bian Tran and a new life were the last few people before her in line, and me. I took a deep breath.

Flight or capture? Nobody would ever know. Nobody would know that she wasn't in the hands of Iraqi kidnappers. Nobody would ever know she was alive and hiding out in Vietnam. And nobody would know that Sean Drummond had put his heart above his duty.

Three more passengers entered the boarding walk. Bian and her mother took a few more short steps, closer to freedom.

Possibly it was my ego, but I just could not believe Bian was a ruthless killer. And I knew what would happen if I apprehended her—a certain conviction for murder, possibly treason, and a slew of lesser charges tacked on for good measure by an overeager prosecutor. While I doubted she would get the chair, I was sure she would never leave Leavenworth and she would know I had sealed her fate.

Could I be responsible for that? What would I do if the love of my life died because a bunch of venal bureaucrats back in Washington were playing career games? I didn't know for sure, and I hoped I would never find out. But I would like to believe I would've found some clever way to make them pay.

So that was it; I would let her go, but first, I would have a word with her. I wanted to tell her I knew what happened. I wanted to tell her how sorry I was for her pain. But, most of all, after all we had been through, after all we had shared, I *needed* to say good-bye.

I stepped forward, when suddenly a hand grabbed my arm. I turned around, and a man in a dark suit said, "Excuse me, sir. Detective Sergeant Jones. Would you please step over here?"

The suit looked nice and expensive, and the man was about my height, only larger, with more powerful shoulders. "Why?" I asked him.

"A lady reported that she was assaulted by a soldier in uniform. You fit her description."

"I have no idea what you're talking about."

"You know what?" He smiled and tightened his grip. "They never do."

I looked and saw that only two people were now ahead of Bian and her mother. I said to him, "Show me your badge."

"Sure. After you come with me."

"Just give me a moment. I need to say good-bye to a friend, then I'll tell you why you're full of shit."

"I'd rather learn why I'm full of shit now."

This guy was as sarcastic as me, and thus equally irritating. I looked again and Bian's mother was handing her boarding pass to the gateperson. I tried to tug my arm away, but he tightened his grip and said, "Don't make me cuff you. Come on, pal . . . do us both a favor."

"Get lost."

He pointed down the corridor and said, "My partner's with the victim. Let's give her a quick look-see. If it wasn't you, you're on your way."

Bian now was handing her pass to the lady at the gate. I reached over, twisted his wrist, and pulled my arm away, saying, "Don't make me hurt you."

I felt something round and hard press against my back. He said, "I won't." He jammed the barrel harder into my back and said, "Let's not upset the tourists by making me shoot you. Walk slowly—let's get this over with."

I looked and saw Bian's back disappear through the doorway and down the gangway to her flight, her new life, and out of my life. *Shit.*

The detective remained behind me as we walked back to Gate 20, where another man in a dark suit stood beneath a Starbucks sign, holding a conversation with a mildly attractive young lady also in a dark suit. The detective stayed behind me and said to the lady, "Is this the man who assaulted you? Take a close look."

She examined my face a moment. Sounding annoyed, she said, "No, the man was short and slightly overweight. I told you that."

I felt the pistol disappear. I turned around and faced the detective. I said, "Who put you up to this?"

"Don't get worked up, pal. Shit happens."

We stared at each other a moment.

The young lady said, "I told you, Officer, it wasn't that bad. Maybe the soldier was having a bad day. Let's forget this. I don't really want to press charges."

As I suspected he would, the detective shrugged, turned to his partner, and said, "Well, what can you do?"

The woman walked away, headed in the direction of the transporters back to the main terminal. I needed to call their bluff and said to both detectives, "Show me your badges. I intend to file a complaint with your department."

The one who'd been standing with the woman looked at the guy with the pistol. He gave me a nasty smile and answered for both of them, saying, "Fuck off and have a nice day."

They both walked away, and I stood and watched their backs until they were out of sight. I can usually smell cops and these two weren't cops. And neither was the young lady in the dark suit a victim.

I wanted to be mad, but what came out was a smile.

Bian Tran had outfoxed and outwitted me, for the final time.

CHAPTER FORTY-ONE

I unlocked the door to my apartment, threw it open, and flipped on the lights.

The first thing I noticed was good and bad news. Nothing had changed in my absence. The place was a complete mess, so obviously my maid hadn't come and straightened things up, which I guess I understood since I don't have a maid.

If you're interested, I tend to be very neat and tidy, which is maybe my only virtue, but in my rush to prepare for Iraq, the place looked like Berlin after the Russian army sacked it. If you're still interested, my apartment is small, with a few pieces of ratty, cheap furniture I had purchased at a secondhand store, thrown around an outrageously expensive big-screen TV—bachelor chic, I believe it's called.

But Army life is migratory, Army movers are endlessly cruel, and only hopeless optimists buy nice or expensive furnishings. I take my chances with the TV.

The second thing I noted was the envelope that had been slipped beneath my door, which I stooped down and picked up. It was the plain white variety without an address, stamp, or return address.

My name was written in small neat letters, so I knew who it was for, and I had a fairly good idea who it was from.

I placed the letter on the kitchen counter, threw my duffel on the couch, pulled three Michelobs from the fridge, and headed straight to the bathroom, peeling off my smelly combat uniform as I walked. I twisted the cap off the first beer and stepped into the shower, where I remained until three dead soldiers littered the floor, and the last Iraqi dirt and sand had been scrubbed and rinsed off. My motto is always wear the dirt from where you are, not where you've been. I wish life was that easy.

I dried off, threw on clean sweats, and returned to the kitchen. I poured a tall glass of scotch, threw in a few ice cubes, sat at the dining table, and opened the white envelope. There were six handwritten pages, and I read:

Dear Sean,

I won't apologize.

By now, I'm sure you've figured it out. At least, most of it.

After Mark died, I thought I would go mad. Actually, I did go mad, and once you've been to that dark place, I don't know if you ever fully return. You once asked me about my dreams. So, I'll tell you now the dream that comes every night: Mark dying in an ugly street, in an ugly city, in an ugly war, because of an ugly act.

General Bentson believed my best hope of recovery was here, near my childhood memories, near my mother, with a job where the most stressful thing I would deal with was some randy old colonel who chased a female underling around his desk. It wasn't working, it would never work, but at least I made it through the days without crying. My nights, well, they were another story.

Six weeks after I returned, Diane Andrews, who had been the CIA courier, contacted me. During her frequent trips to Baghdad, we became friends. When she learned about Mark, despite being under orders not to discuss this with anybody, she couldn't live with herself. She invited me to dinner at her apartment, and over a bottle of Chardonnay, she cried and told me about Cliff. She had no idea why she had an affair with him, or why she ever trusted him, or why she told him about the exploitation cell; she knew men didn't find her physically attractive, and she was desperate, she wanted to impress him, and acted stupidly. Nor was she sure that Cliff was the source of the compromise. But her instincts said it was him.

She said she knew her career was over, it should be over, and she would handle this in whatever way I decided. I told her to confront Daniels, and she agreed. But he wouldn't return her calls, so she accosted him one night at the Pentagon exit as he was leaving work. He denied everything, so she threatened to turn him in, thinking it would force his hand, because an innocent man wouldn't care. He became enraged. She was thankful they were in a public place, because he threatened to kill her, which terrified her, and she literally ran from him.

So it was in my hands, she said. I asked for a few days to make up my mind. Little did I know, I was about to become responsible for another death.

The next morning, browsing through the morning newspaper, I saw that Diane had been murdered the night before. I waited two weeks to see if the police or the Agency would figure it out. They didn't. So Daniels was about to get away with Mark's death, and with Diane's murder.

I couldn't let that happen.

I sipped from my scotch before I flipped to the next page. I had been right about Diane's murder and that was gratifying. In retrospect, it seemed so obvious—now, at least—that Diane had sought out Bian and voluntarily turned her on to Cliff Daniels. And likewise, as her former lover, it was logical that Cliff Daniels knew when and where Diane jogged. Having already sold his soul to his ambitions and then descended to treason with Charabi, it was a short step to the next level, murder, and Daniels made that leap.

By eliminating Diane, he thought he had covered his tracks, he thought he was free and clear; in fact, he invited his own murder.

I continued to read. Over the next two pages Bian described how she approached and entrapped Cliff Daniels, first locating his office in the Pentagon, and from there following him to his car, to his apartment, learning where he got his hair cut, shopped for his groceries, bought his hooch, and she even followed him on a date with one of his mistresses. Then, after a week, in one of the Pentagon cafeterias she fell into a chair at his table, struck up a conversation, and asked him out. What followed was a blow-by-blow account of where and when they went, and what they did. I wasn't sure why she felt it necessary to include all this detail, but maybe the explanation would come later. Interestingly, she never wrote that she slept with him—she used more delicate expressions like "the evening ended on a romantic note"—but I understood.

I thought of that pig having sex with Bian, and *I* wanted to kill him.

I got to that night, and it read:

I took him to dinner at a local bar where I handled the bill. With cash, as I always did. He liked it when I paid. It appealed to his vanity and his selfishness. As usual, the jerk got drunk, and kept putting his hands all over me while I had to act like I enjoyed it. I promised him a night he would never forget, and I meant it. The fool laughed.

Maybe you've already figured this out—but why that night? I knew the maid was coming the next morning and I needed to be there when the police arrived. So I kept him out till midnight, until almost all the other residents of his apartment complex were in bed and asleep. I slipped on a blonde wig and long silk gloves before we got out of the car, and told him this was part of what I had planned for him, which he liked. He had kinky appetites, but I don't think you want to know the details, and I damned sure don't want to recall them.

Upstairs, I asked him to get me a drink of water, and while he went to the kitchen, I went to the bedroom, got his pistol from his bedside table, screwed on the silencer I had earlier ordered via the Internet, and chambered a round. When he came into the bedroom, I told him to undress and get on the bed. He was so excited he nearly ripped his clothes off. I turned on the radio, found an easy listening station, and did a slow striptease that got him more excited. He lay back, fondling himself and watching me. I really hated him, Sean. He kept making obscene comments, telling me the things he was going to do to me, and all I could do was imagine what I was about to do to him. I was down to my bra, my underpants, my wig, and my gloves. Believe me, he was even more disgusting, more selfish and corrupt than you were told. I still didn't know all the details about how he caused Mark's death, but I was sure he did, and I knew he murdered Diane—he split open her skull and left her like garbage in the woods.

So I climbed on top of him, and he told me he loved me, and I told him how happy that made me as I reached for the Glock I had pre-positioned under the mattress. He didn't even notice when I held it by his head.

The moment of truth. I thought about not doing it; it wasn't too late to just turn him in. But not very long and not very hard. I thought about telling him everything. How gratifying would that be, to watch his face as I let him know why.

But in the end I simply said, "You're going to die," and then I blew his sick brains out.

I stared at the wall for a moment. I was sure that Bian had never killed before, though it didn't sound like she was very troubled by guilt, which I guess I understood. But also, no matter how much she detested this man, in the end, she couldn't force herself to mentally torture him. Good people may do bad things, but they don't have to enjoy it.

She then briefly described how she straightened up afterward, getting dressed, taking Daniels's cell phone, and she then sat down and accessed his computer—trying to learn who he had colluded with—only to discover an impenetrable roadblock: the encrypted files. So she placed the computer inside the briefcase and positioned his briefcase in the place where I first saw it, with the corner sticking out from beneath the bed. She continued:

> *I drove back to my apartment, showered, changed into my uniform, drove back, and then I sat in my car in the parking lot, waiting for the maid, and then for the police to arrive. I thought about what I had done, and about what I still had to do. I knew my career was over, and that was okay. My career was over the instant the bullet tore through Mark's heart. I knew what would happen if I got caught, and that, too, was okay. There were still so many unanswered questions and guilty parties. And it wasn't just about Mark. Not anymore. It was about all our soldiers in Iraq, who trusted people in Washington to do what was right. So that was my plan. Involve myself in the investigation, find out who did what, and punish them. I would be the avenging angel. Nothing and nobody would stop me.*
>
> *Enter Sean Drummond. I didn't like you much. Not at first, anyway. You annoyed me and you frightened me, and worse, you nearly figured it out. My God, you came close. Then I found myself liking you too much. You are so much like Mark. I thought I was with a ghost, or that maybe Mark's spirit had sent you. I know, silly. The problem is, Sean, once*

you've committed murder, there is no going back. And once I had a better inkling about what Daniels had done, I couldn't let myself go back. I was falling in love with you, but it was too late for that, because it was too late for me, which meant it was too late for us.

So, there it is. To be truthful, I don't regret it. Except for one thing. You. Also, you might be in career trouble because you were my partner, and because you might be blamed for things that went wrong, like the leak. Thus, this letter—this is your alibi and this should help you clear up any loose ends about the investigation. I've laid out everything in a way that should be easy to verify.

Don't waste your time looking for me. You won't find me. I love America, and I will miss it, and I will always regret losing the chance to see if it would work between you and me.

But I need to start over.

Love, Bian

I put the letter aside, refilled my glass with scotch, and walked out to my small porch. I looked down on the traffic, at the lights and sights of northern Virginia, at my busy cross section of America.

Bian Tran had taught me something about myself, and if people in Washington were paying attention, she had taught them something as well.

War, they say, is supposed to be an extension of politics by other means; for those who are fighting it, though, and for those who love them, it becomes an affair not of the mind but of the heart.

Before you open the gates and unleash the dogs of war, it is wise to remember that the dogs have a mind of their own.

Bian was not starting over; she had returned to the beginning.

CHAPTER FORTY-TWO

It was the last thing I needed to do, the final mystery that had to be solved.

I pushed open the glass door and entered the restaurant. Seated at a table near the back was my date, Phyllis, alone, sipping tea and studying a menu.

She was dressed conservatively in a smart red wool suit, with a colorful scarf pinned around her neck by a shiny brooch, and I, more casually in a blue blazer over a polo shirt and faded jeans.

I fell into the chair directly across from her and asked, "Come here often?"

She looked up from the menu and said, "My God, Drummond, I do hope you've never *actually* used that line."

"Never," I lied.

She flagged down the waiter, who happened to be the same gangly kid with purplish hair who had served Bian and me. Phyllis said something to him in Vietnamese, which surprised me; another reminder of how little I knew about this lady.

The kid looked equally surprised, but he recovered quickly, smiled pleasantly, and they chatted back and forth for about three minutes; for all I knew, Phyllis was recruiting him to go back to Vietnam and overthrow the commies.

I quickly got tired of listening to a conversation I didn't understand, and I turned my attention to the menu—still no red meat, still no cold beer. I really wanted a hamburger. I really *needed* a beer.

Earlier that afternoon, I had made the quick trip to Arlington National Cemetery and located the grave of Major Mark Kemble. It was raining and windy, and I saluted his grave, and then knelt down and we had a long, amiable chat. Maybe Bian had found time to stop here before she fled, maybe not. So I told Mark that he would be proud of Bian, and I told him everything she had done, and I confided how jealous I was of him.

The kid was laughing at something Phyllis told him, and then he disappeared back into the kitchen. Phyllis mentioned to me, "He recommends the freshwater white fish. It's the house speciality." She then reminded me of how well she knew me and observed, "But you don't like fish, do you?"

I asked her, "How long have you known?"

"About the white fish?"

"I'm tired of the games, Phyllis."

"Humor me about the fish, anyway," she replied. "I was first introduced to it in Vietnam. Did you know I spent five years there? During the war, of course. I loved the country, and especially, I loved the people."

Phyllis is not much for small talk, so she was leading up to something, and I had to let it play out.

She looked at me and said, "I wish I could say I look back fondly on those years. I don't, though."

I was obviously expected to ask why, and I did.

"I could say because it was such a horrible and ill-conceived tragedy for our nation. That's how Americans look back on it. We lost fifty-eight thousand lives. I knew some of those people . . . I knew very many of them, actually."

"One of my uncles is on the wall. As are the fathers of several of my friends."

"Not many fathers are on the wall. They were mostly so young." She looked away for a moment, then said, "At least we were able to fit all our dead on a wall. They lost two million lives, and we left millions of southerners to a hellish fate. What about them?"

Usually, Phyllis's ulterior meanings are more nuanced and subtle than this. What it boiled down to was this: The two people at this table knew enough to possibly force a premature end to this war as well. She wasn't going to insult my intelligence by lecturing me about

American honor, or the geostrategic stakes, or even my security obligations. I appreciated that. I know my duty, and I do it—most of the time. I would've told her to screw off, anyway.

So I told her something she already knew. "You knew about Bian from the beginning."

"I knew more than you knew."

"Then why?"

"Why did I let Bian into the investigation in the first place? Why did I allow her to go with it? Why didn't I confide in you?" She paused, then asked, "Or why did I let her slip away?"

She sipped her tea, obviously pleased that I had figured out this much. After all, no boss likes to think they hired a complete idiot—it makes *them* feel stupid. At the same time, she was testing me.

"Start with *how* you knew."

"Well . . . like you, I wondered why an MP officer was at a civilian murder scene." She added, "When I saw how very determined she was to become involved . . . Let's just say that aroused my curiosity all the more."

"Because, unlike me, you knew this was the second related murder."

She did not reply.

"Reason to be suspicious, right?"

"At least reason to dig a little deeper," she acknowledged. "From a background check at Army personnel I learned about her former job in Baghdad. General Bentson is an acquaintance. I called, and he told me the whole sad story."

"And you already knew how her fiancé died?"

"Did I forget to mention that I'm in charge of that investigation, too?"

"In fact, I think you did fail to mention it."

"Well, I'm mentioning it now. We spun our wheels for two months, Sean. All the resources of the Agency, and we couldn't figure out who compromised this very sensitive and important operation, or who murdered Diane. How frustrating. Embarrassing, too."

"But then, you were pretty sure you had your murderer."

"I thought I had a reasonable suspect."

"Why didn't you have Bian arrested? I would."

"It was all circumstantial. No evidence linked her to Diane's murder, and Daniels's case could have been suicide." She picked at something on the table, a piece of lint, maybe. "You yourself told me that it looked like suicide."

Actually, I had said that it was murder made to *appear* like suicide. Phyllis has an amazing memory for details, incidentally. I nodded anyway.

She said, "In my judgment, a premature arrest was too risky." She smiled and added, "She would have lawyered up, and you know what a mess lawyers make of things."

I nodded again, though this was not exactly true. The toughest part of a homicide investigation is finding a suspect and a motive. There are no perfect crimes, only unsolved ones, but sometimes you have to find the suspect to find the imperfections. Detective Barry Enders, in fact, absent both suspect and motive, had already collected evidence sufficient for any competent prosecutor to put Bian away for a long time. Every criminal investigator knows this, I knew this, and I was sure Phyllis knew this, too.

I said, "Regardless, you had to understand the dangers of placing a murder suspect inside an investigation about a crime in which she had a conflict of interest. She was the killer, after all."

"Turn that logic on its head—can you think of a better place to park a suspect than right under your nose?"

"How about in jail?"

The boy reappeared with a plate of appetizers, a combination of squiggly dead things and rice squashed into marble-size balls. Phyllis said something to him in Vietnamese, and he laughed and scampered back into the kitchen. The kid was obviously charmed by her. I really needed to have a talk with him.

Phyllis speared a rice thing with a chopstick and handed it across the table. She said, "Try one of these. They're marinated in vinegar and sugar. Quite tasty."

I bit into it. Not bad. An interesting combination of sweet and sour, yin and yang, sort of easy and hard to take at the same time—like Phyllis.

She speared another one, popped it into her mouth, chewed, and swallowed. She said, "Putting Bian into the investigation was the key that unlocked everything. We learned how the leak occurred, who was responsible, and why."

"And what about the collateral damage?"

"I don't worry about that." She noted, "The country doesn't really understand this war. Nor does it seem to care to. Turki al-Fayef was right about that. Forgive my cynicism, but our people are more interested in Tom Cruise's silly antics on Oprah's couch than who's giving secrets to the Iranians. In a week, the Saudi princes will be forgotten, washed away by a hurricane or a gruesome murder somewhere. And Mahmoud Charabi, should he ever come back to Washington, will be welcomed like a visiting dignitary."

Sad. But also, I thought, probably true. But I was also sure that she understood that at some point, America could care. And if what happened in this case ended up on the front page of the morning newspaper, that point might be tomorrow night. That's why she and I were sharing this table and pretending to enjoy each other's company. Phyllis had been dispatched to make sure I kept my mouth shut.

"So why did you pick me?" I asked her.

"I trusted you to do the right thing. I still do."

"And what is the right thing, Phyllis?"

She did not answer. She didn't need to.

I asked, "Why didn't you tell me about Bian?"

"I needed you to learn the truth about the compromise of our intelligence, and about Mahmoud Charabi."

"Instead of discovering my partner was a murderer."

"Yes. Our job is intelligence, not law enforcement. I warned you about that at the beginning, Sean. You should have listened." She added more warmly, "You should be proud of all you accomplished. I'm proud of you."

"Can we cut the crap? You're here to make sure I don't squeal and to find out what it will cost."

She studied her chopsticks, then looked me in the eye and asked, "What will it cost?"

"More than you can offer. Important people have done bad and dishonorable things. They deserve to be punished. They *need* to be punished."

She speared another rice ball and studied it a moment, which I guess was easier than studying me. She said, "The Director and I were at the White House all afternoon. The President and his National Security Advisor were fully briefed on everything."

"And were they shocked?" I asked in an appropriately sarcastic tone.

She put down her chopsticks, wiped her lips with her napkin, and seemed to think about it. She informed me, "Thomas Hirschfield has been offered a prestigious position outside of the Defense Department. An offer that, he was warned, expires tomorrow. And Albert Tigerman came to the awakening this afternoon that he needs more time with his family. His wife and children, he was told, feel neglected. The President will regretfully accept his resignation in the morning."

I was a little surprised to hear this. But neither was I fully satisfied, and I said, "That's it?"

"Stupidity, no matter how big, is not criminal behavior, Sean. Think of it this way: Thousands of good soldiers have given their lives to make Iraq a success. It no longer matters how we got into it, or even the stupid things that happened in between. What matters now—all that matters—is how we get out, and what happens if we leave too soon."

We were now at the heart of the matter. I wasn't going to tip my hand and Phyllis wasn't going to rush things.

Phyllis said, "If you think about it, all wars are a failure of policymakers at some level. Pearl Harbor didn't have to happen. The attack on Korea was the result of terrible stupidity in Washington, and China's entry was a blunder on top of a blunder. And then, there's Vietnam . . ." She took my arm. "Do I really need to explain this?"

"And what does the Agency get?"

"The pride of a job well done."

"Say again."

"We did not blackmail the administration, as you seem to be suggesting. The guilty parties are being punished. That was all we wanted, and that's all we asked for. We're satisfied. You should be, too."

"Well, I'm not." I mentioned, "Besides, you forgot somebody."

"Did I?"

"You know you did. Mahmoud Charabi."

"Oh, him. Well, there are twenty thousand jihadis in Iraq who dream every night of killing him. Eventually, somebody's going to get lucky. Trust me on this."

That usually is the kind of statement you take at face value, but considering the source, maybe not. I didn't want to know.

The kid reappeared with white fish and rice for Phyllis, and on a separate plate were two Big Macs, a sack of fries, and two cold Budweisers for me. Phyllis laughed and informed me, "The boy remembered you. The entire staff remembers you."

So we ate and we chatted. To keep the meal pleasant, we spoke of other matters, which did not include shoe sales at Nordstrom, so I did not have to reach across the table and strangle her. Phyllis predicted the President would win tomorrow's election, and in her salty opinion that was fitting because he had created the mess and he should have to clean it up. And so on.

But I had asked one question that Phyllis had skillfully evaded and never answered: Why did she let Bian get away? That was okay. I had already figured it out.

Because after I departed Dulles International for my apartment, I put two and two together and finally got four. The "detective" in the expensive suit, his partner, and the victim weren't working for Bian. They were Phyllis's people, a tail team that had probably followed Bian from the moment she set down in Delaware, and their job was to ensure that Bian made her escape. When I stepped forward and it looked like I was going to stop her, they stepped forward and stopped me.

That still didn't answer the why behind the why. Nor would Phyllis ever tell me; not the truth, anyway. Because, though she would never admit this, Phyllis is not as coldhearted or as jaded as she likes to pretend. But nobody fears a dragon lady with no teeth.

Like me, I was sure she sympathized with Bian, and maybe she felt guilty that her beloved Agency had played a role in Mark's death, and maybe she decided the country owed Bian Tran a chance to get her own little slice of justice, and then the chance for a new life. Of course, it helped that Bian's intense personal need for retribution coincided with Phyllis's own very intense professional need to learn what had happened.

I recalled the moment at Camp Alpha when I walked into the conference room—when Bian had been showing her Mark's picture—and I recalled the misty look in Phyllis's eyes.

The plates were cleared. Coffee came. The aimless chatter was over, and Phyllis came to the point and said to me, "You told me in Iraq that you want out. Do you still feel that way?"

"Here's a hint. I cleared out my desk this afternoon. There's a brief letter under the blotter on your desk."

Obviously she already knew this, and she said, "One should never make important choices on emotions."

"I knew you'd say that."

She looked me in the eye and added, "I would hate to lose you."

"You'll get used to it."

She lifted up the coffee carafe and asked, "Another cup?"

"You made me the man in the middle, Phyllis. You and Bian both. You kept me in the dark, fed me bullshit, and played me for a fool."

"So this is about hurt feelings?"

"No. Yes."

"Can I at least interest you in one final mission? Your country needs you."

"Give somebody else a turn."

"A few short weeks. That's all it will take. You owe me two more years. Do this, and I'll arrange a good assignment with the Army if that's still your wish. You have my word."

"You'll release me now."

"Or what?"

"Or I promise you the two worst years of your life. You know I can do that."

She smiled at this threat and said, "Aren't you at all curious about the mission?"

"I was curious last time. Send somebody who still trusts you. Somebody who doesn't know better."

"That's not an option, Sean."

"Because nobody trusts you?"

"Because nobody else has the right background, your credentials."

"Then change your requirements."

She bent down to her purse and withdrew something. It was a white envelope, which she studied for a long moment before casually sliding it across the table at me. I did not pick it up.

She said, "Are you afraid to look?"

"Is the job in Bermuda?"

"No."

"Then it's in the wrong place. Forget it."

She explained, "It's a simple recruitment mission. An asset we're intensely interested in. We have reason to believe it won't be a tough sell."

I made no response.

She said, "The weather there is wonderful at this time of year. Warm breezes, tropical sunsets, attractive natives, glorious beaches."

"That means the place sucks."

"No, it's lovely."

"That's what you said when you sent me to Iraq."

"Well . . . okay, the country does happen to be under an oppressive dictatorship, and maybe it's a little dangerous. You'll need a good cover and strong support from our people in the embassy. And if you're caught, the prisons are absolutely abysmal." She added, "You'll have to be careful."

"Stop trying to tempt me."

"This is a very important job. American corporations are very interested in this place, as is our navy. Its future strategic value could be enormous."

"Phyllis, you're not listening. Take this job and shove it."

I had exhausted her patience. She leaned across the table and, with real steel in her voice, said, "Drummond, open the damned envelope. Now."

Well, why not? I opened it and saw that it contained a first-class plane ticket, a brief description of the mission and the mission number, as well as the name, current address, and a little background about the target for recruitment.

Phyllis was right. It did not look like a tough sell. Plus, the recruit would make a fabulous asset.

I set it down on the table and said, "You're trying to get me out of the country for a few weeks while this thing blows over."

"I won't deny it."

"I won't be bribed."

"Don't be stupid. We all have a price."

"How do I know the address is correct?"

"Trust me."

I stared at her very hard.

She quickly said, "One of our people from the embassy was waiting when Bian landed in Saigon . . . known these days as Ho Chi Minh City. That's a horrible and unfortunate name, if you ask me. I have such fond memories of when it was still Saigon—"

"Phyllis."

"All right. He followed them." She added, "The address is an orphanage run by Bian's aunt, her mother's younger sister."

I placed the ticket and information in my breast pocket.